W9-BTB-577

RAGE
SLEEP

ALSO BY C.W. MORTON

Pilots Die Faster

Sea Trials *(June, 1999)*

C.W. MORTON
AND JACK MOBLEY, M.D.

DUNNE
BOOKS

St. Martin's Press/New York

A THOMAS DUNNE BOOK.
An imprint of St. Martin's Press.

RAGE SLEEP. Copyright © 1998 by C.W. Morton. All rights reserved.
Printed in the United States of America. No part of this book may be used
or reproduced in any manner whatsoever without written permission ex-
cept in the case of brief quotations embodied in critical articles or reviews.
For information, address St. Martin's Press, 175 Fifth Avenue, New York,
N.Y. 10010.

Library of Congress Cataloging-in-Publication Data

Morton, C. W.
    Rage sleep / by C.W. Morton & Jack Mobley. — 1st ed.
        p.   cm.
    "Thomas Dunne books."
    ISBN 0-312-19321-1
    I. Mobley, Jack.   II. Title.
PS3563.0244R34   1998
813'.54—dc21   98-7900
                                                           CIP

FIRST EDITION: October 1998

10   9   8   7   6   5   4   3   2   1

JACK MOBLEY, M.D.:   An anesthetic agent such as Anaex is the surgical Holy Grail. Talking through the consequences of side effects with my daughter has been truly enjoyable, and I'd like to dedicate this book to my few remaining old friends. Stay tuned for my next book: *The Sex Life of Abraham Lincoln's Doctor.*

C.W. MORTON: My thanks to the rest of the team: George Wieser, my agent and hero. Melissa Jacobs, a truly superb editor who stunned me with her work. Any errors that remain are solely mine and are probably the result of not taking her advice at some point. I want her written into my next contract—we come as a package from now on.

Linda Coffman, who heard the story first. Mom and Dad, to whom the real thanks are due for good genes. Dad, we wrote this during a tough time—I hope it made things a little easier.

Most of all, my family: Heather, Daniel, and Ron. Your patience, tolerance, ideas and proofreading made the difference. Thank you.

My e-mail address is: MortonCW@aol.com. Spelling counts.
Snail mail address is:

C.W. Morton
C/O Melissa Jacobs
St. Martin's Press
175 Fifth Ave.
New York, NY 10010

Drop us a line.

PROLOGUE

Algerian secretary of state Pierre Tshoma gazed out over the crowd packed into the square, barely seeing the thronging masses. His thoughts were focused on the razored scimitar in his right hand. The gold alloyed handle cut with delicate ridges into the soft skin of his palm. Sweat slid down and around the meld between flesh and metal, chasing after a purchase.

The ceremony droned on. The entourage was clad in traditional desert clothing, complete with the ceremonial weapons that had survived for centuries. It was a unique blending of Catholic mysticism, French formality, and Algerian native traditions.

He saw his moment coming, careening toward him relentlessly. It had come to him last night, finally, the thought of what he must do this day and the exact moment at which it must occur. Somehow fitting—righteous, in the most terrible sense of the word.

The salute—now. Pierre raised the scimitar, clenched palm upturned and tucked in close to his chest. As the music crescendoed, he twisted his wrist and extended his arm to his right.

There was time for one harsh cry from the security force. The president turned toward him, a puzzled expression on his face. Pierre brought the blade down.

Ice-edged sharp, the metal sliced cleanly through the scalp three inches back from the president's hairline. Its downward motion slowed slightly as it bit into the skull. Then it was through the half-inch bone that sheltered the brain and bisected the cerebellum. The corpus callosum, the thick integument that connects the two sides of the brain, snapped back.

Blood spurted from the intricate web of arteries and veins, arcing through the air, driven by the president's heart. The adrenal glands had just begun responding to the threat, increasing circulation and dumping adrenaline into the president's body.

The blade continued downward, severing the cerebellum from

1

the anterior limbic portions of the brain, gaining speed now with the full force of Tshoma's weight behind the blow. He found himself noting dispassionately that the scimitar had severed the optic nerve and that the eyeballs had popped out of the president's head.

It jarred against the jawbone, splintering the bone and shattering teeth. The force deflected the blade slightly to the rear.

As it cleared the jaw, it continued down. The trachea and larynx parted. The blade grazed lightly against the cervical bones high on the president's neck then hit the scapula.

Blood was landing on the president's body, and involuntary reflex coupled with the force of the blow toppled him forward. The body was moving in the same direction as the blow now, lessening the cutting power of the blade. That, coupled with the resistance from the scapula, proved too much. The blade stopped, wedged deeply in the bone.

The president's head fell backward, his neck a raw gaping wound. The head remained attached to the torso by a broad strip of skin at the back of the president's neck and by the cervical vertebrae. It flopped back, exposing the twin tubes of the trachea and larynx.

The jugular and the carotid, under full pressure as a result of the adrenaline, pumped blood out in long arcs, spattering the crowd gathered nearest the dais. The president's body slammed down onto the wooden platform, twitching and convulsing.

Seconds after the blow struck, the crowd began to move. Shock, the beginnings of wails and screams that would soon fill the square. The spectators nearest the platform surged back, ran into a solid phalanx of people behind them, and panicked.

Rage and fear swept through the crowd.

The ceremonial guards were finally moving. They piled onto Tshoma, dropping him to the wooden surface. His face ground into the boards, the light coating of sand that permeated all flat surfaces in Algeria grating against his skin.

"*Non! Ne le tuez pas!*" the leader of the ceremonial guards shouted, demonstrating an exceptional presence of mind under the circumstances. One subordinate ignored him and drove his knife deep into Tshoma's lower back. It sliced through a kidney and continued on to embed itself in the wood, pinning Tshoma down.

Three minutes after the first blow, the platform was clear. Guards rushed both the wounded Tshoma and the very dead president off the platform, crashing through the other dignitaries and guests fleeing the platform.

That evening, Pierre Tshoma was formally charged with assassinating the president of Algeria. Operating under the Napoleonic Code inherited from France, the presiding judge set the trial for five days hence.

ONE

The air rolled up from the steaming ground in fetid waves, moist and hot. Lieutenant General Thurmond S. Boothby could feel the thickness of it in his throat, heavy and cloying. The Humvee carved a path through rotting ground cover, airborne diseases, an undertone of human waste and sickness.

There were few good wars left since the demise of the Soviet Union, and an Army officer on the fast track had to make do with what the world provided. Korea, a godforsaken peninsula that should have been napalmed into the Stone Age forty years ago, was one of the commands that broke you out of the pack.

Boothby slammed on the brakes. The Humvee skidded to a halt ten feet from the cluster of men. He ignored the stifled oath from his chief of staff in the backseat and vaulted out of the driver's seat.

"General, we're in the open." The chief of staff's voice was low and insistent. "Sir, please."

Boothby pointed at the soldier motionless on the ground. "He walked this perimeter. And you want *me* to hide?"

The lance corporal lay in a crumpled heap. The right side of his face was missing, a bloody, still-liquid mass in its place. Flies swarmed, cloaking waves of black noxiousness.

The field ambulance stood fifteen feet away, siren now stilled. Two medics crouched on the ground beside the soldier. Boothby did not need to look at their faces to know that it was too late.

Should have solved this problem the first time we were here. Should *have*.

Impotent rage flooded him. These soldiers deserved better than the treatment they got from the Army, better than being used as the Army's trump card, better than being stationed here on the border between the insanity of the north and the obsequious resentment of the south. Korea was a holding action, one that had gone on far too long, in his humble estimation.

It wasn't fair, expecting them to sit there and take the repeated insults and slights the North Koreans offered at every opportunity. Not with so much of the military force of the most powerful nation in the world under his direct and immediate control. He was Lieutenant General Thurmond Sherman Boothby, West Point '64, Vietnam '65–'68, on the way to four stars and command of the whole goddamn United States Army. It just wasn't fair.

Or right.

"Move him," Boothby said finally.

They know. Know, and will never say a word. If the general showed up intoxicated at the evening brief, that was the general's affair. There would be a reason for it, one that might or might not involve them, but a reason none the less. Their faith in him, in the Army, in his ability to lead and in the idea that he would never call them to the ultimate sacrifice without just cause was evident.

It was perhaps the finest compliment they had ever paid him.

Commander, Combined Forces Korea (CFC) owned the Eighth Army, the Seventh Air Force, and US Naval Forces Korea, as well as the actual forces responsible for security along the DMZ, a battalion called CSCT-1. The Red Dragon Brigade, formally known as the 501st Intelligence Battalion, fed CFC a wide range of intelligence reports, from electronic sensors planted along the DMZ, dedicated satellite feed, dedicated surveillance flights, and a host of other sensors. The Red Dragon's reports went directly to Boothby's staff, but were also routed to the Eighth Army and, via the Third Military Intelligence Battalion, to Headquarters, US Army Intelligence and Security Command (INSCOM) at Fort Belvoir, Virginia.

Controlling the scenario in Korea meant more than coordinating American subordinate commands. The four-star Korean officer who commanded all ROK forces was double-hatted as Deputy CFC. As Boothby's deputy, the Korean general was supposed to be the American's direct tap into the intricacies of Korean politics and the UN Peacekeeping Force that patrolled the JSA—the Joint Security Area. In reality, the ROK commander was an incompetent, a drunken playboy who thus far had been more than willing to rely on the 501st intelligence assessments and the recommendations of Boothby's staff. His stamp of concurrence on Boothby's plans ensured UN support for whatever position Boothby advocated.

The briefing chart in front of Boothby summarized the escalating intensity of the skirmishes with the North Koreans. His rules of engagement promulgated by the joint chiefs were increasingly hampering his ability to respond.

Was it intentional? His fingers stopped their relentless drumming on the table as he considered the extent of the conspiracy back in the States.

Of course it was. The events on the Korean Peninsula were undoubtedly being orchestrated by jealous powers back in the Pentagon, the same officers who had tried to derail his rapid rise through the ranks and his assignment to this position last year. They were the real aggressors in the border skirmishes that kept his troops constantly in a heightened state of alert, on edge and vulnerable to attack.

And President Williams had done nothing to stop them.

A disgrace, that was. The president had done his time in Vietnam, gone into politics when his first and only hitch was up. Nothing wrong with not staying in the army for twenty years, but at least he ought to keep faith with the men in the field.

Not that the South Koreans weren't at fault themselves. No, it was clearly a joint effort. A joint problem, one that demanded a complete solution.

Another possibility. Had they been involved in the incident with his son? Boothby rubbed his face with his hands, aware of the itchy, oily sheen of sweat coating his scalp at the hairline. It wasn't like him to show signs of tension, was it? In his years in the Army, he'd always been known for his clear head, his ability to call in fire accurately and precisely while under attack himself, his nerves of steel. And now he was letting another border skirmish get to him.

And his son. He'd never once in the last ten years raised a hand against the child, nor struck his wife. Yet both had happened in the last week. His conduct horrified and disgusted him, but at the same time had felt oddly comfortable. A release of tension, a giving in to some impulse that had lurked deep inside him for decades.

It *was* possible that he wasn't fully responsible for either incident. Alicia had been behaving oddly for several months, and the boy—well, what had been that business with the fighting in the school? Brett had come home with both eyes blackened and claimed he got jumped by some bigger boys who'd teased him about being a general's kid.

The more he thought about it, the less probable his son's story was. The men and women under his command were soldiers, *good* soldiers. They raised good kids, army brats who knew how the world ran. Their kids would never have attacked his, no more than their fathers and mothers would have raised a hand against their commanding general.

So it came down to Brett. Brett, the problem child.

He felt a sense of relief as he arrived at the decision. Yes, something had changed about Brett, perhaps as a result of meddling or manipulation by those same Pentagon dickheads who'd tried to get him. The obscenity skated through his mind completely unnoted, although normally General Boothby censored his own thoughts even more stringently than the language of his subordinates.

And they'd succeeded with the child where they'd failed with the parent, then used his *own child* to maneuver him into a compromising position. He could see it all plainly now, the nasty little rumors and innuendoes that would soon skitter around within the closed community on base.

It wouldn't work. He wouldn't let it.

And after he resolved the little crisis brewing in Korea, he'd settle their hash. He'd find out exactly who was orchestrating this campaign to discredit him and take care of it in his own time, his own way.

After the briefing, General Boothby returned to his government quarters. Brett's bike was in the driveway again. The general crushed it with his Humvee. He stormed into the boy's room, jerked him out of bed, and slapped him across the face, then flung him against the wall. Brett hit awkwardly with his arm pinned behind him. The delicate bone, still soft on either end as a result of the child's rapid growth, snapped.

He remembered the rest as a series of brief, unconnected snapshots. Brett writhing on the floor, screaming. His wife Alicia screaming, flailing at him with small fists, then leaning against the doorjamb, her face cold and white. Blood streaking her face. A hard, uncomfortable chair at the emergency room. More wine.

The next morning, the general blamed his entirely uncharacteristic fit of rage on stress and swore to his wife and ten-year-old son that it would never happen again.

The general was wrong on both counts.

Terribly wrong.

TWO

"The Secret Service stole his brain." The guest speaker's voice intoned this statement as though it were indisputable fact, ignoring the muffled round of chortles and chuckles from one side of the packed conference room.

Dr. Christopher Thorne could barely repress the gleeful urge to wiggle in his chair. The flyers advertising the guest speaker's topic had been almost too much to hope for. And so far, the man looked like he'd be just what the doctor ordered after a grueling week in his new position at Murphy Medical Center.

The fascination with conspiracies and assassinations had taken root in his undergraduate years at Millsaps College, when a history professor had expounded on how a single event could spark political conflict into war. The archduke Ferdinand, the sinking of the *Lusitania*, the assassination of John F. Kennedy—the effects were far out of proportion to the event.

That his undergraduate major had been history that rather than biology or chemistry had provoked endless caustic comments from his medical school professors. In the long march through the rigors of medical school, the grueling years of internship and residency, and the final ordeal of job hunting, he'd had little time to indulge his passion for history. Even the engineers and computer geeks got more respect.

But wait—there was more. The guest speaker fumbled with his notes on the battered school lectern and stared out at the assembled group with a challenging air. He gripped both sides of the podium, leaned forward, and said, "The government's seizure of the Zapruder tape is simply the next step in an all-encompassing government conspiracy to suppress the truth about the JFK assassination."

Well, at least that point had some validity. Thorne himself had been surprised at a new development in a case now more than forty years old.

One thing was certain about the monthly assassination theorists' meetings: there was rarely a middle ground between the loons and nutters. The Zapruder tape, a home movie that had captured the actual assassination of President Kennedy on November 22, 1963. Forty years later, controversy still raged over every single frame of the tape.

In 1997 the Zapruder tape, owned by Mr. Zapruder's heirs, was subpoenaed by the still-existent House Select Committee on Assassination, commonly known as the HSCA. The controversy broke out anew.

JFK assassination buffs fell into two broad groupings, although many were clustered along the spectrum between the two extremes. The loons, as they were called, believed devoutly that an international conspiracy was responsible both for the death of the president, the assassination of Lee Harvey Oswald by Jack Ruby, and for all the cover-ups that followed. They pointed to segments of the tape that they claimed proved there was more than one bullet at work on that fatal day.

The nutters, on the other hand, ascribed to the theory that Lee Harvey Oswald was one lone nut operating on his own. They, too, extracted particular frames from the Zapruder tape to prove their theories.

Dr. Thorne glanced around the room, noting the predictable reactions from each of the factions. Most of the nutters were to his right, the loons to his left. It was fitting that he himself was seated somewhere in the middle. Had he been pressed to the point, Thorne would have described himself as a nutter with loon leanings. The conspiracy theories appealed to him at some level. It was simply inconceivable, somehow too gigantic to comprehend, that a president such as John F. Kennedy could have been felled simply by one person working alone. It gave life a sense of fragility that he found both unsettling and yet terribly familiar.

On the other hand, gazing at the faces of the conspiracy theorists around him, he also found it inherently incredible that any group of people could have kept so much secret for so long. Certainly not any of the fanatics who attended the regular monthly meetings could have been capable of such a feat.

The nutters, on the other hand, dismissed most of the inconsistencies in the evidence with the simple conclusion that the government was inefficient. Thorne found this equally difficult to swallow. Numerous inconsistencies in both Oswald's history and in the assassination itself simply could not be dismissed out of hand by such a pat answer. What about the claims that Oswald had talked to Elrod, his cellmate at the Dallas jail? And the possibility, often discussed but never proved conclusively, that a Soviet agent had taken over the real Oswald's life sometime after Oswald's trip to Russia? Furthermore, the assassin's extensive connections with the FBI and the CIA still caused Thorne a great deal of concern. Certainly, if there had been a conspiracy, Oswald would have had the contacts to be a part of it.

Thorne settled back in the metal chair, switched his mind into neutral, and paid attention to the speaker. To this day, the JFK assassination, the reams and reams of physical evidence and controversy surrounding it, and the extent of the impact on the course of American history remained one of the most intriguing and puzzling of events. Sorting out the competing claims, poking holes in each theory, and generally speculating on the deeper motives of everyone from J. Edgar Hoover to Fidel Castro was a welcome relief from the pressures of practicing medicine—a hobby.

After reading his introductory comments, the speaker quickly abandoned his prepared text and launched into one of the passionate tirades that usually characterized the club's guest speakers. The lecturer's eyes were backlit with fanatical fury as he outlined all of the probable participants in this latest conspiracy to suppress the truth, the grave damage done to the First Amendment by the government's seizure, as well as a probable link—and this was as tenuous as it ever got, Thorne admitted—between the Kennedy assassination and the Clinton Whitewater cover-up. Any second now, he would—ah, yes, there it was. Thorne chuckled to himself as a reference to the Branch Davidians in Waco, Texas, inevitably surfaced.

He felt the grin spread to his face as he settled into his chair, eagerly anticipating even more outlandish evidence that every bit of wrongdoing in the world was connected to one giant plot.

An hour later, no more knowledgeable about the Zapruder issues than he'd been before but definitely entertained, Thorne joined the growing crowd around the punch bowl and plate of stale cookies that was invariably served as the club's after-speech refreshments. They were always provided by one of the members who owned a catering service, and Thorne was convinced that they were often leftovers from some previous event. Tonight, each cookie was inscribed with a pink heart etched in frosting framing the initials M + M. Thorne scooped up two, took a proffered glass of punch, and retreated to a neutral corner to watch the fun.

The loons and nutters had already broken into their groups and were staring at each other across the room. A few opponents were engaged in one-on-one debate, their voices occasionally loud and strident over the general buzz of conversation. In another few minutes, the two sides would begin mingling, each longtime member seeking out his usual adversary to debate the finer points of the lecture.

Not that there were finer points, Thorne concluded, washing down a bite of stale cookie with the light purple punch. Each side relied more on passion than reason in presenting its case.

A short, rotund man appeared at the edge of his field of vision, and Thorne turned to find Jim Harley making a covert approach from behind him. Thorne crammed the rest of the cookie in his mouth and held out one hand, lightly dusted in crumbs.

"So, Scoot, are you ready to see the light?" Harley joked. His fat, moist fingers closed around Thorne's hand and bore down.

Thorne winced, as much from the old college nickname as the pressure on his fingers. He'd been able to shed most of his Mississippi accent and all of the prejudices he'd grown up with in the Delta, but not the moniker the Millsaps football coach had tagged him with.

Thorne tried to withdraw his hand. "Careful, buddy, I'm a working man."

Harley snorted. "Not a surgeon, though. Don't know why you're so worried about those damned hands of yours."

Thorne smiled at the normal opening gambit. Among all the diehard enthusiasts in the club, Jim Harley was one of the most devout. He worshipped at the altar of the loons, although he possessed amazing insight into the validity of certain nutter positions. When pressed privately, Harley would admit to certain nutter theories being somewhat persuasive. But never in public. No, never in public.

"The Zapruder business does concern me," Thorne admitted after they'd exchanged initial pleasantries. "Not because I think the film is going to get doctored—they've had forty years to do that. But it's chilling that the government can seize evidence like that. And why do they need the original? Enough copies have been made to provide one to each citizen in the United States."

"Exactly my point," Harley boomed. His voice was surprisingly rich and deep for such a short man. "If nothing else, I think both sides need to agree on this. We cannot countenance such government conduct. No longer."

"I don't recall anyone asking us," Thorne pointed out mildly.

"And that's just the point. So what if the government offers due compensation for it?" Harley argued, always ready to pursue the refrain of governmental misconduct. "If we let them get away with this, then who knows where it will end?"

Another recurrent theme, Thorne thought. Slippery slopes, mudslides—however you wanted to characterize it, the loons were convinced that the world had been going downhill since the assassination. Every governmental atrocity that had occurred since then was linked to it. The Branch Davidians, Ruby Ridge, the Oklahoma bombings—the loons saw those as the logical result of a governmental conspiracy to assassinate the president so long ago. Had they been stopped then, the argument went, none of the subsequent events would have happened.

"Joining us for coffee later?" Harley asked. A number of the members routinely gathered at the local Denny's to continue their arguments over more substantial fare.

Thorne shook his head. "Not tonight. Hot date with the hospital. I'm on call starting at eight P.M."

"You ever sleep?"

"Nope." That had been one of the primary lessons of his years as an intern and resident, living on a minimal allotment of sleep that would have horrified any outside observer.

Harley took a step closer as though readying himself to impart some confidential information. "You keep an eye on those people, Doc," he said confidingly. "They know you're one of us—don't ever doubt it. Hell, they know better than you know yourself, right now."

Harley drifted off, his attention captured by a disagreement that had almost escalated to physical violence. Thorne watched him go, vaguely bothered by the obscure warning. What exactly did Harley mean?

Nothing, he finally concluded. If there was one thing he knew about Jim Harley, it was that he saw conspiracies in everything from the construction of the trolley system in San Francisco to the latest amendments to the Internal Revenue Code. Harley was convinced that he himself was under surveillance, and always took a circuitous route to these meetings in order to shake anyone following him.

Just another loon fantasy. That's all it was.

From the back of the room, Tom Wallinger, head of security at Murphy Medical Center, watched.

Barely two hours into his night on call, Thorne was back in the operating room. An emergency appendectomy, an interesting change of pace amidst the normal run of late-night motor vehicle accidents and shootings. The Murphy maintained a nationally rated trauma center and served as a major resource for their particular area of northern California.

Thorne scrubbed by rote, carefully forcing soap and hot water under his fingernails, sloshing and scrubbing up to his elbows. An appendectomy—an uncomplicated procedure that would probably hold none of the traps that trauma patients laid for the unwary anesthesiologist.

Even better, Debbie Patterson was the surgeon on first call tonight. He sloshed off the last of the soap suds, used his elbow to turn off the water, then gowned and gloved. The heat he felt in his face wasn't directly related to the temperature of the scrub water.

"About ready?" Attila Kamil grinned at him. The tall Algerian surgical resident shoved open the door to the OR with his foot. Kamil had been at the Murphy for a year, and was already deeply involved in the research program that Thorne had been recruited to join. The two had taken an instant liking to one another. After only one week, a solid friendship was already in the early stages. Kamil had shown Thorne around the lab, outlined the protocol, and generally helped him get oriented.

Thorne followed Kamil into the OR and took his place at the head of the table. The ether screen, the piece of fabric that separated the patient's head and anesthesia gear from the surgical field, was already positioned at the patient's neck, protecting the anesthesiologist from exposure to the blood in the operating field itself. He looked down at the rest of the surgical team and felt a stupid smile start at the corners of his mouth.

How did Patterson manage to pull it off? She looked like she belonged on a beach in San Diego, not in the sterile white-tiled OR. Short blond hair swept impatiently off her face, those angelic blue eyes, freckles spritzed across her snub nose, the way she—

"You want to get in the game, Thorne?" Patterson's voice cut through his fantasy, as hard and cold as the scalpel in her hand. She tapped the back of the scalpel on her patient's belly. "I'd rather not do this while he's awake."

And that. The cold hard professionalism while she was in surgery, as hard and aggressive as any surgeon he'd ever met. She slipped it on with the gloves, he guessed.

A contradiction—maybe a mystery. She intrigued him the way that conspiracy theories did.

Thorne slipped the needle out of the supply port in the IV then turned to look at the oximeter. "He's under. Vitals good, good O₂ saturation." He nodded to Patterson. "All yours."

"Nothing heals like cold steel." Patterson drew the scalpel toward her in one quick, practiced motion. Skin and subcutaneous fat sheared cleanly away from the blade and folded back loosely from the incision. Her second stroke sliced through the abdominal muscles, exposing the peritoneal cavity covered with its thin protective membrane.

Patterson's brows drew down over her nose and a line furrowed the center of her forehead. She fingered the flap of severed skin with her free hand, testing the resistance of tissue and muscle to movement and distension. "Jesus, Thorne, did you kill him? I've had roses that didn't unfold as easily as this lummox's belly. Zero rigidity—I've never seen relaxation this good. How sure are you he'll come out of anesthesia?"

Thorne leaned over the ether screen. Dark red muscle covered with a thin white membrane then the translucent peritoneum that enclosed the organs in the abdomen were folded back from the incision. Blood welled from a few minor leakers, small severed blood vessels that Patterson hadn't yet cauterized. The large bowel was nicely exposed, the incision just long enough to allow Patterson complete access to the appendix.

"Damned if I even need these," Patterson muttered, working a small appendicial retractor through the incision and down into the abdominal cavity. With the instrument properly placed, she nodded to Kamil across the table from her. "Now."

Kamil grasped the uppermost retractor then reached across and grabbed the second one. He pulled the retractor slightly out and upwards, rolling the tissue back from the incision.

Patterson nodded approvingly. "With the amount of muscle this guy's got on him, that's a damned fine retraction. Smooth, easy—the last appendix I did was about the same size and I had to use the self-restraining retractor on him." She glanced up at Thorne. "Nice work."

"I'll pass it on to Dr. Gillespie. He was right about this one."

Patterson picked up the cauterizer and attacked the bleeders. The pungent odor of burnt tissue flooded the surgical suite. "As if he would admit it if he weren't."

"Don't start. I owe him a lot."

"And that wasn't doing you a favor, in my humble opinion. You ought to be in surgery every day instead of wasting time on rats. You've been here how long—two weeks?—and you've probably seen more rodents than patients."

Thorne shrugged. "Research is worthwhile. You're seeing the results right now."

Patterson looked up at him sharply. "You're using something experimental on *my* patient?"

"Anaex. Like the name? It's short for Anesthetic Ecstasy."

"And you were going to tell me about this *when?*" The bantering tone vanished from her voice, replaced by the one that her residents knew well.

Thorne stiffened. "Since when is the anesthesiologist *required* to get the surgeon's advice on which drugs to use?"

"It's *my* patient, Thorne. Before, during, or after surgery. You got that?" Patterson's voice was hard. She looked back down at the patient. "He's got a shit-eating grin on his face. Is that your work?"

"Maybe. It's hard to tell when rats are smiling."

"Is there anything else you'd like to share with me now? If not, I've got some work to do." Patterson surveyed the team arrayed around the surgical table. Thorne saw her eyes narrow as she assessed the team's quiet amusement at the conflict between the two doctors. "You people find something funny about this?" She pinned each member of the OR team with a withering glare, extorting head shakes of denial in response.

Satisfied, she looked back down at the patient and slipped back into her teaching mode. "You realize, of course, that a lesser surgeon would have gutted this guy like a fish. When the appendix wraps back around the caecum, it's a bitch getting it out. Observe before you probably the finest example of how to do this right. I'll be available afterwards for autographs." Patterson slipped her index and forefinger into the incision and gently lifted the appendix away from the bowel, delivering it into the incision. "Voila. One hot appendix, just as I promised."

"Don't know how the ER missed it," Thorne said, trying to placate her. While he was well within his rights to plan the course of anesthesia without consulting her, Patterson *was* a senior surgeon. And cute as a—don't go there. Not now. "Now that you look at it, it's obvious."

Dr. Patterson shook her head. "No magic to this. With a white count of over sixteen thousand, anyone could tell the appendix was hot. It's only when it's retrocaecal that the diagnosis is a bit more difficult." She paused from slicing through the peritoneum and pointed the scalpel at Kamil. "*You* should always suspect retrocaecal appendix with the absence of the rebound reflex and the presence of every other classical indicator of appendicitis. If you suspect it, slap them over the right kidney. When you peel them off the roof, you know you've got a hot one and you can plan your incision accordingly. Lower, longer—like this one."

Kamil had an expression of fierce concentration plastered on his face. Good move. Thorne had seen Patterson turn into an unholy bitch if she thought her pearls of wisdom were not being appropriately treasured by her residents, and Kamil had been the victim on more than one occasion. Patterson had the power to get rid of her research surgeons virtually on her own whim. Kamil had confided early on his intent to do everything in his power to placate her, both in and out of surgery—and he'd advised Thorne to do the same.

Dr. Patterson rotated the appendix toward the surface. The caecum, the bridge of tissue connecting it to the body, was short. She judiciously worked her way down it with hemostats, putting a chromic ligature around each hemostat at the point it was holding the appendix between the tissue and the caecum. She put a submucosal circular stitch around the base of the appendix, clamped the caecum a quarter inch above the base of the appendix, then severed the connection between the two. "An ugly one." She held it carefully over the surgical tray.

A normal appendix was about the size of a small child's little finger, a healthy white color with a slight pink due to the blood vessels within it. This one was bigger than her middle finger, angry red and purple, with a small extrudant of puslike material coating its exterior.

"You know, of course," she said to Kamil, pointedly ignoring Thorne, "that the easiest way to get sued is to break one of these over the field. That's why getting it out cleanly and into the pan is critical."

"That's never happened to you, though," Kamil said immediately.

She shook her head. "No, but if it ever did, I'd get everyone to swear it was ruptured before I took it out. You break one of these open, this fellow here's going to be sicker than hell for two or three weeks. We might even get the pleasure of opening him up again to drain the abscess." She opened the forceps and the appendix dropped into the pan with an unpleasant squishing sound. "You don't want to do that. Reeks something awful. The only thing worse is the smell of an infected chest. Describe for me the preferred course of treatment in such a case, Dr. Kamil."

While Kamil reeled off aggressive antibiotic regimes and supportive measures, Patterson deftly stitched the peritoneum closed with 3-O chromic sutures. She interrupted him as he segued into postrelease cautions with, "Close?"

"Thank you, Doctor." Thorne's surgical mask hid a smirk at Kamil's toadying. "If it's all right, I'll close the skin with clips."

"Why would you do it any other way?" Patterson stepped away from the table, peeled off her surgical gloves, and stalked out of the OR.

Thorne peered over the ether screen and watched Kamil carefully place two Allisis clamps, one at each end of the incision. The instrument nurse applied slight tension to each clamp. Eight staples and five seconds later, the abdomen was closed.

The patient twitched once, moaned, and opened his eyes. Kamil started. "Jesus! He's already waking up." He stared down at man on the table. "I just put the last staple in two minutes ago."

"Breathing good, vital signs stable. Just a fast emergence," Thorne said.

"Dr. Patterson thought he might be dead. Now, I'm wondering if he was ever out." Kamil glanced over at the anesthesiologist. "What the hell did you guys do to the anesthetic mix?"

Thorne shook his head. "Bite me, buddy. You're starting to sound like her—and I don't have to take it from you."

"She has that effect, doesn't she?" Kamil muttered. He shucked the gloves from his hands. "Just wondering in case I get another pop quiz from her on it. Come on, Scoot, tell me something that'll make me look smart when she asks. You know she will."

Noting the conciliatory note in Kamil's voice, Thorne eased up. "Okay, here's the magic phrase: Anaex is both a paralytic agent and a sophoric in one. It's going to revolutionize anesthesia. Dr. Gillespie told me we'd see an astounding emergence in people, but you can't ask rats if they're awake." He nodded at the patient. "Go ahead. See if he's responsive yet."

Kamil touched the patient lightly on the right shoulder. "What's your name?" he asked softly.

The patient's eyes fluttered, and then opened. His eyes were still unfocused, but he twisted his head in the resident's direction. "Pietre. Pietre Danoff." The words were slurred, tinged with an odd accent, but recognizable.

"Recognize the name?" Thorne asked Kamil. When the surgeon shook his head, Thorne smiled. "I'm not surprised. If I worked for Patterson, I'd be lucky if I could remember my mother's name. But remember this one—you'll see it again. It's *Prime Minister* Danoff of Ukraine."

Kamil took one step back from the table. "Hell, Scoot. You could have told me before. What if I'd—"

Thorne frowned. "What if you'd *what?* What difference does it make in patient care? There's nothing we'd do differently, either in surgery or in postop. If celebrities make you nervous, get over it."

"Now who sounds like Patterson?"

Thorne laughed, then patted the prime minister gently on the hand, a pleased expression on his face. "Besides, he came out of it just fine. People are always better than rats."

"But not always by much," Clarissa Howling, the instrument nurse, chimed in. "And I'm not too surprised it works the same in rats and men—they're pretty close kin."

"Let's get him down to recovery," Thorne said.

As they left surgery, two men in dark suits fell into step with them on either side of the gurney. Anesthesia posed particular problems with patients who had arcane and esoteric security clearances. Under the influence of preop medication or during emergence, patients often babbled. With the higher cognitive functions of their brain still under the influence of the drugs, they often could and did talk about their work.

In many cases, somber-suited men and women sat by the bedsides of his patients, carefully taking notes on postoperative ramblings. Most of the time the language was English—sometimes it wasn't.

Thorne had heard fascinating tidbits of information he was sure were classified. Sometimes it made sense—most of the time it didn't. Nevertheless, he'd had to sign statements after each exposure, detailing what he'd heard and swearing not to divulge the information.

Dr. Gillespie's new anesthetic was undoubtedly related to the continuing problem of security. That it had beneficial effects during surgery, such as the increased degree of relaxation of abdominal muscles, was merely a fortunate side effect. The faster emergence was the real objective, an increased ability of the patient to safeguard classified material. That it would also relieve anesthesiologists and nurses from the interminable process of being debriefed was also an unexpected benefit.

Dr. Patterson leaned against the nurses' station counter and stared down at her tape recorder. The words were coming quickly, automatically, spilling off her lips almost without conscious effort as she dictated postoperative notes and orders on what had been a routine appendectomy. Neat, clean, and quick, as it ought to be. And just in time—another couple of hours and that gut would have been a mess.

The noise of the gurney caught her attention. She turned away from the tape recorder to see Thorne and one of the nurses wheeling her appendectomy out of the OR and into recovery, what was now called the postanesthesia care room.

"You want to hold on a second?" she said. Thorne—what the hell was he doing moving the patient out that quickly? Sure, that agent he'd used seemed to be exceptionally effective, but it bothered her that he hadn't discussed it with her beforehand. Not that he *had* to, but *still*. If he'd been one of her doctors, she would have busted his chops over that.

She studied Thorne for a moment. Tall, topping out a little over six feet tall, she guessed. Muscular frame, but the lean kind. Like a swimmer. That fit, too, with the unruly hair, dark brown but spattered at the ends with sun highlights, just a shade darker than his eyes. Yep, she'd bet on him being a swimmer. A one-man sport, in keeping with the independence he'd already demonstrated in the OR. Not many research fellows would have stood up to her like he had.

"Dr. Patterson, you have look at this," Kamil called out. "He's already talking."

Patterson laid her tape recorder carefully on the nurses' station and walked over to the gurney, edging one of the security men away from the table. He resisted for a moment, then shifted one step toward the foot of the gurney. The metal rails were up around the sides and the patient was beginning to move restlessly. The odd smile on his face was fading.

Patterson shot a quick glare at Thorne, then turned back to Kamil. "Is he already feeling pain?"

Thorne ignored the snub and answered, "He looks like it, and he's already reaching for that quadrant. I'm going to try Fentanyl instead of using morphine. Less mental confusion—shame to waste the excellent emergence we've got so far, and I want to see how fast he comes out of it."

"What about postop pain medication?" Patterson asked, finally acknowledging Thorne's presence. "No special side effects from this wonder drug?"

"No, none. At least," he amended hastily, "none we've been able to determine on the rats."

Patterson glanced back at the nursing station. "I need another five minutes to finish up postop notes and orders," she said. "I'll stop by recovery as soon as they're done." She picked up the recorder and resumed dictating, her eyes still fixed on the gurney.

Thorne walked at the head of the gurney as the nurse and two orderlies pushed it into the postanesthesia care room. The grin was now completely gone.

"You hurting?" Thorne asked his patient.

The prime minister grimaced and twisted a bit on the gurney. "Yes."

"I'm going to give you something to take care of that in just a second," Thorne said reassuringly.

The postanesthesia care unit was located immediately off a wide corridor that divided surgery. From the nursing station, Patterson could see all three surgical suites as well as the curtained-off preop area and the entrance to the postanesthesia care room. In these days of modern medicine, the euphemism had replaced the old term she favored—the recovery room.

"Space number two," the recovery room nurse said, gesturing to an empty spot in the room.

Thorne slid the gurney smoothly into the spot and hooked up the blood pressure cuff, the pulse oximeter, and the EKG. "Bring me something to sit on," he said to the nurse. "As fast as he's coming out of it, I don't want to take my eyes off him."

Thorne tried to restrain his growing sense of elation. Two milligrams of Fentanyl IV push—that ought to be enough to control the pain without fogging the patient out entirely. He picked up the syringe and slipped the thin needle into the rubber nipple covering the side port on the IV tubing into the man's arm and watched the clear liquid merge into the stream of Ringers' lactate.

Moments later, Prime Minister Danoff quit thrashing and moving about on the gurney. His face relaxed, although the smile he'd had during surgery didn't return.

"Feeling better?" Thorne asked.

The prime minister nodded. "It still hurts, but not as badly."

Thorne turned to the recovery room nurse. "I know it's a bit unusual, but I think I'd like to go ahead and take him up to his room now. It'll upset the routine, but I'll sign the orders."

The nurse nodded. "As long as I've got your signature, I'm covered." She glanced curiously over at space number two. "You sure don't waste any time. What was that?"

Thorne could no longer contain the smile that threatened to cut his face in two. "This is your lucky day. You'll be telling student nurses about this for the rest of your life. We're setting a the new standard for all anesthesia."

The nurse regarded him cynically. "Guess I've heard that one before."

"But not from somebody who meant it."

"Vitals every fifteen minutes," Thorne said, handing the floor nurse Danoff's chart. "Consciousness assessment, a quick look at his mental state. Call me immediately if you have the slightest question or if anything looks even mildly unusual. You got it?" He scribbled his beeper number on the top of the first sheet.

The floor nurse nodded. "What's so special about this one?"

Thorne glanced at the two security men. One had stationed himself by the door to the room, the other next to the head of the bed.

"Everything," Thorne answered. "Absolutely everything."

Two traumas, a cardiac tamponade, and one ruptured spleen later, first call finally ended. Thorne made final rounds on his postsurgical patients, checked out with the ER and OR, then trudged down the passageway that connected the hospital proper to the professional building. His chief would be in his office now, and would be expecting a report on the Danoff procedure.

Very little within the confines of Murphy could force Dr. Gillespie to vary from his daily schedule, and even Thorne, the newest arrival, knew it. In early, an hour or so to straighten out paperwork and review any charts left for him the night before, then in the research lab until just before lunch. Gillespie would see his patients then, keep office hours after lunch, then spend late afternoon and into the evening in the lab.

Anaex was only in limited use in Murphy thus far, and that Gillespie had allowed him to use it unsupervised Thorne took as a vote of confidence. He had almost expected his chief to be in surgery watching. But Danoff's appendix had gotten critical far more quickly than they'd planned.

"It was remarkable," Thorne said, concluding his summary of the surgery. "Absolutely remarkable relaxation and emergence."

Dr. Gillespie shrugged. "About what I expected."

"I wouldn't have thought—" Thorne began.

"No one did. That's the essence of research, Doctor. Looking where no one else has thought to look. Small changes, little deviations—the body is a remarkably fine-tuned instrument, and the link between what we do to the corpus and mental state is even more delicate." He spread his hands in an expansive gesture. "Look at how little it takes to alter emergence. Anaex comes from the same family as PCP. It's so similar to it that we were able to get fast-tracked with the FDA. A few molecules here and there, and you get an entirely different result. You've seen the early research protocols. This agent is so safe and has such a small incidence of side effects that we're talking record-breaking speed in getting it approved."

"When will you publish?"

The senior doctor's frown deepened. "You haven't talked to anyone about this, have you? I've made it absolutely clear to you that I expect complete confidentiality on all my projects."

Thorne shook his head. "Dr. Patterson had some questions about the degree of relaxation. I told her just what you told me, that it's a new agent we're approved to use on humans. She seemed satisfied with that."

Gillespie snorted. "As if a surgeon would understand any explanation more detailed. If they can't see it and cut it out, they don't care about it."

"Nothing heals like cold steel," Thorne said, echoing Patterson's words.

"Nothing kills like it, either. They conveniently forget that part of the equation, particularly when they're trying to blame a bad result on the anesthesiologist." Gillespie leaned forward and rested his elbows on the desk. "Don't forget that, Doctor. Surgeons are *not* your friends, no matter how congenial they may seem. When it comes to facing a mortality and morbidity panel, they'll sell you out faster than a used car salesman. Stick with your own community."

As he stepped out into the hall outside Gillespie's office, Thorne was convinced that he'd made the right decision coming to Murphy. The things he could learn from this man! Gillespie's reputation as a researcher and doctor was sterling—better than sterling, solid gold.

Thorne saw his career stretching out before him, the promotions and accolades that would come to him under Gillespie's tutelage. The older doctor would be warmly approving, perhaps in time coming to look on him as the son he'd never had. It would be the kind of mentoring relationship that his professors at Harvard had talked about wistfully when recalling their own early days, a relationship that transcended medicine and professionalism. And Thorne would be worthy of it—he would *make* himself worthy of it.

Father and son—just too trite, wasn't it? A smile quirked at his lips as he considered the myths he could feel himself creating.

Gillespie, the driven genius who'd never had time for a family. His equally brilliant protégé, Thorne, whose own father had not lived to see his son's achievements. His father had been an internist in a MASH unit during Desert Storm, and one of the first to fully document the effects of exposure to low levels of nerve toxin.

Document it—and die from it.

Just last year, decades after Desert Storm, the Army was just beginning to admit that they'd fouled up badly. Another conspiracy at work, or just simply the unimaginable inefficiency of bureaucrats? Whatever the explanation, Thorne's summer vacation scut work helping his father monitor the long-range health effects of the toxin had been at least partially responsible for a devoted history major applying to medical school.

Thorne glanced down at his watch—thirty minutes until he could reasonably start rounds. What better time to get started than now? He'd go down to the lab, spend a few more minutes getting familiar with the research protocols on the Anaex trials.

Good reports would filter back to Gillespie about the new doctor on his staff who was so dedicated, spent so much free time in the lab. If anything would win Gillespie's approval, Thorne thought it would be that.

THREE

Heart and soul, Sergeant Nigel Carter belonged to General Boothby. He had ever since the general had sprung him from some entirely unwarranted disciplinary charges. Why striking a master sergeant should warrant felony charges against him, along with the threat of a lengthy stay in Leavenworth, Carter had never entirely understood. It wasn't as though the master sergeant hadn't deserved it.

Still, the Army took such matters seriously. Far too seriously, in Carter's opinion. If there were more guys like General Boothby in charge, he had a feeling that the Army would be a whole hell of a lot better off.

Two months ago, General Boothby had seconded Carter into an elite, off-the-books special Operations Team, outside normal Army channels and chains of command and responsible only to General Boothby himself. The major in charge—hell, even he was just one of the guys. There might be some people who would think they were a bunch of misfits and losers, but Carter knew better. No regular unit could have accomplished what the ten men in his platoon had, not with the bullshit regulations and restraints on their conduct. Rules of engagement—Carter snorted. As though there should be *any* rules when dealing with those slanty little bastards. And that included the chickenshit gooks that were supposedly their allies.

General Boothby, now, there was a man who knew how to treat the troops. Carter never had to worry about having the finest in combat gear available, never had any of the dogshit details that had plagued him as a regular soldier. No more night guard watches, no more latrine cleaning or showing up for morning muster. The Alfa team ran by a separate set of rules, ones that centered on simply getting the job done. And the job was defined as whatever General Boothby said it was.

Today, that included teaching the northern gooks—the enemy, as opposed to the southern gooks who were supposedly their friends—

a little lesson in military courtesy. Yesterday, when the general had driven down to the fence to inspect the troops, one of the northern gooks had spit on the ground at the general. Sure, they'd been pretending they didn't see him, but every last one of them knew exactly what had been intended. An insult.

Well, enough was enough. Carter smiled and ran his fingers lightly over the well-oiled barrel of his Chinese RPG, the weapon of choice in the North. In some parts of the world, such an act would have been grounds for immediate execution.

Unfortunately for the North Koreans, Carter's little corner of Korea was one of them.

Carter waited for the light to fade before he moved out. He left his barracks and made his way toward the entrance to the underground tunnel just fifty feet outside the base's perimeter fence. The northern gooks had built it two years ago, and Carter was reasonably certain that they didn't know he'd discovered it shortly thereafter. In all the time he'd been in Korea, he'd never caught one of the little bastards actually using this particular tunnel. Even the telltales he'd left behind, the twig carefully positioned on a rock, the snippet of fishing line draped over the edge of the concealed opening, had not been conclusive. Given the weather, they might have been moved by natural forces.

Then again, maybe not. You never knew for sure, not in the complicated game of bluff and counterbluff that passed for politics in the Republic of Korea.

Carter paused near the stand of low brush that concealed a spider hole leading down into the tunnel, then paced off ten careful steps back toward the North Korean side. He dropped to the ground and pressed his ear against the dirt.

Some of the tunnels that ran under the fence and onto South Korea's soil were manned continuously. He knew that for certain, had eavesdropped from above on the harsh chatter of the little bastards as they whiled away the hours on duty as soldiers in any nation did. He listened to them argue, gamble, snore, and fart with the same dispassionate clarity that he used to listen to the master sergeant's orders.

The content didn't matter—only the existence of the sounds intruding into his reality.

The hard-packed dirt carried sounds for long distances. He could hear the grumbling moan of the base generator, the harsh chuffing of trucks starting and rolling across the packed dirt. Later in the year, when the rains came, it would be more difficult. The camp would be coated in a perpetual layer of sticky, foul mud. It still carried sounds a long distance, but it was hell digging it out of his ears afterwards.

Silence. Nothing moved directly below him. He stayed supine, ear pressed to the ground and eyes closed for twenty minutes, concealed from the rest of the camp by brush as he listened. Finally, he was satisfied. If there were soldiers on duty below, then they were far more professional than any he'd encountered to date in Korea.

So at least his end of the tunnel would be unoccupied. Good—that made it easier. In his experience, the tunnels were either occupied or they weren't. It was unlikely he'd encounter northern gooks further up the tunnel, although it was always possible. Assuredly the other end would be guarded, but that posed no major problems for him either. At least, it never had in the past.

Carter waited outside the tunnel until the sun finally set. There would be a quarter moon tonight, but the low-hanging clouds would block out most of the light. As he heard the sounds of the changing of the watch on his side of the fence, Carter slipped underground, his field knife clenched between his teeth.

Four hours later, he was back. He rested outside the tunnel for a few moments, catching his breath and letting the adrenaline fade out of his body. Exhilarating—God, but it was good to do the work he'd trained for. Be all that you can be—in the Army.

He wiped the bloody blade off on his trousers, mentally reviewing how he'd present the results of his little foray to the general. That was another of the general's rules, that the general was to be immediately and personally briefed after the completion of every mission by the man actually executing the mission. Though what was so critical about burning down food storage sites, Carter had never been told.

After he was satisfied with his version of the debrief, Carter set off back into camp proper. He nodded to the sentry, presented his ID card, and was waved through. Most of the camp knew better than to mess with Carter, although few knew why it was forbidden. The sentry had looked askance at the mud and grime covering Carter's field uniform, but hadn't asked a single question.

Carter trotted back to the barracks and made the obligatory telephone call to the general's office. He was patched through immediately, and the general ordered him to report to the usual location for debriefing in ten minutes.

God, it was good to be appreciated.

"The southern end of the tunnel was unoccupied," Carter started, unfolding the map he'd drawn as he spoke. "I encountered light resistance at the northern end of the tunnel, and neutralized the threats immediately."

"Before they could sound the alarm, I hope?" The general's voice sounded pleased.

It wasn't really a question, Carter knew. Of course he'd gotten them before they'd had a chance to squeal—otherwise, he would have had to abort. No, what the general was really asking for was the details. The gory, up-close-and-personal details of how he'd taken out two gooks in the close confines of the tunnel.

Carter obliged, swelling slightly with justified pride as he did so. The general nodded appreciatively, occasionally asking a clarifying question, but mostly letting him proceed at his own pace. The general seemed particularly interested in the dry storage warehouses Carter had torched. It was less a briefing by an enlisted noncom to a senior officer than two buddies trading war stories, glorying in the details.

Finally, Carter was finished. Total body count: fifteen gooks, including two from the south who'd spotted him leaving the brush around the tunnel. He hadn't been exactly sure how the general would react to those two, since Alfa Team supposedly tried to avoid killing the southern gooks. But there really hadn't been much choice in the matter this time. He had seen it in their eyes that they were going to ask difficult, pointed questions about the condition of his clothes and the blood spattering his face and hands. He'd taken the initiative, tried to make the decision that the general himself would have made if he'd been present, and Carter was relieved to see the expression of approval on the flag officer's face.

After Carter left, the general drew the bottle of wine out of the desk drawer and poured himself another eight ounces. He swiveled his chair around to stare out the window at the clouds, hoping to catch a glimpse of the stars. His fingers tapped out a soft, random rhythm on the chair's worn brown leather.

Maybe some more wine—he lifted the tumbler, discovered it was empty, and turned back to the desk to refill it.

Wine was a tool, one he'd long used, sparingly, to defeat ingrained Army ways of thinking. It silenced the governor, the one that stifled innovation and daring, and allowed his mind to roam free over the vast expanse of history. A few glasses and he could visualize the lines of cause and effect that were the fiber of modern conflict, insinuate himself into the opposition's mind.

Never had this ability been so critical to success as now. There were too many players in this game, entirely too many, and they weren't confined to the deceptively shabby corridors of the Pentagon. The complexity forced him to sort out pressure points, and analyze and reduce weaknesses to single pressure points he could influence.

Carter and the rest of Alfa Team were tools, too. Surgical instruments he could bring to bear on those critical junctions of political power and military capability, scalpels that would sever cause and effect chains, and reshape the playing field without alerting the actual players.

The most critical player right now was the 501st Intelligence Brigade. A gamble, trying to pull this off under their scrutiny, but a necessary gamble. The spooks that analyzed every truck convoy, every troop deployment, and even the routine maintenance actions across the border had to support Boothby's analysis of escalating tensions along the border.

So far, it was working. The 501st viewed the series of inexplicable fires in food warehouses with a cynical eye, and were culturally conditioned not to believe North Korean claims that South Korean and American forces were behind the destruction, particularly when General Boothby and JSOC—the Joint Special Operations Command in the States—denied any involvement.

If U.S. and ROK forces were not at fault, then the North Koreans were. The only question was: Why?

The 501st rarely believed in coincidence. They knew how desperate the North was for food, and found it improbable that the North was intentionally destroying stockpiles. No, the food must have been relocated somehow, convoys delivering supplies actually carting them away, relocating them to lay the groundwork for the buildings to be destroyed. And, more importantly, providing a reasonable, non-provocative explanation for the massive convoys to the DMZ. Operational deception—after two months of careful work by General Boothby and his Alfa Team, the 501st was convinced that North Korea was transporting weapons, armament, and reinforcements to the DMZ under the cover of replenishing destroyed subsistence supplies. To intelligence specialists, reinforcing the DMZ was as dangerous as tracer fire overhead.

Boothby was pleased with the 501st's conclusions, and drafted his own reports to his superior, CINCPACFLT, lauding their efforts. He'd also made sure the Chairman of the Joint Chiefs of Staff, General Jerry Huels, was kept informed, relying on their long friendship to slip information to Jerry outside normal channels.

Boothby sipped the last of the wine and allowed himself a moment of quiet self-congratulation. Just a few more months at the most and everything would be in place. As Korea went critical, Boothby would recommend that he make his reports directly to JCS, bypassing CINCPACFLT, on the theory that a shorter chain of command would enable the president of the United States to more skillfully shape America's national strategy. Boothby himself would fly back to the States and brief the President in person. No one would ever suspect that the first shots in the next—and final—Korean conflict were fired by the United States.

An old Army adage sprang to mind: Tracer fire works both ways.

FOUR

Between his beeper and checking on Danoff's recovery, it was another four hours before Thorne had a chance to get down to the lab. He'd long since passed the point of tiredness and was operating in the twilight state of intellect alone that he'd come to know too well as a resident.

The lab's foyer was a small featureless cubicle. A window looking onto the actual reception area dominated one wall. Thorne tapped lightly on the glass.

Gilbert Lanelli looked up from his desk, stood, and walked over to the desk in front of the window. The senior lab technician assigned to the Anaex project was a sparse man, thin muscles corded over heavy bones. With his short-clipped red hair speckled with gray at the temples, hard, bony nose, and thin lips, Lanelli *looked* like a man who'd spent most of his days working with lab animals. The tech's usually dour expression was no more readable that a rat's.

"Dr. Thorne?" Lanelli's voice was tinny over the speaker set into the glass. Thorne saw the technician look pointedly at the clock. Dr. Gillespie wasn't the only one who believed in the sanctity of a well-ordered schedule.

Research occupied an entire wing of the E-shaped center building. The lower levels and the basement were windowless and exquisitely climate-controlled. Cipher locks and key-carded steel doors barred casual visitors from access, and the basement levels were further fortified by armed guards.

During Thorne's first interview, Dr. Gillespie had alluded only vaguely to the research conducted there, mentioned that most of it was sponsored by the Department of Defense. He'd dismissed further questions with assurances that there were no biological or chemical warfare agents involved, but refused to answer further questions on the grounds of national security.

At the time, Thorne had simply absorbed the information. The possibilities in his new position were too exciting and demanding. Besides, he'd already been told during his initial interviews that he'd be expected to comply with a number of unusual security precautions while treating high-ranking military and diplomatic personnel. As part of his pre-employment screening, he'd undergone a thorough security investigation. At one point, he'd been amused to find out he would be evaluated for a Q-clearance—code-word access on a need-to-know basis for the United States's most secret military projects.

"Just stopping by," Thorne said immediately, annoyed at the defensiveness he heard in his own voice. Why should he have to explain to a lab technician what he was doing in his own lab?

Not his *own* lab, technically. The Anaex Protocol was Dr. Gillespie's project, although Thorne was an associate researcher. That Gillespie had allowed him to perform today's procedure on Prime Minister Danoff was a vote of confidence, even though Gillespie himself had made all the decisions ranging from course of treatment, to obtaining patient consent.

"Everything's fine, Doctor," Lanelli said. "I would have called Dr. Gillespie if it weren't."

Not you. In the two weeks Thorne had been at the Murphy, he'd already learned that what Lanelli didn't say was often more important than what he did. The lab tech had a way of making his point as he just had—if there had been a problem, Dr. Gillespie would handle it, not his new, wet-behind-the-ears research associate.

Thorne smiled politely. "I'm sure you would have. I had some extra time and thought I'd stop by, that's all. Let me in, please."

Lanelli made no move to reach for the button that would buzz the security door open. "Dr. Gillespie doesn't like a lot of people wandering around the lab."

"I'm not *wandering*. Dr. Kamil let me in yesterday—what's so different about today?"

"What do you *want?*"

The hostility in the lab technician's voice took Thorne aback. "I don't think I'm required to justify my presence in the lab to you. Now open this door. Immediately."

Lanelli frowned. "I think you'd better talk to Dr. Gillespie first. My orders don't say anything about letting you in any time you want to *wander* around."

Thorne could feel his temper sliding around the edge of control. First Patterson, then the surgical resident, now a lab technician—was there anyone in the hospital who didn't feel justified in treating him like an idiot? "I am *assigned* to this protocol at Dr. Gillespie's request, and I am the associate researcher for this phase. There is absolutely no reason that—" His words skidded to a halt as he saw Lanelli shaking his head.

"I am going to see Dr. Gillespie right now," Thorne said finally, his voice tight with anger. "Your conduct is outrageous, and we will settle this matter immediately."

"You do that, Doc. And if Dr. Gillespie says to let you in any old time you want, then you'll get it. Until then, I've got work to do and you've got patients. Unlike you, I don't have time to wander around spying on people."

The lab tech left the window and stalked off toward the glassed-in area holding the rows and rows of rats.

Thorne stared at the window in disbelief, then wheeled around and left. He slammed the outer door on his way to the elevator.

By the time he'd reached his chief's office in the next wing, Thorne had cooled off. Maybe Dr. Gillespie *did* have some rule about spending time in the lab outside of scheduled protocol evaluations, a rule Lanelli knew about and Thorne didn't. Dr. Gillespie hadn't said anything about it. But then again, Thorne hadn't mentioned his intention of spending every free moment in the lab. He felt chagrined as he contemplated just how thoroughly his plan to impress the chief had gone off track.

Still, if there *were* restrictions he wasn't aware of, better to find out now. And from the source, so that there would be no need to endure that insufferably condescending tone in Lanelli's voice again.

So much for the technicians feeding back good reports to Dr. Gillespie.

"So I'm not allowed in the lab by myself?" Thorne heard the note of challenge in his voice and tried to moderate it.

"We have technicians for that, Dr. Thorne. It's not a cost-effective use of your time. Daily inspection visits are outside of protocol."

Thorne felt his face flush. "I just stopped in for a moment."

"Time that could have been better spent with your patients." Dr. Gillespie sighed and put down his pencil. "Research is a demanding specialty, Christopher. Not every doctor is well suited to it. It requires a particular turn of temperament, an ability to detach oneself from the experimental subjects and remain objective at all times." He held up one hand, forestalling a response. "It makes the technicians uneasy, you know, having us around the lab at odd times. They start to wonder if we don't trust them to do their jobs. And there is the very real danger that you will taint their formal observations of the animals by discussing the progress of the project with them. The Hawthorne Effect, as well as a number of other well-documented research pitfalls. You ask questions, the technicians discern what you *hope* the results will be, and they start interpreting the animal's behavior in light of those expectations. You could be doing serious damage to the protocol, you understand, even operating under the best of intentions."

Dr. Thorne felt angry. "I'm aware of those factors, Doctor, and I assure you—"

Again Dr. Gillespie cut him off. "I'm not casting aspersions on your intentions at all. But understand, the entire project is my concern." His voice softened slightly. "Thorne, I'm pleased to have you as part of the team, and I think you'll be able to get past this issue without any problems. You're a fine anesthesiologist, and you're going to be a superb research physician. There is a reason, however, that you're not the supervising physician. It's your first major research project, and I think you must grant the possibility that I know a bit more about these matters than you do. I must insist that you adhere to protocol. To be blunt, please stay out of the lab unless your presence is required for a protocol milestone. Once you stop and think about it, I think you'll agree that that's best for both you and the project."

Dr. Gillespie regarded him gravely as though weighing alternatives. Finally, he leaned back in his chair and sighed. "Unreasonable son of a bitch, aren't I? Going on about surgeons earlier, and now keeping you from doing the very job I hired you for."

Thorne started to protest, then shrugged, a rueful expression on his face. "It's your lab, Doctor. How you want to run it—none of my business. I just work here."

Gillespie sighed. "I was afraid of this. The last thing in the world I want to do is discourage your enthusiasm and initiative. Listen, Scoot—may I call you that? I've heard that's what you go by." Receiving a grudging nod of consent from Thorne, Gillespie continued, "Scoot, there's a lot you don't know. And there are reasons for my reluctance to give you free run of the lab, ones that really don't have anything to do with you." He appeared to struggle with himself for a few moments, then continued. "What I'm going to tell you is completely confidential, you understand. Not a word to anyone else, in the lab or outside of it. If word got out—well, you'll understand after I explain." He fixed the younger doctor with a considering stare. "I'm taking a risk doing this, but . . ." Gillespie took a deep breath and began. "You know, of course, that you aren't the first associate on the team. When we first started the animal trials three years ago, I hired another bright young doctor to assist. Frank Hardy—Boston College, Grays—an impeccable background and a real flair for research. He didn't have your skills with patients, though. All he was interested in was pure research."

Thorne nodded. He'd heard Dr. Hardy's name mentioned once, but hadn't heard anything about him beyond that.

Gillespie stared off in the distance. "Two months after he started work here, Frank Hardy showed up late at night in the lab with a team of animal rights activists. By the time security got around to investigating the late-night entry into the lab, they'd managed to free forty cages of cats and destroy at least a year's worth of data. We had to terminate the entire phase and destroy the animals. Without data, there was no point in continuing—we had to start all over. That's one reason for the security, and I'm not willing to change that requirement just yet." He smiled weakly. "Give me a break, Doctor. I lost a year's worth of work because I let a new associate have free run of the lab. As soon as your final clearance investigation comes back clean, we'll discuss it, but for now . . ."

"I understand," Thorne said. And, as much as he hated to admit it, he did. "They said it would take six months, minimum."

Gillespie nodded. "I'm sorry about the restrictions, but I just don't feel comfortable lifting them. Not so soon after Hardy."

"Understandable. Not pleasant, but understandable. Doctor, you mentioned another reason as well?"

Gillespie grimaced. "This one's even more of a judgment call. You know why we've got such solid funding for the Anaex Protocol?"

"Department of Defense, right?"

"That's right. What I said about the chemical structure of Anaex is true—that alone might have been enough to get us fast-tracked to do preliminary trials on humans before we do in-depth primate trials. For once, the military is cutting red tape instead of generating it. Partnered with them, the hospital developed the formula, completely bypassing the pharmaceutical companies. Sure, we've contracted out some of the actual production, but it's our drug. Ours, and the Army's. With a successful track record in Army field applications, Anaex will be approved for general use, and we'll be the ones licensing it to drug companies. That's our payback for being the first ones willing to go this route with the military. But with DOD pushing the development, it was a foregone conclusion.

"Since Anaex combines both paralytic and sleeping agents, it's ideal for front line surgeries. Less equipment to transport, more stable in long-term storage, and faster emergence. The last reason is probably the most important—field hospitals can get men in and out quickly, then safely transport them to rear area facilities after they're patched up. The advantages over normal anesthetic protocols are astounding."

Gillespie leaned across the desk toward him. "Scoot, isn't this why we're in research? To save lives? It's not a flashy, glory-hounding calling like surgery, but the benefits from proving out Anaex will do more in one year than a surgeon could do in an entire career."

"You know that's why I wanted to work with you," Thorne said quietly. "I told you during the first interview. Research—it's always been my first choice. I'm good with patients, I know that. Getting to practice here while working on the Anaex project is a bonus."

"The people you'll help first are the men and women on the front lines of a battlefield. And civilians, later on. But the military has first cut on this, and right now they're very concerned about the incident with your predecessor. It was a hard sell, convincing them to let me hire a replacement." A singularly weary look crossed Gillespie's face. "If they had their way, they'd lock me in the lab alone until all the protocols were done."

"But if I pass their security check, then surely they'll be convinced? What more could they want?"

Gillespie nodded. "That's what I'm counting on. But you can see why there are some restraints on your movements just now. You've only been here a few weeks. I know you're impatient, ready to charge in and get started, but I've got to ask you to live with this for now. I'll do what I can to speed up the process, but I need your cooperation on this."

"How about this?" Thorne suggested. "Lanelli is cleared, right?"

"He's been with me since the beginning," Gillespie answered.

"What if you were to ask him to make himself available as an escort? Sir, I sincerely doubt that I'm going to have much free time—I've seen the schedule you've got me on. But when I *do* have a few free moments, I'd appreciate the opportunity to get into the lab. Just to keep my hand in while we wait for the bureaucracy to do its thing. Would that be acceptable?"

Gillespie nodded slowly. "I think so. Lanelli is busy, no doubt. But he ought to be able to spare some time for you. As long as it's not every hour."

Thorne shook his head. "As I said, I've seen my schedule. I just want to be able to keep my appetite whetted."

"Okay, Doctor." Gillespie reached out and tendered a handshake. "You've got a deal."

FIVE

Thorne left his chief's office and for the second time that day felt a warm rush of optimism about being at the Murphy. Gillespie's reasons made sense, and so did the work-around solution they'd come up with. Sure, it would take some time, but he'd been warned about that, hadn't he? And after the chief's experience with his last research fellow, you couldn't really blame him for being cautious.

Well, if he couldn't hit the ground running in research, then he might as well start earning his reputation caring for his patients. Thorne headed for the surgical ward to check on Danoff.

Thorne tapped lightly on the door, then pushed it open. He paused at the entrance to the room and assessed his patient. From the looks of it, his patient was doing even better than the rats.

Danoff was sitting up in bed watching the television. His color was excellent, his face, arms, and hands the same burnished gold color they'd been when he'd checked in. A definite improvement over surgical pallor. His breathing appeared regular and easy, another positive sign. Too often patients experienced mild respiratory distress following surgery, a result of the paralytic agents used to control their involuntary movements while they were under the knife. If Danoff's lungs sounded as good as Thorne suspected they would under a stethoscope, he'd escape the normal postsurgical course of respiratory therapy.

Danoff was watching him, another surprise. This soon post-surgery, he should still have been woozy, sleeping off the effects of the anesthetic for at least another day. The painkillers Thorne had prescribed should also have contributed to the general decrease in consciousness, but other than a slight sluggishness in his attention response, Thorne found no deficiency.

Thorne crossed over to the side of the bed and pulled up the straight-backed visitor's chair. "How do you feel?"

Danoff shrugged. "Sleepy. Tired. The pain medication, I suppose." A guttural roundness haunted Danoff's vowels, but his English was precise and clear.

"Any pain?"

Danoff shook his head. "A little sore—that is all."

"May I take a look at the incision?" Thorne always made it a point to ask. Too many doctors simply walked up to the patient and pulled aside the sheets and gown to examine their handiwork. It was as though they felt they owned the patient's body—a true statement while the patient was unconscious and on the table, but an abysmal practice with a conscious patient.

"You'll feel a bit drowsy for several days," Thorne said as he studied the incision. Kamil had done a good job, and it showed in the careful matching of one side of the incision to the other. Clear plastic tape covered the healing incision, a porous membrane that would gradually dissolve over the next few days. The subcutaneous stitches closing the underlying layers of skin would as well, although the skin clamps holding the epidermis together would have to be manually removed. Still, there was every chance that in a few years the prime minister would barely be able to see his scar.

Thorne touched the incision lightly, feeling around the edges for any indication of swelling or pus. He glanced at Danoff to check for pain reaction and saw his patient grimace. "That hurt?"

"A little, but, Doctor, you mentioned feeling drowsy. I—I had the strongest dream today. A nightmare really. Absolutely terrifying." Danoff's voice was harsh.

Thorne moved his hand to the prime minister's wrist and felt the pulse hammering away. Around 110 beats a minute, far too fast for a man who'd been lying in bed all day half-sedated. "Wow. It's really got you concerned, doesn't it?" That was important, always to acknowledge the patient's concerns as valid.

Danoff inclined his head slightly. "It was so vivid."

Thorne felt the pulse pick up another notch under his fingers. "I've heard that from patients before," he said. "Postop nightmares are fairly common and nothing to worry about. It's the anesthesia—we have to use it to make sure you're out for the surgery, but the brain objects fairly strenuously sometimes after it's over."

Danoff looked unusually vulnerable, his face openly frightened. He locked gazes with Thorne. "You're certain?"

Thorne smiled. "Absolutely certain. The dreams can be quite realistic and frightening, I've heard. But it's not indicative of any underlying psychological problem or of some deep-seated wish to do something horrible, believe me. It's a little bit like the rage reaction that occurs when we first put you under in the operating room." He felt the pulse slow slightly and saw a trace of relief cross the prime minister's face.

"Rage reaction? That sounds like the dream I had." Danoff

started to say more, then pursed his lips and shook his head slightly. While his face still bore the marks of fear, his eyes were now blank and uncommunicative. His pulse continued to slow.

Encouraged, Thorne resumed examining the surgical wound while he explained. "Another odd but completely normal part of anesthesia. Can I bore you with some trivia from my field of expertise?"

"Please do."

"Most people think that anesthesia just means feeding you some sort of gas through a mask to make you sleep. Actually, it's a bit more complicated than that. I think you'll understand why the dreams are so normal when I explain it.

"First, all you get from the face mask is pure oxygen. All the anesthetic and paralysis agents are liquid. I slip tiny amounts of them into the IV, first to put you under and then to paralyze you.

"There are really four stages of sleep, and each stage has several subdivisions, called levels. For surgery, we want you in the third stage, second level, what's called surgical sleep. But to get there, I have to take you through the lighter stages of sleep, and what the brain remembers can cause the nightmares you're describing. It's because of the stages of sleep you go through, that's all.

"The very first thing I do when I slip the mask over your face is slip you a mild sleeping drug through the IV. That puts you out and into what we call the first stage of sleep. You're asleep, but just barely—almost like daydreaming.

"The second stage of sleep is probably what you're remembering in your dreams. It's a little like—well, have you ever woken yourself up by having a muscle suddenly jerk or tense up? Second stage is characterized by those involuntary muscle contractions. You're restless and uneasy, but still asleep. To prevent them, I give you a tiny bit of a drug that prevents your muscles from responding to your brain. You're already drowsing, so you don't notice it, but you're paralyzed. I handle all your breathing for you while you're under anesthesia, which is the reason your throat feels a bit sore."

"The drug—it is like curare?" the prime minister asked.

"Something similar, but the one I usually use is called Norcuron. It's got another purpose as well. As you leave the second stage of sleep and head for what we call surgical sleep, your body goes through an involuntary anger reaction. We don't know exactly why. It may be some form of survival instinct to resist being forced that deeply into sleep by an outside force. Whatever it is, it makes the patient flail around violently on the table. Without the Norcuron, you'd probably be able to land a fairly decent punch on most of us. Not something you ought to be doing to a woman who has a knife in her hand."

Danoff smiled slightly, his tension clearly easing. "Most particularly not with Dr. Patterson. I suspect she can be rather—formidable."

Thorne shot him a guarded glance. He'd heard many patients report what they seemed to have overheard during surgery while they were supposedly asleep. Had the patient overhead his sparring with Dr. Patterson and somehow filed it away in his subconscious? Entirely possible. Better to not reinforce *that* memory. "Exactly. Adults pass through the rage stage fairly quickly, but kids are another case entirely. They have to be managed much more closely than adults do. If you buy the theory that the brain remembers absolutely everything you've ever experienced, then you can see how this would cause the kind of nightmares you're talking about. On some level, your brain has stored a memory of your being involuntarily sedated and paralyzed and injured. Regardless of how you consciously interpret it, those memories are there. And of the rage stage as well."

The wound appeared to be healing just as it should. It was still red around the edges, but no more than it should be immediately postop. There was no sign of infection or seepage, and Danoff's chart indicated that he'd experienced no more than a few degrees of normal postoperative temp spike.

Thorne nodded his approval, gently pulled Danoff's gown shut, and rearranged the sheet as he'd found it. "It's healing up just fine."

"This rage reaction," Danoff mused, obviously reassured by Thorne's explanation, "it happens as the patient—as I—regain consciousness as well?"

"Yes, as you pass back through that stage from surgical sleep into normal REM activity. I don't let you leave the operating room until you're through it." Thorne thought back to Danoff's rapid recovery. "You came out of it quite quickly."

"Thank you. I believe your explanation is quite accurate." All traces of fear had faded from the prime minister's face. "And I am feeling a bit drowsy now."

"I'm going to leave a prescription for pain medication and for a sleeping pill if you need it. I don't think you will, but if you have any problems getting back to sleep tonight, don't hesitate to ask for it. I doubt you'll have any nightmares at all, but this will certainly prevent them completely. Any questions?"

Danoff's eyes were already drifting shut. For Thorne, it was reassuring to see him look more like a normal postsurgical patient. Thorne stepped away from the bed and took one step toward the door when Danoff's voice stopped him.

"Earlier, you mentioned that there were four stages of sleep. What was the last one?"

Thorne cursed himself for having started his explanation out with that bit of anesthetic trivia. He waited for a moment, hoping, then heard Danoff's breathing deepen into sleep. Good. It was a question he hadn't really wanted to answer.

The fourth stage of sleep was clinical death.

SIX

As soon as he'd shooed Thorne out of his office, Dr. Gillespie headed for the basement. His section of the research area was located one floor beneath ground level. A large chunk of money had been sunk into the most advanced climate control system available, ensuring that the temperature and humidity remained at rat-optimized constants. That the lab technicians and doctors who had to live in the spaces were also comfortable was merely a fortunate side effect. People didn't matter. The rats did.

Gillespie glanced into the glassed-in reception area that overlooked the foyer as he started punching his security code into the cipher lock. Lanelli was not at his desk. The door opened before Gillespie could enter the last digit.

"There's a problem, Doctor." Lanelli's voice was pitched higher than normal. Gillespie noted with clinical detachment that his pupils seemed slightly enlarged, a normal stress reaction, and his skin looked pale. The chemical structure of adrenaline and its clinical presentation automatically cycled through his mind.

"Describe it," Gillespie said, his voice tart. The man's imprecision was irritating. Gillespie had worked with him on two projects so far, and each time he'd carefully explained to Lanelli exactly how to report his observations. Time, place, physical observations, a litany of evidence carefully stripped of emotion and prejudgment. While Lanelli's written notations on the animal behavior had improved markedly, the man still hadn't mastered the art of giving a succinct verbal statement.

Gillespie watched Lanelli take a deep breath and nodded in approval. Hyperoxygenation would aid in the more rapid burn-off of the adrenaline and restore some measure of the man's intellectual equilibrium. At least the lab tech had retained that much of Gillespie's lectures.

"At 1455 this afternoon, I was weighing the rats and checking their postsurgical healing, as per protocol number seven. As I reached for specimen seventy-three, the animal attacked—I mean, bit specimen seventy-four around the area of the cervical spine. Seventy-four went limp immediately, and seventy-three dropped her body. There was no further movement from seventy-four. I immediately donned my protective gloves and opened the cage and extracted the body of seventy-four. I bagged her, labeled the specimen container, and placed her in the refrigerator. Seventy-three has been immobile in one corner of his cage every time I've observed him since that time."

"You didn't call me," Dr. Gillespie noted. He looked at the clock. "That was twenty minutes ago."

"Dr. Thorne was down here. I got rid of him, but he said he was going to see you. That's why I—"

"I've discussed the matter with Dr. Thorne. In the future, please ensure that you personally reach me immediately. I define immediately as meaning as soon as possible after the situation is stabilized. Is that clear?"

Lanelli nodded. "I'm sorry, Doctor. I thought—"

"I don't care what you thought. Just make sure it doesn't happen again." Dr. Gillespie stared at the far wall. Was it just coincidence that Thorne had been down at the lab then? Concocting another incident to justify firing another research assistant would be a problem. Not an insurmountable one, but a problem none the less.

"Doctor, as long as you're here . . ." Lanelli's voice trailed off uncertainly.

Dr. Gillespie snapped his attention back to the technician. "What is it?"

"There've been three other incidents since then."

Lanelli carefully positioned the damp rat bodies on surgical trays. He gave each one a final pat with a brown paper towel, then carried the trays into the lab's small surgical suite. Droplets of water pooled up on the steel.

"That's all of them?" Gillespie asked.

Lanelli nodded. "Just four. I cleaned them up—you couldn't see the wounds the way I found them."

Gillespie studied the first one without touching it. Even from this angle, he could see the ragged gash arching across its throat. The neck veered off at an odd angle from the rest of the body, broken, obviously.

He turned the first one over, handling it gently, probing along the length of the body for other injuries. Another long wound rounded under the belly, and a piece of intestine protruded.

This had been a large rat, an anomaly in a strain of lab animals that were bred for uniformity. This particular animal had dominated his cage mates, and Lanelli had even suggested at one point that they eliminate the specimen from the protocol. Gillespie had vetoed, determined not to allow any opportunity for experimental error or criticism. The animals that started the protocol all stayed.

Gillespie touched the unscarred portion of the rat's pelt, stroked it, then again with more pressure, palpating his way down the spinal column. There were small lumps under his finger, barely larger than grains of sand. Were they related to the injury? Some disease process starting? Or a result of the rat's repeated exposure to Anaex?

"Bag them. I'll want to do a complete dissection, but I don't have time now," he said finally. He stepped away from the table and peeled off his gloves.

Lanelli nodded and was already producing prelabeled bags as the doctor crossed the room for the wash basin.

Gillespie washed his hands thoroughly, forcing the Betadine into every crevice and under his nails. The ubiquitous yellow antiseptic killed almost every dangerous organism that a hospital could generate, with a few notable exceptions.

He reached for a paper towel, stopped just short of pulling one out of the container. What were the odds that whatever was affecting his rats was some form of nosocomial infection? Was it possible? He considered the matter, water running down his arms and dripping off his elbows onto the linoleum.

There were always cases of nosocomial infection in any medical facility, illnesses picked up by patients while in residence. Those were the most dangerous ones, germs and viruses that had survived the constant barrage of sterilization, antibiotics, and general antiseptic procedures in the hospital. The survivors thrived in weaker patients, often immune to the normal broad spectrum antibiotics that were successful on their less-virulent brethren.

It *was* possible. The aberrations he'd noted in their behavior might be entirely unrelated to the protocol. In fact, they probably were. It was simply inconceivable that Anaex could have any effect on an animal six months after it'd been used, simply not possible. There was no record of any anesthetic agent ever causing that sort of long-term psychological damage, none.

He returned to the sink and shoved on the long faucet handle, carefully avoiding touching any surface with his hands. This time, only the hot tap. Another scrub wouldn't hurt, not if there was a chance of a nosocomial bug floating around the lab. He gritted his teeth as he plunged his still-damp hands under the steaming stream of water.

It had to be nosocomial. It had to be.

And if Anaex were everything he suspected—*is*, he corrected—then the ensuing professional demand for it would far outweigh any minor infringement of patient rights.

As if his patients even understood most of them. He'd seen the blank incomprehension on their faces as he'd explained the risks of surgery and anesthesia, watched them scribble their initials so hastily on the consent forms with hardly a question. Only occasionally would a patient actually ask him a question about the risks or the consent form, and then it was generally an easy one: Should I do this?

He always answered in the affirmative. Had the patient's condition not been more serious than the danger from the surgery, they would not be there. Ergo, surgery *was* in their best interest, always. And if he managed to find a way to get Anaex to the OR even faster, so much the better. Using it, really, was doing good rather than harm, since the rate of postsurgical complications was so significantly less than the standard anesthetic agents.

His eyes were flooded with tears by the time he drew his hands out from the hot water.

SEVEN

A strange sense of unease began to permeate General Boothby's staff. At first, the general chalked it up to an increase in tensions in the area wearing on his staff's nerves. Since Sergeant Carter's last foray over into North Korea, the nature and severity of border incidents had escalated markedly. No longer an occasional sniper attack, a few shots fired out of anger and frustration—no, the Demilitarized Zone was raked with automatic weapons fire, the volume of the music and propaganda blasting on the speakers increased until it was almost impossible to hear oneself think. A host of minor training accidents and maintenance failures contributed to the ever-present sense of personal danger.

The feeling was more than just the normal tension of soldiers in danger. Like many great generals before him, Boothby had always been able to engender a sense of immortality, of immunity from enemy action in his forces. The thirty-two thousand men and women stationed in South Korea had always known that America would win, that should the unthinkable happen and the North Koreans come storming across the line of no return, American forces would strike back in devastating and complete annihilation. It was not so much their firepower that they believed in, it was the sheer inevitability of American triumph. As real as the danger always was, they had complete and utter confidence in their ability to overcome it.

But now, it seemed that something was eating away at that conviction of moral superiority. Boothby noted it first in the daily staff meetings—voices higher, questions sharper, and slides sometimes prepared so hastily to reflect the latest incidents that the computer-generated graphics were replaced with scrawled, hand-drawn figures.

His own sense of danger was deepening as well. He saw obscure meaning in the most trivial of stats, read hidden intentions in the late submission of paperwork or in the timing of a briefing phone call from the field. More and more, he became convinced that they were not accidents, that events were moving in some sort of synchronicity toward a final, culminating incident.

The media was no help at all, of course. They exacerbated the problems, reporting each incident as though it were the opening shot of a new Vietnam. Boothby had tried limiting their access, and found that the rumors and speculations that they generated when deprived of facts were even more despicable than the ones they normally reported. He'd gone back to briefing them daily, and had been relieved to see the venom in their dispatches and wire reports diminish slightly.

As a student of military history, Boothby understood America's role in Korea and the virtual impossibility of finding any lasting peace in the region. Certainly not given the imposition of outside forces, nor the enforced stalemate that the U.S. demanded. That itself was a relic of the Cold War era that they would never see again. But that war was an inevitable condition of the human race seemed just as irrefutable. Why, then, were they here? What possible purpose could be served by placing these fine men and women in harm's way, subjecting them to the ever-increasing dangers of this no-man's-land?

Particularly not when they were specifically ordered to avoid international incidents whenever possible. Boothby snorted, acknowledging the impossibility of that as well.

The central conference table at which the two sides met to resolve disputes was perhaps the most pointed demonstration of that. It was bisected by a white line painted on it, divided precisely into identical halves. Over the years, the table itself had become a symbol of each side's rigorous enforcement of the actual boundaries. Any encroachment had political implications and was taken as an intentional act of aggression. Only two months before, a junior lieutenant had reached across the thick borderline that ran down the middle of the table to retrieve a pencil that had rolled across onto the North Korean's side. Weapons had been drawn, rounds chambered, and a diplomatic mission had instantly escalated into an armed confrontation.

He pulled out his standing orders again, reading through guidance from both his operational commanders and the commander in chief. Of all of them, the president's message seemed most obscure. He studied it again, trying to tease meaning out of the tortured diplomatic phrases that sounded much more elegant than the information they conveyed warranted.

He had read these words thousands of times, but never in this particular light. He lingered over each phrase, praying for divine guidance as to his commander's intentions.

Suddenly, he saw it. Saw what should have been so obvious to him for the last five years. The true meaning that had evaded him, as well as all of his subordinate commanders—it was there, plain on the face of the document if you had the courage to look at it.

If there was one thing that Boothby had, it was courage. Moral courage, of a variety that few other officers could ever understand. He felt the weight of his knowledge settling on him now, a heavier burden than he had ever carried before. So obvious, yet so subtly hidden in the text itself.

A cold chill shot through him. To resolve this tactical scenario would take every bit of training and experience he had, every skill that thirty years in the military had brought to him. It would be dangerous, so dangerous—and it had been years since he had faced personal danger himself. Even here in Korea, he was sheltered from actual attack by the cocooning strength of the division around him. For the

North Koreans to reach this far, there would have to be a serious failure of command.

But this—he shuddered and tried to pull away, but duty dogged him inevitably into those quiet places in his mind where his strength resided. He took a deep breath, concentrated, and tried to clear his mind.

There could be no conference, no staff meeting, and no consultation with higher authority. For all he knew, they were all in on it. He looked at the black binder that contained guidance from the Joint Chiefs of Staff and wondered whether or not deeper study would reveal secrets there, as well. He was almost afraid to look—almost, but not quite. A soldier had no choice when faced with fear.

An hour later, when the sun was already tipping down to scald the horizon, Boothby shut his command folder slowly. The operational orders and rules of engagement confirmed his suspicions about President Williams. Once you knew what to look for and could read between obfuscatory propaganda generated by the Pentagon, you could see the truth. There would be another Korean conflict, this one bloodier and far more deadly than the last.

No. It would simply reinitiate the cycle his troops were trapped in now. A bitter victory, one that would never lead to lasting peace. Americans had no business here, and it was time someone said so.

He knew what he must do now, his path was clear. He would see the president, look him in the eyes, and remind him of what the man must have learned on the ground in Vietnam. There was only one person behind this insanity, and Boothby must confront him personally. Confront him, and force him to deal with the facts.

Boothby sent a short prayer of thanks, offering up his anguish to the Lord, that he had been the one so chosen to make this stand. Here, where it all must end.

For the first time in their short but intense relationship, Sergeant Carter looked uneasy. He spat on the ground, scratched uneasily behind one ear, and then framed his answer to the general while staring off at the distant pine trees. "I don't know, sir. This one might be a little bit tougher."

"Are you afraid?" the general asked calmly. He noted with approval the effect his question had on the sergeant.

"I wouldn't call it that," Carter answered. A mild note of annoyance in his voice, enough to indicate that somewhere within the psychotic framework of his mind he still had enough pride to resent being called a coward. "No, wouldn't call it that at all."

"Well." The general let the remark stand as a rebuke. He ran his finger over the line marking off the border between north and south. "It's not even real, is it? Just an imaginary line drawn through a few gullies and dry streambeds. Not even there at all," he said musingly. He glanced up at Carter to see if his sergeant understood the real meaning behind that.

"General?" It was clear from the look on Carter's face that little made sense.

Boothby stood, felt the small bones in his back creak as he stretched. He rolled his shoulders back, flexed his neck from side to side, driving away the tightness accumulated there from bending over the hood of the Humvee. "Quite a simple plan, as I see it."

"You're not the one who has to execute it. With all due respect, General." Carter's voice left little doubt that respect had nothing to do with his answer.

"To the contrary." Boothby felt an enormous relief verging on exhilaration course through his body. To be back in the field, reliving those first days he'd spent in Vietnam with his platoon, moving silently as a snake through the bush—ah, this was the right answer. He felt it with every atom of his being. "I'll be going with you on this one."

"You've gotta be shittin'," Carter said. He shook his head emphatically from side to side. "No way. These diversionary tactics, that's one thing. Man like me, I know how to get in and out, execute the plan, and not leave a trace behind. Besides, I get caught, I figure I can fight my way out. Like last time in the tunnel. But you—come on, you're a general."

"The best leaders lead from the front," Boothby snapped, angered at the insubordination.

"And just how long has it been since you've been in the field?" Carter sneered. "Got those nice BDUs of yours dirty, waded hip deep through stinking mud and rattlesnakes? Just how long, General?" Carter continued shaking his head, the motion making the general oddly dizzy. "No way. Not taking you in, man."

"Do you really think you have a choice?"

Carter glanced up, startled. Boothby stared at him, a cold, granite figure of a senior officer, one larger than life as the result of the accumulated decades of military experience. Clearly, he must stop this now. Must put an end to any remaining delusions in Carter's minuscule brain that they had anything in common beyond the mission that faced them. He had had some hopes about the man, futile perhaps. The weight of his duty descended upon him again, cutting him off from all human contact, isolating him as effectively as internment in a POW camp would.

One final demonstration. As quick as a river snake, Boothby slid his pistol from his holster. In one motion, he chambered a round and slammed the muzzle into Carter's thick, simian skull. "You will meet me here at 2100 hours," the general ordered calmly. "Is that understood?"

"Yes, General." All trace of defiance and insubordination was gone from Carter's voice.

"And if you do not, I will put a bullet through your brain. Is that understood?"

General Boothby parked his Humvee behind a thick stand of pines. He drummed his fingers on the steering wheel rapidly, the sharp staccato sound eerily unnatural in the forest. The closer they got to their objective, the more convinced he was of the righteousness of his cause. The words in the president's message echoed in his mind, beating in rhythm with his heart. Now, more than ever, he saw the clarity of his choice.

"We could wait until it's a little darker," Carter offered. Seated in the passenger seat of the vehicle, he'd been silent, disgruntled the entire drive out from the base. "Make it a little harder to see us."

Boothby nodded reluctantly. The sergeant did have a point.

Boothby had spent too many years in the field to ignore the advice of a seasoned trooper in a tactical scenario. "How much longer?"

Carter shrugged. "Thirty minutes, maybe. Give the moon time to go down." He pointed at the half crescent near the horizon. "No clouds tonight, so we'll have to go for the reduced ambient light."

"At least show me the entrance now," Boothby said. It wasn't quite an order. He was willing to listen to Carter's advice if he had anything worthwhile to say about it.

Carter stubbed out his cigarette and dismounted. "Okay, sir," he said with a surprising lack of argument.

Maybe he understands, Boothby thought, studying the grizzled field veteran carefully. When he'd put his plan to Carter that evening, the sergeant had been disbelieving at first, defiant after that, and had finally settled into a surly acceptance of it all. Boothby hadn't had to push the ultimate threat—to reveal the details of Carter's other nocturnal forays into North Korean territory. A good thing, too. While Boothby had some doubts that any court martial would ever believe Carter's claims that he was acting on the general's orders, there was no point in pushing it. There was a certain sly furtiveness to the man that gave Boothby reason to believe that he might have evidence hidden away somewhere.

Yet it was not a certainty at all. Carter was smart, but it was an intelligence borne of field operations, a tactical sense of terrain and territory honed to a level that made it more instinct than intellectual exercise. Away from the eternal verities of ground warfare, mired in the intricacies of political and legal responsibility, Boothby doubted that Carter would have the slightest clue as to how to proceed.

Still, there was that chance. Thankfully, it hadn't gone that far.

"Check weapons," Carter said, automatically assuming the role of leader now that they were on his territory. "Extra clips." Carter touched his own hanging off his 782 Gear web belt. He waited pointedly for Boothby to verify the location of his own extra rounds.

After that, Carter walked carefully all the way around Boothby, checking for anything that might betray them on the mission. He submitted to a similar examination from the general, standing patiently with the air of one who has done this far too many times before.

Finally, both men were satisfied.

"Let's get the gear," Carter said. He reached into the back of the Humvee and extracted a large canister, struggling with it more due to the awkwardness of its shape than its weight. He finally settled for tucking it up under one arm. Then he looked at the general. "From here on out, it's hand signals only. You remember them?"

Boothby grunted. "Knew them before you were ever enlisted."

"Fine." Carter moved out silently through the brush, quickly disappearing from view. Boothby noted with a dry, dispassionate evaluation that the word *sir* had been missing from the soldier's last two sentences.

Boothby gave him a decent head start, then fell in at standard trail interval behind him. Within the first few minutes, he had to admit that Carter was good. Very good—damn near better than any soldier Boothby'd ever seen. The man was a ghost in this territory, moving silently through the forest without as much as a trace of noise or a furtive movement of the underbrush to betray his location.

Boothby let the familiar feel of silent movement creep back over him, rusty from long disuse, but quickly coming back to him. He noted with approval his own ability to mimic Carter's movements. Not as good—he never would be, nor did he need to be. He was a general, not a field soldier.

Then what the hell was he doing here? The question confused him for a moment, then he almost let slip a chuckle at his own foolishness. Of course—he had to be here, didn't he? There was no one else he could trust, not Carter, not any of the other men who had been reluctantly dragged into his small militia. No, the matter was entirely too sensitive.

Nor was it one he could execute alone. He knew that now, watching Carter move invisibly through the brush.

Finally, they reached the edge of the small stand of trees and underbrush. The general moved slowly and carefully up on Carter, aware that the man knew that he was there and was tracking his every movement by the small, almost undetectable noises he made. As the general settled in beside him, Carter drew him slightly deeper into the brush. He positioned the general's head carefully so that he could peer through a natural break in the underbrush, and pointed.

For a moment, Boothby was alarmed. Whatever it was that Carter was pointing at was invisible to his untrained eyes. Finally, as the moon sank below the horizon, he saw it. A vague, darker black square buried within the other patch of underbrush.

In the shifting moonlight, it had simply appeared to be a pattern of irregular shadows, composed of the odd shapes that made men in the brush think they were alone. But here, in the utter darkness, he saw it clearly.

The entrance.

Back at the base, Carter had assured him that none of the other patrols had discovered this most recent North Korean foray into their territory. Carter himself had only discovered it two weeks ago, and had carefully withheld the information from his platoon leader on the off chance that the general might wish for Carter to use it personally for one of their more sensitive missions. Boothby had congratulated him on his discretion at the time—now, he was quietly pleased with his own foresight. How could he have known back then that there would be a time when the general desired a covert entry into North Korea, a tunnel not yet monitored by the U.S. forces.

Boothby settled into the thick underbrush to wait for the last traces of moonlight to disappear.

Carter touched his arm lightly. Time now. Boothby nodded his understanding and rose slowly out of the low crouch he'd assumed to wait, cursing the right knee joint that popped and complained as he did so. Carter glanced once back at him and grimaced, shaking his head slightly.

Too old. Or so you think. The general shook his head in denial. No, he was not too old, and he never would be.

Carter led the way again, taking them on a slightly circuitous route to skirt around the edge of the clearing and approach the tunnel entrance from the side. Once there, still creeping through the thick underbrush, they quickly cleared a path down to the entrance.

A heavy wooden door barred their way into the tunnel. Carter motioned for silence, then laid his fingertips gently along the wood. He shut his eyes, and his face assumed an expression of concentration. Boothby watched, half-spooked by the thought that the man was capable of determining if the tunnel was occupied solely through the vibrations that reached his fingertips.

Carter took a step closer to the door then and plastered his ear to it, keeping his fingertips resting on the old wood. He stood there motionless for five minutes, then drew back, evidently satisfied.

They'd gone over this particular point several times, the general drawing on highly classified intelligence databases to confirm Carter's firsthand experience. When the tunnels were guarded, it was by regular troops. There were no sophisticated electronics or listening devices in the North Korean inventory, not for this sort of duty. If there were no men there, then this end, at least, was not guarded.

Carter wedged a machete in between the two halves of the door and lifted slightly. Boothby could hear wood scrape wood as the crude restraining bar on the other side of the door lifted on top of the machete. Carter moved the blade up approximately one foot, then applied gentle pressure to the right-hand side of the door. It swung inward quietly, the hinges evidently well prepared for use. No trace of squealing metal or rasping wood betrayed their presence, and Boothby only hoped that the ambient light outside was so low as to show no distinguishable change in the light inside the tunnel as well.

Again they waited while Carter brought his finely honed senses to bear on the tunnel. He nodded once and slipped into the opening. The general followed close behind him.

Inside the tunnel, the general had expected to find complete and utter blackness. Instead, he could still see Carter's form, even when the soldier slipped the wood door back into place and barred it as it had been before.

As they progressed along the tunnel, the general saw the reason why. Once they were safely under the DMZ, a series of small skylights brought traces of starlight into the tunnel.

They moved down the tunnel quietly, although Boothby thought certainly that his harsh breathing must have been easily audible to anyone within a hundred yards. The dirt was soft and loamy under his boots, absorbing the sounds of his footsteps. An occasional trickle of dirt and dust from the walls of the tunnel startled him, sending the adrenaline flooding through his blood into a keening frenzy.

He saw the vague form that was Carter slow, and matched his own pace to the sergeant's steps. Carter held up one hand, signifying a halt. Boothby stopped dead, and waited.

Again, the interminable silence broken only by the sound of their breathing, of his heart hammering away inside his ribcage. The slight hand motion: forward.

They moved up a slight incline that brought them to the opening at the surface. Carter paused one last time while they were still hidden in the shadows of the tunnel and listened. By now, Boothby fancied that he himself could mimic the soldier's skill. When the signal came to move out, he was ready.

To his eyes, accustomed to the deep dark of the tunnel, the starlit night was immeasurably brighter. He could pick out each distinct shape of a tree, the tracks vehicles had cut into the ground. Carter motioned him over to cover forty yards away from the entrance to the tunnel. They settled in behind a fallen tree, facing the American side of the DMZ, and waited.

Boothby saw Carter grimace before he even heard the noise the other men made as they approached. Branches snapped under the Americans' feet and rocks clattered as the two men patrolled opposite them on the American side of the border. Loud, careless—excellent targets. Had they always been this sloppy? Boothby made a mental note to reinforce basic field skills upon his return to his post.

Carter withdrew slightly from the fallen pine, careful to avoid rustling any of the low underbrush that surrounded them. He motioned to Boothby: this one's all yours. That had been part of the agreement. Carter, horrified beyond what Boothby would have thought possible, had flatly refused to do anything more than put Boothby in position. The rest of it was up to him.

He should have stayed current on the rifle range. He really should have. Another point to emphasize to his officers—one never knew when such skills would come in handy.

Boothby slipped the gas mask off of his web belt and pulled it over his face. He could feel the air stir behind him—Carter doing the same, he suspected. Boothby glanced back to confirm that and then wished he hadn't. Carter wouldn't have had to.

Boothby stood, careful to make his movements slow and deliberate. He heard the patrol distinctly now, a whispered, off-color joke passing between the two soldiers bored with the routine patrol along the DMZ. He waited until they were directly opposite him, then pulled the pin on the canister and lofted it over toward the DMZ.

The sharp clang of metal on rocks brought an immediate and surprised reaction from the patrol. He heard their frantic scuffling movements as they scuttled for cover, heard a sharp, obscene oath break the silence. Boothby felt the night breeze on the back of his neck. He waited.

The breeze must have been no more than five to ten miles per hour, but it was sufficient to carry the pale yellow gas spewing out of the canister over South Korean soil. A chorus of gasps and hacking coughs erupted from the American side of the DMZ, followed by stifled yipes of pain. The underbrush in which the Americans had sought cover erupted into movement.

Boothby dropped back down and balanced his weapon on the tree trunk. He waited until the first soldier darted into view, took careful aim, and fired.

The sharp, flat crack of the weapon brought an immediate response. Automatic weapons fire chattered across the area, shredding the bushes around them.

Boothby had dropped back down behind the fallen trunk for cover, and he felt the soft pine wood chatter under the impact. Splinters and chips flew over their heads to ricochet harmlessly off the trees around them.

Beside him, Carter swore quietly. Boothby made a sharp gesture with his hand, demanding silence.

The weapons fire ceased. Good—perhaps they thought they'd shot him. Another point to remember to bring up with his officers— never assume the enemy is dead. Boothby poked his head cautiously back up above the tree trunk.

The man still under cover was wheezing and moaning from the

effect of the tear gas. Boothby saw a rustle behind one tree and fired again. Then he bracketed the tree, nailing the other side. He was rewarded by a hard, shrill yell of pain.

Carter tugged at the general's sleeve and motioned frantically toward the tunnel. Boothby nodded reluctantly. They had to leave now before the radio call summoned in an entire company to execute a complete and thorough search of the ground. It was standard procedure after the skirmishes that frequently erupted between the two sides, but Carter and Boothby had to be back on the American side before it commenced.

They retraced their steps quickly, gas masks still in place. The tunnel seemed shorter returning to the U.S. side than it had venturing into North Korea, and they were soon at the heavy wooden gate.

Carter popped the latch and led them out into the open field. This was the most dangerous part of the entire evolution—the chance that someone might see them emerging from the tunnel and shoot them before they could be identified as U.S. soldiers.

Or that they might see them emerging at all. It would spawn questions, too many questions. Better that they come and go like ghosts.

"Hey!" The hoarse cry, filled with pain and fear, startled him. "Hey, you over there."

Damn. Now what was he supposed to do? His contingency plan came immediately to mind, and he tried to dismiss it. It was not so difficult standing on the other side of the border when the soldiers were anonymous, camouflaged shapes. But, here, face-to-face, it was another matter entirely.

Or was it? He considered the matter as he approached the soldier lying half concealed by the scrubby pine. If he was willing to sacrifice his own troops by ordering them into enemy action, he'd reasoned earlier, then was it so different to sacrifice them to a higher purpose in this matter? It was simply a matter of will, of having the moral courage to do what was necessary. And ultimately it could not matter whether their deaths came at long range or short range.

The soldier was curled into a fetal position behind a tree, his face marked with camouflage paint. As he saw Boothby approach, he let out a low, muffled groan and tried to reach for the pistol at his belt. His M16 lay two hand lengths away from him where he'd dropped it.

"It's all right, soldier," Boothby said. The American accent had the immediate effect of calming the soldier's movements.

"Bastard shot me," the soldier groaned. "Bad. The radio—" He motioned toward the brush that concealed a canvas pack.

"It's going to be all right," Boothby said soothingly. "Everything's fine." He walked over to the radio, using the movement to conceal his own actions in chambering another round.

He picked up the radio, walked back over to the soldier, and knelt down beside him. "Everything's fine." He placed the muzzle of the pistol against the side of the man's head and gently squeezed off another round.

In the last eight months in Korea, Alicia Boothby had become intimately attuned to the odd creaks and groans of their house. The two-story, military construction senior officers' quarters was far more luxurious than the accommodations most of the troops enjoyed, but two cuts below what they would have rated in the States. Still, it was more solidly constructed than many of the notorious white elephants at Fort Benning, Georgia, where Alicia had been forced to live while her husband was a mere lieutenant colonel serving a seemingly interminable stint as commander of the infantry officer's basic course. The World War II–era buildings were aptly nicknamed. The drafty, creaky affairs had inlaid oak flooring that had been polished to a thin veneer over the decades, oversized windows that were expensive to curtain, and the broad verandas that were de rigueur in the South. Intended to shield the house from the blistering summer sun, the porches proved to be such luxurious housing for insects that humans rarely ventured onto them.

It wasn't the noise of the heavy front door opening that awoke her, nor was it the gentle tread of the general's boots on the stairs. Given his odd hours and the demands on his time, she'd long ago become accustomed to sleeping through both.

No, what finally brought her wide awake from a sound sleep, jerked her upright into a sitting position in the bed, and tweaked her nerves and internal sense of danger into a high state of readiness was the sound of her son's door opening.

It was at the other end of the short second floor hallway, and not in any particular state of disrepair, but she as much felt as heard the door to her son's room open, as though some psychic bond between mother and child had been gently plucked.

She slipped quickly out of the bed, not bothering to don slippers or robe, and moved to the open bedroom door. At the end of the hallway, she could see her husband's broad, tall form almost filling the other doorway. His shape was fuzzy and indistinct in the almost lightless corridor.

She started to speak, to call out his name, but something odd in his stance gave her pause. She stood where she was, transfixed, not really believing what she was seeing. Then, without a sound, driven by some sudden feral intensity, she darted from her own bedroom down to the doorway of her son's.

"My God." She reached up with both hands, grabbed him around the wrist, and, putting all of her weight behind it, jerked his hand down. The sharp crack of gunfire almost deafened her. Brett awoke, screamed, and shrank back to cower against his headboard.

Alicia Boothby was not a brave woman by nature, but she had grown up in an Army family and had spent the last twenty years married to an Army officer. She knew how to stand her ground, and there was no force in this world or the next that would get past her to harm her child.

Particularly not her husband. "Give it to me," she ordered, insinuating her fingers around his clamped down on the Beretta's grip. "Thurmond, now." There was an unmistakable note of command in her voice.

Thurmond Boothby started, as though awakening from a bad dream. He gazed down in horror at the hole in the wooden floor, then back at Alicia. "What happened?"

"Give me the gun first."

Evidently bewildered, Boothby shifted his gaze to his hand. He saw the gun, then looked back at Brett. A dawning look of horror crossed his face. His grip on the pistol softened, and Alicia immediately plucked it from his fingers. She took two steps back, keeping her body between him and her son. She checked the gun, ensuring that there was not another round chambered. Finally, she turned her gaze to her husband.

He stood before her, a massive man clad in filthy, mud-spattered camouflage uniform, pants bloused into his boots. The combat boots were caked with mud, and one leg of his trousers had pulled free from it. He reeked of something primitive and dangerous. Black stains covered his camouflage, continuing up onto his face. Camouflage greasepaint? She studied his face, memorizing the details without acknowledging the look of stricken horror on his face.

No, not the familiar patterns of gray, white, and black that she'd come to associate with night camouflage makeup. God knows she'd seen it enough in her thirty-five years of life. This was something different. It wasn't painted on in those teasingly irregular patterns that the Army favored for concealment, the ones they tried so hard to keep from patterns. No, this ran in broad slashes, the lower edges marred by what looked like trickles.

That was it. He was spattered, and whatever it was ran.

Sick horror overtook her. Somehow, a new Thurmond inhabited her husband's body, a crazy violent man who magnified the old Thurmond's every minor character flaw. Rage instead of pronounced irritation, Brett's broken arm instead of stern lectures and a spanking. How far would it go? She'd never thought her husband capable of killing someone, not outside of the strictures of his profession of arms, but instinctively she knew that this new Thurmond was capable of anything.

Anger replaced fear. With her son threatened, so was Alicia.

The gun butt was clammy and sticky in her hand. Holding it carefully in her right hand, she lifted her left hand and examined it with her peripheral vision, careful to keep her eyes fixed on her husband. A dark stain, coppery and pungent. The same substance spattered his clothing and skin.

With a muffled groan of disgust, she rubbed her hand frantically on her nightshirt, all the while keeping her eyes and her gun firmly fixed on her husband.

"Where have you been?" she said finally. "Thurmond, what have you done?"

He started to walk toward her and she raised the gun, keeping it pointed dead at his chest. "No closer. Tell me."

He stopped, frozen in place by her rage. He looked down at the hole in the floor once again, as though to reassure himself that he hadn't imagined it, then back at her. "He grabbed my hand," he said at last. "That's why the weapon discharged."

She shook her head, not even minutely tempted by his explanation that tried to do so much and yet failed so miserably. "The gun was loaded," she said levelly. "It was pointed at Brett. I'm not talking about that. Earlier tonight, where have you been?"

He looked down at his uniform and ran his hands over it as though he would find the answer in the rough ripstop cloth. His hands paused as they crossed over the dark blotches, and he brought one hand to his nose to sniff deeply. He grimaced, much as Alicia had done.

Finally, he said, "I don't know. I was at the office—there was another incident today. And then . . . I don't know."

He looked back at her, fear now mingling with the horror. "Jesus, Alicia, what have I done?"

She heard the other steps now, the hard clatter of military boots coming up the stairs. What had taken them so long? Surely it had been hours since she'd first seen Thurmond standing at Brett's doorway, since the shot had been fired? Where was his aide, and the housekeeper? Why weren't they here?

With a start, she realized it had been less than a minute. Less than a minute for twenty years of marriage, forty years of a good life, to unravel and lie in tatters around her.

"General?"

The aide. Her Army instincts kicked in. Keep the Army staff out of it, keep family secrets in their place. "Tell him," she hissed. "Tell him that nothing's wrong."

The general cleared his throat and said, "Everything's fine, Turner. Don't come up—damned fool accident. I was cleaning my gun and I didn't check it first. Must've gone off."

The steps continued up the stairs, cautiously now. "General, are you certain?"

Alicia could almost feel the sergeant waiting, straining to hear the code word that every member of the household had been taught. It was changed every month, and served as a signal that they were answering questions under duress or were otherwise constrained from freely talking.

"Nothing's wrong at all," the general said, a note of command returning to his voice. The shaken, bewildered man who had stood in front of her faded away and was replaced by the solid, brilliant officer she'd known and loved for twenty years. "We're not under duress—icebreaker," he added, giving the code word for all clear.

Alicia heard a sigh of relief in the hallway, then the sound of weapons being reholstered.

"General, can't I—"

"No," Boothby said sharply, now finally seeming to realize the extent of the situation. "Everything's fine, just a stupid accident, Sergeant. One I'll be embarrassed about tomorrow. Go back to your post."

There was a long silence, and she could feel the hesitation on the part of the sergeant. If anything were wrong and he didn't intervene, there would be hell to pay. Finally, the question she'd dreaded. "Mrs. Boothby?"

She spared a moment to admire the sheer nerve of the soldier, daring to challenge his superior to ascertain the safety of the wife. "I'm fine," she said, marveling at how calm and steady her voice sounded. Where had it come from, this seeming wellspring of strength? By any standard she would have used, she should have been shaking uncontrollably and crying by this point.

"Pekinese." Her own personal code word followed.

"Yes, sir. I'll be downstairs if you need anything." The sergeant's footsteps faded down the stairs, headed to his post on the other side of the house.

Boothby drew in a deep, shaky breath and turned to his wife. "I have no idea what happened," he said calmly. "And what are you doing with my gun?"

He held up one hand and motioned for her to return it to him. He was, she noted, not so foolish as to take a step toward her. "Put that down, you'll hurt someone," he said sharply.

She started to laugh, then caught herself. "Not a chance, Thurmond." She motioned at the door. "Go get yourself cleaned up. We'll have to do something with your uniform. Put it in a plastic bag, then put it in the closet. I'll take care of it later. We can't very well leave it for the laundry, can we?"

He looked down at his uniform and back at her with a dawning admiration. "No, I suppose not."

"Do it, then go to bed." She motioned at him with the gun as though emphasizing her point. She heard Brett whimpering behind her. "I'm spending the night in here, and I won't sleep."

Without a word, the general turned and walked out of the bedroom. She heard him walk down the corridor, the squeak of their door, then the soft snick as it closed.

At that, she walked to the door and gazed down the hall to make certain he was not standing on the other side of the door. Finally satisfied, she let her gun hand waver.

"Mommy?" Brett's voice was thin and wavery, keening almost out of control. "Mama?"

Without a word, she drew her son to her and held him tightly. "Go back to sleep, baby. Tomorrow, we're going home."

General Boothby stretched out naked on his back. He stared up at the speckled plaster of the ceiling, trying to decipher a pattern to the intricate swirls. The figures defied him, a random collection of arcs and swoops that seemed to possess no master plan other than a simple desire to confuse the mind.

As so much of this week had been. It had passed as a quick collection of snapshots, a series of images no more real than a cartoon. It was as though he had taken a series of still shots and flipped through them rapidly, creating the appearance of motion when there was none.

Alicia—damn, what a soldier she would have made. He paused for a moment to admire the determination he'd seen in her eyes, her courage in standing up to him. Twenty years ago, he would never have expected her to be capable of it. But something in motherhood had brought out a new ferocity to her, an instinctive protectiveness that was more binding and powerful than any bond he'd ever seen between soldiers in the field. Yes, if you could capture that, what a division he would have.

And Alicia had made her choice. Brett over Thurmond, son over father. He understood it in a way he could not have explained, but nevertheless was certain that she must bear the consequences of that decision. She could not see the unfolding of the higher plan, would not have understood the complexities if he had explained them to her. There had been little opportunity to, at any rate. It had been only earlier that evening that he had understood it himself, followed that with his foray into the field with Sergeant Carter, and came to the final and stunning conclusion that what destiny required of him was so much more than he'd ever thought possible.

Abraham and Isaac. The altar and the son. His mind flashed back to his earliest Sunday school teachings when he'd understood the harsh obedience God exacted of his most chosen servants. To be called to sacrifice one's son—now that was a crucible.

Would God have stopped him? He wasn't so certain, and in the end it did not matter. Alicia, she'd interfered with the plan, prevented him from knowing whether or not he'd ever be worthy to prevail in that final test. For that alone, he damned her.

Boothby rolled over on his stomach and tucked his arms under his pillow. Tomorrow would be soon enough to deal with the details. Alicia and Brett would be returning to the States—he'd seen that in her eyes and knew it was probably the best solution at this point. Fewer distractions, less interference. If he were to fulfill his mission, he must eliminate the fog of war, most particularly in his own house.

He put aside all of the smaller concerns to concentrate on the spine of his story, on the one compelling objective that had been made so clear to him earlier that evening. The situation in Korea was not one of conflicting political philosophies or warring cultures. No, it was a carefully orchestrated plan implemented by the highest possible levels of the government. The very highest levels.

If this night had taught him nothing else, it had confirmed what he'd already deduced, made certain what had been strong suspicion.

One man was responsible for this situation, one man alone. And General Thurmond S. Boothby knew who it was.

EIGHT

Thorne knew the new instrument nurse was in trouble the moment she stepped into surgery. There was an air of hesitancy about her, a tentativeness that he suspected would wilt into panic under the demands of the six-hour surgery in front of them. He glanced over at Patterson, saw the almost imperceptible shake of her head. Patterson was no slouch—she'd have picked up on the new nurse's aura the minute she stepped into the room.

Not that either Thorne or Patterson was really the new nurse's problems. But Kamil—

As much as Thorne liked his friend, there was a streak of implacable pettiness that ran deep in the man's character. Arrogance, but distinct from that usually found in surgeons. While Kamil outwardly rejected the pomp and circumstance that accompanied his position as a member of one of the most powerful families in Algeria, Thorne felt certain he must have internalized at least a significant portion of it.

Clarissa Howling, the senior nurse in the surgery department, stood across the table from Kamil, ready to step in if the new nurse fumbled. Thorne heard her sigh and felt a flash of dislike pass between Patterson and Howling. Thorne kept his eyes carefully neutral, but let the smile spread slightly behind his surgical mask. For all of the evident dislike between the two women, they had so much in common that it was almost scary sometimes. Now he could see that Patterson was irritated that Howling's take on the new nurse was exactly like her own.

"Welcome, Janice," Patterson said calmly to the new nurse. "I think you know everyone here."

"Yes, Doctor," Janice said softly.

Kamil pointed at the instrument tray. "I like my nurses in surgery before I arrive. Gives them a chance to correct any mistakes they may have made." Kamil sailed on into a brief lecture on the instrument nurse's responsibility, ignoring the dark looks that Howling shot at him across the table. As if her nurses would make any mistakes.

"Ready?" Kamil asked and looked over at Thorne.

Thorne nodded. "As ready as we'll ever be."

The moment came eventually, as Thorne had known it would. Kamil muttered a command, and Janice slid the instrument off the tray and tentatively tapped him in the palm with it.

Kamil's fingers closed around it, slender even in surgical gloves. He stopped for a moment, stood completely still, then looked pointedly down at the instrument in his hand. "I believe I said retractor," he said sharply.

"I thought you said—"

In one violent motion, Kamil threw the instrument across the table. He whirled on Howling and snarled, "Why is this idiot in here?"

"You said retractor," Howling said calmly. She was already moving out of her observation position and around to ease Janice gently out of the direct line of fire. In one practiced motion, she pulled the correct instrument off the tray without looking and slapped it into his hand. "Here it is."

"Get her out of here," Kamil ordered. "I will not be distracted like this."

"Doctor," Patterson said. Her voice was hard and cold. As senior surgeon on staff, she was technically in charge of the operation. Kamil was listed as assisting, and she had chosen to use this operation as a teaching session. "Your patient doesn't have time for this." She glanced pointedly at the clock on the wall.

"This woman has—"

"Continue, Doctor." Patterson's voice brooked no argument. "Continue or step aside and let me finish the procedure."

Kamil lashed out and knocked the instrument tray stand over, scattering the stainless steel surgical instruments across the cold tile floor. "No one speaks to me like this," he screamed.

"That's enough." Patterson's voice had gone beyond frigid. "Get out of my OR, Doctor. I'll speak with you later." She turned back to Thorne. "Vitals?"

"All stable," Thorne reported promptly, knowing that she was simply giving Kamil an opportunity to leave before the argument escalated. Despite the volatile personalities at play in any operating room, the middle of surgery was no place for an argument. Not with a patient under and his gut sliced open from sternum to pubis.

"Very well. Retractor," she said, not bothering to look over as Howling slapped it out.

Patterson continued with the procedure and waited until Kamil had left the OR. After allowing everyone time to settle down, she turned to Howling and murmured, "Let's have Miss Brady step back in. This is a teaching hospital, after all." Howling shot her a grateful look which Patterson pointedly ignored.

Three hours later, Thorne helped wheel the patient out of OR and into postsurgical care unit. He stayed by the man's bedside for a few moments, watching him emerge from the anesthesia. As before, the rapidity took him aback. If Gillespie's formulation continued to provide this sort of result, it would revolutionize surgical anesthesia forever.

"He's finished," Patterson said as she walked up behind him. "No resident pulls that kind of temper tantrum in my surgery."

"Kamil's an all-right guy most of the time," Thorne said, finding himself on the defensive already. Patterson had a way of doing that to people. "There's something bothering him. I don't know what it is, though. He hasn't talked to me."

"I don't care about his personal problems. You leave that at the door. What if he pulled that kind of stunt when I wasn't around?"

"Who do you think he learned it from?" Thorne asked. The words were out before he thought them through.

"Just what the hell are you implying, Doctor?" She was facing him across their patient now, one hand clutching the bed rail, the other pointing an accusing finger at him.

Silently, Thorne pointed down at her hand on the bed rail. The fingers were stark white, clenched into a fist around the metal strut.

Patterson glared at him. Then, the slightest softening in her body posture indicated she got the point. "He's been scrubbing in with me for a year." Her fingers slowly relaxed. She shifted her gaze back down to their patient. Finally, with an unusual note of hesitancy in her voice, she said, "Talk to him if you can, Thorne. A temper tantrum . . . word gets around. This is the first time he's ever gotten tossed in the middle of a procedure, and it'd better be his last. If this continues . . . " Patterson didn't bother finishing the sentence since they both knew where she was headed. If Kamil continued to be a disruptive force inside the OR, no matter how brilliant or how well connected he was, he would be out of the Murphy. With no chance for a residency anywhere else.

Thorne nodded, aware that he'd just skirted perilously close to the edges of Dr. Patterson's tolerance. "I'll try. Like I said, he's really a good guy."

"I don't care if he's a good guy," Patterson said crisply. "All I care about is if he's a good surgeon."

"Speaking of personalities, how well do you know Dr. Gillespie?" It was an awkward transition, and Thorne winced inwardly as he asked the question. Still, he trusted Patterson's judgment. She might not come right out and say that Gillespie was acting oddly, but he thought she might trust him enough to give him at least a hint of an honest reaction.

"Why do you ask?" Thorne watched Patterson draw back slightly, as though reluctant to get into a discussion of her fellow chief. However, since Patterson had imposed on his good offices to help her solve the problem of Kamil, he felt no compunction about asking her a favor in return.

Briefly, he outlined his conversation with Gillespie over the military security aspects of his job and touched on his lack of access to the lab. Patterson's face went from politely neutral and aloof to distinctly curious.

"I don't understand that," she said when he'd finished. "We routinely get interim clearances for our residents and interns. Why should it take so much longer for a full-fledged doctor? Unless," a guarded look crossed her face, "there's something in your background that's holding it up."

Thorne shook his head. "Not a damned thing. That's what's so strange. If I'd ever done anything to give them a reason to be suspicious, I could understand it, but aside from a couple of parking tickets and one speeding ticket when I was seventeen, there's nothing."

"This is for the Anaex Protocol, isn't it?" Patterson said, changing directions. Thorne suppressed a smile. It was like her, the mercurial change of direction that often led to intuitive insights. "How is the protocol going?"

Thorne sighed and shrugged. "It seems to be going well—you've seen the results in surgery."

"Any postop complaints?"

"Not a one. If anything, our patients recover faster and with fewer side effects than do patients on the traditional anesthetics. No, I don't think the answer's in the protocol. I get the feeling there's something else on Dr. Gillespie's mind. I just thought you might have a hint as to what it might be."

Patterson shook her head. "Nothing occurs to me." She glanced up at him and her eyes riveted him in place. She seemed to extract a promise from him that this conversation was just between the two of them. "I could let you know if I think of anything," she said noncommittally, her eyes still locked on his. "Maybe."

Thorne stood and tugged down on the hem of his green surgical blouse. "I'd appreciate it, Doctor," he said more formally.

"And let me know how it goes with Dr. Kamil," she responded.

Quid pro quo.

As Thorne watched her walk away, a tangential thought struck him. He wondered, if his and Kamil's situations were reversed, whether Dr. Gillespie would be as concerned about his future.

Thorne finally tracked Kamil down to the emergency room. As a senior resident, Kamil was often summoned to handle surgical traumas at their ever-expanding regional trauma center. Funding for the program was a small but significant portion of Murphy's revenues, and Kamil took every opportunity available to establish his presence there.

Kamil was just walking out of trauma three when Thorne spotted him. His white disposable gown was spattered with blood, and Kamil was stripping it off and stuffing it into a sealed biohazard trash bin.

Thorne debated briefly on the best way to approach his friend, and finally settled on what had worked before: simple honesty. He followed Kamil into the ER lounge and flopped down on the couch across from him. "So what happened in there?"

Kamil glared at him. Thorne met his gaze levelly. Finally, the truculence faded from his friend's eyes and he sighed deeply. "I shouldn't have been in surgery today. I knew it before I went in. I shouldn't have been operating."

Thorne felt a trill of concern. "What's wrong?"

Kamil shook his head slowly from side to side and then buried his face in his hands. Thorne gave him time, and waited for him to proceed. He heard a muffled snort, and the realization struck him that Kamil was crying. Thorne stood up and walked over to sit down on the couch beside the Algerian surgeon. He patted him gently on the shoulder, and then continued in a softer voice. "Come on, buddy. What's wrong?"

Finally Kamil raised his face from his hands. "It's my family," he said dully. "My uncle."

"Is he sick?"

A harsh sound that could have been a laugh escaped Kamil's lips. "Nothing so simple," he said bitterly. "It's a good deal more serious than that." He glanced sideways at Thorne, as though checking to see whether or not he was embarrassed by the Algerian's emotion. "You are the last one who ought to be asking about it."

Now that puzzled Thorne. Just what exactly could Kamil mean?

"After all, you're the assassination buff," Kamil continued. "That's probably why you're talking to me now, isn't it? Hoping to get a little firsthand insight into what makes men go insane and kill presidents." Kamil stood abruptly and stared down at Thorne. "God, and I thought pathologists were ghoulish. Did you hunt down his medical records yet? He was here—but I'm sure you know that by now. It's not likely you'd let the opportunity to get a close look at an assassin's medical records get past you."

Now distinctly angry, Thorne stood as well. "What the hell do you mean?"

"Don't tell me you haven't heard. It was on the news this morning. And if I know you, you've been just dying for a chance to ask me about it. What did you do, tell Patterson, too?" Kamil was now clearly angry, with veins bulging along the sharp-boned jaw.

"I don't know what you're talking about," Thorne snapped. "I came down here to see if there was anything I could do. Like a friend would. Obviously, that's not something they understand in Algeria." Thorne turned and walked briskly toward the lounge door.

"Wait," Kamil said suddenly. Thorne turned back to him.

"What?"

Kamil studied him for a moment, then his expression suddenly cleared. "You haven't heard," he said softly. "I don't believe it."

"If you ever bothered to check the schedule, you'd know I was on call last night—all night. I got maybe two hours' sleep, and I sure as hell didn't spend that time watching CNN."

Kamil sighed, a wrenching sound that seemed to break loose from deep inside him. He walked over to Thorne, slung one arm companionably over his friend's shoulders, and guided him back over to the couch. "Sit with me a moment, then," he said, that oddly foreign inflection popping up in his voice again. "I will tell you how things are in Algeria.

"Yesterday evening, the president of Algeria was assassinated."

Thorne sucked in a hard breath. No wonder Kamil had thought that Thorne would know about it. Thorne's interest in the JFK assassination had quickly become a standing joke within the ranks of the Murphy's doctors. "Did you know the man? Of course you did. Kamil, how could you think that . . ." He let his voice trail off as he realized what Kamil must have thought.

"There's more," Kamil said levelly, his voice just barely steady. "The president was killed with a ceremonial scimitar. The assassin split his skull open. Death must have been instantaneous," he added almost as an afterthought.

"How could he have gotten so close to him?" Thorne asked, his mind already racing through the questions about Oswald's access to the Texas Book Depository. If there had been a conspiracy, obtaining access to favorable firing positions had been one of the key parts of the plan.

Kamil shook his head slowly. "It wasn't very difficult. You see, the assassin was his secretary of state."

Now it was Thorne's turn to look aghast. "The secretary—*your uncle?*" He stopped in horror as he realized the strain Kamil had been working under. For his family back in Algeria, this must represent the ultimate in disgrace. Their family honor, their standing within the nation would have plummeted overnight. For all he knew, members of Kamil's family had been executed in retribution.

"I'm so very sorry," Thorne said finally. "And I can understand under the circumstances why you would think—but I wouldn't, Kamil. You ought to know that. Is there anything I can do for you?"

Kamil shook his head and his voice broke as he said, "There's nothing any of us can do. Why he would—it makes no sense. No sense at all. Oh, they had their political differences, but they would not have been resolved like this. Especially not with my uncle."

"Your uncle. How is he? I assume you've called home."

"No one knows," Kamil answered. "He's been held incommunicado since he was arrested. There's a very good chance that he'll be executed himself within the next week or so."

"That fast?" The odd juxtaposition of the essence of speedy trial with Jack Ruby's murder of Lee Harvey Oswald struck Thorne. "There'll be a trial, won't there?"

Kamil grimaced. "Not a long one. The whole thing was broadcast live to the rest of the country. And in Algeria, there aren't quite as many appeals in the criminal justice system as there are in the United States. There's only one, actually. And it'll be denied."

"Oh, Jesus," Thorne said, slumping down on his side of the couch. "Kamil, I swear to you, I had no idea."

"I know you didn't." Kamil's large, moist eyes sought his out. "Thorne, thanks for tracking me down. I guess I just needed to talk to someone about it."

"Do you need to go home or something?"

Kamil shook his head. "I could never get there in time to see him alive again. Besides, if anything, I should be working on how to get the rest of my family out." His eyes focused on a point somewhere off in the distance. "The executions—they're not like here. Everything is so very different in Algeria. You cannot understand. Everything. The death sentence is much more quickly carried out. In a way it makes sense to me. The crime, the trial, the punishment—people have a chance to see the results. And no secret lethal injections, either. It will be a public execution, most probably a beheading."

Thorne stared, now more deeply horrified than he'd been before. "My God."

Kamil tendered him a bitter smile. "Not yours—ours."

"You eat yet?"

Thorne turned to find Debbie Patterson leaning against the corridor wall. It was an oddly relaxed pose for her, at odds with her normal reservoir of controlled energy.

"Not yet. In fact, I was just thinking—would you—the Dry Dock is just—I mean . . ."

Patterson laughed. "Let's go, Doctor. And I hope your conversational skills are better once you get some food in you."

Patterson sat across from him, her eyes locked on his face. "You going to eat that?"

Thorne shook his head. "I don't think so. You know how it is after a certain point, the idea of food just doesn't sit right."

"How long has it been?"

Too long. Between the call schedule, moving here from Boston, and about a hundred other things, it's been—

"Thorne?" Patterson prompted. "Sleep, when's the last time you had some?"

"Ah." Thorne could feel the flush surging through worn-out capillaries. "About forty hours, I guess. Somewhere around there."

"Are you a swimmer?"

For a moment, he was vaguely annoyed. The first thing to go is always patience—she should know that. And what was this, jumping around subjects like a hummingbird? Had he been mistaken when he'd heard a double entendre in her earlier question?

Slow down. Concentrate.

"I used to swim in college during football off-season. Slacked off during medical school, and just never got back into it." A brief, rueful smile, an acknowledgment of how much of life medical school prevented.

Patterson leaned back against the worn orange vinyl booth. "Me, too. I tried to get back into it a couple of years ago." A brief, rueful smile. "The mind remembers longer than the body."

And there it was again—was he imagining it?

"So what do you do, when you're not being Gillespie's favorite son? And what was all that with your buddy today? Frankly, I was a bit surprised. He's always been fairly competent in surgery."

From her, that was a stunning compliment. Almost as shocking as her question to him about his off-duty hours. There was an odd undercurrent in her voice, something warm and rich and husky just below the normal cool, sardonic tone characteristic of surgeons. Still trying to puzzle it out—was it really what he thought it was?—Thorne answered the second question first.

"You know about his uncle?" Thorne asked.

She shook her head.

He filled her in briefly, sketching in the family connections and the sequence of events as Kamil had related them to him. He finished with, "If you can cut him some slack . . ."

Patterson nodded slowly. "I hadn't realized . . . of course I can." She shot him a sly, conspiratorial glance. "It won't look like it. And don't tell him. But yeah, of course I can."

"Thanks. It'd mean a lot to me. I sure wasn't much help to him today."

"What do you mean?"

Thorne sighed. Would she think he was odd, off-kilter somehow? "I've got this hobby," he said. He hesitated, wondering how far to go.

"Does it have to do with long, sharp knives?"

"Almost. Ever since I was in college, I've been one of these conspiracy nuts." He forced a chuckle, trying to diminish the importance of it. "You know—like the people who claim JFK was killed by the CIA. Or Johnson. Or the Cubans. Like that. Kamil thought I knew about his uncle, figured I was trying to get an inside scoop on it."

"Were you?"

Thorne shook his head. "I didn't even know about it until Kamil told me. I've been on first and second call for the last two days, remember?"

"Wow." Patterson toyed with a piece of bacon.

"I hate to admit it, but Kamil was partly right. If I'd known it was his family . . ." His voice trailed off as he contemplated his probable lack of tact in broaching the subject with his friend.

Patterson patted his hand lightly. "You've got morbid interests, Thorne. Doctor's orders: take up swimming again instead."

He pushed his plate aside. "Maybe so, but there's something absolutely engrossing about political assassinations. World wars have started over them, and entire countries are changed. One crazy nut, one bullet, that's all it takes to change the course of history."

He leaned across the table. "And this is even worse—I wish I could have been there at Dealy Plaza, to see it all for myself." Seeing the look of shocked horror on her face, he stopped himself. "I know, I know. But there're still so many mysteries so many years later," he continued, now oblivious and totally caught up in his own passion. "The medical evidence alone—when you read the coroner's report and the surgical reports, there are so many unanswered questions. Like why the neck wasn't bisected to determine whether or not it was an entry or exit wound. That alone would have proved conclusively how many shooters there were, and whether or not—" He stopped as Patterson stood.

"Get some sleep, Thorne," she said, not unkindly. "The mysteries of the Kennedy assassination have waited for over forty years, and they can wait for another couple of days."

He rubbed a hand over his face absentmindedly, feeling the rough bristle beneath his fingertips. He had a confused feeling that he'd just failed some sort of test. "Look, I'm sorry. I'm running on about nothing."

She shook her head, a rueful note in her voice. "My fault. I'm the one who should know better than to try to hold an intelligent conversation with someone coming off back-to-back calls."

"But I wanted—"

She leaned forward and put one finger over his lips. Her touch burned like ice on his tired flesh. "So did I. But it'll keep, won't it? Now go get some sleep. By yourself. For now."

Stunned, Thorne watched her walk away, stop at the cashier and pay the bill, and leave. Too late, he realized she was picking up the tab for his breakfast as well.

Patterson cut off two old ladies in an ancient Chrysler and then switched back into the fast lane.

Why, oh why? It was a stupid idea, and I just made a fool of my-self. Over someone who was just a resident a few months ago! You'd think I'd learn, but—

She concentrated on her driving, slowing down from vicious to merely reckless as she contemplated the problem of Christopher Thorne, Murphy Medical Center, and all the intricate unspoken rules that governed conduct between the senior staff and the research fellows.

Stupid rules. Fraternization, improper relationships—there were a lot of names for it, but far too few answers for a woman at the top of the food chain at Murphy. No, there was no absolute *rule* against dating a research fellow. They were, after all, full-fledged doctors, part of the teaching staff. It was just discouraged, that was all.

Now nurses—for male doctors, that was entirely different. Not as incestuous as research assistants, and an unwritten privilege that came with a medical degree. But only if you were male. Female doctors were expected to keep their hands off all of them.

And why hadn't she realized just how wrong the moment was? It'd taken a few minutes of screwing up her nerve even to ask him— *ask him*—because she damn well suspected that the good Dr. Thorne would never, ever get around to it himself. But she should have known—postcall, barely even thinking past his last patient, Thorne needed sleep more than a flirtatious breakfast date with—

With what? Ah, now we come to the crux of the problem, don't we?

With an older woman. There. She could admit it. It's not like the age difference was that great. What, maybe seven years? Not enough to matter.

To me.

But maybe it does to him.

It should matter, she supposed. Their relative positions within the pecking order at Murphy, the fact that she would have at least some input into decisions about his career there. Anesthesiologists, especially very junior ones, couldn't survive long without at least some support from the surgeons.

How long had it been since she was someone besides a surgeon?

Years. She'd been too good too early on, a superb surgeon with excellent political connections. Her career had fast-tracked while her personal life shriveled. Her peers, the ones that might have been her natural source for relationships, had been her competition for jobs, promotions, and research grants.

Until this year, she'd been too busy to realize what was happening. The unfulfilled needs had accumulated, pressure building, until she'd recognized the edgy, forlorn moods for what they were—loneliness. By then, the edge she'd cultivated in order to survive in the male-dominated field of surgery had hardened into a shell. It was as though she were trapped behind glass, staring out at life swarming around her, unable to break through the barrier she'd created.

The way Thorne stood up to her in the OR, wasn't afraid to challenge her, she'd thought he might be able to help. But she'd fouled it up, making a clumsy run on him postcall, a time when she should have known all he'd want was sleep. Maybe on some level she'd planned it that way, approached him when she knew he was least likely to respond.

Neutral ground, that's what she needed. Somewhere that she could slip out of the surgeon persona and find out who was underneath. A place without patients, beepers, or surgery.

A simple prerequisite—and one completely unlikely to be met anytime in the future.

NINE

General Boothby glanced around the assembled staff, glad that he'd foregone his new noontime ritual of a few glasses of wine. By now the entire base knew that Mrs. General Boothby had departed for the States, length of stay unknown and reason unknown. The circumstances had produced the usual flood of wild rumors across the small, insular base, but nobody on the general's staff was talking. Least of all the orderly who'd heard the gunshots that night and observed Mrs. Boothby as she departed the residence.

Yet it seemed to make no difference now. Not here in this room. The entire division was outraged at the apparent attack by the Korean forces the night before.

Gone were the vague hangdog looks he'd begun to notice, the edgy fearfulness and apathy. In its place was a revitalized, aggressive group of officers eager for action. The names of the two men who'd died were spoken in hushed, reverential tones as befit a warrior. The stimulus of their deaths had bonded the twenty-two men and women now sitting in his conference room into a tight, cohesive, and effective force. He felt a profound gratitude at having been selected to be their leader.

"You all know what happened," he began gruffly as the noise died away. He let the silence sink in for a few moments, then continued. "The 501st Intelligence Brigade estimates indicate that they're moving south even now, reinforcing all operational battalions with additional logistics and resupply companies. If anything, this will leave the North Korean civilian population in even more dire straits. Starvation, pestilence, death on a scale that we cannot begin to imagine as every last resource is mobilized to support the hordes now streaming toward us.

"There is one additional fact that cannot have escaped your notice." He took a moment to study each face quickly and then nodded. "Yes, I see you understand. The simple fact is that we cannot withstand a determined attack of the complete North Korean forces. The defense cutbacks, our own logistical tale—even the finest fighting force, when outnumbered twenty to one by a fanatically desperate enemy, must suffer atrocious casualties."

The mood in the room was now somber as each officer considered the facts. They were indisputable, the results of decades and decades of intelligence analysis and battle estimates. It cut each of them to the very core. They lacked sufficient force to execute their mission.

"We fight or we die," the general concluded quietly. "That's all there is to it."

"With what?" his operations officer asked, his voice determined. "General, I—"

Boothby cut him off with a wave of his hand. "Of course there are options," he continued, glad that the man had provided a natural transition to his follow-on orders. "I have spoken with the chairman of the Joint Chiefs of Staff this morning. He is in constant contact with the president, as you know. We have received, much to my delight, a change in our rules of engagement. Given the seriousness of the operational scenario, the president has authorized us to take whatever measures are necessary to hold our line." He saw a few startled looks in the room and ignored them. "In other words, ladies and gentlemen, the best defense is a good offense."

Of course, there had been no such conversation. The chairman of the Joint Chiefs of Staff, General Jeremy Huels, was an old friend of his. Jerry would have been the last person to condone such a course of conduct, even if Boothby had been able to make a persuasive case for it. And no president since Eisenhower would have dared placed such broad political power in the hands of a military man. Particularly not this president.

Yet as he spoke the words, he knew that every officer in the room would believe them. Believe them because they must believe them, because they wanted so desperately to believe that their cause in Korea was not completely doomed. That generations and generations of American fighting men and women had not wasted their blood in vain on this thin and rocky soil. That there was a way out—both for them personally and for the men and women they were responsible for. Yes, they would believe—they would believe because they had to.

"There will be very little message traffic on this," Boothby continued. "Politics are a delicate matter. But I am pleased that the president has understood our situation and granted us the power to resolve it. Naturally, we must go through the motions." He made a vague gesture, which they all appeared to understand. "I will go to the conference table in thirty minutes to meet with my opposite number. We know it will be futile, but we must observe the formalities of the protocol we have worked out with the North Koreans. But," and he let the smallest of grim smiles flicker across his face, "in my absence, you will begin the planning process."

Every head nodded slightly. They understood all too well. There were contingency plans upon contingency plans for the peninsula of Korea, all of which had been staffed down and worked in infinite detail. Logistics, air support, even authorization to recall the reserve units already trained to augment his staff and support units in the field—although not additional combat troops. Everything was already in place. A straightforward problem for this staff already immersed in the tactical details.

Yet every crisis held its own peculiar requirements, and this was no different than any other had been. Units would have to be assigned to the skeleton plans, taking into account those which were minus men and assets for maintenance, due to casualty, or for any one of another million reasons. There would be additional forces to be requisitioned, maritime preposition assets to be brought into play eventually, although that too would have to be authorized by his superiors. But no plan can ever completely account for all the preconditions that will exist at the beginning of conflict.

"You have six hours," Boothby said.

The operations officer stood and walked formally over to the planning clock. He positioned the counter at six hours, turned to the general, and waited.

Boothby nodded. "Begin." As he left the room, he heard the officers falling into their well practiced planning cells, pulling out charts, logistics tables, casualty figures, and beginning a drill that they had practiced innumerable times before. The six-hour planning process was underway.

By the time he returned from the conference table, his intents would have been fleshed out into an operational plan, complete with follow-on objectives, target lists, task force organization, and Army Reserve mobilization requirements. With a little bit of divine guidance, it would work.

Boothby turned to his aide. "Call me when they're done."

As he climbed into his Humvee, the general thought back to Sergeant Carter. He felt a moment of regret that he had not killed the man when he had the chance.

Now, if Carter had been wounded, even slightly, that would be a different matter. Boothby's hand went unconsciously to his own flat stomach and traced over the scar from his appendectomy four months ago.

Why are they all named Kim?

General Boothby's counterpart from the north sat across the neutral zone table, his face impassive. He was tall for a Korean, and bore himself with an air that Boothby had immediately recognized. General Kim was a field soldier, not a denizen of the cliques and gangs that passed for a political circle in the tumultuous north. Kim was someone whom, within the constraints of both of their political systems, Boothby could deal with. They might not agree—and indeed, their differing perspectives made it almost inevitable that they would not—but they would understand one another. Understand, and anticipate.

The appearance of his briefing team here today bore that out. The requisite notices, statements of disagreements, and other formalities of the process had been observed with minimal quibbling. The reason for that, Boothby understood, was that both men knew this was serious. The current crisis went beyond the normal flurry of gunshots and woundings, sniper fire and harassment that constituted a daily part of life on the Korean peninsula.

Boothby could see that Kim was troubled. Troubled and suspicious—whether of the American forces or of his own troops, it was impossible to tell, yet. Boothby had expected this, that Kim might know that American forces were behind the last attack. But he would never admit to it—he couldn't, without losing substantial face. For American forces to slip through the tunnels—which the North Koreans claimed still did not exist, and if they did, they'd been built by the South Korean forces—eliminate two North Korean soldiers, and execute an attack against their own side would be to admit that the North Korean border forces were incompetent. Inferior, at the very least.

In fact, Boothby was somewhat surprised that the Koreans admitted the incident had occurred at all. They were being forced to choose between admitting that the Korean forces could not control their side of the border or, even worse, admitting that a North Korean force had executed the attack. An interesting applicational feint and double-feint, Boothby thought.

The room was plain, devoid of ostentation or comfort. It had taken years of wrangling to work out the location of the room, a plain cinderblock building exactly bisected by the line between north and south. A long conference table had been placed in the middle of it, again, exactly on the dividing line.

Each side lined up on their side of the table, and cold formalities were exchanged. They waited until the flurry of scufflings from their aides died away before beginning.

Kim took the initiative, surprising Boothby by leaning forward slightly. Boothby heard one of his aides suck in a surprised breath. But the North Korean's face was grave, more serious than Boothby had ever seen it before. His mind raced as he tried to anticipate the next move.

"There has been an incident," Kim said calmly. He let the sentence hang in the air while the translator echoed it. "Two of my soldiers on routine patrol were shot."

"So I've heard." Boothby said. Let the Korean play it as he would.

"You are at fault," Kim said bluntly. He eyed his counterpart directly, a cold scowl on his face. "You jeopardize everything that has happened here, General."

The American staff stirred angrily. Boothby ignored them. "A preposterous claim, considering two of my soldiers are dead."

"And two of mine as well. But we were not the aggressors in this." Kim motioned to one of the men standing behind him. The man stepped forward smartly, passed him a thin brown folder. Kim made a show of opening it slowly, extracting a single piece of paper. He laid it on the table in front of him, turned it so that Boothby could read it across the line that divided them. It would not be passed across the table, not without permission. To do so would constitute an invasion of South Korean soil.

Boothby allowed no surprise to show on his face. When had they learned that he could read Korean, he wondered. No matter, that card was being played now to give added validity to whatever intelligence the message contained.

Boothby scanned the message quickly, then looked up at Kim. "I'm afraid I'll need my translator," he said blandly.

Kim shook his head. "I will explain to you the points that may be unclear. First, an analysis of the trajectory of the two bullets indicated that they came from *our* side of the border. Second, chemical weapons detectors indicate that your troops were attacked with tear gas."

"Exactly the points I made in my protest," Boothby said.

Kim shook his head. "You intentionally misunderstand. We do not have tear gas readily available to us. Only the American forces do." He eyed Boothby coldly. "If we wanted to break the protocols, we would do so with a much more significant attack. Not this." He gestured in disgust at the message, still turned around so that Boothby could read it.

A murmur from his side, the American intelligence officer scratching quick notes. In intelligence terms, this was pure gold. Not only had the North Koreans admitted that tear gas was not available— if that could be believed—but they had made the bold statement that their attack would have been with some substance far more deadly. That alone was sufficient to cause deep concern on the American side of the table. While they had long suspected—with the speculation bordering on certainty—that the North Koreans were willing to use biological and chemical weapons, never had their suspicions been confirmed quite so baldly.

General Kim stood suddenly, breaking the well-established protocols that passed for peace here. "You cannot afford this war any more than we can. Do not push us any further."

Kim slammed his chair back against the table and stalked out of the room, followed by his cadre.

The American team sat stunned. Finally, Boothby stirred. "We're wasting our time—let's get the hell out of here."

As they filtered out to the fleet of Humvees parked on their side of the border, Boothby felt a surge of joyous rage shoot through him. It wouldn't take long. Not long at all.

Boothby spent twenty minutes meeting with his staff, providing additional guidance, and tentatively approving the plan that was being developed. He made only one substantive change—insisting upon the early call-up of the reserve units designated to support a full-scale war in Korea, particularly the MASH units, pending approval for mobilization of reserve combat troops from the States.

"Medical units alone will get some public attention, but not the general outcry that combat troops would," Boothby pointed out. "It will play well in the media, emphasizing the commitment to take care of casualties. Besides, we'll need the doctors in place to start screening the combat units as soon as they start arriving."

His emphasis on quickly escalating the number of combat troops in Korea chilled the entire staff. The nervous murmur that ran through their ranks was finally stilled by one quick glare from the general.

Operating on too little sleep and too much adrenaline, General Boothby was beginning to feel the drain. He could feel the leaden dullness nibbling on the edges of his concentration and the hard knot in his stomach that indicated it had been too long since he'd eaten. He left the staff abruptly, rustled up his driver, and ordered him to take him home.

Boothby left his driver outside waiting in the car while he went into his quarters. The rooms were still and silent, dust motes floating in the shafts of autumn sunlight streaming through the old glass. There was a chill in the air already, an indication of the winter that would not be long in coming. Winter—the favorite time for the North Koreans to attack. With the ground hard and frozen, the swamps that were impassable during warmer months would form wide, broad avenues for armored vehicles and troops. They could move quickly, much more quickly than they could during the summer.

He went to the kitchen and fixed himself a sandwich, carelessly slapping mustard and mayonnaise onto two pieces of slightly stale bread. He swore mildly when he saw the state of the refrigerator. Have to get his aide to replenish it. Tomorrow was Alicia's shopping day. With Alicia gone, along with Brett, his housekeeper might have less to do, but the cook would have additional duties. Alicia had always liked to cook—had made a point of not relying too heavily on the enlisted men and women assigned to their household staff. He experienced a brief pang of regret at the changes Alicia's departure would work on his personal life.

No matter. He bit deeply into the sandwich, barely chewing as he gulped it down. A soldier could survive on field rations for months and months, and often did. As a worst case, he could always requisition a case of MREs—Meals Ready to Eat—from the supply officer. He chortled, almost choking on another bite of the sandwich, as he thought of the commander of all forces in Korea being reduced to field rations within his own house.

Washing down the last bites of sandwich with a beer, he wandered from room to room with the remains of the sandwich in his hand. Crumbs dropped on the immaculate floors behind him.

He experienced a moment of sanity, a deep welling of extreme regret that his wife and son were gone. The pictures flashed back into his mind with stunning clarity: Alicia with a gun. Brett's cold, frightened face. His own face, as though seen from a distance, twisted and angry. What in the world had possessed him? How could he have even brought his gun into his son's room?

He ran up the stairs, suddenly certain that perhaps it had all been a dream. None of it had happened—Alicia and Brett were still here, simply out of the house for a few moments. Some activity on base— perhaps the wives' club was meeting, a soccer game, one of the innumerable visits Alicia made to the other Army wives on the post. They would be back soon.

He ran down the passageway and stopped dead in Brett's room. The beautiful illusion he had started to craft in his mind, a coherent explanation for everything, crumbled into shards. The room was rumpled, the closets empty, a bullet hole in the floor. Toys and one pair of shoes remained scattered about, but the essentials were gone. Brett's closet was virtually empty, only a few suits of winter clothes remaining.

Boothby howled, an ancient, primal scream torn from deep in his soul. He was still keening when he heard the door downstairs burst open and his driver clatter into the hallway and up the steps.

The mask slipped back down over the general's face. By the time the orderly reached the top of the stairs, he was as cool and collected as ever.

"General?" the driver panted. "I thought I heard—" He stopped suddenly, confused.

"Yes?" the general asked calmly. "What did you hear?"

Now thoroughly baffled, the orderly shook his head. "Nothing, sir. Nothing at all."

"Fine. Back to headquarters, then." The general strode down the stairs without waiting for a response, followed close on his heels by the baffled sergeant.

The revised plan, as the staff presented it, was a good one. Boothby listened carefully, asked several sharp questions, and finally nodded in approval. "Good. We will execute in one week."

A sharp gasp somewhere in the back of the room. Boothby whirled and searched the faces for the offender. "Problem?" he snapped.

The operations officer cleared his throat, then said, "Not at all, General. We were just wondering—at least some of us thought—"

"You've got a format for thinking, Colonel. It's called the deliberate planning process. Or, in this case, the crisis planning process. That's how wars are executed—six hours to plan, six months in the field. Or am I the only student of military history here?"

"But one week? General, why? Of course, there have been some incidents, serious ones at that. But full scale mobilization and wartime preparations? Are you sure . . . ?"

The silence in the room was palpable. Every officer sat frozen as though afraid to draw attention to himself or herself by the slightest movement. Boothby stared at them, a blunt, broad-shouldered man—an icon—in many of their minds.

"One week," he repeated. He turned and strode from the room, leaving a puzzled staff behind him.

TEN

Thorne had spent most of his day off sleeping, eating, and attending to the myriad household problems that seemed to accumulate every time he had first call, a thirty-six-hour stretch at the hospital as the duty anesthesiologist. In the midst of collecting laundry, soaking dishes, and hunting for clean towels, he felt a moment of envy for the married doctors on the staff, the ones who weren't married to other doctors. At least *they* had someone to throw out junk mail before it accumulated to unmanageable levels. It was almost a relief to roll out of bed at 4:00 A.M. the next morning and head for the hospital.

He made rounds and checked the surgery schedule, hoping to run into Patterson somewhere along the way. The hospital wasn't that big—she had to be in the area somewhere. Kamil caught up with him near the pharmacy, spouting effusive and heartfelt apologies for his outburst earlier. Still wondering where Patterson was, Thorne hurriedly reassured him and made some excuse to return to surgery.

She still wasn't there. Annoyed at himself, and at her, he headed for the professional building. If she wasn't there, then at least her secretary would know where she was. With a poignant thrill, he realized that it mattered to him that he didn't even have her beeper number.

Thorne knocked lightly on the solid door separating Patterson's office from the rest of her suite. When there was no answer, he turned the knob and pushed the door open slightly, intending to stick his head in and see if she was available. Patterson was slumped down, elbows on the desk, her head resting in her hands.

In two quick steps, he was by her side. As she heard him enter the room, the surgeon started, quickly rearranging her face into an expression of neutrality.

"What's wrong?" Thorne asked. He dropped into a chair in front of her desk.

Patterson's expression suddenly changed. "Oh my God," she said softly. "You haven't heard, yet."

Thorne took a deep breath. "I spent most of yesterday sleeping. That, and trying to figure out how to apologize for being such lousy company the other day." The words were coming out easier than he'd thought they would. "Could we have dinner tonight, maybe? I should be done by six, and . . ." His voice trailed off as he realized she was staring at him with a stricken expression on her face. She passed him the piece of paper she'd been holding. It was addressed to several individuals, one of them a resident in her department. Halfway down the list, he saw his own name.

"Don't you ever watch the news?" Patterson's voice held an incredulous note. "Jesus, I know you had call, but, Thorne, Korea's issued an ultimatum to the United States. They're saying it wasn't anticipated, but somebody must have known. My uncle—he would have said something, I know he would have. But this—I just can't—" Patterson finally broke off the beginning of a tirade and watched him silently.

In official capital letters, the message notified the addressees that they were being mobilized to active duty with the United States Army in support of operations in Korea. They were given seventy-two hours to report to the nearest reserve processing facility, and were admonished to report with a complete inventory of personal gear and such other necessities that might be needed for a six-month activation to Korea.

"But they can't—I'm not—" Thorne tried to prod his brain into action. When was the last time he'd had any contact with the Army Reserve? At least a year ago, he figured. There'd been some bit of official correspondence, a new claim form on which he could claim his hours of grand rounds and continuing education.

Back when he'd been in medical school and a newly minted resident, the seven hundred dollars a month that the Army sent him for maintaining his proficiency in anesthesia had seemed like a princely sum. Some months, it had paid the rent, allowed him a few luxuries that other residents didn't have.

However, since then, the sum had been hardly significant compared to his normal salary. He'd taken to banking the monthly checks, occasionally forgetting to fill in the correct forms and even send them in. Still, the checks arrived, and Thorne duly deposited them in his savings account.

As much as he'd forgotten about his Army commitment, it appeared the Army had not forgotten about him.

"Medical teams are always the first recalled," Patterson said. She crossed the room and slumped down on the leather couch that graced one wall.

"I can't go," he said finally. "I just got here. Surely they don't expect us to—"

Patterson let out a low, cynical chuckle. She levered herself up from where she'd been stretched out on the couch and smoothed her skirt down over her legs. "You don't have a choice. Look at it this way. You're new at the Murphy, still waiting for your security clearance to come through. If you fail to report as ordered, the Army will chalk that up as a desertion. Hell, if this thing with Korea gets serious enough, they may even come looking for you.

"If you don't go, you'll never have a chance in hell of staying at the Murphy. Gillespie will fire you in a heartbeat with the complete support of the board. Most of them, in case you haven't noticed, are retired military doctors. And there's the matter of our military contracts—a major source of revenue for us, as you well know."

"Is that all you think about? Then what was all that about the other day?" Thorne snapped. "Do you know I don't even have your beeper number?"

Sudden, deep silence engulfed the room. Thorne's annoyance turned into horrified embarrassment. He took a deep breath, tried to get his bearings. "Never mind, Doctor. I'm sorry, I was just a little surprised by all this. I just—"

"Two-two-one-zero."

"What?"

"My beeper extension. The standard switchboard number, then two-two-one-zero." Patterson stood, crossed in two graceful steps to stand in front of him. He started to step back, stopped when she grabbed his lapel with one strong hand. "And you didn't misunderstand. Not today, not yesterday. The question is, where do we stand now?"

"I—"

She sighed, let go of his jacket, and stepped back. She crossed the room to her desk and stared down at it. With her back to him, she said, "Don't talk right now, Thorne. Not if you don't understand what I'm saying." A harsh sound escaped her, then she continued, "I suppose you could even be contemplating a lawsuit for sexual harassment right now." She turned back to face him. "Are you?"

"No. Of course not."

"Good. You'd lose."

"Probably."

"Certainly." She crossed the room to stand directly in front of him, so close that he could feel her breath tickle his neck. "I always win, Thorne. Always. Don't ever forget that." She slid one hand up behind his neck.

It seemed to be the most natural act in the world, to let his arms go around her and pull her into him. He barely had to bend down to find her mouth with his, and the kiss deepened from exploratory to demanding. Within moments, he could no longer tell where his body ended and hers began, where her hands were touching him and his were touching her. He lost his breath, couldn't find any rhythm except the deep demands of his body moving with hers.

Patterson gasped, then pulled away. Her eyes glowed brilliantly. "Not here. Not now."

"When?"

"I'll take you up to San Francisco to check in."

"Get out of town so no one will see us?" Thorne asked.

Patterson nodded. "That's part of it."

"And the other part?"

"We'll both be different people if we're away from Murphy. Too far away to be paged or called in. You'll see." She laughed, then stretched, rolling her neck from side to side as though to ease a muscle cramp. "You're still new at being on staff, Thorne. You don't even feel it yet, the way you're tied down right now. Come on, let me take you to San Francisco."

"That's *days* from now."

"You'll live." She came close again, so tantalizingly close he could barely stand it. "Besides, you're going to be busy getting ready to go. You better go break the news to Dr. Gillespie before he hears it from someone else."

Thorne leaned back in the chair and tried to absorb the situation. The last thirty-six hours were quickly blending into a haze of emergencies, hasty decisions, and crises, capped by this latest, life-altering stunner. "Oh, man," he said softly. "Gillespie—he's going to be seriously pissed."

Patterson stood in the middle of her office, smiling as Thorne pulled the door shut behind him. As soon as it clicked shut, the smile faded from her face.

Dear God, what have I done? And just where did all THAT come from? Her shoulders slumped. She walked unsteadily back to her desk, uncertain of what she'd just committed herself to and quite sure that she'd just made a complete fool of herself.

But this was what she'd wanted, wasn't it? Time away from Murphy, away from the world that kept her trapped in the surgeon role. How could she have imagined that she could pull this off?

But she had. She hadn't imagined Thorne's response, could still feel the hard power in his arms as he'd pulled her close, his warm breath on her neck.

The hero off to the war, one last fling with his woman. Was there really a grain of truth behind the cliches that had fueled so many scenes in so many war movies? Evidently so. The knowledge that Thorne was going to Korea, that he might be in danger over there, had enabled her to break through the wall long enough to make the first move.

So what now? "We go to San Francisco," Patterson said aloud. "We go, and we see what happens. When he comes back from Korea, we see where we stand."

A faint glimmer of hope now, the possibility that this might be the first step in breaking her own pattern of isolation. After all, she'd made the first move, hadn't she? Even if she'd preceded it with that bitchy little sermon on sexual harassment.

And if she could make the first move this time, then maybe she could again. She stretched in her chair, feeling gloriously alive and excited for the first time in years. Maybe she was capable of more than she'd expected of herself.

Forty-eight hours later, Patterson picked him up in her red BMW and drove him to the Army Reserve center in San Francisco. They talked shop, desultorily, avoiding the subject of their relationship. Patterson dropped him off and told him to beep her when he was done with his in-processing.

Once there, much to his annoyance, he was poked, prodded, immunized, and issued new uniforms. He also learned, to his surprise, that he'd been promoted to major two years earlier. The notification had never reached him.

Thorne moved through the day with mechanical disbelief. It seemed that at any moment, someone—perhaps an official from the Army, perhaps someone from the hospital—would pop out from behind a door, laugh hysterically, and proclaim it all a joke. That he could actually deploy to Korea as part of the medical unit there seemed simply unbelievable. Aside from two brief weeks in officer indoctrination training and one long summer spent at the Army's camp, Thorne's major source of information on his prospective assignment was watching old *M*A*S*H* reruns.

Crammed into a massive drill hall with four hundred other mobilized reservists, Thorne raised his hand and repeated the oath that countless doctors before them had taken. Now reactivated in the Army Reserve, he was given a forty-eight-hour pass, told to return home and tie up any loose ends, and ordered to report at 0800 on the third day for deployment to Korea. A stern master sergeant explained patiently that that meant eight o'clock in the morning.

Thorne found a pay phone, beeped Patterson, then went out to wait for her. He sat down on the curb, a massive sea bag full of new uniforms and paperwork crouched beside him.

Patterson's car pulled up. She stuck her head out the window. "Hey, soldier, new in town?"

Thorne tossed the sea bag into the backseat. "Reality overload. Let's get the hell out of here.

Patterson worked her way through the gears on the car, sliding smoothly in and out of traffic. "No reality for the next two days." She turned toward him, her eyes concealed by mirrored sunglasses. "Agreed?"

"Agreed."

During the next forty-eight hours, Thorne came to know a different Debbie Patterson. Away from the hospital, she shed the cool demeanor that was her professional trademark. While he'd been at the procession station, she'd checked them into a hotel, given the telephone number to their answering services, gone shopping, and made reservations for dinner.

The restaurant—Thorne could remember nothing about it, not the name, the location, or even what he'd had to eat. What had started as anticipation grew to a hunger that was barely controllable over dinner. By the time they'd finished and paid the check, he was slipping out of control.

He kissed her in the parking lot, let his hands play over her as they drove to the luxury hotel. By the time they'd gotten to the room, the current coursing between them had been overwhelming.

Now he had new images to remember, ones that replaced those of her in surgery. Patterson. He laughed at that, still thinking of her by her last name.

They lost track of time, ordered room service, and spend most of the two days naked. Thorne had clicked on the TV at one point. Patterson snatched the remote from his hand, turned the TV off, and pinned him to the bed. "No TV. No sleeping. There's time enough for sleeping after we're both dead." Her mouth descended on his, cutting off his response.

Finally, a little before 0800, they pulled into the parking lot of the Reserve center. Four hours later, now with final orders and sea bag in hand, Thorne climbed aboard a bus that ferried him to Castle Air Force Base. Along with his fellow reservists, he was herded aboard a transport aircraft, ordered brusquely to buckle in, and was underway. Thorne fell asleep shortly after takeoff.

Sixteen hours later, after one stop for fuel, he was in Korea.

ELEVEN

"Welcome to Korea. I am Lieutenant General Boothby." The words from the ancient loudspeaker were broken with static. As the general leaned forward over the podium, an ugly, painful scream of feedback assaulted the newly activated reservists.

Thorne winced as he studied the man on the podium in front of them. Standing in the fifth line of the assembled ranks, he had a clear view of him. Shortly after they'd landed, a grizzled sergeant had insistently herded the disorganized gaggle of civilians into an arrangement assembling a formation, tried quickly to tutor them on the finer points of standing at attention, then thrown up his hands in disgust and settled for a cautionary, "Now hold still, sir, ma'am. Just hold real still and look at the front of the room."

The military music flared suddenly and a group of official-looking officers paraded in. Thorne saw the sergeant snap into a sharp salute. He tried to follow suit, then noticed that no one around him was mimicking the motion. He let his hand fall to his side.

The parade of officers was headed by the man speaking now. Through a haze of fatigue and frustration, Thorne tried to take the general's measure. As a student of history, Thorne knew just how much of this current conflict depended upon the personality of the man in charge. Despite his rather precarious involvement in what seemed certain to be a war, Thorne felt a slight thrill that he would at least experience this one firsthand. Stories to tell his not-yet-born son, actual experience to round out his extensive reading and studies.

"I know most of you are probably in a state of shock at this point," the general continued. "Most of you were civilians up until less than a week ago." He paused and appeared to study each one of them. Thorne felt the general's laserlike gaze flit over his face and move on to the next officer. "We'll do what we can to ease the tension, but you must understand this, the tactical situation here in Korea is critical. In other words, I intend to get you farmed out to your respective posts and rely on my subordinate to do a crash indoctrination. If you have questions, speak up. They'll do their best to answer them. In the mean time, I expect you to behave as professional Army officers and to do your damnedest to keep my people alive. That clear?"

Thorne heard a murmur of assent and found himself nodding as well. There was something oddly compelling about the general, a quality of charismatic command that hooked deep into his soul. Patton, Eisenhower, Rommel, Bismarck. The names of great military men from the past echoed through his mind. This was what it had been like to follow such men in the last wars, to experience that bonding and leadership.

"Now, the actual details of each operation are still classified at this point. You'll be briefed later, but for the time being all you need to know is that you've got to be ready. The ground troops are going into harm's way soon. I expect to take casualties." For a moment, the general's face settled into a bleak mask. "And I expect you to care for them as they deserve to be cared for. These are the best fighting men and women on the face of this earth. I expect them to get the best medical care possible. You'll get tired, you'll get frustrated, you'll probably start thinking that you're dealing with an unending tide of injured humanity, one that you can never stem. You will care for them under field conditions, in the hospitals, on the transports back to the U.S. Every second you're doing it, you will remember what I expect from you. More important, you will remember what they deserve— the very best. Is that clear?"

A hushed pause, completely devoid of the scufflings and quiet whispers that had characterized the formation earlier. Thorne stood a little straighter, felt a part of the entire operation.

"Now, are there any questions I can answer?" The general stepped away from the podium and looked at them expectantly.

No. Among other bits of hastily conveyed information, the sergeant who'd lined them up had been abundantly clear on this point. The general would ask if there were any questions, and each one, sir, ma'am, yes that includes you, Doctor, was to keep hands at side and not to ask any questions. As the sergeant explained it, if the officers had any real questions—as distinguished from gripes, moans, and miscellaneous bitching about the Army—then there were corps and corps of people whose very job was to answer those questions. Not the general. He would be consulted only after the chain of command had done its very best to resolve the situation.

But the entire conduct of the war depended on the decisions that General Boothby would make. Standing in ranks, enthralled by the man's charisma, Dr. Christopher Thorne forgot all that. He raised his hand.

The general looked slightly bemused. "Yes, Doctor?"

"General, I'm Christopher—well, Major, I guess—Thorne. Are we going to Yalu or stopping at the narrow neck?"

There was a brief, horrified silence among the regular Army officers assembled. Boothby's face went blank for a moment. The sergeant who'd been herding them about for the past six hours twitched and made a motion as though he would step forward and personally take charge of Thorne's eventual fate, senior officer or not.

Then Boothby laughed. It was a brief chuckle, more a signal to the rest of the assembly than any real trace of amusement. "I was told you people were all doctors and nurses," he said, waving the crowd instantly into silence. "But I suppose there's no reason a doctor can't be a student of military history as well. Dr. Thorne, is it? And yes, young man, those are the insignia of a major."

The spell was broken. Thorne was now thoroughly embarrassed. The sergeant's caution that real questions were *not* asked from the ranks while in formation echoed in his mind. His first day back in a uniform he barely knew how to wear, and he'd already marked himself as one who had no understanding of military protocol—nor the sense to follow good advice from a sergeant.

Was there a way he could suddenly sink into the worn linoleum under his feet? To his surprise, however, the general was answering his question.

"Most of the actual details are so highly classified that I could order you shot for simply asking about them," Boothby continued. He smiled, indicating he was joking. "However, since I'm in charge around here, I have the option of practicing an old Army tradition." He paused for a moment. "So let *me* ask *you*, Major. What do *you* think of the two options? Assume for the moment those are the only two."

"The narrow neck," Thorne said promptly. "It was the mistake we made last time, not stopping there. Along with misinterpreting Russia's intentions."

"Ah. Yes, you do know your wars, don't you?" Rather than sounding patronizing, the general's voice held a note of warm approval. "Well, historically speaking, I agree with you. But the first mistake most commanders make in warfare is to fight a war as though it were the last war fought. In our case, that has certain implications that have guided my staff planning thus far." The general paused, turned, and spoke briefly to an aide. He then turned back to the assembly. "Too much of a general's life is ruled by his staff. I'm afraid I can't go into details at this point, but I thank you for your question. And your analysis. Are there any other questions?"

Quailed into submission by the glares of the assembled staff, the entire formation froze. Thorne had been lucky to escape without public humiliation, but his question had had the effect of breaking the thrall General Boothby had held them in.

Boothby thanked them for their future service and once again welcomed them to Korea. He departed quickly after that. His aide lingered behind.

As soon as the staff left, the sergeant dismissed their formation with instructions to return to the drill hall at 0800 the next morning. As the orderly lines dissolved into knots of prior friendships and newly discovered common specialties, the sergeant advanced on Thorne, murder in his eyes.

The general's aide reached Thorne first. Coolly dismissing the sergeant, the aide stood nose-to-nose with Thorne. Thorne glanced down at the man's collar, noted the bars of a captain, and returned the glare in full measure.

"The general," the aide said, his smooth words at odds with the irritation on his face, "would be pleased if you would join him for dinner this evening. Your question," and the expression of distaste deepened, "intrigued him. General Boothby has quite an interest in military history, and he would enjoy discussing these issues with you."

The aide's tone of voice made it clear that he himself would have nothing to do with a reserve officer ignorant enough to ask the general a question.

Thorne was fairly sure that he was senior to the captain. "I'd do something about that facial tic, Captain," Thorne said. "Could be a sign of a serious neurological problem. And yes, I'd be honored to have dinner with the general. Please thank him for the invitation."

As advised by the aide, Thorne reported to the general's house at exactly 2000 hours. He was met on the doorstep by the aide and shown into the house's spacious library to wait for the general. While he waited, Thorne examined the volumes crowding in on every available surface in the room. Mostly military history and operational art, but the general evidently had eclectic reading tastes. A number of best-sellers as well as a few books on geopolitics were included in the mix.

The general appeared at the archway leading into the room, neatly dressed in civilian khaki pants and a light sweater. In his hand he held a glass of red wine.

Thorne immediately felt overdressed in his uniform. The general, noticing his discomfort, waved it off immediately. "A man's never out of place in a uniform, Doctor. Particularly not around here. Besides, it will be good for you to get back in the habit of it. Me, I always feel a little uneasy out of it."

"Another history buff, General," Thorne said. He felt uneasy with the general in civilian clothes—just how was he supposed to address him?

"Study it or repeat it," the general said, gesturing at the books. "There are lessons to be learned about Korea, and about the rest of the world as well. Tell me, what's your particular interest in military history?"

Thorne thought for a moment, then finally admitted, "The Civil War. Probably because it struck so close to home. I was born and raised in the South, in Mississippi. You see the reminders of it all over the landscape."

The general studied him for a moment. "Something peculiarly

101

fascinating about brother fighting brother, isn't there? Especially when it hits home."

Thorne nodded. "I've always been fascinated by how differently other parts of the United States see the Civil War," he said, warming to his subject. "Up north, it's barely talked about. Out west, it could have happened a millennium ago. But in the South—we lost more people, I suppose. Proportionally, at least. There's that parallel to Russia in the Great War. And it changed our whole way of life."

"Should the South have been allowed to secede, then?" Boothby said.

Thorne shrugged. "It's a moot point now, I suppose, to most people. But I personally find it odd that the United States is so bent and determined that every nation in the world will experience self-determination—except its own."

The general laughed. "You buy that, do you?" He waved one hand, encompassing the whole of Korea around them. "Then what are we doing here?"

"Protecting democracy?"

Now the general roared. He was, Thorne thought, in person and off duty an entirely different fellow. Brilliant, yes, and as massive as he'd seemed from the podium. He did not bother to wonder at the oddness of a general speaking so frankly with a newly mobilized reserve major.

"The United States supports self-determination when it furthers U.S. national interests," the general said, settling down on the couch next to Thorne. He plunked the wine bottle down on the table in front of them and handed Thorne an empty glass. "But you know that, don't you? At some level."

"I'm not sure I've ever heard it put so bluntly. At least not in public."

The general's face took on an annoyed look. "We're not in public, are we? A general officer must speak to his staff with the utmost frankness if they are to carry out his wishes completely." The last phrase had an odd, memorized sound to it.

"Of course, General." He held up his glass as the general held up the bottle. The rich, ruby wine poured into the glass unsteadily. With a shock, Thorne realized that the general was more than a few glasses ahead of him.

"And you are on my staff," the general added as the liquid reached the brim of Thorne's glass. "As of two hours ago."

"Beg pardon?" Thorne steadied the glass to keep it from spilling. "I assumed I'd be sent to a MASH."

"You were sent to me," the general said firmly. "Nominally to the MASH, perhaps. But where my officers serve is my decision. Oh, I'll take some flak from the divisional surgeon. The man's an idiot—a couple of days out in a tent might do him a world of good."

"Sir?" Now Thorne was distinctly uneasy. Annoying the divisional surgeon wouldn't make much difference if he were just on a week's tour of active duty, but if the war in Korea dragged out for months and months the senior medical man on post would no doubt find ways to exact revenge. Thorne recalled one of the few adages he remembered from his indoctrination training: No good deal goes unpunished.

"What else?" the general asked. "The Civil War, you've explained that. But what else?"

Back to history, then, Thorne realized. He stared at the man sitting opposite him, stunned at the sheer amount of power he had. While he'd understood the military organization before, it had never really sunk in, the amount of control the general had over the daily lives of each one of his officers. "Uh, the JFK assassination," Thorne said, grappling to keep up with the change in subjects. "Assassinations in general, I suppose."

Whether the general knew it or not, there was a similarity between Thorne's history interests and the situation now at hand. Perhaps that was the reason he'd posed the question first during formation. The power of an individual to affect the course of the affairs of an entire nation raised particularly compelling questions. Had Kennedy lived, what might the country have become?

And here in Korea, it was General Boothby's decisions, tempered only in small part by the controls of his superiors, that would determine who lived and who died. Who won and who lost. The course of the conflict, which side would mount the first offensive, how the intricate web of strategies and deceptions would be woven, all those decisions would be made by the man sitting before him. Indeed, from what Thorne had heard from the soldiers on his troop transport aircraft and in the barracks, the medical personnel now flooding into Korea had been mobilized at Boothby's request, approval granted immediately by the Joint Chiefs of Staff in reliance on Boothby's summary of the tactical scenario. Despite advances in electronic surveillance, intelligence networks, and diplomacy, military operations still depended on the judgment and assessment of the general officer in the field.

"Ah, yes, the JFK assassination," the general said. "Tell me, which camp do you fall into?"

Thorne smiled, now on familiar ground. "I'm a skeptic, through and through. Briefly, I find it difficult to believe that the amount of people needed for a cover-up could have kept silent for so long. Yet, the coincidences, the unexplained bits of the story, truly concern me. The missing bullet fragments, for instance."

"And what would that be about?" The general drained his glass in one gulp and then refilled it. "I thought they were all accounted for."

Thorne shook his head. "Not at all. One FBI report indicates that when JFK's body was unrolled from the sheet, a missile fell out. There's been a debate raging for years on whether missile refers to a complete, unexpended bullet, or merely fragments that were dislodged from the skull."

He launched into a description of the conflicting theories on the matter, ending with "Of course, we can't duplicate some of that, since JFK's brain is missing."

"What?" The general set his glass down with a sudden thump on the coffee table.

"His brain. It was there at the autopsy, and removed sometime before JFK's burial."

The general sat there as though in stunned silence. His gaze fixed on something long off in the distance, and his mouth twitched slightly.

Finally, Thorne said uncomfortably, "General?"

With a start, the senior officer appeared to return to reality. He stood suddenly, tipping over the entire glass of wine in the process.

"I'm afraid dinner will have to wait. There's something I must attend to." With that, the general strode immediately from the room.

Thorne watched him go, now completely bewildered. What had he said? He'd been elaborating on a couple of his favorite conspiracy theorists' points, and something appeared to have disturbed the general.

Had he offended him somehow? Thorne replayed the conversation in his mind, trying to discern the reason for the general's sudden agitation.

Finally, after a few minutes, the general's aide appeared at the arched doorway to the library. "Do you have a field uniform?"

"Is that the camouflage-colored one?"

The aide looked disgusted. "Yes, the one with the neat tree patterns on it. Sir."

"Yes, I have one."

"Well, Doctor, have someone show you how to wear it. The general would like you to accompany him on field maneuvers in approximately six hours. You've got time to get home, get some sleep, and be back at division headquarters no later than 0130. Think you can manage that? Sir."

"Look, I don't know what your problem is, but I'm having a tough time keeping track of things here," Thorne began angrily. "I mean, I know I'm in the Army, but—"

"You'll want to get some sleep," the aide said, cutting him off. His expression softened slightly. "Come on, I'll have the sergeant take you home. He can make sure you've got all the bits and pieces of the BDUs, and show you how to wear it. Just don't be late, Doctor. The general hates tardiness almost as much as he hates Koreans."

Thorne let the old sergeant lead him out to his vehicle and drive him back to his room. They traveled in silence, Thorne too preoccupied with his own thoughts to do much more than respond minimally to the sergeant's polite comments. Finally, with an evident sigh of relief, the senior enlisted man lapsed into complete silence.

In the darkness it was impossible to tell the general from the rest of the men. They moved as silent shapes, night camouflage uniforms blending with the broken rocks and the narrow strip of coarse sand edging the water, occasionally vanishing from view as the shadows caught them. The six boats pulled up onto the beach were equally difficult to make out, more odd shapes protruding from the water than recognizable vessels.

Thorne stood back from the preparations. Exactly why he had been tapped to accompany this elite cadre on their covert mission had never been addressed.

Nor was there any apparent concern about the general's involvement. Thorne had imagined that the general would remain ashore, waiting impatiently with Thorne at his side for the raiding party to return. Again, something in the general's manner discouraged questions. With their uniforms completely devoid of identifying insignia, the general was just another career soldier hardened by years of duty on the Korean Peninsula.

Except that he wasn't. Nor was Thorne the competent soldier he was pretending to be. For different reasons, both were so markedly out of place on that cold beach as to defy explanation.

One of the men drew him aside. In a harsh, hurried whisper, he gave Thorne a hurried brief on the details of the operation, field hand signals, and basic infantry skills. Thorne nodded, trying to absorb enough information to stay alive.

Boothby motioned Thorne into the rubber boat he was boarding. The only indication of his rank was that the other soldiers allowed him to enter first. A flash of something he'd learned at officers' indoc course: *First in, last out.* In order of seniority, like so many other evolutions in the army.

Thorne moved quickly down to the edge of the water, feeling the awkwardness in his movements, wishing he could mimic the easy grace of the men he'd watched prepare the boats. But the rocks strewn about the beach shifted uneasily under his feet, threatening to topple him into the sea. He slowed down, took a deep breath, and reminded himself: *You don't know what the hell you're doing.*

Finally, he reached the edge of the boat and slipped easily over the side and into a spot next to one inflated wall. The general nudged him, pointed toward the center. Thorne moved over, leaving room for the more experienced men to board. He felt a slight shimmer of shame—the place of protection in the center of the boat, one from which he could not so easily be catapulted into the sea.

The general leaned toward him and spoke quietly. "You stay with Sergeant Carter," he said, pointing at the man in the bow of the boat. "He knows how things are out here. Just do what he says."

Thorne nodded.

The outboard engines, muffled and configured for special operations work, broke through the silence like gunshots. To Thorne it seemed as though the entire coast must suddenly spring to life. Any second accusing spotlights would arc out from the northern coast, pinpointing their exact location for the sniper fire that would follow. The medical details of the damage the machine guns would cause spilled into his mind, vivid and in full color. At least it would be quick.

It seemed beyond possible, but their departure caused no evident reaction from the shore. The boats backed out from the coast, headed quickly out to open water and then fell into a loose column formation as they headed north. Still in the middle position in the boat, Thorne clamped his hands onto the rough planking, holding his butt down on it. The jouncing increased as the boats turned once again, the motion threatening to catapult him out of the boat.

Ten miles up the coast, the lead boat veered back toward land. Large swells gave way to choppier waters and the boats skipped from wavetop to wavetop like pebbles on a pond. A half mile from shore, the engines cut out and the men reached for paddles. Sounds returned, the lap of the ocean against rubber, the hard, even breaths of the men paddling, the constant murmur of breakers against land.

Their progress seemed infinitesimal after the jousting ride through open water. Finally, with one last rush, they were ashore. The other men dragged the boats up and out of view, caching them behind an outcropping of rock and making sure the bow lines were securely tied off. It took just moments, then the hard, forward hand motion from the team leader that only thirty minutes before Thorne had learned meant *Follow me.*

He tried to move as they did, slipping between shadows and moving soundlessly over the broken ground, tracing their steps exactly to avoid known minefields. How and where they'd come by this detailed intelligence he didn't know. Nor, he realized, did he care to know the particulars. For the first time since the orderly had shaken him awake at 0100, the reality of this mission hit him. It was not an intricate war game, carefully staged and planned. Nor was it the operation of a MASH unit, the only skill he'd been taught at officer indoc, aside from a few intricacies of saluting and military courtesy. This was, instead, the practice of real warfighting craft of the most esoteric kind, a covert strike mission intended to partially decapitate the snake that lay coiled to the north of their base.

Or at least temporarily. Thorne had no illusions about the lasting effect of this mission. The decades of warfare between north and south would not so easily give way after a single strike.

With a start, Thorne realized he was alone. The other men had slipped away quietly, seeking cover in the impenetrable night.

What he'd thought was a shadow twitched, then resolved itself into a soldier. Sergeant Carter, the man who'd been in the bow of the boat, the one the general had told him to follow.

"Don't do what they expect you to do, Doc. Or what they want you do to." Carter smiled, an ugly display of stained teeth and jagged incisors. "That way you'll stay alive."

"Thanks," Thorne managed. "I'll remember that."

If he'd had any doubts that he was in the wrong place, the Army sergeant dissolving back into the night had cleared them up. He'd never heard the man approach, not even when he was just inches away.

The first shots rippled out against the silent night like sudden thunder. There was a brief flurry of sound from the trees, birds taking flight and animals seeking deeper cover. Then the silence.

And what the hell am I doing here, anyway? Was that us or them?

"Move!" Carter was back at his side, grabbing Thorne's shoulder and dragging him forward. "We can't stay here."

Thorne followed the heavy pull on his shoulder, stumbling across the terrain and finally fetching up against a tree trunk. He slid down it, turned so that his back was to the rough bark. His breath sounded ragged. He concentrated on slowing it, stilling the fear screaming along his nerves.

Another pull on his shoulder. The sergeant then motioned silently to a fallen tree. Thorne could see a small dugout underneath it, a surface cave carved in black soil. "In there. You wait for us."

Trapped. No, he'd be trapped in place, an easy target for anyone walking by. Even their own troops wouldn't know it was a friendly, not as dark as it was. Regardless of what the sergeant suggested, Thorne wasn't going into hiding.

"No. I'll follow you."

The sergeant shrugged. "Stay close, then. I don't have time to be dragging you around. Get us both killed that way."

Thorne nodded. "I'll keep up."

The sergeant released his grip on Thorne's sleeve and slid silently into the blackness. Thorne followed, trying to mimic his movements. The feet, just so. Arms in close to the body, avoiding nearby branches and leaves.

Thorne lost sight of him once, panicked, and turned to find the sergeant standing motionless off to his right. A short, sharp flash of teeth, then the sergeant said, "Like I said, stay close." He moved out, Thorne following close behind.

Interminable minutes, in which life was reduced to the simplest of actions. Move, check the surroundings, wait for the sergeant to move again. The sounds of the forest were returning now, slowly but noticeably. More cover for any inadvertent noise they might make—cover for both Thorne and whoever waited at the end of this long, stalking existence.

The sergeant froze in position, just when Thorne had been anticipating another step. The automatic weapon was nestled against the sergeant's right hip, his left arm slightly lifted in the signal Thorne had come to understand as *halt*.

Thorne schooled himself into immobility, trying to even stop the heaving motion of his chest as he breathed. His lungs—surely the noise he made breathing was so loud that the others could hear it, hear it so clearly that they could target him even amid the cloaking protection of the trees.

And where were they? The sergeant was still not moving, not even breathing it seemed.

The slightest noise to Thorne's right—a bird? The wind? Or something more dangerous.

Thorne watched the sergeant turn his head slowly, ever so slowly, the motion almost undetectable. More frozen minutes passed.

Not just his head, Thorne realized, almost starting from his immobility as the realization struck him. Not at all. The sergeant's entire body was pivoting slowly in the direction of the noise, the muzzle of his weapon leading the movement. His feet remained fixed in place as his torso rotated.

Thorne contemplated trying to move himself. He could, he thought. As silently as the sergeant had, maybe, since it now seemed like he'd spent months and months following the other man through the bush.

Thorne started to turn.

Automatic weapons shattered the quiet. Bright muzzle flashes erupted from the sergeant's weapon. Sparks answered from fifty feet away. Underbrush splintered as each side fired at the other's muzzle flashes.

A hoarse ragged scream from across the small stream, then another. The brush rustled, harsh exclamations in another language. Thorne sucked in air, unaware until that point that he'd been holding his breath.

The sergeant was moving now, disappearing in pursuit of the sounds fading off into the distance. A voice keened halfway up the hill. Thorne held still, knowing he could never keep up with the veteran of this odd, dangerous land.

A brief chatter of automatic weapon fire, a muffled oath, maybe in English, maybe not. At this range, all Thorne could clearly make out was the pain in the voice.

Two more shots, single ones, fired from somewhere closer to Thorne. The screaming stopped. More sounds of movement in the forest, fading away as Thorne stood frozen.

Finally, silence again, except for a branch shattered in the firefight finally breaking loose from its tenuous hold on its tree, crashing to ground just ten feet to Thorne's left.

Thorne sagged against the tree trunk behind him. He'd spent

hours, maybe a lifetime motionless in the forest while the outcome of the encounter was decided around him.

And where was the rest of the squad? The general, the other soldiers with him? Ever since the sergeant and Thorne had split off from them to take point, he'd heard not the slightest sound to indicate that there were other friendly forces in the area.

Were they nearby, watching? Judging him, perhaps, wondering whether or not he would hold in position as the sergeant had directed?

If so, he'd just failed that test, although he supposed his immobility during the brief battle might count in his favor.

Should he call out? Risk alerting other Korean forces in the area?

No. Better to wait, here in the protection of the tree, until the more experienced men made their presence known. They wouldn't forget him.

Would they?

Ten minutes later, Thorne was not so sure. There'd been no sign of either Carter or the rest of the squad. No indication that they were hunting for him, indeed, no sounds of human movement at all. The forest itself was back in full voice, subtle murmurings of wind and vegetation, the occasional harsh cry of an animal.

The inevitability of it sank in finally. For all he knew, the sergeant had been wounded or killed on his dash up the neighboring hill. The rest of the team didn't know where they were. And if the boonies were still infested with Koreans, they wouldn't be likely to search for him. What was one man, a reservist at that?

He straightened up, stepped away from the sheltering bulk of the tree. Naked, exposed, but moving quietly with the new skills he'd acquired, he started to retrace their steps.

A sound off to his right. Thorne froze, mimicking what he'd seen Carter do.

Again, the faint rustle of brush. Closer now, no more than fifty feet away, clearly audible over the background of night sounds.

Every nerve ending was tingling, so vitally alive and sensitive that it was as though he'd been sleepwalking his entire life. He could feel the forest around him, sense it as an extension of the ground he stood upon, a living entity that he moved through like a symbiotic parasite. The night air fluxed and twisted around him, bringing him the details of the other man's movements.

There, just beyond that bush. Thorne sensed the other man as much as saw him, felt his presence in the disturbed air currents eddying around him, the slight change in the night sounds. Closer than he'd thought before—

Before what? He started to try to puzzle out the changes that had come over him so abruptly, just as he'd heard the first sounds of the other man's movements. But there was no time for it, not now. Whatever it was had happened because Thorne was alone in the forest, dependent upon only his own meager skills for survival.

Thorne moved now, feeling the uncanny grace and stillness in how he turned, how he felt the effects of his own movement in the forest. Slowly—but quickly somehow, a different type of moving than he'd ever experienced before.

Who was it? One of his own team? Carter, finally returning to retrieve the novice after having a good laugh at Thorne's expense? Or a North Korean, deadly and experienced in this land?

It didn't matter. Whoever it was, he would die. The distinctions between friend and enemy had disappeared at the first surge of adrenaline in his body.

He was closer to the cover that edged each side of this trail now, sliding through the brush and foliage with barely a discernible rustle. It felt safer already, deeper into the woods. Finally convinced that he was not a clearly visible target, Thorne edged the pistol out of his holster, cursing silently at the sibilant noise metal sliding over nylon fabric made.

Across the path, the brush shifted. The vague outline of another man. It was a Korean, clad in camouflage, carrying an automatic weapon.

Thorne brought the pistol up, sliding it over to bear on the other soldier. His finger caressed the trigger, lighting gently on the worn arc of metal. Squeeze, don't pull. He remember that much from indoc, the growled admonitions from the master gunnery sergeant who'd supervised their cursory weapons familiarization course.

Squeeze.

Thorne increased the pressure slightly, felt the trigger resist and then start to move. A few more seconds, slowly.

A chatter of gunfire off to his left startled him. His finger jerked off a round. The gun recoiled in his hand, almost skittering loose from his grip.

An inhuman, anguished howl from across the path. The brush shook violently as the other man crashed through it and out onto the path. He lay across the path, bisecting it, both arms curled protectively around his gut.

Thorne brought the pistol back down to point at him, intent only on ending the danger now, before it could end him. There were no longer any sides. Not since he'd been left alone.

The man on the ground writhed, curling around his shredded midsection. Thorne could smell the stench now, the characteristic bowel smell he knew from surgery when the intestines are perforated and the contents exposed to air. Thorne moved closer, his weapon still up and centered on the man, torn between the need to make some last-ditch, futile effort to save the soldier and his own newly-discovered self-preservation instincts.

This far away from a trauma center, or any hospital at all, the wound was fatal. Feces and urine mixed with blood washed over all the internal organs, spreading the seed material for an infection that the soldier would not survive. Not that there would be time for that to kill him. He was bleeding out, soaking the rocky dirt and pine needles as Thorne watched. A minute, maybe two. No longer.

The man was moaning louder, words distinguishable amongst the animal sounds coming out of his mouth. His eyes were open now, unfocused and staring. He was trembling, turning paler even as Thorne watched.

Thorne started toward the soldier again. He had done this. Taken this life. No matter that there was nothing he could do, that the soldier would have killed him had Thorne not fired first. The body on the ground was no longer any threat.

I killed him.

Gunfire again, this time so close as to be deafening, stitching a seam across the Korean on the ground. Thorne whirled to face the new danger, pistol firing wildly.

The Korean groaning on the path abruptly stopped.

Dead silence.

"Thorne, come on out of there." The voice was low, sliding into his ears as though it were part of the jungle. "Come on, point the weapon at the ground and move."

Still Thorne stood frozen, held motionless by the new caution the jungle had taught him. Danger surged around him, indiscriminate and pervasive. To move was to give up the only advantage he had left, the concealment of the brush.

"Come. They're gone. It took us a while to find you, but we're here now." The voice insinuated itself past the new reflexes of the forest, patiently drawing him back to that other world, the one he'd left so recently. "The weapon, Thorne. Point at the ground and move."

Reality surged back in as suddenly as the forest had. The pistol in his hand, burning his palm. The Korean, a massive bloody field where his abdomen should be. The voice.

He could place it now, the voice. Not Carter. The first man who'd spoken to him on the beach, the one who'd taught him the hand signals.

A friend. That realization came last, along with the ability to move again, to override these new reflexes with his intellect.

Thorne moved, just slightly at first, just enough to give away his position. Emboldened by the fact that he was still alive, he stepped out onto the rutted path.

"Killed your first one, did you?" The other soldier slid out of the trees as though he were surfacing from a deep lake. "Should have finished him right away, though. The screaming draws others."

"I—I didn't know who you were," Thorne said slowly, as though that would explain everything. Why the Korean lay on the ground. Why he'd been hiding. Why he was in Korea in the first place, for that matter.

The other soldier nodded. "I know. Come on, let's get back to the boat. We don't have much time." He stepped off the path and back into the forest.

This time, Thorne could see him. Follow him, keeping up far more easily than he had earlier with Carter. The new understanding of the land they traveled stayed with him, overlaying the more ordinary world with a patina of awareness. Thorne quit trying to understand it and just accepted it for what it was. There would be time later, perhaps, to think about it.

By the time Boothby returned to the boat, Carter was already there, leaning against the side of the vehicle and clutching his left shoulder with his right hand. His camouflage uniform was stained dark black under the starlight. Carter's face was pale beneath his camouflage paint.

"How bad is it?" Boothby asked. He peeled the sergeant's fingers away from the wound. "Let me have a look."

As he moved closer to the soldier, Boothby felt the blunt muzzle of a pistol jabbed into his gut.

"Un-unh," Carter grunted. "Not after you killed that soldier last week. One of *ours,* General."

"Don't be a fool," Boothby said. "Put it down. I need to see—" Boothby knocked Carter's arm away.

Carter swore, twisted away, brought the gun to bear on Boothby, and fired. Boothby hurled back, then slumped down onto the ground.

Shot the general.

But then, hadn't the general killed one of his own as well?

What real choices had he had, though? Carter shook his head, suddenly weary to the bone from shock and loss of blood.

The general was on his feet again, moving quickly toward Carter like some prehistoric beast. Boothby barreled into Carter, knocking him down into the surf. Carter felt the general's hands go for his throat, encircle them, and squeeze.

The rest of the team was returning to the boats in a flurry of dark, quiet movements. Now, Carter could not even groan, and hardly had the will to even try.

The crushing pressure on his throat lifted. Carter rolled away from the general, deeper into the pounding surf line.

Carter felt hands lift him, and realized that they'd picked him up and slid him into the boat. "We'll be back real quick," a voice said. "You just hang on."

Thorne shivered in the night air as the last traces of adrenaline faded from his body. He stepped out of the jungle and onto the narrow verge of beach that separated it from the sea. The darkness around him shifted as though an unexpected night wind had blown in and the rest of the team joined them.

He joined the others wading waist high into the breakers, manually shoving the now-unwieldy boat out past the surf then vaulting into it. This time, he was allowed to remain on the outer rim of the boat. The injured Carter was stretched out at an awkward angle on the wooden-planked floor. As they paddled back out into the surf, Thorne examined him. No imminent danger, although shock was always a risk. A pressure bandage stanched the flow of blood, and there was little else that Thorne could do until they returned to base. Carter kept his eyes fixed on the general as he refused morphine for the pain.

They reversed the process by which they'd entered North Korea, paddling out against the surf, firing up the engines only when well clear of the shore. Again he marveled at how completely covert the boats seemed to be, at the lack of reaction from the shore. They made a quick dash toward open ocean then turned south.

The sergeant seated in the center of Thorne's boat watched his handheld GPS intently. A few moments after their southerly turn, he looked up at the general and nodded. The general spoke the first words Thorne had heard from him since they first walked out onto the southern beach: "Do it."

The sergeant nodded and toggled a switch. Thorne heard distant thunder. A few moments later, the coast to the north exploded into activity. Flames shot up from somewhere inland, searing his night vision and turning the air around him black. Guns spattered the water far behind them, sirens wailed, all the sounds of a camp awakened to emergency quickly fading out behind them. For the first time, Thorne appreciated how quiet the special forces boats really were, that he could hear the cacophony behind him at all.

The trip back seemed to take longer than the trip north. Forging into shore now seemed like a common event and he did his part in helping haul the boats back into their storage sheds. A few puzzled soldiers assisted them.

"Well." The general studied him for a moment. Thorne noted the high color in the man's cheeks, the glints in his eyes. "Your first field experience. How did you like it?"

"It was . . ." Thorne fell silent for a moment, unable to define precisely how it felt. Surely this wasn't it? "I didn't have time to be afraid," he said finally.

That seemed to sit well with the general. He smiled broadly, encompassing with a motion of his hand the team now unpacking the gear they'd taken with them. "They're good men. All of them." The general threw an arm over Thorne's shoulder. "Come on, come back to my quarters, we'll have a drink."

Boothby drew back for a moment and looked at Thorne again. Something in his face amused the general—he roared with laughter, drawing the attention of the rest of the team.

"Look at him, he's still in shock!" the general chortled. The other men crowding around slapped Thorne on the back, punched him on the shoulder. "Still doesn't realize what hit him!"

Something shuddered and snapped inside Thorne, cascading out in a warm rush of exhilaration. "I don't believe this shit," he said, trying to absorb it. "We actually—" The significance of the muffled thud he'd heard finally sunk in. "You blew the shit out of their command post."

"We, Doc. We blew it. That's the rule, everybody on the mission takes full credit. Just like the guy that sat up in the *Apollo* while the other two went down and walked on the moon," the sergeant explained.

"Wow."

The general's hand clamped down on Thorne's shoulder, the fingers cutting deep into his flesh. Thorne yelped, tried to jerk away, but the general's fingers clamped down even more. Then the general's beefy form slammed into him and slid down to the bottom of the boat.

Thorne shielded his eyes from the harsh glare of the ambulance's rotating lights. The stretcher slid in and he followed it, leaping lightly up into the back of the vehicle. It had been years since he'd made an actual ambulance run. At the hospital, he'd been the one waiting inside the doors for casualties, not the one arriving with them.

He murmured commands to the two medics, keeping his eyes on Boothby's face. The general was still conscious, had been the entire time except for those first few moments when he'd fallen to the floor of the boat to lie next to Carter. Everything had happened quickly after that—the sergeant shouting, dragging the general into the nearest building, Thorne following and praying that there was no spinal cord injury.

It was the general himself who, having regained consciousness shortly afterward, had cleared up the mystery. By then Thorne had already discovered the hot, wet wound in his shoulder, weakly pulsing blood. The taut BDU fabric was already glued to his skin with dried blood. Thorne probed it gingerly, and was relieved to find that the bullet had missed the bone. A flesh wound, one that would heal easily.

"Right before we nailed those bastards," the general said, his words coming out in a monotone from behind clenched teeth. An odd, satisfied smile, almost a grimace, suffused his face. "We turned south and they fired."

Thorne remembered the sound of the Korean's attack and how close it had been. The rounds could have hit the boat, ripped one of the thick canvas sides into shreds, if they'd been close enough to hit the general. He focused on the injury, the simple basics of first aid, not even searching for the bullet once he'd ascertained the general was in no immediate danger. More extensive evaluation would wait until they were at the base hospital.

The ambulance screamed through the chill night air, a peculiarly American sound cracking open the normal nighttime silence. Carter went first, then the general was loaded into the second ambulance.

Thorne braced himself against the bench, experienced an odd moment of flashback to the rocking motion of the boat, and watched as the orderlies cut away the general's shirt. They peeled the shirt away from the gaping wound, exposing the torn and bloody flesh. Thorne checked to see that no major blood vessels were involved, applied a direct pressure bandage to the entrance wound, then rolled the general slightly to his side to examine the exit wound. It appeared to be clean, the projectile passing through flesh and muscle without shattering the bone or severing an artery.

Satisfied that the general was in no danger of bleeding to death, Thorne proceeded to a quick cursory exam of the rest of his body. He ran his hand over the general's other extremities, checking for broken bones or wounds, then finished with a quick examination of the head. As far as he could recall, the general had not struck his head when he'd fallen against him. Nor had he hit his head at any other time during the evolution. The sudden unconsciousness was understandable, given the stress, strain, and amount of blood loss, but at this point he was not prepared to rule out any more serious damage.

The first sounds of the siren seemed to rouse the general slightly. His eyes moved back and forth under his eyelids, and he let out a low, guttural moan. His fingers flexed, one hand lifting slightly as though he were reaching for something. Thorne leaned forward, intending to murmur some reassuring words and motioned to one of the medics to prepare the pain medication.

The general's eyes snapped open, vague and unfocused, then quickly sharpened into a maniacal glare. He focused on Thorne's face, his eyes darted, and the vague, wheezy moans slipped down lower in the register into something far more ominous. The general's lips drew back from his teeth in a rictus of a smile. The hand that had been flailing ineffectually in the air shot out and clamped down around Thorne's throat.

Thorne let out a surprised squeak, all that he could manage with his air supply choked off. He jerked back, trying to dislodge the general's fingers, but it was as though a steel band had been placed around his neck. The thumb was digging deep into his larynx now, trying to crush it back against his spine.

One of the medics swore and jumped forward, grabbing the general's arm by the wrist and forearm. The medic jerked, working his pressure against the weaker thumb joint. A brief trickle of air ran down Thorne's trachea, followed by a wash of coolness as the arm was jerked away. Thorne fell back, gasping and staring in shock.

The general was now sitting up, reaching with both arms toward Thorne. He unbalanced the stretcher, tumbling off and onto the floor of the ambulance, evidently oblivious to the excruciating pain the fall must have caused his injured shoulder.

Boothby scrabbled to his knees, threw himself against Thorne, knocking them both back down to the floor with the general on top of him.

Thorne fought back frantically now, flailing at the larger man as the implacable hands sought his throat again. A hard knee rammed into Thorne's groin, once again shutting down his air supply in a paroxysm of pain.

The two medics were on top of the general now, wrestling and swearing and trying to drag him back off the doctor. The general seemed oblivious to them, his sole intent evidently to strangle Thorne. Fragments of his uniform clung to him where the medics had not yet finished cutting it off, one pant leg flapping vaguely behind him like a tail.

Both of the general's hands found Thorne's neck this time, and the pain was intense and immediate. Thorne felt soft tissue crack and give way as the general's fingers tightened around his neck. His vision started to gray out, fading away from the sight of the red, enraged face of his commanding general.

Just as Thorne was sliding into unconsciousness, the general's grip suddenly relaxed. The general roared, struggled to stay conscious, then slumped heavily to the metal deck beside the doctor.

One medic held up a now-empty syringe. "Plugged him as soon as he started, Doc, but it takes awhile to take effect."

Thorne drew in a deep, shaky breath, violently nauseated by the blow to the groin and the lack of air. He rolled over on his stomach, turned his head to the side in case he puked, and waited for the red haze that surrounded him to fade away. The pain went on for hours, days, it must have been—but finally it seemed almost possible that he could move without dying. He slowly uncurled from the fetal position.

The medics had already wrestled the now-unconscious general back onto the stretcher. Heavy plastic straps like garbage ties secured his wrists to the metal railings. His feet were similarly secured to the other end of the stretcher.

"Vitals all good," the first medic said. "How are you?"

Thorne shook his head tentatively, and tried to speak. A weak, rasping sound issued from his damaged throat. The medic offered him a cup of water, which he sipped gingerly.

"Let me look at you," the second medic ordered. He grasped Thorne by his shoulders and turned him around to face him. The medic's fingers expertly probed Thorne's throat, assessing the damage partially by Thorne's evident signs of discomfort. Nothing moved or grated under his fingers. Finally, he peered down Thorne's throat with a flashlight, holding his tongue out of the way with a piece of gauze. "We'll want to get some X rays, maybe an ultrasound," the medic said finally. "Looks like you got off lucky. The general's a strong man."

Thorne sat back down with a thump on the floor of the ambulance. He took a deep, shaky breath, repressing the waves of nausea washing over him. The ocean roared again in his ears, the heavy steady sound of waves on shore. The boat, the landing—how much of this was really happening at all?

"Doc?" the first medic asked. "Don't go fading out on us, we're almost there."

Stop it, Thorne told himself. The general—

He levered himself up and leaned back over the stretcher. "What did you give him?"

"Valium IM."

"Good. That'll put him out for a while. Let's take another look at him before he comes out of it." Thorne resumed the examination which the general had interrupted. The shoulder—the general's attack had dislodged the pressure bandage on both sides of the wound. Thorne repacked it, checking again for significant bleeding. He concluded his examination, with unremarkable results. Finally, he returned to the general's head, searching for any sign of a head wound.

That could have been it, he reasoned. A blow to the head, coupled with pain—would that have been enough to cause the general to lapse temporarily into raging insanity? He started to shake his head, then remembered the nausea that movement had induced last time, and settled for a frown.

No, it didn't make complete sense, but then what about the brain did? The general's reaction reminded him of two PCP users he'd seen brought in by the cops last month in Merced. The violent rage, the superhuman strength—if that's what it was—it was a wonder the medic had been able to subdue him in the first place.

He glanced over at the medics, saw the closed-in, impassive look on their faces. No doubt they were thinking the same thing.

"Maybe a concussion," Thorne offered, aware as he said it how lame that explanation seemed. Still, after trusting the general with his life not an hour before off the coast of Korea, he felt a compelling urgency to stifle the rumors that would inevitably be flying about the base.

"Sure, a concussion." The older medic looked directly at him, then shifted his gaze to the younger man. "That's what it was. You understand?"

The younger medic looked puzzled for a moment, then his face cleared. "A concussion it was," he agreed heartily. He returned his eyes to his patient and began checking the vitals again.

The older medic looked across the stretcher at him, and Thorne saw the same concerns mirrored in the medic's eyes. "The general," the medic began slowly, "takes good care of his people. Best general there ever was."

Thorne nodded, and felt a small trickle of amusement. Whatever his concerns had been about protecting the general's reputation, those went double for the medic. Confronted with an unknown quantity, a reserve doctor just recently reported to Korea, the medic wanted to make absolutely sure that Thorne understood the ground rules. He would take care of the younger sergeant, his eyes told Thorne. But the new doctor better understand that what happened in that ambulance was between them alone.

"A concussion," Thorne agreed. He held onto the stretcher as the ambulance executed two sharp turns and then pulled into the emergency bay at the base hospital.

"And you suffered a training injury of some sort, Doctor," the medic continued, reaching out to touch Thorne's throat gently again. "We'll take care of you, too. And Sergeant Carter."

The emergency room was swarming with senior doctors, staff officers, and a myriad of other personnel assigned to the base who deemed it in their utmost interest to be present and by the general's side. The chief of staff quickly took charge of the horde, brusquely dismissing most of them, and deftly winnowing out the people who really had a need to know. Another team attended to Carter.

Thorne, oblivious to the political and diplomatic machinations taking place in the outer foyer, briefed the staff doctors on Carter's and Boothby's conditions. Two of them immediately took charge of the general while a third shuffled Thorne off into a separate room for an examination of his injuries.

"A training injury, you said." The staff doctor—Gilliam, Thorne read on his nameplate—regarded Thorne thoughtfully. "Odd sort of accident."

"It was." It was getting more difficult to talk by the minute as the swelling increased, bruised tissue crowding the narrow airways.

"Well, you know what we're going to do at any rate," Gilliam continued, dropping down in the chair beside the examining table. "Watch the swelling, do the X ray and MRI routine. You want anything else?"

Thorne shook his head, willing to trade a fleeting spiral of nausea for the pain of having to try to talk. "Well." The doctor gazed down at the tile on the floor for a moment as though gathering his thoughts, then looked back up at Thorne. "You're new here, Doctor. Brief refresher on Army medicine—your record's not completely confidential. You probably remember that from training, but I thought I'd reinforce a teaching point." The doctor smiled briefly, then continued. "However, there are secrets and then there are secrets. What I need to know is how you got those injuries. Not so I can cause any trouble or place anyone in legal hot water, but so I can figure out what else might be wrong with you." He raised a hand to forestall Thorne's protest. "No names, you understand. Just tell me what happened. It won't go down in the record, but you should know that I need to know."

Thorne considered the matter for a moment, then made his decision. He understood the doctor's position, and in the same spot he felt that he himself would undoubtedly have tried the same sort of reassuring tactic. But as the chief of staff had said, it was a small post. Rumors traveled faster than the insistent north wind blowing down on them.

"You're going to see bruises around here," Thorne said finally, pointing out the ring of painfully reddened flesh around his neck. "Excessive force—think of it as a ligature if you like."

Gilliam nodded. "About what I suspected. And it wasn't thin, like a piano wire. No garroting, I mean."

"No. The, uh, instrument was perhaps one inch wide," he continued, summoning up a picture of the general's massive fingers. "Variable, I'd call it."

"Well, that settles it." Gilliam put aside his chart and examined Thorne's neck again. "Did you lose consciousness?"

"No."

"Any trauma to the head?"

"No."

A final check of the pupils. "Equal and reactive," Gilliam pronounced them, and the examination was complete except for the MRI. "I want to keep you overnight," Gilliam said, scratching his notes in the temporary chart. "The swelling still worries me. Gets any worse, we might have to trache you."

"God, no."

"You'd rather suffocate?" Gilliam slammed the metal folder shut and tucked it under his arm. "Doctors are the worst patients."

"How about this?" Thorne said, an idea occurring to him. "I'll stick around the hospital for forty-eight hours—hell, you can even give me a bed. But we both know I'm not in any immediate danger. I'd like to have a chair set up in the general's room. Keep an eye on him this evening."

Gilliam looked startled, then frowned. "No need for that. He'll have a private duty nurse on with him all night."

"The general might wake up a little confused," Thorne said hesitantly, feeling his way through the now-treacherous ground of the general's stability. "Disoriented, maybe. As you said, there are secrets and there are secrets."

Gilliam looked at him, a strange expression of incredulity and outrage on his face. "You don't mean that. You want somebody there who was with him tonight?"

Thorne nodded. "I'll bet if you could ask him, that's what he'd say."

Now it was Gilliam's turn to look uneasy. "The general's not quite himself at this point," he said carefully.

"Keep him in restraints," Thorne said. He resisted the impulse to touch his throat. "Restraints, and I'll stay in the room. That way, we contain the problem."

Finally, Gilliam nodded. "I'll have to run it by the senior medical officer, but it sounds like a reasonable idea to me. However, you start to have the slightest difficulty in breathing or swallowing, and I want to hear your finger slamming down on the call button. Got that?"

"Got it." For some reason, Thorne found Gilliam's capitulation gratifying for the oddest of reasons, the feeling that he was protecting the general.

Late that night, with the lights in the general's hospital room dim and the muted padding of soft crepe shoes up and down the passageway a delicate counterpoint to the intermittent clicks of the general's bio-stat machine, Thorne dozed off. He awoke when the general uttered a fretful noise, followed by a low moan. Thorne stood, ignoring the pain now pounding in his neck and shoulder where he'd hit the ambulance floor. "General?" he said softly. He reached for the general's wrist and felt the pulse strong and steady under his fingertips.

"The brain, not the brain," the general moaned. His eyes struggled open, he blinked several times, then focused a confused gaze on Thorne. "Where am I?" The words were weak but understandable.

"In the hospital, General. There's nothing wrong with your brain, sir," Thorne said. He discreetly pressed the call button located near the general's head. "You took a bullet in the upper shoulder, nothing serious," he reassured the man as a look of alarm spread across the general's face. "No major vessels, no bone damage. It'll hurt like hell, but heal up just fine."

The general frowned. "Where's Carter? He was wounded, too, wasn't he?"

"He's fine. He'll need surgery. The bullet impacted the rotator cuff. You were the lucky one this time. The one with your name on it passed through flesh and missed the bones."

The general appeared relieved. He relaxed back onto the pillows, then tugged with one arm as though to raise his hand to his face. He jerked again and then, puzzled, looked down at his wrist. The restraining strap still held it securely to the bed railing.

"Take this off." The note of command was soft but definite.

"You were a little confused when you woke earlier, General." Thorne paused and then ran through a quick mental assessment. "Do you remember anything of what happened?"

The general frowned for a moment, then his face closed over. "The boats. We went north," he said finally. He looked over at his left shoulder as though trying to see the wound. "The bastards shot at *me*?"

Thorne nodded, relieved that the general's memory had returned. "Do you know where you are?"

"The hospital, of course." A note of impatience was in the general's voice.

"And what day is it?" Thorne pressed, conducting the quick mental orientation routine. "Do you remember?"

A look of comprehension dawned on the general's face. "It's Thursday, at least I think it is. It was Wednesday night when we made the plans, early Thursday when we deployed, and probably Thursday when we returned." He frowned slightly as though displeased. "There's a little part I can't remember, but it must be Thursday, unless I slept through until Friday."

A nurse appeared at the door framed by two orderlies. A look of relief settled into professional calm as she strode into the room. "Awake now, are we?" she said briskly. She reached for the restraining straps at the general's wrists. Thorne caught her hand and held it for a moment, shaking his head almost imperceptibly.

The nurse appeared about to object, then drew back slightly.

"And who is the president?" Thorne said, turning back to the general.

"Williams. He won the last election, he's Republican, and there've been no new tax increases. Tabitha King's latest book is at the top of the *New York Times* list, and "You Can't Take It with You" is number one on the country and western charts. Convinced I'm oriented?" the general said, his voice now returning to normal volume.

"One last question," Thorne said. "Do you know who I am?"

The general fixed him with a steely glare. "The only doctor in this hospital that understands military history. Now turn me loose."

Within the base hospital, General Boothby was clearly not in charge. He still rated a certain degree of deference, and his opinions and wishes were carefully acknowledged by the staff. But all medical decisions were theirs, including the necessary treatment of Sergeant Carter.

"He's special Operations Team," Boothby said once again. "I want him at Murphy. You know the reasons why."

The head trauma surgeon and the anesthesiologist glanced at each other, then back at the general. "Of course, sir. We could treat him here, though."

Boothby shook his head forcefully. "I know more about what this soldier's done for our country than any of you," he snapped. "He gets first class treatment, not field services."

"Now, just a minute—" the surgeon began, then fell silent as he realized just who he was talking to. "I'm sure our standard of care would provide excellent results," he finished stiffly. "With all due respect, General."

The general's expression softened slightly. "I'm sure it would, soldier," he said gruffly. He placed one massive paw on Carter's uninjured shoulder. "But he's going to be getting pain medications, right?"

The trauma surgeon nodded. "Oh, definitely. For at least a week."

"There are things he can't talk about." The general's tone of voice brooked no argument. "Even here. Especially here." He shot a significant glance at the South Korean maintenance worker emptying trash cans at the south end of the hall. "You understand, right?"

Not that it matters if I do, the surgeon thought bitterly. *He called me soldier. Damn it, I know I'm in the Army, but I haven't been called that since basic.* "Of course, General, if you think it's necessary for national security reasons. However, I have to justify it on the transfer orders. Is there anything specific you can tell me?"

The general leaned closer to the surgeon, and the doctor was all at once aware of the sour stink of old alcohol. He blinked once in amazement, then carefully concealed his expression.

"Special Operations Team—that's all you need to say. Any questions?"

Defeated, the surgeon shook his head. "Medevac flight tomorrow. I'll make sure he's on it myself, General."

The general slapped the surgeon on the back. "Good man. And you tell that flight crew that I want Sergeant Carter to have the best treatment possible at all times. You tell them, Doctor."

Numbly, the surgeon nodded and watched the general stride away down the hall. Distinctly relieved that his commanding general was now gone, he turned back to Sergeant Carter. "Well, it looks like you've got yourself some friends in high places," he said to his patient.

A vague, distant expression on his face as a result of the pain medication, Carter nodded. "General's a helluva guy," he said, his words slurred. His eyes were slightly out of focus and looking in different directions.

The surgeon slipped the hypodermic into the IV access port and depressed the plunger. He watched the vague look of anxiety on Carter's face ease out and smooth away into a chemically induced slumber.

The general hadn't had to say it specifically, but the surgeon had caught the message. Sergeant Carter would be in no condition to talk if the surgeon had anything to do with it. Not until he was safely ensconced at Murphy Medical Center in Merced, California. For not the first time that evening, the surgeon wondered just who the hell Sergeant Nigel Carter was.

TWELVE

If anything, the general was more impressive wounded than completely whole. Thorne watched him move restlessly about his office, stopping to touch a memento on the bookcase with his good arm, the awkward motions as the general inevitably forgot that he was injured and tried to do something with his right arm. With a clinical eye, Thorne noted that Boothby's ruddy complexion was tinged by an undercoating of pallor, the change almost completely obscured by the nervous energy that radiated off the general in waves, encompassing everyone around him.

In truth, Boothby's recovery had been remarkable. Over the objections of the staff doctors, and conditioned solely on Thorne's promise that he would keep a close eye on him, the staff doctors had reluctantly released him to full duty. At the general's insistence, they had scratched through the typewritten notation on his discharge papers indicating restrictions on mobilization and an order for light duty.

Now, standing in the doorframe and watching the general pace restlessly, Thorne smiled inwardly at how futile the doctors' attempts to control the motions of their patient had been. There was nothing on earth that could restrain General Boothby, no known human force. He was too elemental, too much the distilled essence of a driven, committed soldier ever to submit to the limitations imposed by mere flesh. The reputation and the aura of invincibility that had surrounded General Boothby since his earliest days as a second lieutenant had its basis in the solid iron bedrock of the man's very essence.

The general waved him in briskly, indicating a chair in front of his desk. Thorne walked to it, stood with his hand on the back of it, unwilling to sit while the general paced. He felt awkward, weak, and oddly at risk so close to this fusion reaction wearing army green.

"How are you feeling, General?" Thorne said finally. The general had just started to reach for a book on his shelf and had uttered an annoyed oath at the sling and restraint strapped around his chest and arm. "Any pain?"

The general turned and glared at him. "Of course it hurts," he snapped. "It always does. Not when it happens, but afterwards."

"Even generals need time to heal," Thorne said, aware of the risk inherent in his words. He was treading close to the line of insubordination, trying to balance his duties as a physician with his obligations as a subordinate officer. It was a line, he suspected, that the general's usual doctors had never been able to discern. "If you don't let it rest, it won't heal up."

Unexpectedly, the general laughed. He gave a resigned shrug and walked back down to his desk, pointedly sitting down in his chair. "That make you happy?"

Thorne nodded. "It's a start. I'd like to have a look at the wound, if I might."

"I'm busy."

"It's me or the hospital, General." Now feeling that he was on solid ground, Thorne made his voice firm. "There's always a danger of infection with field wounds. It won't take but a minute."

The general waved away Thorne's assistance and fumbled with the buttons on his blouse. He slid it off, exposing the underpinnings of the sling. Thorne stepped up, unbuckled the strap, and peeled the tape off the edges of the dressing. The general bore his attentions stoically.

Thorne examined the wound. The edges were firm, clear, and pink, with no trace of redness indicating infection at the edges. He pressed lightly along it, noting the absence of any exudant from the wound.

"It looks excellent, General. Nothing at all to be concerned about."

"I could have told you that." Boothby shrugged back into his clothes, surprisingly deft for having the use of only one arm. Again, Thorne resisted the impulse to help him.

"So what did you think of it?" Boothby said. Now fully dressed, the fleeting aura of vulnerability Thorne had seen during his examination passed.

Thorne slid back into his chair. The general was asking about the raid, and Thorne was uneasily aware that he'd consciously avoided analyzing his own reactions to the entire mission. Much of it was a confused jumble in his mind, a patchwork of brilliantly detailed frozen tableaus interspersed with the muddle of noise, flashes of fire, and overriding—what?

With a small start, he realized that was exactly what he'd been avoiding. That emotion that had seized him during the onslaught, that oddly exhilarating combination of fear and bloodthirst that had buoyed him up during the charge. He was a doctor, forbidden by the Geneva Convention from taking part in those very acts he'd observed. He should feel revulsion, hate for the human emotions that inspired such violence, compassion toward the injured.

The Korean—dead and bleeding in the dirt.

Thorne looked up to find the general's eyes locked on him.

The general's eyes stripped him bare, exposing far more of Thorne than the general had in the act of undressing. Hard blue eyes, blazing with a maniacal sort of glee, poked and prodded inside Thorne's head, noting his reaction and glorying in it.

"You felt it, didn't you?" Boothby said. It wasn't a question as much as a statement. "What happens out there."

Thorne's throat felt suddenly dry, too parched to permit even a monosyllabic reply. Yet, his own emotions that he saw mirrored in the general's face were still too much for him to face. He let the moment slide into seconds, time stretching out as the two men stared at each other, one acknowledging the common bond, and the other fighting to deny it.

"I thought you might," the general said finally. He shook his head slightly as though marveling at his own insight. "As much as you've studied military history, your fascination with the Kennedy case—it was there, I could see it. It's too bad you're a doctor, you would have made a hell of a fine infantryman."

The cold-blooded conclusion snapped Thorne out of his momentary paralysis. "I shouldn't have been there last night," he said. "Not there."

The general's face iced over. "Oh, but you do belong there. It was evident in every move you made, in the things you noticed and you didn't. You've got the instincts, Major Thorne, whether you want to admit it or not."

"Instincts for what?" Thorne burst out, sickened by the truth in the general's words. "I'm not a killer. I'm a doctor." He felt that last word settle on him, seep in through his skin and somehow magically make him a whole being again. What had happened on the raid—no, never again. It wouldn't happen.

"We need medical people on the battlefield, too," the general continued as though Thorne hadn't spoken. "Do you know how many lives you could save if you treat them quickly? That's how we lose most of them, you know, in the time it takes to get them to a field hospital. You could be out there. Hell, I'll order you to be. For the good of my soldiers." The general paused, as though waiting for a reaction.

Tempting, so tempting. To be back out there so close to death and yet more intensely alive than he'd ever been at any point. Where survival was not measured by grants and money, paychecks and pensions. No, survival meant merely drawing another breath, hearing the screams and dying cries of those around you who wouldn't.

On the other hand, the general had a point. After all, healing shattered bodies, that was his calling, wasn't it? No one need know how he felt out there. No one would ever suspect.

Even if they did, they'd simply chalk it off to a case of adrenaline junkie, or dismiss his eagerness to be at the front as dedication to duty. No one would ever know.

Except himself.

Slowly, Thorne shook his head. "I can't do it." With a sudden flash of insight, he realized the general knew exactly what he meant.

Not couldn't—wouldn't.

He would make this choice, this time.

"I could make it an order."

"And I could disobey."

Surprising even himself with the strength of his resolve, Thorne stood. "Your shoulder looks fine, General. If that's all?"

The general recoiled. A flash of anger flashed across his face, to replaced immediately by the stony look Thorne had already come to know so well. "Dismissed, Major." The words held a cold, harsh bite that had not been there earlier. "Maybe you're not the man I thought you were."

Thorne fought back an impulse to argue the point, to say yes, I am, and that's exactly why I won't go there again.

After Thorne left, the general reached into his lower desk drawer and pulled out the trusty bottle of wine. More and more often as of late, it seemed like only alcohol would blunt the edge on the daily indignities of life. He rushed through the ritual of savoring the bouquet, trying to convince himself that he was indeed the connoisseur he aspired to be. Yet the movements were hurried now, lacking the slow, leisurely pace that he strove for.

Finally, the first precious sip, turning into a gulp before he gave it any conscious thought. Delicate fumes seemed to flow straight from his mouth to his brain, blurring the hot rage pounding in his mind to a dull, dissatisfied ache.

How could the man be such a fool? Did he really think he could continue to fool himself—and to fool General Boothby? No, it was far too late for that, had seen it in the doctor's eyes, literally felt it in that psychic bond of communication that runs from a general through the ranks down to his very best soldiers. It was more than just a common bond of men under enemy fire, a closeness that transcended distinctions of rank, education, and breeding.

Boothby had felt it with Thorne, and he knew Thorne felt it, too. He tossed another gulp down his throat, all his good intentions of savoring the fine vintage gone completely.

If only Thorne had been willing to talk. Boothby had seen the confusion in his eyes, as he'd seen it before in too many men. He knew what to do, how to shepherd the young man through the coming-of-age ritual that was as old a part of mankind as war. If Thorne had stopped to talk, had just admitted to himself and to the general what he'd found out himself to be, then it could have been dealt with. Examined, explained, put into perspective by one who'd seen it too many times before. It would have molded Thorne from merely another officer—albeit a good one—into the sort of force that General Boothby would need on his side in order to finally settle this question.

And to settle the score with the man who'd caused all this. Who'd failed to put an end to it over fifty years ago, who'd left American men and women to live and fight and die on this desolate peninsula.

But what to do with Thorne now? Reluctantly, he considered his alternative courses of action. It had happened before, this turning away from one's destiny. Not nearly as often as the man—and yes, one woman—had accepted it, gone on to become a superb soldier. But once or twice before, yes, Boothby had seen it happen. And in each case, the results had been far from satisfactory.

Was this what had happened with President Truman? Time became a bit unstable for a moment as the general considered the character of the commanders in chief who'd gone before and after. Had each one faced this moment himself? Faced it, and found himself wanting? He thought so. Just as Thorne would ultimately feel the pain of his own struggle, so must each of them have faced it. Faced it—and lost.

Once tested, once plunged into the fire for tempering, there was no going back. Fire was the key. It yielded either the hardened soldier, the one that could be burnished and whetted to a razor's edge, or a chunk of worthless metal, more dangerous to its bearer than its absence would have been.

Such was the case now with Thorne, he concluded, and not without a bit of regret. He could have been so good, so potent. Instead, whatever potential he'd had would be wasted. And knowing as he did now the process he'd been forced to undergo, the tempering, and knowing that he himself had failed, Thorne would be more dangerous than useful.

He would have to go. For a moment, the general considered his options. An accident, perhaps? Or simply a bullet in the brain late one night while returning from the hospital.

No, he finally concluded. Neither one. There were both practical and moral difficulties, beginning with the absence of Sergeant Carter, his most trusted agent in such cases, and ending with an instinctive aversion to fratricide. However much he might wish it, however appropriate it would be to destroy the flawed weapon that Thorne had proved himself to be, the general simply could not bring himself to do it. Or to order it done, for that matter.

Fortunately, in Thorne's case, there was an easier solution. It would be a waste, but better a waste than a more righteous cause of action.

The general slid the bottle of wine back into his desk drawer and nestled the now empty glass in a towel next to it. He wiped his mouth with the back of his hand, took a sip of water from the carafe at his side, and punched his intercom button. The chief of staff answered. Boothby asked him to step in for a moment on an urgent personnel matter.

"One of the reserve doctors, a fellow named Thorne—he was here a little earlier," the general began. He paused for a moment, wondering if this were the only solution. He would miss their discussions of military history, the fascinating possibilities that the Kennedy assassination had held for conversation. For a moment, he was tempted to forego what he had planned, to give in to the weakness inside himself and the longing for companionship. No, that would make him as weak as Thorne himself. Better to do what must be done now before he changed his mind. "He's not working out," Boothby continued abruptly. "Put him on the next plane out of here."

"General?" The chief of staff's large bushy eyebrows quirked up slightly. "But he just—"

"Send him home, Erwin," Boothby interrupted. "He's got no business being in Korea."

And neither do the rest of us.

Thorne drummed his fingers impatiently on the desk as he waited for the sergeant to put him through to the chief of staff. He'd put in a full day at the field hospital, checking on the soldiers injured in training mishaps and even overseeing the daily sick-in-quarters call. When he'd run out of make-work and tasks with which to occupy himself, he'd given up and headed back to the quarters, not at all eager to be alone with his thoughts. The message from the chief of staff had waited for him there.

Finally, the slow southern tones of the chief of staff had come on the line. "Dr. Thorne?"

"Yes, sir. This is Dr. Thorne." The absence of his military title jarred slightly on his ears.

"The general has ordered you released from active duty," the chief of staff said with no preliminaries. Intoned in the soft cadence of an Alabama accent, the words sounded like a commendation.

"He what?"

"You're going home, Doctor."

"But why?"

The chief of staff's voice took on a wary note. "I'm not in the habit of questioning orders from my commanding general, Major. Nor is he required to provide you with any explanation. To assuage your curiosity, however, in reviewing your field record, the general noted that you are on staff with Murphy Medical Center in Merced, California. Having once been a patient there himself, the general has a particular soft spot for that institution. Given your wide range of experience there, the critical nature of the Murphy should hostilities break out here, and your own lack of field experience, he felt you could better serve the nation by returning to your civilian career. Get packed, Major. You're on the first transport out tomorrow."

Thorne stammered out something that might have been a thanks or a protest, he wasn't sure which. Joy warred with offended honor. He wouldn't be trapped in this lonely and desolate outpost, a remnant of America's Cold War and containment policies, wouldn't be forced to confront the final decision himself. The general knew him far better than he had known himself, and had removed his choices.

Removed his choices, or removed a danger? In trying to come to terms with his own participation in the raid, Thorne had become increasingly convinced that for General Boothby to participate in the mission himself had verged on professional insanity. The general was too important to be risked on such a foray, no matter how sensitive and no matter how skilled a field soldier the general was. There were other people to take those risks, and Thorne's study of history convinced him that General Boothby knew that.

He'd also felt the judgment in the general's final discussion with him about the raid. Thorne had come away from the meeting feeling as though he'd been judged and found wanting in some way.

Risks. Did it make sense for Boothby to have done any of this? Particularly when the general might have had some lingering physical weaknesses or incapacity. The chief of staff had mentioned that Boothby had been a patient at the Murphy. Had this been some sort of test for Boothby himself, a personal challenge to prove that he was still a soldier?

"Colonel?" Thorne asked as the chief of staff was about to break the connection. "When was the general a patient at the Murphy?"

"I don't know what business that would be of yours. Mind telling me why you want to know?"

Thorne thought quickly, searching for an explanation, any reasonable facsimile of a reason that would justify his request without involving the raid. "Depending on what he was there for and how long ago it was, it could have implications on how his wound heals up," he said finally, aware of the possibility that there might be a grain of truth in his response.

Maybe.

A silence, then, "I doubt it. Four months ago, the general had his appendix out. He was in northern California visiting relatives when it happened. Given the sensitive nature of his duties here, it was felt best that he be treated at the Murphy. I'm sure, as an employee of that institute, you can understand those reasons."

"Of course, of course. And you're absolutely right," Thorne said soothingly in his best bedside manner, "an appendectomy should have absolutely no effect on treating a shoulder wound. But I had to ask, you understand."

The chief of staff's voice was gruff. "Go back home, Doctor. This isn't the place for you. You want to do something, you just take the best care possible of our men and women when they start showing up there. You understand?"

"I will. And if you would, thank the general for me."

As Thorne replaced the receiver, he couldn't decide whether to be outraged or grateful. But he knew what would decide him. He made a quick call to let Dr. Gillespie's office know that he was returning to the States. Gillespie's secretary informed him that the doctor was out of town for another day, attending a research conference in Denver, but that she would pass the message on. Thorne hung up, then dialed Patterson's number.

The telephone line buzzed with the distinctive two-ring undulating tone of an international call. Patterson picked it up on the third ring, and the sound of her voice immediately brought back the sheer rightness of this decision. What he had experienced was simply transitory madness, the emotions of a man caught up in the sound and fury of a battlefield.

"Want me to pick you up in San Francisco?" Patterson's voice made it clear that a repeat of their parting was in order, and more than acceptable. Thorne felt a grin spread across his own face, a flooding sense of relief that washed away the last traces of battlefield madness.

"No, not that I wouldn't like it. But the schedule's too fluid. The chief of staff said I'd be out of here tomorrow, day after tomorrow at the latest, but I don't know exactly when we'll be in. Besides, I need to get back to the Murphy."

"God, I'm glad you're going to be here. Just hurry up, Thorne."

When he hung up, Thorne felt the transition from military officer to civilian doctor begin. A reordering of priorities. A feeling that the universe was once more back in sync with what it had been for the past thirty-two years. It would be good to be home.

He reported to the airfield as ordered at 0800 the next morning. The airfield struck him as strangely busy, although he was forced to admit he wasn't a particular expert on operational tempos at the airfield. After only one week in country, he was hardly in a position to say what was normal and what was not.

Still, there was something in the air that gave him pause. A feeling of urgency, a new briskness to the movements of the noncommissioned officers and senior sergeants teeming both in the operations center and on the airfield. They barked commands, sending schools of troops scurrying first in one direction then another on obscure missions that made sense only in the minds of the sergeant majors.

Two dots on the horizon, slowly growing larger, resolved themselves into the shapes of two enormous transport carriers. They lumbered down to the airfield, impossibly awkward and ungainly this close to earth. First one then another touched rubber to tarmac, the squeal of friction audible even over the thunder of their engines. They stopped quickly, using up only half the runway, before slowly turning and taxiing in to the terminal area.

"There's your ride home, Major," one of the sergeants said, pointing to the transport aircraft. "Gotta get her unloaded first, though. Shouldn't be ready to go before noon."

"Then why did I have to be here at eight?" Thorne asked, realizing as he voiced the words that there would be no reasonable answer. He had to be there because that's what the orders said: Report at 0800 hours. No matter that the aircraft would be tied up for hours for servicing and unloading.

"Usually the case," the sergeant admitted. He stared out at the ramps now lowering from fore and aft the cargo ship. Men loaded with field packs pounded down the ramps, forming an orderly, instep single-file procession toward the terminal. "Normally it's a fast turnaround. And a different aircraft."

"What's that one, anyway?" Thorne asked, feeling that he ought to know at least something about the Army.

"C-17," the sergeant answered. "Biggest transport plane in the inventory. We just got word last night she was coming in here."

"It's not a usual flight?"

"Same time. But not the same loadout. Usually we get just a normal load of pax to replace troops that are rotating home. But this" The sergeant stopped, waving at the continuing progression of men and equipment off the aircraft. "This is something different. All new troops, none ordered in as relief. The general is puffing up the regiment to full strength. Canceled all orders for those who were rotating home, too. Pissed a lot of soldiers off."

"No one else is leaving?"

The sergeant shook his head. "Just you."

"And all those soldiers are arriving?"

The sergeant shot him a disgusted look. "Those aren't soldiers, sir. Those are marines."

Interminable hours in the air, an unexpected diversion to March Air Force Base and two MREs later, Thorne was back on American soil.

The change in landing sites was actually a benefit—March was only a hundred miles or so from Merced.

With pay to date for his tour in Korea jammed in his wallet, Thorne splurged on a one-way rental car at the nearest office. The closer he got to Patterson, the more it seemed that events were conspiring to keep him away from her.

Finally, clutching his sea bag in one hand and his contract in the other, Thorne headed out for his rental car. Two hours, maybe three, and he'd be home.

THIRTEEN

The cage was too small. The rat clamped his front teeth on one thin aluminum bar. The strut flexed slightly under his teeth. His teeth cut easily through the top layer of shiny metal then chipped as he hit the hard inner core.

The rat jerked backwards, putting every bit of his six ounces of body weight behind the motion. The soldered joints affixing the bar to the top and bottom crossbars flexed. The rat paused, took a deep breath, then tugged again.

"What are you doing, Andy?" Lanelli flicked at the rat's grip on the bar with one finger. "What's the matter, our accommodations not good enough for you?"

The tip of his finger hit Andy's sensitive snout. It hurt—hurt like hell. The rat recoiled from the pain, then threw himself at the metal bars again.

The technician grasped the cage firmly on either side. He shook it. "Come on, now. Stop it."

The motion threw the rat off its feet. He tumbled into the far corner of the cage, and fetched up against another bar. It hit him in the back of the head. The indignity only heightened his fury.

He started to sink his fangs into the bar again, but a slight motion on the other side of the cage caught his attention. Another target, one more yielding and pliable than the bars around him. He knew her familiar scent as well as his own, the low, musky odor that enabled him to pick her out of any pack of rats. His injured nose wiggled, and the scent grew more intense, approaching the levels that drove him with single-minded passion during her estrus cycle.

Andy wheeled around and stared at his mate.

She cowered in a far corner of the cage, small pink eyes staring at him fixedly. Her scent changed, now dominated by the rank sweetness of fear. Andy took a step forward. An involuntary shiver shook her small body. She weighed four ounces. On her best day, she was no match for Andy.

It was less a conscious decision and more of a reflex. The male rat sprang across the cage, landed on top of her, and buried his front teeth in her neck. The yellow, slightly elongated incisors passed through skin and muscle easily, meeting in the middle just millimeters above her spinal cord. He jerked his head upward, lifting her off her feet. Her paws scrabbled frantically at the air. Andy snapped his head back and forth, whipping her tiny body through the air. Her tail hit the bars of the cage, and they gave off a soft ping.

"What the—" Lanelli grabbed for the heavy rubber gloves in his smock pocket.

Still carrying his mate, Andy took two steps forward. He reared up on his hind legs, her body dangling limply from his teeth. With all the force and drive that six ounces of sheer fury could manage, he slammed her head into the wire mesh bottom of the cage.

"Patterson." Her voice was clotted with sleep but still recognizable.

"It's me. I'm back."

A yawn, then, "What time is it?"

"Three A.M." Thorne felt a wash of guilt. "I'm sorry, I guess I could have waited."

"Maybe you can. I'll be there in ten minutes." The phone went dead.

The alarm clock jerked him back into consciousness. Thorne bolted upright as the mattress trembled slightly. By the time his eyes focused, Patterson was already standing next to the bed, looking down at him.

"Dibs on the shower," she said.

Thorne groaned and collapsed back down on his pillow. "I need sleep."

Patterson grabbed his wrist and pulled him up out of the bed. "You can sleep when you're dead, love. Now get your butt up and get moving. I expect coffee brewed by the time I'm out."

Thorne pulled her to him. "I've got a better idea."

Patterson frowned slightly. "Another time, Scoot. I've got to get back to my house and change."

"You should have brought clothes with you."

"Hey, you're the one who woke me up last night. Be glad I made it at all."

"Come on, woman." He tightened his grip on her. "Is that any way to welcome back a war hero?"

Forty-five minutes later, showered, shaved, and ready to go, Thorne was back at the Murphy. Gillespie being out of town was a lucky break—he'd have a chance to get back up to speed before his boss returned.

Thorne's first stop was at the ER to check on new admissions and to find Kamil. The charge nurse told him that he'd just missed Dr. Kamil, who'd had call the night before and was now on rounds on his surgical patients from the day before.

"But we do have one new admission," she said. She pointed to the line that an orderly was just erasing from the board. "Not particularly a usual one—a helo transport from Castle Air Force Base."

"What's so unusual about that?" Trauma cases from the military were routinely admitted through the ER.

"This one's a lot less serious than most of them are," she said. She passed the chart over to him and waited while he flipped it open. "Gunshot wound, nothing a good orthopedic surgeon can't fix in an hour. Dr. Kamil did him early this morning. But the weird thing is, this guy was medevacked from Korea."

"Korea?"

She nodded. "According to the notes, he was shot two days ago by a renegade border patrol. The other two guys were killed. I guess the brass in Korea figured he deserved first-class treatment."

Thorne frowned as he replaced the chart in the stack next to the nurse's computer. "But why just a regular soldier? That doesn't make sense, not with a less serious injury."

The nurse leaned forward across the counter and said quietly, "The medic told me he was with special operations. He's got the usual guards on his room."

"This fellow have a name?" Thorne asked.

She nodded. "Carter, Sergeant Nigel Carter."

As soon as the elevator doors opened, Kamil knew there was trouble on the ward. Brown-shirted security forces crowded the passageway outside Carter's room, and the incessant beeping of a medical warning device cut through the muted snarl of terse orders that characterized chaos in any hospital. Kamil shoved his way toward the middle of the pack and was stopped by a line of security guards.

One gruff, Irish-looking fellow took note of the obligatory stethoscope hung around Kamil's neck and drew him aside and away from the entrance. "Can't go in there, Doctor. Not safe right now."

"He's my patient," Kamil snapped. From his point of view, that explained everything, including his ultimate authority over the security forces.

The friendly light in the officer's eyes dimmed. "You get him to quit cutting up the nurses, then."

Kamil's jaw dropped. The Irishman regarded him with a look of satisfaction. "They gave him breakfast. When the guy came to pick up the tray, your patient took him on with his knife. Slashed him up pretty bad—he's down in the ER right now. The nurse heard the screaming and called security. Good thing she did. The guy's still weak and they were able to get him trapped in the room."

"He's postsurgical. He can't—" Kamil started.

"He certainly can," the Irishman said, evidently losing the last bit of patience he possessed. "See for yourself." He led Kamil back to the entrance to the room.

Carter was crouched in a corner of the room, barricaded into his position by the bed. He leaned against the wall and braced himself against it, holding his breakfast knife in his good hand. His face was pale, clammy-looking, eyes slitted and focused on the three burly orderlies arrayed in front of him. The security guards hung back, evidently torn between protecting their charge and intervening.

"Let me talk to him," Kamil said, shoving his way into the room. He stopped short, right behind the orderlies, and studied the patient for a moment.

He's going into shock, one part of his mind noted clinically. Given enough time, the plummeting blood pressure would resolve the situation quite handily. He considered for a moment letting events progress in that manner, and then dismissed it. Shock so soon after surgery could have fatal consequences.

"Mr. Carter," Kamil said quietly, trying to inject a note of authority into his voice. "I'm Dr. Kamil, I was your surgeon. How does that shoulder feel right now?"

Carter's eyes darted around the room and then settled on Kamil, a sly, feral look taking over his face. "Get rid of those goons and we'll talk."

"Will you put down the knife?"

Carter snorted, as though choking back a laugh. "Knife's the last thing you have to worry about, Doc. I wanna hurt you, I don't have to use a knife."

"Why would you want to hurt me?" Kamil asked.

Carter studied him for a moment, then seemed to lose interest in him. "I've got to get back to my unit."

"What unit?" Kamil asked, trying to find some thread into the man's mind. If he could get him talking about anything, anything at all, it might lead to a better resolution of the crisis. He noted clinically that Carter's sweating seemed to have increased, and his pupils were slightly dilated.

"Recon. Special recon," Carter said, putting emphasis on the first word.

"What is special recon?"

"You don't want to know. Let's just say it's real . . . special." An ugly smile spread across Carter's face. "Special enough not to need no stupid knife."

"Special enough to get sent to the Murphy instead of to an Army hospital, then," Kamil continued. "That's where they send most people, you know."

Carter nodded in agreement. "The general fixed me up, I'll bet. General Boothby," he added, evidently noting the look of incomprehension on Kamil's face. "That's who we're special for."

"So what started all this?" Kamil said, gesturing at the orderlies in the crowded hallway outside. "Can you tell me?"

A look of confusion spread slowly across Carter's face. His lips started moving as though he were talking to himself, although no words were audible. Even watching his lips, Kamil could make out no discernible words.

"Mr. Carter?" Exasperated, Kamil nudged one orderly slightly aside. "Look, if there's—"

With a snarl, Carter sprang on him. He moved faster than Kamil would have thought possible six hours postop, still groggy from the effects of the anesthesia and with a shoulder and arm bound tightly up. He launched himself in midair at the doctor, the knife extended in front of him.

One of the orderlies reacted instantly, nailing Carter with what must have been a linebacker technique learned years ago. The two men tumbled over and over, the orderly bringing his greater weight to bear on the weaker man. Carter's hand flailed free for a moment, then drove the knife deep into the orderly's back. The orderly howled and smashed Carter's head on the floor just as a second man grabbed Carter's arm.

Still frantically flailing, occasionally managing to throw one of the orderlies off balance with a sudden flex of his body, Carter continued to fight.

Kamil stared in horror, then snapped at the nurse, "Versed, now!" She slapped the syringe into his hand.

"Hold him." Kamil advanced on the still-struggling man, trying to stay clear of his flailing arms and legs. Seeing an opening, he jabbed the hypodermic into Carter's naked butt and drove the plunger home.

Carter howled, a cry of sheer animal fury and hate.

"Hold him down," Kamil ordered. "It'll take some time to work."

He turned his attention to the injured orderly. "Shit. The spleen, I think. Get the surgeon on call."

Finally, ten minutes later, Carter's frantic maneuverings slowed. Blood coursed down his arm and soaked into the thin cotton gown that covered him. The stitches had broken loose.

As soon as Carter began to experience the effects of the Versed, Kamil nailed him again with another five milligrams. This time, the effect was more immediate. Within a few moments, Carter subsided into unconsciousness.

"Move him now," Kamil ordered. "This stuff doesn't last very long. Full restraints." He turned to the Irishman who'd first met him at the door. "I want a guard on this door for now."

"I'll try to find the guys who brought him in. He arrived with his own security force, just like a lot of them."

"What is he, some high-ranking officer?" Kamil asked. Security detachments were not unusual at Murphy.

"No. According to his records, he's a sergeant. And with recon, just like he said." The security officer went off to find the men who'd brought Carter in while Kamil and the nurses supervised placement of the restraints. Kamil was careful to ensure that the buckles were out of reach of Carter's fingers.

Two orderlies transported their injured colleague to a trauma room. The commotion faded away and the ward resumed the normal rhythms of operation.

Kamil slumped down into the chair in Carter's room. Tox screens. He should have ordered them first off, but it hadn't seemed necessary. He stared at the recon soldier—special recon, he reminded himself—and wondered just when the hell shoulder injuries led to psychosis.

FOURTEEN

The crowd surged around the podium, a wild mixture of traditional Algerian dress and Western garb. A babble of languages arose, ranging from heavily accented French to native dialects bearing little resemblance to any modern language. Vendors wound their way through the crowd, offering cold drinks, skewers of spicy cooked meat, and odd trinkets of memorabilia to commemorate the occasion.

A massive bell mounted on a platform in the center of the city squares began tolling out a slow, steady refrain. At first, its peals were almost drowned out by the noise of the crowd.

Almost, but not quite. Gradually, the assembled mass grew still until only the joyful cry of children and the incoherent ramblings of the elderly disturbed the hush.

The bell picked up speed now, until the rich metallic tones were almost one continuous hum. The sound permeated the crowd, reaching down through skin and flesh to invoke some ancient, fundamental resonance within their bones. A few prayed quietly, their lips moving silently, but most turned toward the podium and waited. It was something they were good at.

Algerian justice required little of it, though. Behind the podium was a whitewashed stucco structure that somehow managed to blend both and French and desert influences. A thick wooden door opened slowly. A drummer stepped out, clad in the traditional array of the Algerian presidential service. The bell in the center of the square fell silent. The drummer picked up the beat, the lighter, higher-pitched tone of the snare bouncing off the surrounding buildings and echoing throughout the area. The crowd breathed a sigh of relief as the last echoes of the larger bell faded away.

The soldiers came out of the door two by two, goose-stepping slowly to the cadence of the drum. Four sets of two, followed by two priests and their attendants waving intricately fashioned crucibles of incense. The hush grew deeper, and even the children fell silent. Their parents pulled them close, turning them to face inward and holding their hands over their eyes.

Finally, the prisoner shuffled out, supported on either side by two more guards, each with an expression of disgust on his face as if to touch the man would be to risk eternal contamination. His feet dragged across the ground, his elbows held high by the guards, each of whom had one arm supporting his elbow and the other just forward of his armpit. His feet moved as though to keep step, but his legs could barely support the weight of his body.

147

Four more sets of soldiers followed afterward, with an impressive, portly figure in an intricately worked uniform bringing up the rear, the new president of Algeria.

The president's face was grave, as befit the leader of a great nation. Just two hours before, he had signed the warrant authorizing the immediate execution of Tshoma. Word had spread quickly about the town, and within thirty minutes the crowd began to form. Now the square was packed, with barely room for the small procession to pass. The people drew in on one another, somehow pulling back and creating a clear path to the hastily erected podium.

One final man exited the bold wooden doorway and stood for a moment, blinking in the sunshine. There was a sound like the wind, the noise of twenty-five thousand people simultaneously sucking in an involuntary gasp. The executioner stood there, letting the sound wash over him, unknowable and impassive beneath the black hood.

The drum continued beating, and the executioner finally moved, walking behind the procession to take his place at the farthest end of the podium away from the stairs. In his hand he held a giant, jeweled scimitar. The blade caught the hard African sunshine, flashed out across the crowd occasionally, momentarily blinding the spectators. Children quivered and buried their faces in their parents' legs. The adults stared, an odd combination of fascination and fear on each face.

The executioner held the scimitar with both hands curled around the pommel and rested the razor-sharp point on the wooden planking. Or so it appeared to the crowd. In reality, he bore its entire weight and kept the point just slightly above the boards.

At the foot of the stairs, the two priests crowded close in front of Tshoma, enveloping him with a cloud of the pungent, heavy incense. There were low murmurs from them, and the nearest spectators could see Tshoma's lips moving in response.

Tshoma himself was a shadow of the man who'd been secretary of state of Algeria. His face was cut and bruised, and flies buzzed around him, drawn by the scent of fresh blood. He was pale and sweating, and his eyes had a glazed, unfocused look to them. His gaze drifted from the priest to the podium to the executioner standing at the far end of it, and then back to the crowd as though searching for something.

One priest shook his head solemnly. The other continued to nod, in an odd counterpoint of inconsistency.

Finally, the younger of the two priests reached out and traced the sign of the cross on Tshoma's forehead. He reached into one of the deep pockets of his vestments and pulled forth a tiny vial, opened it, and sprinkled a few drops of holy water on the condemned man's head.

The procession at the base of the podium turned for a moment as the participants rearranged their position within the queue. The pairs of soldiers stepped apart, forming a corridor for the condemned man to pass through. He still walked unsteadily, and was passed along from pair of hands to pair of hands toward the base of the stairs.

As he reached the first step, he paused, unable to summon the strength to mount it. The two end soldiers kept their grip on his hand and unceremoniously dragged him up the eight steps. All pretense of walking on his own was over and his shins banged against the stairs during the ascent. The two priests followed him up.

As they mounted the podium, the soldiers marched him forward to the executioner. The priests stopped just on the platform and stepped away to either side. The president finally followed, his steps slow and certain as he ascended. In front of the executioner was a freshly hewn tree stump. Sap oozed from the bark, and a few rugged knotholes glistened with its residue.

The soldiers loosened their grip on his arm and Tshoma dropped heavily to the deck. He clawed at the stump as though to pull himself to his feet and face these last moments with some semblance of dignity, but his strength was not sufficient. He settled for draping himself half on the stump, raising himself to the highest position he was capable of attaining. The executioner stared down at him impassively.

The newly appointed president turned and faced the crowd. "Algeria stands for justice." He cleared his throat and stared out over the crowd as though to make a further statement, then simply took two steps back from the edge as though realizing that statement stood alone quite well. He turned and gestured to the executioner. "Begin."

The two soldiers reached down and each grabbed the elbow he had so recently turned loose. They yanked to the side, and Tshoma's head and chest plummeted forward, landing on the fresh stump with a sickening smack.

"Move him back," the executioner said, speaking for the first time.

The soldiers struggled with what was now almost dead weight, finally positioning Tshoma to the executioner's satisfaction. They stepped away to the back of the podium and took up positions on either side of the president.

A low roar arose from the crowd, spreading from the far corners inward to the closest spectators. It was a primal sound, one ripped deep from the guts of each man and woman, a low, incessant roar that gradually deepened into the very substance of fury. It grew louder and louder until it seemed impossible that the sound could have been emitted from any group of human throats.

The president seemed taken aback slightly by the noise and shifted uneasily between his guards. He made a small movement as though to glance down and make sure that the rest of his escort was waiting, then stilled the motion before any but the closest onlookers noticed it.

The executioner stepped forward, still holding the sword in front of him. The new angle rotated the different facets to the sunshine, and glares of red, blue, and green flickered around the pommel as though by magic.

Even the executioner now seemed discomfited by the scream of the crowd. He shifted from foot to foot as though finding his balance, then brought the sword down slightly. He paused with the pointed tip poised just above Tshoma's buttocks. Then, in a quick motion, he jabbed forward with the sword.

Tshoma was weeping now, but the pain from the slight prick of the sword evoked a sharp, hard gasp. He flinched involuntarily, stretching to his full length and straightening his neck out as his head thrust forward.

It was the movement the executioner had been anticipating—and counting on. For several centuries men of his ilk in every nation had known that this small ritual of preparation would cause the victim to extend his neck to its full length, thus opening up the cartilage between the cervical bones and permitting easier entrance of the executioner's blade.

He brought the sword up high in one lightning motion, then slammed it down in a straight arc to Tshoma's neck. It penetrated between the second and third vertebrae, slicing through the cartilage easily. The executioner had spent the previous night honing the blade to an absolute perfection of sharpness, and his efforts paid off now.

The spinal cord was no more than butter under a hot knife and parted easily, the severed edges clean and straight with no trace of raggedness. The blade continued downward, biting into the back of the larynx and trachea, moving a little faster now as the executioner reached the full force of his downward swing and the soft tissue was replaced by the empty airspace of the two tubes.

Finally, three quarters of a second after he'd started his downward swing, the blade cut through the last bit of flesh on the front of Tshoma's neck and buried itself in the tree stump. A cascade of blood poured out of the severed neck. The edges of the wound were even, evidence of the sharpness of the blade.

Tshoma's head paused for a moment on top of the stump, wobbling unevenly on forehead and nose. Finally, its center of gravity, newly reoriented to somewhere just behind the mouth, took charge. The head tilted off the nose and forehead, rolled to the right, bounced once, then wobbled toward the edge of the podium before it came to a stop.

Tshoma's eyes were open, fixed, and unseeing. The skin at the back of his neck was deeply tanned and creased. Fresh acne was spattered over it in small patches. Blood continued spurting out of the rest of the body, slower now as the heart seemed to realize that there was simply insufficient volume to support its normal functions. It was coming faster, in smaller spurts as the body emptied. Finally, the shock of decapitation made itself felt and the heart quit.

The executioner stepped back from the stump to avoid the streaming gushes of blood and then the growing pool that soiled the fresh-cut boards. He'd often wondered about this moment, the first minute after an execution. Although it had been years since one had been performed in Algeria, he'd often discussed the matter with other men of arms.

Under normal circumstances, it took the brain four minutes to die from lack of blood. It was a hotly debated point among the executioners and other soldiers over whether the same standard of time would apply to an executed prisoner. Could the blood remaining in the head keep a man conscious following the shock of decapitation? It wouldn't be due to lack of oxygen if it didn't, it was generally agreed. If that were the case, the executed would die slowly, perhaps even screaming out in their last moments with whatever air remained in their trachea following the severing of head from body, if any part of the vocal cords remained intact.

Staring now at the head facing him near the edge of the podium, the executioner revised his earlier opinions. He watched closely and noted that there were no reflexive or involuntary movements of either eyes or mouth. He had hoped, perhaps, for a slight movement of the lips as though the dead man were attempting to speak, or a fluttering of the eyelids, something to support his position that consciousness remained for some short period of time after the head was removed from the body.

Before, during those discussions, it had seemed like the logical position to him. Now, however, he experienced a vague disappointment that there was no evidence to support his theory. The eyes stared straight forward, unseeing and blank. They were not yet filmed over with the appearance of death, but neither was there any trace of consciousness behind them. He shifted his gaze to the body, which had already slowed the infernal rate of pumping blood. A few muscle tremors there, not that that was any help. The head, now, that was the key. As he watched, the eyes seemed to glaze over and become even more lifeless, if such a thing was possible. He noted the details with infinite care, preparing himself for the many questions that would come that evening, and the detailed recital of facts that he planned to provide to the others.

Yes, he was certain of it now—there'd been a change, however slight, in the appearance of the eyes between the first moment of decapitation and now, almost ninety seconds later. He felt a slight glow of satisfaction. However rudimentary, however limited, there was something in the brain that knew what was happening, perhaps howled in silent protest against the summary, violent death, perhaps offered a last prayer to whatever god the body had followed—but consciousness nonetheless.

The executioner felt a slight glow of satisfaction. A job well done was something to be proud of.

Dr. Kamil was still on rounds, just starting to feel the adrenaline ebb from his system, when the telegram arrived. Unlike the old days when uniformed messengers had delivered the flimsy yellow pieces of paper to the intended recipient, the modern telegram was a telephonic communication. He was in the middle of palpitating an abdomen when the page came over the hospital's loudspeaker system. "Dr. Kamil—two-one-three." The operator's voice announced an extension to which outside calls were routed.

Making his excuses, Kamil left abruptly. The telephone call from his mother last night had prepared him. His mother had seemed oddly fatalistic, almost in shock at the impending death of her brother. The family had ridden so high for so long that the sudden plunge into disgrace following the assassination had virtually numbed them all to further agony.

"Dr. Kamil," he said after he'd dialed the extension. "A message?"

"One moment for an outside call, Doctor," the voice said. He heard the crackle, the sharp metallic ping as the outside call was connected.

"Dr. Kamil?" a new voice said. "Dr. Attila Kamil?"

He acknowledged his name and then waited with numb dread for the message that must surely follow. He heard the shock in the operator's voice as she read the message, the careful effort to keep her words neutral and emotionless.

"At noon today, your uncle was beheaded." A long pause as the ghastly import of that one sentence seemed to echo in the electronic connection between him and the Western Union operator.

"Will there—I mean—is there any response?" she finally said, a slight agitation creeping into her voice. "Forgive me, but it's—"

"No response," Kamil said. He replaced the telephone in its cradle and leaned heavily against the wall. His uncle, his favorite uncle. After the death of Kamil's father, he'd stepped in to be a father to his sister's only son. He'd supported, been there at the critical moments during adolescence and young adulthood, and even attended Kamil's graduation from Boston College and Harvard School of Medicine. Even Kamil's memories of his own biological father paled in comparison to the continuing, unwavering thread of strength that ran from his uncle through his own life.

And now he was dead. Kamil's mind skirted around that most final of facts, refusing to acknowledge either that reality or the horrendous chain of events that had preceded it.

It made no sense. None at all. The Tshoma family had been a mainstay in Algerian politics for decades, only with his uncle's generation rising to the highest pinnacles of power and influence. Following his selection as secretary of state, there had been virtually a year of celebration within the Tshoma household. Kamil had been barely able to contain his own pride and assume the modest demeanor required of one of the country's foremost families.

How could it have happened? The question banged away at him until the refrain became almost unbearable. He slammed his fist into the wall, as much to silence the voices inside of him as to give vent to his anger.

"Dr. Kamil?" a deep, masculine voice said. Kamil barely heard it through his personal hell. A hand came to rest on his shoulder. Kamil turned to face the voice, staring at the figure through the tears that crowded his eyes. He swiped one arm across his eyes and blinked. He took a deep breath and struggled for some semblance of composure. "Yes?"

"Are you all right?" Kamil could place the voice now—Dr. Gillespie. Kamil straightened up and attempted to conceal the emotional storm that threatened to override all he had accomplished in his own life thus far.

"Yes, Dr. Gillespie, I'm fine. Just some bad news from home."

"Nothing serious, I hope." Although Gillespie's voice was patently concerned, Kamil could hear the undertones of vicious glee that permeated the question. Of course he knew. They all did. The entire sequence of events—although not the beheading—had been carried on CNN for the last several days as a lead story.

"I'm fine," Kamil said, avoiding the question. "Is there something I can help you with?" His question seemed almost absurd under the circumstances.

"I was wondering if you'd heard from Dr. Thorne," Gillespie said easily. "I've got a message that he's back from Korea."

"No." Kamil shook his head, unable to remember even when Thorne had left. It had been after the assassination, during that time when life had disintegrated in sequences of hours fogged by emotional pain. He almost laughed at the utter, agonizing absurdity of it all. In Algeria, his uncle was being put to death, and Gillespie expected him to know where Thorne was. It was absurd, some oddly cruel Caucasian ritual for testing mental endurance. As an instrument of torture, it would have been more suited to his native land than to the pristine, sterile walls of Murphy Medical Center.

"Doctor, if you could excuse me—I've had a bit of a shock." He marveled at his own ability to use those words to describe his emotional state, and reflected that perhaps he had spent entirely too long in America.

Gillespie nodded understandingly. He took a step closer to Kamil and laid one moist, heavy hand on Kamil's shoulder. "You look quite unwell, Doctor. Is there anything—"

Kamil knocked his hand away and turned away. He walked quickly down the corridor as though he could leave much more than Gillespie behind.

FIFTEEN

After Thorne checked his mail and notified both surgery and the ER that he was back, he started looking for Dr. Gillespie. He needed to let Dr. Gillespie know that he had returned and, more important, wanted to replace his last memories of Korea with reminders of who he really was. A doctor, not an infantryman. He'd had no business being out in the field like that, none at all.

A flash of the jungle, the preternatural alertness, the sheer aliveness, stopped Thorne stopped in the passageway. The memory washed the color out of his surrounding, mocked who he thought he was.

Enough. He pushed the images away, concentrated on where he was now, willing the unexpected yearning to fade.

He went directly to Gillespie's office, hoping that the doctor was back and adhering to his usual routine. After checking with Gillespie, Gillespie's secretary motioned him in to the inner sanctum.

Dr. Gillespie was seated behind his desk, steadily working his way through a pile of papers. Thorne stared in surprise at the mess scattered around the intricately grained wooden antique desk. His department head was normally the most meticulous of organizers, with folders color-coded and stacked neatly in specific locations on his desktop and credenza. His pen and pencil set, his name plaque, and the other paraphernalia of an office were always aligned in precisely parallel lines, centered between the in and out baskets and perpendicular to the desk pad. Thorne could not remember ever having seen so much as a paperclip out of place.

Now, however, the area looked more like the small office that he shared with Kamil. Papers stuck out at odd angles from file folders. The chairs, always so methodically posed in front of the desk, now formed an odd angle with each other. Reflexively, Thorne reached out and straightened them.

"You're back." Gillespie's voice was flat and emotionless.

"Yes, sir." Thorne moved to sit down in one of the chairs, only to find that it was also piled high with folders, clippings, and books. Gillespie's raincoat was slung over the other one. He settled for standing in a posture that felt increasingly like attention in front of the desk.

"I received a phone call from General Boothby last night. My service tracked me down in Denver to take it." Gillespie looked up now, his face a hard, impassive mask. "Just what the hell did you do over there?"

"I don't know what—"

Gillespie slammed his pen down on the desk. "Don't play coy with me, Doctor. General Boothby filled me in completely. If you think this is going to make getting your security clearance any easier, you might reconsider. Just what the hell were you doing, insisting on going out on a nighttime patrol with those men? According to the general, the patrol started taking fire. He didn't even know you were armed—wouldn't even have approved your going out on the patrol if he'd known."

Gillespie's expression metamorphosed into horrified, righteous indignation. "You killed a man, didn't you? And you call yourself a doctor."

Thorne stared, stunned. "That's not what happened."

"Are you saying General Boothby is lying?" Gillespie's expression made it clear that anything Thorne could say in his own defense would be viewed with a jaundiced eye.

"The general *asked* me to come," Thorne began. The image of the dead Korean soldier rose up in his mind.

"You admit you were there, then." Gillespie's voice brooked no denial.

Thorne nodded. "Yes, I was there. At the general's *request.*"

Gillespie laughed, a harsh, barking sound. "God, man. Don't compound your troubles by lying about it."

Thorne's astonishment now metamorphosed into anger. "I'm not lying. That's exactly how it happened."

"How was the general?" Gillespie said, changing subjects suddenly. "Did he have any complaints about his postsurgical recovery?"

Thorne floundered for a moment, trying to follow the change in subjects. "His shoulder seemed to be healing without complication."

"I meant his appendectomy. The one we performed here. I know you asked about it while you were there."

Stranger and stranger. The chief of staff must have told Boothby that Thorne had asked about his visit to the Murphy. Understandable, but if the general were going to talk at all about the mission into the north, why lie about it? And especially why fabricate a story that was likely to cause problems for Thorne, in light of the fact that the general had seemed to like him?

Liked him, at least until Thorne had turned down the suggestion that he stay in country. Was Boothby really that maliciously petty that he'd try to destroy Thorne in retaliation?

"The general seemed quite well," Thorne said finally. "I noted no restrictions in his movements, no involuntary guarding—nothing to suggest that his recovery was anything but complete and uneventful."

Gillespie nodded, some of the anger fading out of his face. "At least you remember that much about being a doctor."

The utter injustice of the conversation now struck Thorne full force. "Maybe his recovery wasn't as complete as I thought," he said slowly. He let his voice trail off as he tried to marshal the facts in his own mind.

"Oh, please." Gillespie's voice dripped with disgust. "Can't we even discuss a former patient without your scurrying for some rational excuse for your conduct? Listen, Doctor, this will go no further than you, me, and the general." He pointed one accusing finger at Thorne. "Unless you persist in such scurrilous accusations against one of the finest military men who's ever lived. Can you hear how ludicrous you sound? Do you have any conception of what you're saying?" He shook his head thoughtfully and studied Thorne. "How stable are you?"

"I'm fine," Thorne shouted, the combination of emotional turmoil and physical exhaustion now catching up with him full force. It seemed like only hours since he'd been on the ground in Korea, just returning to his room after the nighttime raid. Now he was here, listening to the most utterly ridiculous version of those events that he'd ever heard. "I'm absolutely fine."

Thorne glanced at the television in the corner of Gillespie's office which was turned to CNN Headline News. A story about Korea was flashing across the screen, the announcer's voiceover a muted murmur in the room.

Finally, Thorne's world began to make sense. Everything that had happened to him personally in Korea and the growing tensions between the two nations was a direct result of General Boothby's influence. The man was brilliant, far too astute and capable a military tactician to allow the situation to escalate that far out of control.

Unless he'd wanted it to. And that, Thorne was now convinced, was exactly what was happening. Lying about Thorne's involvement in the raid was part of it, somehow. It had to be.

"I am placing you on medical leave, effective immediately," Gillespie said, his voice harsh. "It's clear to me that you are unstable. Maybe it's just jet lag—I don't know. You will go home, get some rest, and reconsider your rash statements. In view of your recent service to our country—such as it was—I will overlook your remarks. Understood?"

Thorne nodded, now conscious of the overwhelming exhaustion he felt. Maybe Gillespie was right. God knows he could use some sleep. He felt as though he were still running on adrenaline from the nighttime raid, that had been circulating in his system for the past twenty-four hours, waiting for release.

"Thank you, Dr. Gillespie," he said formally, forcing the words out. "I understand completely. There's just one small matter, a request from General Boothby."

"Go on."

"The general asked me to check on a patient here, one of his people. Sergeant Carter, the name was. I'd like to see him before I leave, just because the general asked me to."

Gillespie appeared to consider the request for a few moments, then nodded. "Go ahead. See him, but don't treat him. And then you go straight home."

Thorne called the switchboard from an in-house phone on the first ward he came to and found that Carter had been transferred to the psychiatric wing. A small shiver of fear started down his spine. The sergeant had been admitted for a shoulder wound. What the hell was he doing on the shrink ward?

Minutes later, Thorne was admitted to the locked ward on the strength of his employee ID. He asked an orderly for Carter's location and was shown to a locked, single-bed room at the far end of the corridor.

Thorne stared in through the observation glass. The man in restraints lying on his back in the bed bore only a small resemblance to the combat sergeant he'd seen in Korea.

Carter's face was pale and drawn, with a wasting look to it as though he'd lost massive amounts of weight. He moved restlessly in the bed, tossing continually and pulling against his restraints. Thorne saw thick cotton pads wedged between the straps and his flesh, evidently an attempt to keep him from rubbing his skin raw with the movements.

Thorne tried the door and found it was locked. He walked back to the central reception area and asked for the key. A nurse gave him a skeptical look, then said, "I'll go with you, Doctor. Ward rules."

"I saw other doctors going into rooms by themselves," Thorne argued. Dealing with petty bureaucratic regulations was a bit past his endurance at this point.

"Not in that room." She came around the counter and preceded him down the hallway.

The nurse slid the key into the lock and then shoved the door open. She carefully pocketed the key in her smock and motioned Thorne in. "We never stay too long," she said quietly. "Having people around seems to agitate him."

Carter's restless motion stopped suddenly. His eyes opened and he focused on the two people standing in the door. His eyes lit up with a mad light of glee as his gaze found Thorne. "Come to break me out?"

"I'm Dr. Thorne," he began.

"I know who you are. I remember. Got a little taste of the good life that night, didn't you?"

The nurse looked on in mild surprise. "He's lucid."

Thorne took two steps closer to the bed, then stopped as the nurse laid a restraining hand on his elbow. From three feet away, he asked, "How are you? The general asked me to stop by and see you."

"Oh, the general." An oddly incongruent giggle spilled out from Carter's bleeding, tattered lips. "And just how is the big boy? Still managing an occasional pleasure trip across the border?"

Thorne took a step closer, not heeding the nurse's warning. "How long has he been doing that?" he asked quietly. "The raids, I mean."

Carter's giggle escalated into loud, maniacal laughter. "Is that what you're calling it? Raids?"

"What would you call it?"

Carter paused and appeared to consider the question seriously. "A counteroffensive. A demonstration raid, maybe." He shrugged as best he could within the restraints, appearing to lose interest in the subject. "Just some fun is all. Cross the line, burn a few gooks, come back." A sly look crossed his face. "The general, now, he likes the stories." He winked conspiratorially at Thorne. "But you know what I mean."

Thorne glanced back at the nurse still standing near the door. Her face registered nothing—not comprehension, not shock, not even disgust. All were concealed by the carefully bland façade of her profession.

"When did it start?" Thorne asked. "Has he always been like this?"

Carter shook his head. "About three months ago, right after he came back from the States. He found Jesus back home, I guess." Again the sly look, the hooded eyes sparkling with some private amusement. "And Jesus told him to kill gooks, so that's what we do." Carter made it sound like anyone should be able to understand the reasonableness of his position.

"He wants to start a war, doesn't he?" Thorne asked.

"Don't we all?"

After he left the psych ward, Thorne went back to the small cubbyhole he shared with Kamil. His friend was absent, and the desiccated doughnut on his desk indicated that it had been more than a day since he'd been there. Thorne sniffed at the coffee cup, then tossed it into the waste can next to Kamil's desk.

He slid into his own chair, oddly comforted by the familiar contours of the back and seat. It had been a good catch, finding this surprisingly ergonomic chair in the cluster of castoffs that were used to furnish the research assistants' rabbit warren of offices.

As a medical student on clinical rotation, he'd been appalled at the sick humor he'd heard from doctors and nurses. During that first year, he'd come to understand that it was just their way of coping with the uncontrollable, that vast and awful conclusion of some cases. Over the years, through the rest of school, internship, and residency, he'd found himself slipping into the same sophomoric coping mechanism. Finally, he'd outgrown it, perhaps become callused to it. The death of a patient was still painful, disturbing, but no longer an affront to him personally.

But Korea had been different. As he'd heard one soldier say, it was up close and personal, not merely the last entry on a patient's chart. As it had been in Algeria, both for the president and Kamil's uncle.

It must have been like that for JFK as well, and for his wife. Not a clinical conclusion to life, but the sudden shattering of it.

JFK, Korea, Algeria—for a moment, the three places melded together, connected in some uncertain way he could feel just beneath the surface of the facts, elusive and inchoate. What was it? Something he should recognize, something demanding his attention outside the hospital, and—

The hospital. Surgery. Algeria and Tshoma, Korea and Boothby. Is it possible?

Thorne's stomach lurched sickeningly. According to Carter, the general's forays into North Korea had started shortly after the general's surgery at Murphy. And Secretary of State Tshoma assassinated his president within a few months of being treated at Murphy.

But what about Oswald and JFK? The Murphy hadn't even been in existence back then. If there was a connection, it would be related to medical treatment, not being at the Murphy.

Thorne reached for the phone, dialed for an outside line, then pecked out Jim Harley's number. Two short rings, then the gruff voice answered. "Harley."

"It's Thorne. I need to ask you about Oswald's medical history."

"Finally coming around to our way of thinking, are you?" Harley asked genially. "I knew you would, once you saw the facts."

Thorne ignored the insinuation that he was now firmly in the loon camp and asked, "Did Oswald ever have major surgery?"

"Define major."

"Anything that would require general anesthesia."

Harley's voice took on a thoughtful note. "As I recall," he said slowly, "the only surgery we know about was something to do with his jaw. Hold on, I'll find that section of the autopsy."

I know a man who has copies of Oswald's autopsy. How much stranger can life get? Thorne waited while his friend banged around in a filing cabinet.

Finally, Harley came back on the line. "I was right. Macular degeneration, something like that. I'll spell it for you."

Thorne listened as Harley read off the details from the autopsy, then thanked him for his time.

"Of course, that doesn't account for anything that might have happened in Russia," Harley warned before he rang off. "Oswald spent a good deal of time there. No telling what they used on him over there."

"Would anyone know?" Thorne asked, now intrigued. The Russia connection had not come immediately to mind, but now that Harley mentioned it—

"Only one fellow I know. But he doesn't share his material." Harley's voice dripped envy.

Thorne thanked him again and rang off. He leaned back in the chair as the overwhelming tide of weariness surged over him.

He'd hoped Harley would tell him that Oswald had never had major surgery, at least breaking that part of the nagging suspicion. But even absent the macular degeneration surgery in the States, Harley had raised another troubling possibility. Oswald had spent a significant amount of time in Russia, and that time was poorly documented. Harley's source might have some information, but it didn't sound like Thorne's chances of getting a look at it were good.

Correlation? Or mere coincidence?

Eight thousand miles away, the very object of Thorne's speculations was doing some hard thinking of his own. General Boothby stood at the window to his office and stared out across the compound at the double line of concertina wire that ringed either side of the DMZ. The sniper attacks were coming more often now, and his troops had taken to responding in kind surreptitiously. No one had reported it to him officially, thus permitting him to remain ostensibly ignorant of his own troops' conduct. Still, the daily crack of the long-range rifles irrefutably came from both sides.

Now, at night, the occasional chatter of automatic weapons fire woke him from a sound sleep. At first it had just been the Koreans, with the distinctive hum of the AK-47. Now, more often, he heard the shorter, staccato bark of American weapons answering in kind. What had once seemed to be impressive fortifications on both sides of the border looked like the sheerest, most ephemeral sort of restraints. Barbed wire and mines could come and go, but the forces really at conflict in Korea were eternal. Communism against democracy, good against evil. He snorted, recognizing the fallacy in the argument. It presupposed that the South Koreans were any better than the warlike society that inhabited the northern part of their peninsula.

Increasingly at night, during those lulls in the automatic weapons fire, he found his thoughts turning back to the young reserve doctor who'd been here so briefly. Already the man's name was becoming a blur as it merged with the infinite multitudes with whom Boothby had served during his career. A reservist, where had he been from? Unconsciously, he reached down and ran his hand over the uniform above his scar. That's right, Merced, California. Where he'd had his appendectomy.

It was not the doctor himself who returned repeatedly to haunt Boothby's thoughts, nor the medical care he'd received at Murphy. No, it was something the doctor had said—now what the hell was his name?—during that first dinner here. For some reason, that memory remained sharp and clear, even though he had only the barest recollection of the man's face.

JFK, John F. Kennedy. The doctor had known a little bit about the assassination, more than a little. But it had not been the central facts of the tragedy that had stunned American society back in 1963 that had truly hit Boothby so hard that evening. No, not the assassination at all. The secret to everything—to Korea, to Alicia, even to Brett's odd and difficult behavior—lay in the events that followed. The cover-up, the autopsy, the subsequent obfuscation by the House committee assigned to investigate the assassination.

And, central to the conspiracy, the theft. The word loomed in capital letters in his mind, ringing with the clarity of a bell as it clarified his own thoughts.

The details were unimportant, or so it seemed now. What mattered was the final result. That sometime during the autopsy or shortly thereafter, some party or parties had removed the president's brain and taken it into safekeeping somewhere. It was a mystery that had puzzled assassination buffs and investigating committees for over fifty years—the missing JFK brain.

But Boothby knew. Knew with a certainty that grew out of moral conviction, knew it as completely, absolutely, and certainly as he knew his own name, the details of his own career, and the most effective firing range of a howitzer.

Lyndon Johnson had taken possession of JFK's brain and had traded it to the North Koreans in exchange for . . . in exchange for what? That was the only small portion of the equation that still puzzle him, but he was certain that with time—and the judicious questioning of either the right North Korean or the current United States president—he would know that as well. The North Korean because he would be part of the conspiracy. And the same for the current president. Boothby had no doubt that succession to the office of president involved more than passing the nuclear codes from incumbent to successor. It went far deeper than that. The details of Watergate, the true location of Area 51, and the details of the deal that Lyndon Johnson and his CIA cohorts had cut with the North Koreans. Some day soon he would know the complete truth. One way or the other.

Boothby stared out at the compound and made his plans.

SIXTEEN

It was the noise that caught Lanelli's attention first: one short, sharp squeal that penetrated his glassed-in office. He was poring over the record of expenditures for the last week for the lab, noting the increased cost due to changing brands of food. Dr. Gillespie said that the last batch had been spoiled, maybe contaminated with ergot. That particular mold could produce hallucinogenic effects and might account for the odd behavior of the rats. Lanelli had sent a sample of the food to the lab himself.

Now that had been a useless expenditure. Lanelli knew just as well as Gillespie that there was nothing wrong with the rat chow they'd been feeding the animals for the last six months. Still, Dr. Gillespie had been insistent. It was his project. If he wanted a change of food, that's what he got.

The sound cut through his concentration like a buzz saw. Lanelli's head jerked up and the rest of his body followed it. In two quick steps, he was at the door and out into the animal care lab proper.

He surveyed the cages arrayed around the room, looking for the offender. The rats stared back, dark, beady eyes glistening under lights. Another large expenditure, the multiple sets of natural lighting bulbs that Gillespie had ordered, claiming they simulated a more realistic daytime environment. Lanelli snorted. As though the rats needed to know when it was daylight.

The rats were milling about in their cages as normal, many of them sleeping, curled up in gentle piles of fur and tail. It was at night that they were most active, and the few times Lanelli had been unfortunate enough to be stuck here after 5:00 P.M. on some task, he'd noticed that the rats began to increase their level of activity sometime after 7:00 P.M. Then, their gentle shuffling about the cage, the sound of teeth clinking on a water bottle, or the occasional protesting cry from a rat was not unusual.

But it was nine o'clock in the morning, a time when most of them should have been doing what nocturnal animals do during the day: sleeping.

He went to the first cage, examined it, and then moved on to the next, searching for something out of the ordinary. Rat eyes met human, both sets dark and glittering. Lanelli suppressed an involuntary shudder.

He completed his circuit of the room and went back to his office, puzzled. There were no indications of agitation among any of the cages, and no reason that he could see for the noise he'd heard. Perhaps he hadn't heard it after all, maybe it was just a squeaky bearing on his chair or a hinge on the door. He debated asking the other lab technicians if they'd heard anything, then dismissed the matter as trivial. More important that he get the accounts ready for transmission to their funding agency the next day than track down the unusual sounds of some irritable rat.

He returned to his accounts and was soon deep in the intricacies of matching poundage of food with rat population as prorated over a partial week. When the second noise came, Lanelli was annoyed more than surprised.

It was followed shortly by another, then a fourth and a fifth. The third cry was enough to bring Lanelli out of his seat and back to the lab. As he opened the door to his office and stepped out into the central area, the unholy din stopped him short in his tracks.

The rats in every cage were now awake, pacing and moving anxiously within their enclosures. He heard sudden squeals, the soft impact of body against body, the violent rattling of water bottles and feeders against the thin aluminum bars of their cages.

The motion and stench caught his attention as well. The rats were moving ceaselessly, pacing back and forth in their cages, stopping occasionally to whirl on another and lash out with a quick flash of long incisors. The stink was more pronounced now, too, as agitated rats voided their bladders and bowels.

The sound kept increasing, building to an intensity that Lanelli had only heard before in horror movies that involved rats in sewers. Six months in this protocol, over a year and a half all told on this one project. Suddenly, it dawned on him what was at stake.

He whirled, darted back to his office, and began summoning the rest of the technicians. The rats would have to be isolated, individually caged, each one accounted for and labeled so that the data would not be lost.

The other technicians arrived quickly, streaming in from adjacent wings of the laboratory facility. They moved quickly, confidently, immediately donning the heaviest grade of gloves available after a cursory glance at the cages. Lanelli winced inwardly as he watched them reach gingerly into the cages and try to close their fingers around the quickly moving rodents.

The voices of the technicians added to the babble, too, as they grew increasingly nervous over the aggressive and uncharacteristic behavior of the laboratory animals. He heard a young woman yelp and saw her slam the door of a cage shut and grasp one hand with her other, holding it up for inspection. From his vantage point, Lanelli could see that there was a sharp gouge in the thick, reinforced plastic palm.

"Little bastard bit me," she said excitedly, holding the glove out for inspection.

Lanelli took it, ran his finger over the gouge, and shook his head. "It didn't penetrate, at least."

She glared at him. "Fuck you and your rats." She took off the gloves and threw them on the floor. "Find somebody else to work with these psychos. You need to put them down—all of them."

"Now, just a minute—" Lanelli began.

"I don't think that's going to be necessary," one of the male technicians interrupted, his voice shaken and hoarse. "Look."

The technicians had managed to transfer approximately one-third of the rats to individual containment pens. The remaining two-thirds, some sixty-seven community pens all told, still had their normal quota of inhabitants.

As he whirled and scanned the remaining cages, Lanelli noticed that the noise level in the lab had changed markedly. No longer was it a cacophony of angry howls and screeches of pain. It had died down to a quieter, more ominous level. There was no more frantic activity, no more slashing fangs and wildly flailing tails. Instead, in each cage, one rat remained standing. The others were strewn around the bottom of the cage, motionless. Fur and blood spattered the bars of the cages as well as the linoleum below, evidently flung outside the pens by the sheer force of the attacks.

He took a step closer and examined the first cage slowly. Two rats were dead, a third dying. A white haunch had been ripped from one body and tossed carelessly into a far corner of the cage. The tail, deprived of part of its supporting tendons, hung limply down in the feces collection area from the remaining hindquarters. Intestines dangled as well, and the rat was ripped open from throat to anus in a rough, running gouge. Blood and viscera dripped down onto the sheet metal below.

He walked the cages slowly as he had done half an hour earlier at the sound of the first squeal. In the sixty-six remaining cages, only six rats still showed signs of life. Of those, three appeared mortally wounded. For a moment, he considered telling the technicians to put them down, then dismissed the idea. One small, vicious part of his mind argued that the rats had no right to a merciful death, having so thoroughly and completely disrupted his own day.

The rats in the individual enclosures were faring not much better. They threw themselves against the bars, reaching through with fangs where the cages touched to lash out at one another. Through an interwoven lace of aluminum bars, two of the individually contained rats had a vicious death grip on each other's throats. Blood streamed down their throats, spurting out from the torn flesh in thin streams to spatter on the metal trays below.

Those rats that could not reach an opponent threw themselves against the bars, gnawing at the restraints and inflicting as much injury on themselves as the other rats would have done had they been able.

"What the hell is going on here?" the male technician said wonderingly. He spread his hands out, clearly stricken by the massive carnage around him. "What the hell did you do to them?"

Lanelli shook his head numbly. "That will be all."

The technician shot him a disgusted look. "Okay, don't tell me anything. It's not like it's my project that just went down the tubes." With a last look at the rat carcasses, he left the lab, slamming the door behind him. The glass rattled in aftershocks even as his figure disappeared around the corner. The remaining technicians followed more slowly.

Dr. Gillespie. He had to find the doctor. Lanelli's mind started working again as he searched frantically for an explanation, something to tell Dr. Gillespie other than that his entire project was lost. He battered against that irrefutable fact as relentlessly as the rats had torn at each other.

Two hours later, Dr. Gillespie surveyed the disaster that until this morning had been his pride and joy. His face was impassive as he made a slow circuit among the cages, counting rat bodies and briefly examining tags on their cages.

Finally, he turned back to Lanelli. "Clean them up."

Lanelli nodded. "Dissection preparation for all of them? What about the loose parts?"

"No. I mean get rid of them."

Lanelli stared, dumbfounded for the second time in as many hours. "You're not going to dissect them?"

"If you can't understand simple declarative English sentences, let me know. I'll find someone who can." Gillespie turned abruptly and left the room.

Lanelli stared after him.

He means it. Just to throw them out—no investigation, no trying to figure out what happened.

"He really doesn't care," he said wonderingly to the room that only he and the dead rats occupied. "He really doesn't care."

SEVENTEEN

Thorne woke early the next morning with a sense of dislocation. All was as it normally should be, the bedside clock indicating it was nearly four-thirty in the morning, just two minutes before his alarm would normally go off. The house was quiet, with the peculiar stillness it always had during the predawn hours.

He considered going back to bed for a moment, then dismissed the idea. After finally retiring early the night before, he'd slept nine straight hours, more than enough to wash away most of the effects of jet lag. Only an odd, nagging sort of sandpapery feeling remained to remind him how recently he'd returned from the other side of the world.

He stuck with his routine through breakfast: cereal and fruit, a short stint at the computer to download the latest news and check his stock portfolio, and then a cursory scanning of the e-mail that was comprised almost completely of junk mail. He almost purged the entire incoming array by reflex when one small note caught his attention. Intrigued by the subject line—Genetic Implications—Thorne clicked on the message and scanned the sender's address. Not someone he recognized, but the first few paragraphs intrigued him nonetheless.

It was from a genetic researcher at the Massachusetts Institute of Technology, one who specialized in folic acid deficiencies. The mailing was en masse, probably to every physician who had listed an e-mail address in the latest AMA directory. It was an announcement of a forthcoming paper to be presented at the AMA conference, the same one at which Gillespie was planning on presenting the preliminary data on Anaex.

Dr. Rita Clowers. The name sounded vaguely familiar, but not immediately recognizable. Dr. Clowers' research centered primarily on infrequently reported consequences of nutritional deficiencies during pregnancy. Clowers postulated that a whole host of minor symptoms might be caused by early pregnancy deficiencies in folic acid. Among those she cited fibromyalgia, an official-sounding name for a vague collection of muscular and skeletal discomfort complaints. She argued that while the levels might be beneath those normally considered clinically deficient, even minor variations in folic acid levels could result in problems.

Of course, marked levels of folic acid deficiency often resulted in serious, usually fatal complications. Spina bifida, for instance, in which a portion of the spine failed to grow sufficiently to cover the spinal cord. Without its protective covering, the spinal cord was vulnerable to repeated infections and trauma. Victims required surgery and constant monitoring to ensure that the infections did not become systemic. The most common cause of folic acid deficiency was a radically unbalanced diet on the part of the mother. In particular, pure vegetarian and health food nuts tended to suffer from the syndrome in the United States, although it was quite prevalent among poorer third world countries where a balanced diet was a luxury.

Would it have any effect on a patient's response to anesthesia? It seemed possible. Wide variations in a patient's response to anesthetics made up a well-known facet of practicing anesthesiology. Thorne had even encountered several individuals who lacked essential enzymes in their blood to metabolize normal anesthetics. Those patients never emerged quickly and smoothly from sedation and often experienced a terrifying sensation of paralysis. Patients emerged from sleep states only to find themselves unable to breathe, move, or even communicate their distress to the anesthesiologist. Treatment under those conditions would normally be massive infusions to increase the volume of the blood and aid in the elimination of the anesthetic by the kidneys.

Thorne printed out a copy of the notice and made a mental note to be sure to attend that particular lecture at the conference. As he did so, he glanced at the clock. It was five-thirty, the time when he normally left the house for the hospital.

But not today. Gillespie had been clear on that point, that Thorne was on leave until his emotional stability returned.

For the last ten years, through the grind of med school, internship, and his first position as a staff anesthesiologist, his routine had been driven by the enormous demands of his profession. Even during his short, week-long vacations in earlier days, he'd never been able to leave the hospital and his patients far behind. The constant telephone calls, questions from nurses who didn't realize he was on vacation, and general routine that went along with being a doctor had so continually interrupted his time off that it barely seemed worth it.

The literature search, then. The hospital library wouldn't be open for another three hours, but there was plenty he could do at home. He toggled through the menus until he located the Melvil Medline program and quickly logged onto the massive medical database. Two hours later, the printer finally quit spitting out a steady procession of synopses, citations, and references to aberrant side effects to new anesthetic drugs.

A couple of days to whip through the literature review, maybe another week to put his hypothesis and data together into some form of preliminary outline. Maybe Gillespie's order was actually a blessing in disguise, one that would give him the opportunity to pole vault ahead in his profession by presenting at the AMA.

While he'd garnered a good deal of information off the Internet, there were some sources that still weren't digital. Surely Gillespie's prohibition didn't apply to the medical library—his superior had meant stay out of the hospital proper, Thorne was certain.

He waited for another hour for the library to open, sipping the cooling cup of coffee and studying the data he'd downloaded. Then he drove to the hospital library. A few hours, that's all he needed. Then he *would* stay home and write the actual paper.

As Kamil pulled into the parking lot, he saw Thorne's small gray Cadillac Catera parked in its reserved spot. It was centered between the yellow lines, in a neat and precise fashion that Kamil invariably found fascinating. More than anything else, he suspected, Thorne's method of parking provided insights into his character. Just to get a rise out of his friend, Kamil parked at a jaunty angle in his own space, the chrome bumpers of his Volvo intersecting a plane just perpendicular with the interior edge of his own parking spot. In his own way, he was as precise as Thorne. Just a bit more artistic.

Thirty minutes before he had to be in the ER to commence turnover of the ongoing cases from the preceding shift, Kamil thumbed the car's security alarm, the one that was supposed to deter thieves who were convinced that every car parked in the doctors' parking lot harbored a secret stash of pharmaceuticals. The alarm, coupled with the intermittent patrols by the hospital's security force seemed to deter them.

He angled off away from the main entrance to the hospital and headed for the research wing. If he knew Thorne, he'd be knee-deep in rat records by now, thumbing through their records with the unflagging, determined curiosity that made him such a prime catch for the research department.

Well, the rats could wait for a minute. Kamil had questions about his latest patient from Korea, Sergeant Nigel Carter. He'd missed seeing Thorne around the hospital.

Kamil shoved open the double glass doors and walked into the separate wing, aware as always of how the atmosphere changed as soon as he stepped over the boundary between practice and theory. The research wing had a separate air-conditioning system, installed under the theory that if it were ever necessary to isolate some contagion in either wing, the separate filtering and recirculating systems would make it easier. As a result, the background flavor of air in research always tasted slightly different. Underlying the pungent tang of antiseptics and pine disinfectant was a primal, animal taint to the air. No one had ever been able to devise an air filtering system that completely removed the scent of too many animals kept too close together, but Murphy had come closer than most. Here it was just an odd, background tartness to the air, a peculiar tickle in the nose that Kamil sometimes fantasized was the result of only the smallest molecules escaping the massive banks of filters.

The massive steel doors that separated the Anaex Protocol wing from the rest of the corridor were solidly locked, as they were supposed to be. Kamil tapped on the glass-enclosed reception area to catch Lanelli's attention, then motioned toward the door. Lanelli buzzed him in.

"Dr. Thorne in?" Kamil asked. He looked past Lanelli and scanned the open expanse of the lab and the main work area. A frown creased his brow and he asked, "You guys moving?"

Lanelli shook his head. "No."

"What, did all the rats sign out AMA?" Kamil joked, referring to a release against medical advice.

Lanelli's sullen expression deepened into a scowl. The thin man's dour expression looked almost painful. "No. You have any questions, you ask Dr. Gillespie."

"Well." Aware of Thorne's ongoing battle with the senior lab technician, Kamil decided not to press the issue. "Where's Dr. Thorne?"

Lanelli stood abruptly. "I don't have time to keep track of everybody, Doctor." He waved one hand at the work area behind him. "You doctors have no idea of how much time and attention this requires— no idea at all. Now, if you'll excuse me—"

Kamil's fragile emotional equilibrium fled. He grabbed Lanelli by a lab coat sleeve. "Don't talk to me about how tough your job is, asshole. You don't have any idea how nasty some jobs can get."

Lanelli jerked back, then scampered behind his desk, placing the massive metal government contraption between him and the enraged doctor. "Get out. Get out now."

"Not yet. I came to see Dr. Thorne. And that's what I'm going to do." Convinced that Thorne had to be in the area since it made no sense that something this major would take place without all of the research assistants being involved, even those still under supervision, Kamil pushed past Lanelli and strode into the apparently empty lab. What he saw brought him to a sudden stop, stomach churning as his vagus nerve spasmed.

The carnage was beyond imagining. The long, steel work tables were strewn with partial rat bodies. The carcasses were arrayed in oddly neat rows, with detached rat portions placed near the main fragment of the rat carcass when the relationship between the two was obvious.

On the second table, the illusion of methodical inquiry continued. There, portions of rat bodies ranging from the very smallest scrap of facial skin and whiskers to entire, gutted abdomens were again ranged in lines. The order imposed on the carnage put the largest pieces first in a decreasing size line, followed by the smaller fragments arrayed in similar order.

Why size, one part of Kamil's mind wondered. Why not just an anatomical grouping? All intestines together, all hindquarters. He turned back to Lanelli. "My God. What happened?"

The smaller man seemed to deflate, his anger at being manhandled replaced by something far more genuine. "I don't know," he muttered, shaking his head. Stunned, Kamil thought the man looked like he might cry. "I came in the next day and it was like this. All of them."

"All of the rats?" Kamil breathed. The sheer enormity of the loss stunned him. "Who could be responsible for such a thing? And why?" He waved a hand in the air, indicating the security which surrounded the wing. "Nobody could get in. How could they—"

"Not who, Doctor. What." Lanelli pointed at the dissection tables. "It was them that did it. The rats."

"Call Dr. Thorne," Kamil said.

Lanelli shook his head. "I heard Dr. Gillespie put him on medical leave. Somebody your buddy pissed off in Korea." He shot Kamil a sly glance, already recovering his equilibrium. "That's what happens when a doctor gets too full of himself and gets too much out of line."

Kamil ignored the veiled threat as to the possible results of his earlier conduct. In the past few minutes, his stomach had settled back into a stable state. The pungent, gory smell of raw flesh already beginning to decay, coupled with the ever-present stench of animal urine, was already fading out as his nostrils became accustomed to it. What had almost caused him to lose his lunch only minutes earlier was already part of the background.

"Talk about rotten jobs," Lanelli continued. "I don't see any doctors down here helping clean up the mess."

"What do you mean, clean it up? There's going to be a full workup on each of them, isn't there?"

"I just do my job, Doctor."

Kamil's beeper went off. He glanced down at his watch and noted time for shift change had just arrived.

"Like some people ought to do theirs," Lanelli continued. "So sorry you have to leave, Doctor. I was just thinking you might enjoy giving me a hand with this."

As Kamil hurried down the corridor to the medical wing of the hospital, he tried to make some sense of what he'd just seen before the constant demands of the ER overwhelmed him. The sheer viciousness of what must have been some sort of mass hysteria overwhelmed him. Dead, all of them. How many animals? Judging from the carcasses he'd seen laid out on the dissection table, there could've been well over three hundred of them. Hours of observation, months of planning, and years of actual development—all down the drain. Even a fast-tracked military experimental drug protocol couldn't continue under those circumstances.

He stopped abruptly just outside the door to the ob-gyn ward. Down the drain. What Lanelli had said finally sank in.

There was going to be no further study of the rat remains. No toxicological or chemical workups to determine whether or not there were external factors relating to the laboratory disaster. No further investigation, no serious inquiry into what had happened at all.

As with other branches of medicine, Dr. Gillespie was simply going to bury his mistakes.

And Thorne didn't even know. What had Lanelli said, that Gillespie had placed Thorne on administrative leave? Was it related to the feeding frenzy in the lab? Kamil shook his head as he approached the double doors leading into the emergency room. For now, the answers would have to wait. He pushed open the doors and walked into the ER.

Thorne slumped in the hard-backed chair and shut his eyes. What was he missing? The few possibilities he'd turned up were dead ends. Outside of neurological surgery, he could find no indications that surgery resulted in significant changes in mental state.

He gave up for the day, aware that he was still fighting off jet lag. As he left the main entrance to the hospital, the sky was already leaden and gray with the normal nighttime fog that passed for clouds in Merced six months out of the year.

Although there were plenty of physical resources nearby, Merced itself was notably lacking in any of them. The flat, fertile plain that stretched between the mountain ranges and the sea trapped every passing cloud, concentrating them into a gray layer that hid the sky most of the year. In the summer it was scorchingly hot, and in the winter notably cold for California. In between, it rained.

Tonight, however, the clouds barely covered the half-full moon. As Thorne walked toward his car, he noticed Kamil's Volvo juxtaposed at an odd angle with the lines on his parking spot. Although Kamil consistently denied that he did it just to irritate Thorne, the anesthesiologist had never been convinced that there had been any method to Kamil's parking patterns other than to make people wonder about him. Certainly when he'd carpooled with Kamil and seen him park, there had been no indication of any deficiency in motor skills.

If Kamil knew that his daily parking routine was a source of continual amusement for Thorne, he would have been pleased. Moreover, he would have immediately ceased doing it and found some other way to make Thorne try to puzzle out his motivation.

Thorne beeped the antitheft alarm on his car. As he opened the door, a dark green Oldsmobile pulled into the parking lot. A man rolled down the window and called out, "Are you a doctor?"

Thorne shook his head. Although there were remarkably few incidents in the parking area around the hospital, it was never wise to acknowledge one's membership in the profession at night when one was alone. "Plenty of them in there." He pointed toward the hospital.

The man stopped the Oldsmobile and got out. He cross around to the passenger side, yanked the door open, and jerked a thin, blond woman onto her feet.

The woman was barely able to stand on her own, Thorne noted. She took small, tottering steps, supported at her elbow by the man. He hustled her along, spitting out a refrain of harsh words too low for Thorne to make out. He doubted the woman heard them, anyway. A dull, dazed stare was fixed on her face, as though reality had simply become too much for her. She yielded to his direction passively, obediently. Thorne would have been willing to bet that she had no idea where she was at that very moment.

"Well, if you're not a doctor then find one." The man gave the woman one last shove in his direction, then turned and walked back to the car. The motor started with a rough grind, raced into a full-throated roar immediately. Tires squealed as the man peeled out of the parking lot.

The woman swayed on her feet, still staring in his direction with unfocused eyes. Her equilibrium became increasingly unstable until it seemed as if she must fall. Thorne darted to her side, circled one steadying hand around her back, and asked, "What happened?"

It was a moot question, he knew, as soon as he stared into her face. A raw ring of red, bruised tissue encircled her throat, the huge blotches from the fingertips standing out like separate sores. Blood ran from one nostril, tracing a delicate path around her mouth to a long smear at her jawbone.

"Let's get you inside," Thorne said soothingly. "You need to see a doctor."

The woman turned her face to him, squinting. "It hurts," she said, her voice as much puzzled as concerned.

"Where does it hurt?" Thorne asked. God, he didn't need to be doing a physical exam in a parking lot on a woman who had just been dumped on him. Particularly on one who was bleeding. AIDS, HIV, hepatitis—who knew? For a moment, he considered waiting for a pair of surgical gloves, then pushed the thought aside. "Can you walk?"

She nodded, a slow, hesitant movement. "I—I think so."

"It's just a little ways," Thorne coaxed. He slid his arm up a little bit higher so that his hand curled around underneath her far arm, and let her lean her weight against him. She was light, too light for her height, little but bone and tendon fleshing out the shapeless dress she wore. She had a raw, rank body odor, the aftermath of something recent rather than a prolonged period of not bathing. Thorne steeled himself not to flinch as she leaned against him, and tightened his grip lightly.

She jerked back immediately and moaned.

"Does that hurt?" Thorne asked. She nodded, gasping for breath.

Damn—broken ribs, at least. He wondered what else the man had inflicted on her before dumping her off at the Murphy. At least he'd had the common sense to do that. He focused on getting her moving, shoving away the upwelling of anger he felt at the man who'd done this then dumped her.

"Come on, let's try to walk. If you can't make it, I'll go get a wheelchair for you."

Step by step, linked by the strong supporting weight of his arm, she moved forward. It took them five minutes to negotiate the one hundred years to the entrance of the hospital. As soon as they got within the lighted circle of the driveway, Thorne called out for an orderly.

One appeared immediately. The orderly assessed the situation in one glance, then grabbed a wheelchair and wheeled it out to them. Thorne helped the woman collapse into it, lowering her gently so that she would not jar her damaged ribs any further.

"What's your name, ma'am?" Thorne asked as he took over the handles of the wheelchair from the orderly. "Your name?" For a moment, he wondered whether she would answer. Her expression was increasingly distant, and she seemed even less responsive than she had been at first.

"What does your mother call you?" he asked, trying a different approach.

"Hannah," she said in a high-pitched voice, oddly childlike in its tones. "Hannah . . ."

"That's a very nice name, Hannah," he said soothingly, all the while wheeling her down toward the emergency room. He paused for just a moment as one of her feet slipped off the metal supports, and lifted it back off the floor. "Do you have a last name?"

She frowned, and fear clouded her eyes. "I don't think so," she said hesitantly. She looked up at Thorne, an expression of apprehension creeping into the corner of her eyes. "Do I have to?"

"Not at all."

Finally, they reached the ER entrance. Thorne wheeled Hannah past patients queued up at the triage desk, through the double doors segregating the treatment area from the waiting room, and to the nurse's station. "Who's on?" he demanded. "Some guy just left this poor woman in the parking lot. Broken ribs, at least. Maybe a concussion—she's a little confused right now," he said charitably. The nurse stepped out from behind the desk and knelt down beside the wheelchair, her eyes fixed on the red marks on Hannah's throat and face.

"What's your name?" the nurse asked quietly.

"Hannah," Thorne supplied. "No last name, yet."

The nurse stood back up and nodded. "Room two, please, Doctor. Dr. Kamil is on right now—I'll go get him."

Thorne wheeled Hannah into the room and helped her move from the wheelchair onto the bed. He elevated the head of the bed slightly to make it easier for her to breathe.

"I have to talk to you. Right now. Scoot, the lab—it's—" Kamil's voice broke off as he stepped into the treatment room. His voice lost the urgency it had had just a few moments ago. The surgeon crossed the small room immediately to stand by Thorne's patient, his hands already reaching out to touch Hannah's wrist. "What do we have?"

"Good to see you too," Thorne said dryly, his eyes still fixed on Hannah. "That's what people love about you, your charming, people-oriented personality." Thorne gave a brief summary of his own conclusions about Hannah's injuries as Kamil gently palpated the broken ribs and the woman's battered neck.

"Did quite a number on her, didn't he?" Kamil said finally.

Thorne nodded. "No point in trying to tell us that she just fell down the stairs," he said, pointing to the red, splotchy marks around his patient's neck. "I wonder what stopped him. Why didn't he go ahead and strangle her?"

"Maybe she can tell us," Kamil suggested. He touched Hannah lightly on the side of the face. "Can you tell us what happened?" he continued softly, his voice now full of compassion.

Hannah shook her head, then a small moan escaped her lips. "Don't try to move," Kamil said quietly. "You'll feel better shortly, but you've got some damaged tissue there. Nothing life-threatening, but it's going to hurt for a while."

Hannah's unfocused eyes now sought out his face. "The baby," she whispered. "Is it all right?"

Thorne felt hot rage flood his body. "I didn't know. How far along are you?" He ran his hands again over the abdomen, and now felt the slight swelling that indicated the early stages of pregnancy.

"Three months," Hannah said. Her voice was barely louder than a whisper. "He doesn't—I mean he thinks—" Her eyes squeezed shut and tears trickled out the corners, running down her freshly scrubbed face. "I don't know what I'll do."

"There's no need to worry about that right this second," Kamil said gently. "You'll be in the hospital for a few days. And after that, we have some places you can go. Safe places—he won't even know where you are. I promise you, it will be all right."

While Thorne knew Kamil to be a compassionate doctor, the depth of concern in his friend's voice surprised him. Surprised him, and evoked a slight sensation of chagrin. He recognized at that point the difference between his reaction to Hannah and his friend's. Thorne's had been one of rage, of a strong desire to destroy the monster who had beaten this helpless, defenseless woman. Kamil, on the other hand, was oriented almost entirely toward her well-being. While Thorne could see the anger in his friend's face, Kamil's concern for the woman herself was his first priority.

Kamil turned back to the nurse. "Start O_2, BP, and vitals every five minutes until I tell you to stop. Let's get a hematocrit, hemoglobin, and white count—and a MAC18. Order two units of whatever she is. X rays of skull, jaw, arm, back, ribs, and chest. AP and lateral of right shoulder." Kamil glanced back at Thorne. "I've got to talk to you. Right away."

"The police," Thorne began, "I ought to call them."

"Later. Listen, I've *got* to talk to you."

"He was here," Hannah said unexpectedly. Her eyes roved wildly around the examining room and she tried to push herself up into a sitting position. "Here, here, this room!" Her voice climbed the octaves in a crescendo of horror and fear, her twangy midwestern accent becoming more pronounced as her voice grew louder. "Here!"

"Who was here, dear?" Kamil asked, settling her gently but firmly back down onto the pillows. "Who was?"

Hannah's eyes finally stopped their maddened darting about the room and settled on Thorne's face. "My husband."

Thorne walked back to her bedside and laid a comforting hand on her bruised and scarred arm. "When was he here, Hannah? When?"

"February," she mumbled, evidently having exhausted the limits of her physical and emotional outburst. "An exploratory." She pronounced the word as though it had several more syllables than it did, drawing it out as though the taste of it were unfamiliar on her tongue. "Didn't find nothing, though. Just stitched him back up and sent him home."

"What's your name, Hannah?" Thorne persisted. "Your last name?"

"Greener," she said finally. "Hannah Greener."

Thorne exchanged a quick nod with Kamil. Given her last name, they could track down the rest of her relevant data. However, under the circumstances, he doubted they would be calling her husband as her next of kin.

Something odd in the way that Mr. Greener had carried himself reminded Thorne of General Boothby. There were physical dissimilarities, with the general's physique honed by years of balanced nutrition and exercise, and the deprivations of poverty having taken their toll on Mr. Greener, but the similarity was there. It was in the carriage, perhaps, the way each one stepped out confidently as though he owned the entire world around him. Boothby, while attacking the North Koreans. Greener, while dumping his battered wife on the hospital grounds.

"Listen, she's stable. Come *on.*" Kamil grabbed Thorne by the elbow and pulled him toward the door.

"Okay, Okay." Thorne shook off Kamil's hand and followed him out into the hallway. "So what's so urgent it can't wait? And thank you, yes, I'm glad to be back."

"You might not be. Your pet project—all your little furry pets as well—is done for. You ought to use Lanelli instead. That bastard tried to throw me out of the lab."

"Done for?"

"Unless you know how to figure out which rat is which from body parts. They're all dead. From what I saw, it looked like they simply bit, scratched, and clawed until only one was left standing." Kamil related what he'd seen in the lab, and finished with "And what's this about your being on medical leave?"

"Just a misunderstanding, that's all," Thorne said, brushing away Kamil's last question. "Every rat? Every last one of them?"

Kamil nodded.

"Shit."

"What are we going to do?" Kamil asked.

Thorne swore. "Gillespie's barred me from the hospital. Okay, technically I'm on medical leave, recovering from stress and jet lag, but he's made it clear that he doesn't think I'm in any condition to see patients."

"Are you?"

"A little tired, maybe. That's all."

"Not an excuse in my book. I wouldn't have thought it was in Gillespie's, either. So why are you *really* off the rotation?"

Thorne considered the question. At the moment, all he had was something that he couldn't even prove as a decent correlation, much less a cause and effect relationship. And did that really relate to his status with Gillespie, anyway? His chief's decision was predicated on

Boothby's version of events that night in Korea, not on the connection Thorne had not yet discussed with anyone.

Did he have any right to draw Kamil into this? Probably not, particularly not after what his friend had already been through this month. Kamil's own standing at the Murphy was none too strong right now. According to Patterson, who had eased up his schedule, Kamil was still moody and occasionally prone to temper tantrums in surgery, although not to the degree the day she'd ordered him out.

Still, it involved Kamil's uncle. And if the positions had been reversed, Thorne was damned sure he'd want to know.

"You may think I'm nuts," Thorne said finally. "But what you saw in the lab . . . well, it worries the hell out of me. Here's why." Briefly, he laid out the connections between Boothby, Kamil's uncle, and the Murphy, concluding with his attempt to get more information on Oswald. "Now do *you* think I ought to be on medical leave?"

Thorne could see the doubt in Kamil's eyes. "I don't know. It's a long reach to tie in my uncle," Kamil's voice hitched slightly, "and what happened to the Murphy. And the rats . . . I don't know what to think. You don't have any evidence that Anaex was used on Boothby or my uncle, do you?"

"No. Based on what Gillespie said, Prime Minister Danoff was the first one."

"And you didn't think that was odd? That he'd have you handle the first actual use of it, instead of doing it himself?"

"Not at the time." That wasn't entirely true, though. Thorne *had* wondered for a moment, but had easily chosen the more flattering interpretation of Gillespie's action. That Gillespie trusted him, believed in his skill as an anesthesiologist. "In retrospect, though, yes, it was odd. If I'd been Gillespie, I'd have been there myself."

"Me, too. Tell me, Scoot. What do you have in writing that shows Gillespie told you to use Anaex on Danoff?"

"Nothing. It wasn't necessary, and there wasn't time. Danoff came in with a hot appendix that got bad fast. I called Gillespie, gave him a rundown on the facts, and he told me to go ahead. You know how it is when it's two o'clock in the morning and you're . . ." Thorne's voice trailed off as he realized just what Kamil was implying. "Nothing. Jesus."

Kamil nodded. "And now Gillespie's suspended you. Do you know how that's going to look to a review board? You can tell them all you want that it was because of Korea, but nobody's going to believe it. Not if you used Anaex on Danoff outside of protocol."

Thorne's world shivered, then started to collapse around him. "Oh, man." He swore softly under his breath. "I'm screwed. And if I'm right, nobody's going to believe that, either."

"You have to start covering your ass right now. Those rats—Scoot, Lanelli probably just tossed them in the Dumpster. He'd take the easiest way out to get rid of them, you know what he's like. And since there was no overt evidence of contagious disease, technically he'd be in the clear."

"But where? How many Dumpsters are there, anyway? Do you know what it'll be like trying to find them?"

"Easier than finding another position if the professional review board fires you. Look, I'm tied up here until my shift's over." Kamil sounded apologetic, but convinced. "Go find them, Scoot. Dig out some bodies and wrap them up in plastic bags and put them in your freezer. That way you've got a chance to get some independent testing done on them, get some evidence to support your claims."

"He could have taken them down to the incinerator." The hospital maintained its own facility for disposing of biohazards.

"And risked somebody asking questions? If he did that, you're screwed anyway, though."

"Lanelli's lazy," Thorne said. "He'd take the easiest way out, wouldn't he?"

Kamil nodded. "For your sake, I'm counting on it. Otherwise, the rats aren't the only ones that are dead meat."

Thorne cornered the ER charge nurse and asked, "You got any of those plastic bags around? You know, the ones you use for biohazards?"

She nodded and handed him a single, sealable bag.

"A couple more."

"You run out of sandwich bags at home?" she joked. She dug down into a dispenser and withdrew an entire handful of the slick, clear envelopes. "Here, take enough for a week."

"Want to share my dinner with me?"

She shook her head. "Not if you're keeping it in those.

Six Dumpsters. Thorne stared at them, trying to decide which one Lanelli most likely had used if he had in fact been dumping rats into the Dumpster. He let it frustrate him for a few moments longer, then settled on the obvious. Lanelli would have gone for the closest one. That would have probably been full this late in the day, so Lanelli would have gone to the next—and the next and the next and the next. It was entirely possible that the rats weren't even all in the same Dumpster, that the garbage bags necessary to contain that many dead bodies would be spread out over all five Dumpsters. That thought alone made Thorne's task seem virtually Herculean.

But wait a minute. He didn't need to recover all the rat carcasses. He didn't have the means to store them even if he did. No, all he was looking for was a sample. And from what Kamil had told him about the carnage, all of the lab rats suffered from the same problem.

Two Dumpsters, he decided. He selected the third and fourth in the line, popped the top on the fourth, and was gratified to see that it was only half full. He glanced up at the hospital. If Lanelli were still working, he might even be on his way out to dump another load of rats. Thorne would have to keep a close eye on the door, and take cover at the first sign of someone heading for the Dumpster.

Thorne mounted the rickety metal steps stationed next to the Dumpster, and peered down into the interior. It was a froth of food debris, industrial-strength green plastic garbage bags and the flimsier white ones used in offices. Those he could eliminate immediately.

He pulled out his pocketknife and made a small slit in the nearest green bag. Garbage, nothing more. The task began to look less daunting as he realized that he would need only a small incision in each bag to determine the contents. He doubted that Lanelli would have mixed the rats in with any other trash or undertaken any elaborate subterfuge to disguise the contents of his mass grave. He started sorting through the trash.

What had seemed like a good idea two hours ago was now sheer lunacy. How could he ever scrub for surgery again, knowing where his hands had been? Thorne eyed the last Dumpster with disgust. All of his theories had been for naught. If Lanelli had discarded the rats into the hospital's Dumpster, they had to be either there or in the very first one, the one Thorne had reasoned would be full.

His hands and clothes reeked of everything from remnants from the kitchen to filth the origins of which he didn't even want to imagine. Thank God the hospital was stringent on enforcing biohazard protocols and there had been no needles or sharp objects that had been exposed to body fluids in these Dumpsters. He shuddered to think what one mistake in disposing of a hypodermic needle could have done to him.

He hauled himself up the four steps to the Dumpster, realizing that he should have started his survey of the trash with a quick look at each of them.

As he opened the last Dumpster, his suspicions were confirmed. Seventeen garbage bags were piled along the bottom. Similar in size and shape. After going through four Dumpsters, Thorne knew just how odd that was.

He sighed and lowered himself into the Dumpster. The bags squished meatily under his running shoes, and he mentally added the Nikes to his list of items that would have to be replaced. Thorne leaned over and slit open the first bag with his knife.

Bingo. And it would have to be the last one.

He examined his surgical gloves carefully, checking to see that there were no rips or tears in them. He had already gone through three pairs and had thanked the foresight that had caused him to stick another couple pairs into his pocket. There was no way that he wanted to go back into the hospital to ask for more gloves, not after even his first foray into the Dumpsters.

He slipped fresh gloves on and gingerly pulled away a few rat carcasses. Lanelli must have been as methodical in sorting the bodies into garbage bags as he had been in aligning them on the table. This one consisted of almost complete carcasses.

He filled up six steri-bags, each holding two rat bodies. Then he slipped all six into a larger bag he'd brought along just in case.

Finally, his task completed, he climbed out of the Dumpster and headed back to his car. He paused at the entrance to the parking lot.

Did he really want to get into his car smelling and reeking like this?

He shook his head. A cab wouldn't be any better. Besides, no self-respecting cabbie would let him in as a fare, not the way he looked. Even hospital ID would not be sufficient to convince him that Thorne was a professional, not a professional bum.

Thorne pulled a towel from the trunk of the Catera and spread it over the driver's seat, hoping to spare it the worst of the stain. Maybe a good detailing would take care of the worst of the smell—maybe. The bag containing the rat carcasses he placed in the trunk, double wrapping it in a sheet of plastic he had back there.

He'd given the rat bodies a cursory once-over as he'd stuffed them into the bags, nothing particularly rigorous, but enough to establish that these were indeed the correct rats. Already he knew one thing that puzzled him. Many of the rats had large amounts of fur torn from their bodies, exposing broad expanses of skin. Over most of them, there was an ugly, mottled rash. At first he'd thought it had been trauma related to the forcible removal of the hair, but now it struck him that it was probably more than that. Much more, if it was linked to Anaex.

EIGHTEEN

General Boothby pressed his hands tightly together in front of him and stared at the speakerphone. In the old days, he would never have left a friend on speakerphone, and most particularly not one who happened to be chairman of the Joint Chiefs of Staff.

But these days were different, too different. It was odd that nobody noticed it except he.

"Thurmond, you've got to keep a lid on this for a few more days." The voice that came out of the speakerphone, though scratchy, was plain and firm. "You can't escalate now, not now. The media is already blowing your limited authority recall way out of proportion. I'm spending half my time responding to inquiries about the situation over there, not to mention fielding calls from the White House."

"I hear what you're saying," the general responded calmly. "But you're not in my shoes, Jerry. You don't know what's going on over here."

"Oh, but indeed I do."

The general fell silent for a moment, letting the comment lie in the dead air between them. Just how much did General Huels know? And why was that oddly accusatory note in his voice?

"Thurm? You still there?"

The general cleared his throat. "Of course, sir," he said calmly. "Just thinking over what you said."

"Do more than think."

Now it was unmistakable, the threat conveyed by a man he'd thought was a friend. Boothby interlaced his fingers, digging the nails deep into the flesh on the back of each hand, letting the pain distract him from his irrelevant emotions. Now was the time to play the most delicate game of military cat and mouse, the fine art of appearing to obey orders—or at least avoiding having a superior give them—while doing exactly as one wanted.

"I'm doing all I can to stabilize things here," Boothby began carefully, "but the number of incidents are increasing every day. My people are under almost constant harassment from snipers."

"That's not the way I hear it."

"That's the way it is," Boothby snapped, a little bit more sharply than he'd intended. He drew a deep, shuddering breath, fighting off the effects of adrenaline on his system. This was not the time to be impetuous, to give in to the impulse to smash and destroy the man on the other end of the line. It called for a methodical execution of the plan he'd devised, a textbook example of the fine art of senior officers arguing without ever openly disagreeing.

"Look, I can't put every detail in the message traffic," he started again, striving for reasonability. "Even the classified traffic breaks out to the media eventually. You think you've got problems now, you know what would happen then. And just what do you think the American public is going to say when they hear about the constant harassment of our troops here? Harassment, hell. They're trying to kill us."

"There's no reason for the situation to be deteriorating," the voice fretted. "No reason at all. Every indication is that the North Koreans should be too preoccupied with feeding their own population to move into a more aggressive military stance. That's what's got us all worried."

"And me as well," Boothby said, reinforcing the train of thought. "But just what am I supposed to do, let them shoot at us and not take action? How long until the major assault and my people are unprepared to deal with it? Just how much damage do I have to let the North Koreans inflict before I'm allowed to strike back? You know that the right to act in self-defense is not only a right, it's a duty as well. And one that I have to exercise as the general on the scene, on behalf of my troops. I need those medical units, Jerry. I need them for my people. And before long, unless things change, I'm going to need combat troops as well, so we need to prepare the White House for that possibility as well." He waited for two beats, then played his final card. "What will happen if we start taking heavy casualties and word gets out that the chairman of the Joint Chiefs of Staff told me to cool it?"

A long silence, then, "I'm going to want you back here, Thurm. At least long enough for a complete debriefing for my people, and probably for the White House as well. When can you leave?"

"Just a few days, sir. Let things stabilize a little, then I can leave."

"A few days, then. And be prepared, Thurm. I'm not sold yet, and this is going to have to go all the way up."

Boothby clicked off the speakerphone, luxuriating in the thrill of anticipation coursing its way up his spine. General Huels might not like it, but Boothby had the feeling his boss understood the situation. Smart, not to go into details on the phone, even on the most secure line the military possessed. There was no telling who was listening. The Koreans, the Russians, maybe even the Secret Service.

Soon—very soon.

He stared down at his hands, marveling how the opportunity was so close to falling into them. His short-clipped nails had gouged deep furrows in the flesh. So much for the legendary calm he was supposed to have. He snorted, wondering if any of his subordinates or superiors ever knew just exactly how much this command cost him.

And not just in terms of his family, either. He considered Alicia a threat for a brief instant, then dismissed it. More of his life had been spent in the Army than had been spent as either father or husband.

The Army—for a moment he longed for the Army as he'd known it in West Point, the Army that had been such a mainstay of the history of the United States. In modern times, it had been crippled by a series of incompetent and cowardly commanders in chief. That young officer's story about the theft of JFK's brain came back to mind. A good thing that had been, too. JFK was no General William Tecumseh Sherman.

General Sherman. Now there was a man an Army general could admire, an officer who understood the politics of siege, who knew that the fighting spirit of the South would keep both parts of the country at war for decades unless he could bring the war to the people. Historians had had it all wrong when they talked about Sherman's brutality and the atrocities he had supposedly committed on his march through Atlanta.

No, General Sherman understood war, that it was not for weaklings or those whose minds were clouded with civilized considerations. War demanded the utmost in loyalty and fidelity, marching forward with only one goal in mind: the complete and utter destruction of opposing forces. Razing fields and buildings and leveling the South to ground masonry, shattered columns, and dirt had been neither an act of cruelty nor unwarranted aggression. Instead, it had been the only way to stop the war. To bring it home to the people, and to end it.

General Sherman would have known how to cope with the Koreans. Boothby felt sure that the general would have understood the constraints under which he himself operated, would have applauded the single-mindedness that Boothby brought to this operation.

A small, niggling doubt rose in the back of Boothby's mind. The doctor—Thorne, Dr. Christopher Thorne. A flash of rage surged through him. General Sherman had been allowed to practice their profession as it was meant to be waged, to do those acts that were necessary in the conduct of complete war.

Had Dr. Christopher Thorne appeared one day as a member of

General Sherman's staff, Boothby felt certain the young anesthesiologist would not have survived one week. Nor would General Sherman have been as lenient as Boothby himself had been. No, at the first sign of cowardice, at the first refusal to take up arms, General Sherman would have solved the problem of Christopher Thorne with a bullet in the brain.

A vague nostalgia swept over him. To hell with Congress and those subcommittees constantly gnawing at his ankles, and the political animals that now inhabited the Joint Chiefs of Staff. To the Congressmen, war was a social exercise, the flexing of political muscle. Many of them had never served in the military, and were more interested in the cut of an officer's uniform, the congenial and affable face he could put on for reporters, his performance during the myriad social events required of senior military officers, than they were in his dedication to the profession of arms. The JCS had had little success in educating them in reality.

Thorne—and Carter. Had he imagined it? He shook his head, trying to recall the details of his last conversation with Carter. Even through the haze of morphine, Carter had appeared to understand what Boothby had told him. Understood, and agreed. All that was needed was one phone call now with the code word, the one he'd gone over and over with Carter before putting him on the medical evacuation flight.

Benedict Arnold.

Would it work? He considered the phone for a minute, stretched his hand down and let his fingers rest lightly on the black cold surface. There was only one way to find out—as there was in war. Another phrase flitted through his mind, one that brought a grim smile of amusement. The phrase *surgical strike* was about to take on a whole new meaning for Dr. Christopher Thorne.

Weakling. You whining weakling. The words slid into his mind as though whispered from behind him, insinuating themselves into his thoughts as a second voice. It startled him for a moment, then he relaxed as the hard, jarring northern accent rang in his ears. He felt a moment of shame. General Sherman was right—hesitation kills more soldiers than enemy fire.

He picked up the phone and waited for his aide to answer. "I want to talk to Sergeant Carter. Find him." He replaced the phone softly in its cradle and waited.

War was hell. Sherman, Patton, all the great generals, they understood that. But only Brigadier General Thurmond S. Boothby knew just how personal that hell could be.

After two days in the loony ward, Carter had finally gotten himself under control. Peaceful, that was the password. It'd earned him a ticket back into the general population.

"You've got some important friends," the security guard said as he replaced the telephone in its cradle. He waited until the LCD display indicated that the call was terminated, then rotated and slowly withdrew the STU-3 crypto key from its slot on the side of the secure telephone. "Not often we have SCI calls coming into the surgical ward," he continued, referring to the specially compartmented information circuits that were the military's most highly secure and encrypted telephone lines.

Carter shrugged. The motion twisted his shoulder. His arm was strapped into a splint that eliminated any arm movement and held his right hand firmly against his left shoulder. Dr. Patterson had assured him it was necessary for healing to have complete immobility, but he wasn't so certain he believed her.

Maybe there was another reason.

The surgeon knew this was his good hand, maybe he hadn't been injured at all. Through a postanesthetic morphine cloud, he had speculated on the possibility that the general had somehow betrayed him, had ordered the Murphy surgical center to operate on a perfectly healthy arm and completely disable him.

Crippled. The word sent a cold shudder of dread through him. Well, he was almost as good with a knife in his left hand as he was with his right—almost. He had proved that to the general on more than one occasion.

The army didn't need crippled killers. Up until the moment of the phone call, until he'd heard General Boothby's reassuring commanding voice on the other end, he'd almost convinced himself that there'd been nothing wrong with his shoulder, that Boothby had found a way to take him permanently out of action.

He tried to flex the muscles in his shoulder again, felt the sluggish response, the hard deep ache of severed tissues and nerve endings and the curious numbness just above his elbow. They'd cut on him, no doubt about that.

He considered the general's words for a moment. The details of his transport from Korea were coming back to him now, the memories keyed by the one phrase the general had drummed into his head: Benedict Arnold.

"So what did the general say?" the security guard asked as he resumed his seat in the corner of the tastefully furnished hospital room. "Now that's a hell of a general—he calls to check up on you."

"I want to talk to my doctor," Carter said, ignoring the questions posed to him. "That woman, what was her name? Find her."

Dr. Patterson stood at the entrance to the room and paused before she shoved open the heavy door. There was something about Sergeant Carter that bothered her, bothered her more than it had with any other patient. Carter seemed to have an unusually high tolerance for pain. Most patients who'd had his surgery would have been begging for Demerol.

But Nigel Carter actively resisted the pain medication, even to the point of becoming combative with the night nurse who'd shown up for his evening dose. She'd explained to him several times that pain interfered with his recovery, that there was nothing weak or sinful about using drugs when medically required, but Carter appeared not even to hear her. She'd finally had to insist, threatening to have the orderlies hold him down to administer the medication. His constant fidgeting, his startled reaction to even the most common of hospital sounds was interfering with the recovery. It was more a matter of sound medical practice than consideration for patient comfort.

Maybe she shouldn't have agreed to his transfer off the psych ward. But he'd seemed so rational, so completely over what manic anger had possessed him immediately after admission.

And now he was asking to see her. That, more than anything worried her.

"You asked me how I got hurt." Carter said the words slowly, without emotional inflection. "I got shot."

She nodded. "I figured that after I removed two bullet fragments from your rotator cuff."

He gazed up at her, sullen and close-faced. "You don't know all of it. You don't know anything."

"What do you mean?"

"It wasn't the North Koreans. It was that doctor—the one who was over there. He works here."

"Dr. Thorne?" Patterson frowned, then hastily smoothed her face into a blank mask of professionalism. "That's who you mean, right?"

Carter nodded. "We was out on patrol. He went crazy and shot me. That's why General Boothby sent him home. Not that other story."

"That's kind of hard to believe," Patterson said carefully.

"You calling me a liar?" A new animation flooded Carter's face. "The last bitch that done that's dead now."

Patterson took an instinctive step back from the foot of the bed and glanced at the security man in the corner. The man was paying attention, but still seated comfortably in his chair. Every instinct warned her that Carter was on the verge of an explosive reaction to her words.

"No more medicine," Carter said finally, and she saw in his eyes that he was gratified by her reaction. That sparked a new flare of anger in her gut.

"You'll take what medication I order for you," she said firmly. "If not, we've got bigger men than you around here."

Carter laughed, an ugly, intimate sound. "You just tell 'em, Doc. Thorne, that chickenshit yellow-streaked bastard shouldn't have been over there. Couldn't have shot the enemy—had to shoot one of his own men."

"I need to look at that wound," Patterson said finally.

"You gonna tell them? About Thorne?"

She nodded. "Now let me look at that incision."

Finally, the security man reacted. "You better do what she wants,

Sergeant," he said quietly. There was no mistaking the threat in his voice.

Carter subsided into a surly, angry expression. "Go ahead."

Patterson approached with more confidence than she actually felt. "Keep your hand resting on the opposite shoulder," she ordered. She peeled back the surgical tape, ashamed that she hoped he would flinch at the minor discomfort. He didn't—absolutely no reaction. She peeled back the gauze, studied the incision in his shoulder. There was no redness or swelling. She pressed gently on the edges, and noted the absence of any exudant. "Any pain?" she asked, knowing that there had to be.

Carter shook his head solemnly. "I'm fine. Send me back to Korea."

"Not just yet, I think," she said, carefully redressing the wound. "You've got some fairly extensive damage there. You'll need three to four weeks for the incision to heal up well, then at least two months of physical therapy to get a full range of motion back in your shoulder. With a little luck, you'll have no residual restrictive motion."

"I'm not crippled?" The question was oddly plaintive, the first sign of humanity she'd seen in this unusual patient. "I'll be okay?" She nodded. "If you do what we say. And that includes taking the pain medication I've ordered. I've already told you that pain interferes with your recovery."

"I don't suppose there's any other reason you want me drugged," Carter said. "Is there?"

She stared at him. "What reason could there possibly be?"

Carter appeared to relax. He sunk down lower in the bed and the tension seemed to ease out of his body. "No reason. None at all."

Out in the passageway, Patterson leaned against the fabric-covered wall and let out a deep, shaky breath. She'd made progress in her doctor-patient relationship, at least she thought so.

And Thorne. Just what the hell had Carter meant? She shook her head angrily, annoyed with being drawn into the intricacies of the investigation that would surely follow. It was outrageous, impossible, and completely and totally false, but she had to report it. The regulations at Murphy relating to statements by patients were clear on that.

She glanced at her watch—two hours until she was due in surgery again. She sighed and headed for the security office. Best to get this out of the way now before she got caught up in the rest of her daily routine.

Could she tell Thorne about it? Ask him, get some explanation for Carter's bizarre allegations?

She knew the answer immediately. No.

Within moments of making her statement to security, Thorne's privileges at Murphy would be suspended. There would be a complete investigation, both by the hospital and by the military as well, she suspected. The lawyers would have her ass if she so much as forewarned him about the maelstrom that was about to descend on him.

Choices, always choices. And none of them were ever easy.

With the relationship, they had carefully sidestepped around the proprieties expected between senior surgeons and research fellowships. Compartmentalization, that was the key. If she asked him now, insisted on answers as was her right, whatever they had was over. Irrevocably.

Now, Carter had taken away any choices she had. His allegations might be drug-induced, the ranting of an unstable mind, but he was still her patient. She had to take action—had to, or risked every bit of respect she'd wrung out of the male-dominated world of surgeons.

She walked down the hallway and into the elevator, dreading the next thirty minutes. She would do everything she could to help Thorne, indeed anything that would not compromise her duty to her patient. Including, if necessary, calling her uncle, Jerry Huels.

Thorne was just slamming the Catera's trunk shut when he heard someone approaching. "Doctor Thorne?" Thorne turned to see the hospital's chief of security.

"Yes?" Thorne had met the man on three occasions, two of which had had to do with a delay in Thorne's security clearance. Wallinger, that was the man's name, Thorne recalled.

Tom Wallinger was a large, beefy man. He looked like what he was, a retired cop who'd started out as part of the hospital's security force and worked his way up to commanding an entire department. It was an important job at Murphy, more so than at other facilities, given the nature of Murphy's patients. Wallinger was involved in every major decision involving the hospital, from construction of new physical plants to how the patients were staged among the various floors. His province included not only physical security but avoiding some of the nastier political problems that could arise from berthing a high-ranking Israeli next to a military official from an Islamic country.

"I need to speak with you for a moment, if I may." Wallinger's voice made it clear that it was an order, not a request.

Thorne suppressed a surge of irritation "Can't it wait? I was just headed home."

Wallinger shook his head slowly. "I'm afraid it can't."

Thorne sighed heavily. "I suppose it's about Hannah Greener's husband?" he said, wondering how the ER had gotten word to the head of security so quickly. He wouldn't normally have thought Wallinger would personally show up to investigate a battered spouse case, and the man rose slightly in his estimation.

"I'm not here about your patient," Wallinger said levelly. "I need to talk to you about Nigel Carter."

What Nigel Carter knew about him, Thorne wanted to forget. To forget, and push back into the furthest reaches of his being where it would never, ever surface. If that were possible. Remembering the difference between Kamil's focus on Hannah Greener and his own anger at her husband, he wondered whether it was ever possible.

"He's not my patient," Thorne said finally, suddenly aware of how odd his silence must have seemed. "I ran into him in Korea, but aside from that . . ." He shrugged, wondering just where this conversation was going.

"That's not what Carter says," Wallinger said, a note of steel creeping into his voice. "Dr. Thorne, I'm afraid I'm going to have to ask you to come with me."

"Look, I don't know anything about his case. Nothing at all. And frankly, I don't want to."

Wallinger seemed to grow extremely still. "And why don't you? Want to know, I mean." he asked, his voice a soft, neutral tone. "I would think you'd be interested. After all, you went out on patrol with him." Wallinger drew back slightly, disgust dawning on his face. "What the hell's that smell?"

The patrol—damn it, would it haunt him forever? He hadn't asked to go there, hadn't asked to be in Korea at all. Participating in a midnight raid across the DMZ had been the last thing on his mind— and the last thing he should have been doing as a physician.

"The lab—formaldehyde, probably," Thorne said immediately, hoping Wallinger would let the issue of the stench pass. "About Korea—I didn't have any choice in the matter."

Wallinger's eyes took on a wary look. "No choice? How about if I give you the choice of giving me permission to search your car or waiting while I call in the local authorities?"

"Go fuck yourself." Thorne reached for his car door handle.

Two other security guards appeared on either side of him. One grabbed his right arm, forcing it behind his back, and Thorne felt a cold circle of metal snap around his wrist. He exploded, thrashing and turning away from the man in an effort to pull free, but a third set of hands joined the two guards on either side of him. Very quickly, his left wrist was forced into the handcuffs.

"Why? What is the meaning of this?" Thorne protested. "You can't just—"

"Open your trunk."

"You can't—" Thorne tried again.

"I can. I tried to do this politely, but you should read the sign next to the parking lot entrance more carefully, Doc. You consent to a search of your car and your person every time you drive onto the grounds. Now open it."

The two security guards donned heavy plastic gloves and then gingerly tore open the sack. The stench intensified. One gagged and stepped back. "Jesus, boss, it's—oh God." He turned away and retched.

Wallinger stepped forward to examine the contents himself. "Formaldehyde, huh? Too little too late, I'd guess." He turned to the remaining guard. "Bag it and label it. Establish a chain of custody. Then check out the rest of this stuff."

Thorne stood near the driver's side fuming, watching as they rummaged through the immaculate arrangement of tools, spare tire, and emergency medical kit. As one of them opened his medical bag and began pawing through it, he could stand it no longer.

"There are no drugs in there, if that's what you're looking for," he snapped.

One of the security guards glanced up at him and looked over at Wallinger. The chief of security stepped forward. "I don't need to tell you how serious this is. We were looking for you, and one of the nurses said he'd seen you go out back. We watched you go through the Dumpster—even absent your consent, that gives me probable cause to look for anything else you may have decided to misappropriate."

"I didn't misappropriate them," Thorne shouted. "They were in the Dumpster, damn it. They were garbage!"

Wallinger shook his head slowly. "You want to talk to an attorney, go ahead. But I can tell you what he'll say—that you're in deep shit, Doc." Wallinger let the crudity of the last words sink in before turning back to the car.

"Do you want us to pull the passenger compartment panels off?" one of the men asked. Wallinger glanced back at Thorne, his eyes revealing a malicious glint. "Let me think about it," he said slowly. He fell silent for a few moments, his eyes locked on Thorne's. Finally, he shook his head. "No, I don't think so. We've got what we came for."

Thorne darted over to him. "You don't understand," Thorne said, his voice low and urgent. The seriousness of the situation was evidently starting to sink in.

"I understand everything I need to," Wallinger said.

"No, you don't." Thorne gestured back toward the car. "Do you think I would have taken those rats unless I thought there was a damned good reason? Look at that car. Why in the hell would I keep something like that in there unless there were a damned good reason."

Wallinger shrugged. "Who knows why people do things?" he said philosophically.

"There's something very wrong here," Thorne said. Clearly, it would be useless to try to convince Wallinger that he'd had to take the rats, that something was very wrong with Gillespie's lab procedures. "I can't stop you from what you're doing. I know that. But at least refrigerate them. Please, don't take the chance that there's something in those bodies that we might need later. They're evidence, damn it, but not of what you think they are. Please, put them in the freezer as soon as you can."

Wallinger's face was impassive as he listened to Thorne's pleas. "I'll think about it. That's all I can promise you, Doctor, I'll think about it. The Merced County police are on the way over. Unless they let you post bail, you're going to have plenty of time to think about it, too. In jail. And while you're thinking about that, I suggest you come up with an explanation for your behavior in Korea."

NINETEEN

There was a sameness to institutional smells, whether it was the medicinal reek of the surgical center at Murphy, the vaguely disturbing stench of death in the pathology lab, or the overwhelming miasma of too many people packed too closely together under unsanitary conditions that characterized the county jail. Patterson took a deep breath, letting the noxious odor flood her nose and lungs. Like the sickening stench of an infected gut, the quickest way to quit noticing the smell was simply to overwhelm one's senses with it. Even the most horrendous assaults on the olfactory system would quickly fade to background.

The jail. She glanced around the small waiting room again, trying to find any indication that it had been intended for anyone other than criminals. Putrid orange chairs were bolted to a support framework, locked rigidly into a straight row, as though rebuking the overwhelming sense of disorder and chaos that otherwise permeated the jail system. A philodendron in a cheap green pot stood pathetically alone in one corner, dying a slow and lingering death. Whether from neglect or the unhealthy atmosphere it lived in, she couldn't tell,

The jail clerk behind the bars and bulletproof glass was ignoring her. Dr. Patterson had already posted the bail, which had been accepted with some degree of contempt by the clerk, and was now waiting for Thorne's release. When pressed, the jail clerk would only respond that it would be a while.

Thirty minutes constituted a while, so far. She scuffed uneasily at the swirls of dirt, tracing out the last effort to mop the linoleum floor, wishing she'd had the foresight to bring something to read. How was she to know? It wasn't every day that she was called on to bail a fellow doctor out of jail.

Finally, she heard the harsh, metallic grinding of a motor in poor repair. She stood and walked to one corner of the room where she could peer around an open archway to the small, barred hallway that connected the waiting room to the rest of the jail.

At the far end of the hallway, the door retracted slowly into the wall. Thorne stepped into view, then into the hallway, the sallyport, which was barred at either end. He waited, staring down at the ground, as the bars clanged shut behind him. Only when a red light had illuminated on the wall, indicating that the interior gate was firmly secured, did the bars opening the sallyport to the waiting area start to move.

"Scoot?" she asked uncertainly. He was still, so still, his eyes refusing to meet hers as he stepped into the waiting room. He walked over to her, stood in front of her as though not really understanding that he was now free.

"Are you okay?" she tried again. She reached out and touched his arm above the elbow, then shook him lightly. "Come on, let's go."

He nodded. "I'm sorry I had to call you. Kamil is still on shift at the ER, and . . . well, I didn't know who else would get me out. I'll pay you back, I promise."

As they stepped out onto the city sidewalk, Patterson was aware of the miasma of the jail still clinging to him, along with a more noxious stench. It had penetrated his clothes, nestled its foul molecules deep in his lungs. She wondered how long it would take to dissipate.

"My car is over here," she said, motioning to the paid parking lot across the street. "Come on, you need to shower, probably something to eat. Are you hungry?"

"No. Not hungry." Thorne's voice seemed to come from deep in his belly, a low growl at odds with the normally urbane and sophisticated tones she associated with him. This, more than his earlier unresponsiveness, worried her.

"Well, a shower at least," she said, trying for a light tone. "You smell like you're still in med school," she said, referring to the stench of formaldehyde and decomposition that invariably had permeated their clothes during the first year.

Thorne followed her to the car and climbed into the passenger seat. Finally, he turned to her and said, "I appreciate your doing this. I'm sorry to involve you, I just didn't know who else to call. Kamil—they were after him as they were taking me away. I couldn't . . ." The sudden rush of words tapered off, and Thorne seemed about to lapse back into the earlier immobility that characterized him.

"Not a problem," she said in an effort to keep the conversation going. "You'd do the same for me, I know."

Thorne laughed harshly. The noise startled her.

"You'd never be in this position," he said softly. "You're not that kind of person."

"What kind of person?" she asked.

Thorne shook his head, and withdrew into himself.

"What is this all about, anyway?" she asked, because she knew she was expected to. The sick, twisting feeling in her gut notwithstanding, she had to continue the pretense that she knew nothing about it. "Drunk driving or something?"

Thorne stared straight ahead. "No. Not that at all. I wish it were that easy."

"If you don't want to talk about it, that's all right," she said gently. A moment of relief, a wild hope that he would indeed not want to talk about it. Sooner or later he would know, although Wallinger had assured her that her statement was entirely privileged and confidential. But with criminal charges pending, no doubt sooner or later he would be told.

"Nigel Carter," he said finally. "He told someone that I shot him in Korea."

"Carter is two days postop," Debbie said. "He's still on the pain medication—there's no telling what he'd say."

Not on that much pain medication, one part of her mind said

acerbically. He was refusing it—you forced him on it. When he talked to you, he was completely lucid. If crazy.

He turned to her, his face haggard and drawn. To her relief, he said, "I don't want to talk about it. Not Carter. Not Korea. Not now."

Thorne leaned back and let the steaming hot water pound into the top of his head. It was so hot that the steam and water mist mixed together to create a steam-room-like environment inside the large, immaculate shower enclosure. Water beaded on the pristine white tile, collected in the spotless soap dish. He'd washed his hair three times and could still smell the jail.

He reached out and switched the water to cold, gasping as the icy torrent battered against his skin. Maybe the constricting reaction of his pores would force even more of the residue out of his skin.

He groped for the towel he had hung over the corner of the shower compartment, his eyes burning slightly from the water in them. His hand met only cold glass. He cracked one eye open and saw the towel had fallen down on the floor outside the shower compartment. With the water still on, he cracked the door open slightly and reached out for it. As water dribbled out of his ears, he overheard Debbie's voice.

Who was she talking to? An odd, niggling suspicion started at the base of his spine. She'd insisted he get in the shower immediately, claiming that the smell of the jail was just overwhelming, voicing some concerns about what sort of bacteria and germs he'd picked up while in custody.

He stepped quietly out of the shower, reached over and picked up the towel, and squeezed the remaining water out of his ears. He could hear clearly now, the low urgent tones of her voice. Who was she talking to?

"I don't know, Uncle Jerry," he heard her say. "But is there anything you can do? Can you find out?"

Silence. She was on the telephone then, not talking to someone in person. Thorne stepped closer to the bathroom door, leaving the running water on as a cover. He could hear more clearly now.

"I had to do it," he heard Debbie say, and was oddly gratified by the keen note of regret in her voice. "He was my patient, Uncle Jerry. My patient."

Carter. Of course, Debbie would have been the one to repair his shoulder. A cold chill, not entirely from the icy shower, invaded his body. Debbie and who else? Had Kamil assisted? Who had done the anesthesia? Of course Wallinger would have talked to them about Carter's allegations.

No, the final piece fell into place in his mind. Wallinger hadn't sought them out, Debbie had sought him.

"I don't know how long I can keep him here," she said finally, after an evidently lengthy speech from the person on the other end of the line. "Listen, he's beat—he just got out of that hellhole."

Angered now beyond all reason, Thorne reached into the shower and shut off the water. He picked up his clothes, and ignored the jailhouse odor as he quickly pulled them on. Dressed, he pulled open the bathroom door.

Debbie Patterson was sitting on the edge of the bed, holding the phone receiver in her hand. She looked up him, her eyes deeply troubled.

"I'm leaving," Thorne said. "And I'm sorry to have bothered you. Don't worry, except for the operating room and the hospital, I'm out of your life for good."

He walked quickly to the front door of the house and left, willing himself to ignore Debbie's protests.

"The doc said put them in the refrigerator," the taller of the two security guards said as he handed the plastic bag to Wallinger. The inside of the bags were coated with a thin slime of clear fluid and blood. Suspended inside them and adhering to the walls of the bags were oddly nauseating bits and pieces of rat carcass. Grayish purple entrails spilled from the gaping slash in its gut. The rat's eyes were immobile in death, staring dully ahead. A thin film already coated one eye, and the other was partially deflated from trauma. Oddly enough, the tail was completely unmarked. It coiled gracefully in a corner of the plastic bag, the one piece of its body that might still room to be alive.

"Some messed-up little rodents, aren't they?" Wallinger remarked as he studied the bodies. He prodded gingerly at the side of the plastic bag. "The doc said the rats fighting with each other did this. Looks like this might have been one of the stronger ones. Except for the belly wound, it's mostly missing a lot of hair."

The rat's carcass was oddly mottled with patches of bare skin. Evidently the result of another rat barely missing a death grip on its spine. Thin, delicate skin was reddened and spattered with blood from the gut wound. Through the plastic, Wallinger swiped at one bare patch of skin.

"It looks like its got measles," one of the security men said, bending over to study the anomaly that had caught his boss's interest.

Wallinger moved that bag under a bright study light and examined it more carefully. Assuming that rat skin reacted anything like a human scalp to pulling, there was damage he could not account for. The other man had been right—it did look like measles of some sort. Apart from the reddened hair follicles, huge eruptions cratered the skin, black and pustulant in spots but mostly just an angry red of infection.

"Jesus," the other man said softly. "I had an uncle who had shingles once on his back. It looked like that. I didn't know rats got it."

Wallinger glanced up at him. "How the hell should I know what kind of skin diseases rats get? I know the cause of death, not that I give a damn. It's just a fucking rat."

"Well." The other man shrugged, in acknowledgment of the dismissal. "Guess I'll be getting back on rounds."

Wallinger nodded. He waited until the man left and then began studying the rat again. There was something odd about it, even apart from the absolute savagery that had gutted the rat and almost severed one leg from the carcass. He prodded it again gently, wondering just why Thorne had stolen mutilated rat carcasses from the Dumpster.

Finally, he reached a decision. The white refrigerator in the evidence locker had a strong padlock on it, and Wallinger had the only key. While he could conceive of no reason to refrigerate the rat, better safe than sorry. Whistling a silent tune, he wrapped the rat bag in another evidence container, labeled it neatly with date, time, and place of seizure, assigned a sequential number, and then tucked it into the freezer compartment. Probably no point in it, but better safe than sorry.

General Thurmond Boothby dismounted from the Jeep and walked toward the fenced barrier separating north from south. Aides and a guard force fluttered around him like moths, pointedly interposing their bodies between his and the fence, hoping to shield him from any incoming fire. Boothby ignored them, pushed them roughly out of the way when they impeded his progress. Their concern, yes, he understood it, appreciated it for what it was, indeed would have done the same thing had he been in their place. Nevertheless it broke his concentration, prevented him from reaching that stage of understanding of the battlefield that Clauswitz called coup d'ouiel. It was an ability that for many years he had assumed other officers had, the capacity to assess land and terrain, the relative positions and strengths of forces, the dynamics and correlation of forces that would soon play out in open warfare. Achieving complete understanding of what was to happen—what could happen, what must happen—required physical presence on the ground, evoking that unique connection between terrain and military mind that gave rise to genius.

He hadn't always thought of it in those terms, not early on, at least. As a lieutenant and later as a junior captain, he'd seen terrain in terms of mere tactical value, more as a series of unending traps that might lead his men into disaster rather than as a broad strategic canvas. His early tours in the Middle East had done little to dissuade him from that concept, since the broad, flat, expansive sand and rock offered little in the way of variance in terrain.

He studied the fence and surrounding trees, lost in his own memories of Germany. That was when it had happened, during one of his tours with the now-greatly reduced American forces stationed there as part of ATO. It was then that he had seen how hills and valleys could pose such enormous tactical implications, had truly felt for the first time the reality of the wars that had been so often waged over that soil. It had stunned him at first, the realization that the dirt upon which his boots then rested was soaked in the blood of men such as himself. Generations and generations of men before him—and women too, he supposed—had fought and died on that terrain, swept through its broad valleys on chariots, motorized vehicles, and later tanks through the fertile plains of Ukraine, had fallen back under fierce attack from the Russians. It was terrain such as this that gave rise to generations of warriors. He supposed that was so even today. The fiercest fighters always came from the mountains, like the Kurds and the Cossacks.

Not so in the Middle East. The flat, featureless sand plains did not breed true men of war. Fortunately for his country, that had been proved many times in the last twenty years.

And Korea, now there was a country with terrain. From the jagged, virtually inaccessible coastline to the broad sweep of mountain ranges, Korea posed a fertile training ground for troops. And now, this time—in this next conflict—the terrain would play again. It was something his naval counterparts could never have understood, none except the submariners he supposed. The submariners and the men and women who hunted them. With the surface navy, aside from the electromagnetic spectrum, the world was simply a flat, blue void, defined only by changes in sea state and weather. No, terrain didn't play for the Navy, not the way it did for the Army and the Marines.

And how would it play this time? He elbowed his way past another soldier to gain a clearer view of the surrounding area. Trees, hills, and mountains—indeed, even the buildings counted as part of the terrain now, since they could be used both as shields and reference points for maneuver units.

"General?" His aide approached, positioned himself a few feet away, and waited for the general's attention.

Boothby turned to him. "Yes?"

The aide held out a field secure radio unit. "The command post, General. There's a telephone call for you."

Boothby swore silently, started to vent his annoyance on his aide, and then dismissed the thought. The man was a good soldier. He would have already checked to make sure that the matter was important enough to require the general's personal attention. He paused for a moment and studied the apprehension on the man's face. Yes, he'd been about to lose his patience, and unjustifiably so. This man deserved better.

"From whom?" Boothby asked finally, now comfortable with his own command of himself. "Did they say?"

"Yes, General. It's General Huels. He said it was urgent."

Again, Boothby suppressed the flare of annoyance. When the chairman of the Joint Chiefs of Staff calls, there is little that an ordinary general can do or say to avoid taking the call. General Huels would accept no excuses—as Boothby would not have, had their situations been reversed.

"All right, let's get back to the command post."

Boothby turned and headed back to the Jeep, then paused and assessed the battlefield once again. He had a sudden, chilling premonition: The next time he saw it, he would be fighting for his life.

"Yes, General, I'm here." Boothby waited while radio operators on both ends of the circuit keyed their equipment up to a higher level of security. The odd, warbling tones of crypto gear being placed on line continued for several moments, then subsided into a soft background crackle of static. "We're secure now, sir."

"Secure and private?" There was no mistaking General Huels's hard Arkansas twang.

Boothby glanced around the room and made a motion with his hand. The other officers and men took in his meaning and filed silently out of the room. "Now we are."

"Good. Let's talk frankly, Thurmond. You didn't quite tell me everything last night, did you? No more games. Just what the hell is going on down there?"

Boothby's mind flitted through the possibilities, assessing the probable impact of his last reports of sniper fire, the strategic implications of the latest satellite imagery. Huels clearly had something specific in his mind, and just as clearly, he was doing a reaction check on his subordinate general. Of all the myriad information fed from Korea to the Joint Chiefs of Staff, what was it that was bothering Huels?

"General, I thought we agreed that I'd get things stabilized here and then brief you in DC," Boothby said carefully. Information, he needed information. Just what had gone wrong since he'd last talked to the chairman?

"This Carter thing," Huels continued, not waiting for Boothby to arrive at a conclusion on his own. "Your sergeant, the one at Murphy."

"Sergeant Nigel Carter?" Boothby asked, his mind racing. Of all the possibilities he had conjured up, the medical status of one lowly sergeant was far down on the list. Indeed, it was not even on the list. "I haven't had a progress report on him in several days."

"Progress, hell," Huels snorted. "Next time, get your doctor to shoot him in the jaw. That way he won't be running off his mouth."

Boothby drew in a huge, shuddering sigh of relief. So it had worked. Sergeant Carter had carried out his last assignment. For a moment Boothby felt a warm rush of love for the other man, the deep appreciation of one soldier for another. "I sent Dr. Thorne home as soon as I found out."

"Don't fuck with me, Thurmond," Huels snapped. "Why the hell wasn't I informed? And what in the hell were you thinking, taking that doctor out on patrol with you? Hell, you shouldn't have been there yourself, not if the situation is as crappy as you lead me to believe."

"Is the general suggesting I hide behind my men?" Boothby asked, his voice carefully respectful but iron hard. What did Huels expect him to do, stay cloistered in his office while the world fell apart around him? No, he conceded reluctantly, Huels was a better officer than that, he knew what had to be done.

"You should have told me, Thurmond. As soon as you knew," Huels continued, ignoring the question. "Damn it, was it an accident? Or did he do it on purpose?"

"General, I find it hard to believe that a doctor would shoot an enlisted man on purpose. It was dark, there was a good deal of confusion, and it was Dr. Thorne's first time in the field. He's just a reservist, you know." Boothby played on General Huels's well-known distrust of his reserve forces.

"Which leads me back to my first question: Why was he out there in the first place?"

"He asked to go, damn near insisted," Boothby said. "I let him go because I thought it would be a good idea for him to get a firsthand look at what combat is all about. Obviously I didn't expect a sniper attack."

"So that's your story?" Huels asked. "You came under fire and this Thorne fellow panicked. Is that it?"

"That's all I can substantiate, General," Boothby said. He let the implication hang in the air.

"No games, Thurmond. Have you any basis for suspecting it was something besides an accident?"

"I can't say, General," Boothby answered. "There were a few facts—no, nothing hard I could hang my hat on."

"Quit talking like a lawyer and answer my question," General Huels demanded.

Boothby took a deep breath. This part had to be played carefully, so carefully that Huels would have no idea that he was being manipulated into a grander scheme of things. "There had been a conflict between the sergeant and the doctor earlier on that day," he said carefully, measuring his words and his tone of voice as skillfully as any actor. "Naturally, I backed the doctor—he is an officer, after all. It was just a misunderstanding over weapons safety. The doctor pointed a loaded weapon in Carter's direction. Accidentally, that I'm sure of. The sergeant took offense. He's a good man, Carter, been around for quite a while. Anyway, from what I understand, he called Thorne a few names that the man didn't like."

"Shit." Huels one-word summation of the incident told Boothby he had him exactly where he wanted him. "And the doctor shot him, right?"

"Exactly. So I shipped Carter off to Murphy—on my authorization alone," Boothby continued. "I didn't realize that's where Thorne was from, I just wanted to get Carter somewhere secure so that if he shot off his mouth about the incident it wouldn't make the rounds of the entire Army immediately. I thought I could keep a lid on it."

"Well you didn't," Huels said, a note of disgust in his voice. "Sergeant Carter evidently decided to bare his soul to a pretty young surgeon. The next thing I know, I've got two congressmen calling me

211

asking why our doctors are shooting our soldiers. Talk about your blue on blue in fratricide fiascoes, this takes the cake."

"I'm sorry, sir. You're right, I should have called you immediately. But I thought we had the matter contained."

"Hell. Listen, Thurmond, I'm worried about things over there."

Boothby's antennae were all up now as he noted the change in Huels's voice. "Worried about what?"

"Let me be blunt. I'm concerned about you. Thurmond, this isn't like you. You should've been able to keep the lid on over there. And I know Alicia—"

"My wife has nothing to do with this," Boothby said crisply, calmly. "She's just returned to the States for an extended visit with her parents. Her father has been ill for some years, you know, and it doesn't look like he has much time left. Brett, of course, accompanied her."

"That's not what I hear."

"Beg pardon?"

A long, heavy silence filled the line, seeming to dampen out even the crackle of secure static. Boothby waited.

"Alicia and Gina have been friends for a long time. They've known each other as long as we have, Thurmond." Huels voice took on a gentle note. "Christ, man, why didn't you tell me you were having problems?"

"We're not 'having problems' as you put it, General," Boothby snapped. "And quite frankly, I resent this intrusion into—"

"She filed, Thurmond. Yesterday. She called Gina right after it. Rather than have it go through base legal, I accepted service of the summons and petition for divorce on your behalf. I thought you might want it that way."

"Divorce?"

"She's filed for divorce," Huels repeated patiently.

"But—why would she—" For a moment Boothby floundered. His world, the one he'd spent decades in the Army creating, wavered and threatened to crumble around him. "She can't—I mean it's just—"

"Is there anything you want to talk about?" Huels asked. "Thurm, we've known each other for a long time."

Boothby took in a deep breath, forced himself to stop and think calmly. A divorce. No, it was unthinkable. "I don't know what you've been told, General," he said finally. "But Alicia and I are not getting divorced. Never."

"Well." The word hung between them, heavy with regret and sympathy. "So tell me about Korea."

"It's as I said in my last situation report," Boothby said, relieved to be back on familiar ground. "I was out evaluating the DMZ when you called. I can't pin it down, General, but something's coming. A major offensive. I can see it in the way they walk, in the way they stand, in the satellite imagery on the moving of supplies. You can see them massing. The signs are subtle, but I'm certain of it. Sir, we have to be ready for it. Have preparations been made to get the reserve combat units into the NTC pipeline?" Boothby asked, referring to the National Training Center, the facility used for advanced infantry and tank warfare training. "They're rusty, and I'm going to need them."

There was a long, heavy sigh from the other end of the line. "Not possible. Under the current political situation, I'm afraid I can't agree with your assessment. And, yes, I know about the satellite anomalies. And I received an adequate explanation—a peaceable explanation, I may add—for the movement of supplies and troops. Winter is coming, and the North Koreans are still having food shortages—you know that as well as anyone else. The supplies being transported are simply United Nations foodstuffs, not anything with military value."

"Food is of military value. Sir, the first thing a smart tactician thinks about is logistics, how he'll get ammo and food to the front lines. You know what a logistics tail will do to a fighting force. You know. This explanation about humanitarian relief, it's all bullshit. It has to be."

"Our analysts back here don't agree with you," Huels said.

"Then they're wrong."

Another silence, this one just as uncomfortable as the earlier ones. Finally, Huels said, "Thurmond, I want you to come back here. To DC. Now."

"The situation here, General, it's—"

"Don't make me make it an order, Thurmond." General Huels's voice was final.

Boothby repressed an inner shiver of anticipation. Carefully now, oh so very carefully. "My deputy is a competent man, but I'm concerned," he said flatly.

"He can carry on for a while, Thurmond," General Huels answered, his voice again oddly gentle. "I promise you, at the first sign that things are growing worse, I'll have you back on a transport. Look at it this way—maybe you're right and the rest of the analysts are wrong. You're the one on the front lines, after all. Maybe you're seeing something they don't catch. If you are, then I need you to talk to them, convince them, show them what they've missed. If you really think it's that bad, Thurmond, then you need to get back here even more. Help me convince them that the situation truly is heating up."

"Yes, General, I see your point."

"Good. Then you'll be on the next transport back. Make it fast, Thurmond. If you're right—and you can convince the rest of us that you are—then we'll need every second we have to get prepared for this."

And if I'm wrong, you'll move me out of the field of fire and urge me gracefully to retire, save myself the disgrace of being relieved of my command. But you'll make sure it's not just your decision—no, you'll let me brief the president, won't you? You'll do that for me, won't you, Jerry, old buddy? I know you will, because you're that kind of man.

And that's what I'm counting on.

"First available transport, then," Boothby continued out loud, now barely able to contain the satisfaction he felt. "I can be there day after tomorrow."

"Good. I'm looking forward to seeing you," General Huels said.

As he summoned the men back into the radio shack, Boothby's thoughts turned back to the matter of terrain. He smiled lightly, thinking that maybe the Navy had a point after all. Every battlefield had its terrain, whether a matter of elevations and defilades or the delicate strands of political connections and military power that bound two generals together.

TWENTY

Nigel Carter gave the rolling bedside table a hard shove. Just as it started to move, he caught it with his other hand, stopping it before it could smash into the wall. It was important now to maintain the façade of being a docile, compliant patient recovering from battle zone stress and bullet wounds.

He never should have stabbed the orderly. No, that had been foolish, a plan not well thought out.

The general was always going on about planning, planning, planning, until it made Carter want to scream and smash something. Now, confined to his room with guards outside because he'd overreacted—okay, he hadn't *planned*—Carter understood why.

He slid his bedside table aside quietly, let down the bed rail, and slowly swung his feet out over the floor. God, but it hurt. Less now that he'd started taking the painkillers, but still more than he'd anticipated. Enough to slow him down.

But not enough to stop him. It was just pain, nothing more, something he'd felt a thousand—no, a million—times before in the field. Pain was a distracter, an enemy diversion, something to be ignored. It was no more of a hindrance than sleepiness or hunger.

He let his feet rest gently on the cold, linoleum floor for a moment, then transferred his weight from the bed to his feet. He stood slowly, careful not to let the sudden change of position make him dizzy. He'd learned that lesson the hard way, back in the deep forest of Korea. Postural hypertension—he was mildly pleased that he remembered the words the general had taught him.

After he'd repeated the movement a few times, he eased himself back into a sitting position on the bed, confident of his ability to react quickly. As he reached for the call button, a sudden twinge of pain from his surgery reminded him again to be cautious. He pushed the yellow button and waited.

Moments later, a nurse appeared in the doorway. The security guard seated by the entrance stood, and Carter noted the relative size difference between them.

"Is there somewhere around here I can smoke?" he said, keeping his voice soft and mellow. *Make her think the pain medication has kicked in, make her believe I'm harmless.* He waited, saw the nurse and the security guard glance at each other, and stopped a smile before it started.

"You have to go outside. There's a garden just outside that door," the nurse said finally, pointing at the end of the corridor. She glanced uncertainly at the guard. "But I don't know if—"

"Are you sure you feel up to it, buddy?" the guard asked. Carter saw his hand go as if by reflex to his trouser pocket. He'd already known his guard was a smoker. The telltale scent clung to his clothes, filled the room even during his periods of abstinence.

"Yeah, I do." Carter made a lazy motion with his hand. "Been cooped up here for a while now, I think. I'd really like to have me a smoke."

The guard nodded understandingly. He turned to the nurse. "I'll go with him."

She nodded, still unconvinced. "You didn't have any cigarettes in your possessions," she said thoughtfully.

"Must have lost them on the plane," Carter said, "you know the Army." He turned to the guard. "Tell her."

The guard grunted. "Probably would have taken them off him on the aircraft, especially a lighter or matches," he conceded.

"Nurse—" Carter looked down at the floor, willed an ashamed expression onto his face. "Listen, I don't know what to—I want to apologize, okay?" He lifted his face, let his eyes meet hers and invoked every ounce of sincerity he could muster. "The other day—I was way out of line. That fellow, is he okay? Could you tell him—I mean, he won't want to talk to me, but if you could just tell him I'm sorry, I'd surely appreciate it."

The nurse nodded, her expression cleared. "I know him. I can tell him for you."

Carter let his eyes drop back down to the floor. "Don't know what got into me. My mama didn't raise me to be like that. It was kind of scary, you know. Boom. One second I'm in Korea, the next second I wake up here. I thought I was still back in the jungle, that somebody was shooting at me—maybe the pain medication or something."

"It happens." Her doubts evidently assuaged, the nurse turned back to the guard. "Okay, go ahead and let him go down there. But he uses a wheelchair."

The guard nodded. "You stay here for a moment, I'll go get one."

"There's one at the nurses' station," she said. "Just tell them I said it was all right."

As the guard departed, the nurse moved two steps further into the room. "I'll explain it to Walter," she said. "And yes, he's doing all right."

"Thank you. Will you tell him I'm sorry?"

"I will."

The guard reappeared in the doorway with a wheelchair then nudged it past the nurse to the side of his bed. "Can you get into this okay?"

Carter levered himself up off the bed with one hand and eased his way slowly onto his feet. He tottered for a moment, held onto the bed rail with one hand, then made an evident display of mustering his strength. He managed a weak smile. "Sure, I can do it." He sat down in the wheelchair.

"Off we go." The guard gave the wheelchair a shove, maneuvered it around to face outwards, and headed out the door. "You got some smokes on you?"

Carter shook his head. "Like she said."

"Have one." Carter could smell the eager anticipation on the man, the opportunity to take a smoke break himself in the company of his patient. The longing, the eagerness rolled off him in waves, the compelling call of a nicotine addiction.

"Thanks." Carter took the proffered cigarette and rolled it lightly between his fingers. "I appreciate this."

"No problem, buddy. Say, I saw how you handled yourself back there with that orderly—pretty damned fast, aren't you?"

Carter managed a small shrug with his good shoulder. "I was.

217

But this thing will slow me down for a couple of months anyway. Hell what it does to you. Damned near can't even stand up by myself."

"Well, they got some good doctors here. You just do what they say, you'll be fine."

Followed by the disapproving eyes of the nurses, the guard rolled Carter down the hallway and outside.

A walkway ran between two rose bushes then bulged out into a sitting area ringed with wooden park benches. The guard sat down on a bench and then lit Carter's cigarette. He pulled out one for himself and lit it as well.

The guard settled back on his bench with a small sigh of satisfaction. "Damn places are getting so picky about smoking, you can hardly burn one anymore."

Carter inhaled deeply on the cigarette, felt the rush of nicotine hit his brain seconds later. He could almost feel the blood vessels contracting, the flow of blood to his brain accelerating and sweeping away the medication-induced lethargy. He sucked in deeply, held the smoke in his lungs, choked back a cough.

The guard leaned toward him. "I heard about you the other day," he began in a companionable fashion. "I was in the marines myself. First Marines. You ever work with them?"

Carter shook his head. "Mostly Third Marines—Korea, you know."

The guard nodded. "Never got over there myself. I heard it was pretty nasty, though. What's it like these days?"

Carter shrugged again. "About the same as always—maybe a little worse. Beer's more expensive, women cheaper. That's about the difference."

The guard laughed. "Say, I had this buddy who was over there. He was—"

Carter waited for the moment. The guard's eyes unfocused slightly as he recalled his past military service.

Carter's hand plunged under the side of the hospital gown and sought out the dinner knife strapped to the inside of his leg with two small pieces of adhesive he'd torn from his surgical bandages. He ripped the knife free and in one smooth motion lunged across and buried it in the guard's throat. He twisted the knife, felt the serrated edge grate on cartilage and bone, then sawed viciously into the loose flesh and fat around the man's neck.

The guard gurgled, his hands reaching for Carter. He managed to grab Carter's arm, then his hands went to his own throat. The spray surging out of his severed veins spattered against his open hand, directing the spray back on his own face. As the light faded from his eyes, he jerked at the handle of the knife and pulled it free. Carter saw his lips move as he tried to speak, but with the trachea severed and blood now spilling down into his lungs, the guard could manage only a brief strangled sound.

Unconsciousness followed swiftly, but Carter didn't wait to see it. He was already standing, moving away in the ground-consuming run that he'd learned in Korea. This was no different than dodging tunnels and snipers—enemy terrain was enemy terrain.

He spotted the parking lot that contained the more expensive vehicles and headed for it. A small sign confirmed his first suspicion. This was the doctors' parking lot. He darted in between two vehicles and waited. He used the knife to cut away the tape holding his injured arm immobilized, then tested his range of motion. Not great, but it would have to do.

Fortune was on his side. Moments later, a new Mazda Miata pulled into the lot, bright red with a convertible top. A casually dressed woman was behind the wheel.

Carter waited until she pulled into her assigned spot, got out of the car, and was starting to head toward the hospital, a jaunty, expectant look on her face. Her expression changed immediately as he rose between the two parked cars in her path.

"The keys," he demanded. He held out a hand. Her face paled. Silently she proffered the dangling keychain in her fingers. Something in his expression warned her not to run.

Carter nodded approvingly. "Smart woman. You know I can catch you, don't you? Catch you with no problem at all, even with this shoulder. Catch you and kill you."

Now she was shaking as the shock set in, her blood withdrawing from her extremities and pooling in her vital organs. Still, to her credit, she did not panic. Not that it would have done her any good.

"Just the keys, that's all I want," he said calmly. He took a step toward her. Now she moved, a survival reaction more than anything. Despite his calm words, something in his eyes told her, called out to her that she was in mortal danger. The calm broke and she turned to run.

In two quick steps, Carter was on her. He grabbed her by the short hair high on the crown of her head and jerked her back down. She screamed, a sound abruptly cut off as Carter clapped a hand over her mouth. He dragged her back in between the parked cars and crushed her larynx with one hard chop.

Her eyes were frantic now, mouth gaping wide under his mouth. He could tell she knew what he had done, realized that her crushed throat would not longer support life. Unless she had a tracheotomy, and quickly at that, she would soon suffocate.

He wished her well. She'd been brave, after all, but fate was what it was.

Whistling a soft tune, he bounded back to the Miata, ignoring the sharp lancing pain in his shoulder. Bone grated against bone, the cartilage that should have separated them carved away by the surgeon's knife.

Still, it didn't matter that much.

As he pulled out of the driveway and onto the interstate, he glanced back at the Murphy. Sure, security was fairly tight there, but there was one problem. Whoever had designed it had planned only on keeping bad guys out—not keeping them in.

Thorne slipped around to the back of his house and retrieved the key he had hidden under a cement planter. Not a particularly imaginative spot, but then again he wasn't really expecting anyone to try to break in. He slipped the key into the back door and turned the knob. The blinking red light just inside the door indicated that the security system was still on. He had thirty seconds to disable it and call the alarm company to let them know he was home, using his code number.

Thorne did so, then finally allowed himself to collapse. Sheer nervous energy carried him through the last twenty minutes—his abrupt departure from Patterson's condo, the quick jog from her house back to his. He'd covered the three miles in a little over twenty minutes. Not bad for someone running in blue jeans and his everyday Nikes. Fortunately, no cruising patrol car had stopped to ask him exactly why he was running in that attire.

He slumped into one of his comfortable kitchen chairs and tried to make some sense of it all. The allegations about Carter—they had to come from Debbie, of that he was certain. Not that he blamed her, not that he meant to, at any rate. In her situation, with allegations of a gun fired by a doctor at a patient, he would have had to do the same thing. Which was go directly to Wallinger and report the incident.

But who would she be talking to on the phone? His mind turned that one over and over, trying to make sense of it. Something she'd said a long time ago, about the connections of people who worked at Murphy. Was someone in her family military? Had she called them to damn him? Or to save him?

It had been when she'd found out about his recall. An uncle or something, someone who would know how long Thorne could expect to be in Korea.

Korea, the firefight, the woman who was thrust on him in the parking lot, and the jail. The pictures flashed through his mind, all mixed together in one long series of unrelated scenes and disasters that made a lousy nightmare—and a worse reality.

At least he was out on bail, he had that much to thank Debbie for. And he'd had a shower. As the adrenaline ebbed out of his system, he became aware of how desperately hungry he was. How long had it been since he'd eaten? He cast his mind back. There'd been a sandwich, hadn't there? Something he'd grabbed from the hospital cafeteria at some point?

He rose, walked over to the refrigerator, and pulled out one of the many reputedly healthy frozen dinners stashed there for just this sort of emergency. The prospect of waiting the entire eight minutes it would take for the dinner to heat in the microwave oven suddenly seemed unbearable.

He popped it in and stood opposite the microwave as though he could will it to cook faster by watching it carefully.

The phone rang. It startled him, and he was surprised to realize how on edge he was. He waited until the answering machine picked up and then heard Kamil's voice. He cut the machine off and lifted the receiver. "I'm home."

"Thank God," Kamil said. The relief in his voice was evident. "What in the hell happened?"

Thorne shook his head numbly, unable to marshal all of the events of the past thirty-six hours in any sort of coherent form. "I'll be damned if I know," he said finaly. "Listen, I've got to eat, get some sleep. What did they say to you?"

"They searched my car, damn it." Kamil's voice was tight.

"Jesus." The bone tiredness that had faded somewhat during his quick run home now came back with a vengeance. The more he thought about it, the more confused he became. Finally, he gave up. "Listen, we have to talk. But not right now."

"Yes, right now. There's something you don't know. It's Carter."

"Carter? What about him?"

"He's gone. Thorne, you've got to be careful. I don't know what the connection is between you and this man, but he left the hospital about thirty minutes ago. He killed a guard, crushed an orthoped's throat. Jesus, if he's after you—"

An image of Carter slipping in and out of the jungle at will, silent and undetectable, came to Thorne's mind.

"What happened in Korea, Thorne? You haven't said a word— hell, you barely stepped foot back in the hospital when—"

The insistent chiming of the microwave oven interrupted Kamil's flow of words. "I can't talk now, I can't even think."

Over Kamil's protestations and offers of assistance, Thorne gently replaced the telephone in its cradle. Eat first, then think. He held back a huge yawn that threatened to crack his jaw.

If Carter really believed that Thorne had tried to kill him, wouldn't he want to stay as far away from Thorne as possible? Or would he be seeking vengeance, trying to right some wrong that had occurred only in Carter's own twisted mind?

Food, his stomach insisted. Food first, and then he could think.

Behind the bushes in his backyard, near the planter he'd so recently disturbed, something moved.

"Dr. Kamil? You're due in surgery in thirty minutes." Kamil nodded at his secretary, briefly contemplated restoring some order to his cluttered desk, and then gave it up as a lost cause. It was something he'd been meaning to do for days, weeks—hell, even months.

Thorne would never have tolerated his desk being in this condition, any more than he would have parked his car sloppily in his assigned spot. It just wasn't in Thorne's nature.

Nor was shooting at a patient. Admittedly, a man who hadn't been a patient at the time, but still.

After one last look at the desk, Kamil slipped on his comfortable running shoes and headed down to surgery.

Inside the prep room, he was surprised to see Dr. Gillespie scrubbing at the next basin over. Kamil tendered a polite greeting.

"Bad business with that Carter fellow," Gillespie said as he took his place at the head of the table. "I can understand it, I suppose. If a doctor had tried to kill me, I'd be leery about staying in the same hospital, too."

Despite Gillespie's calm words, there was a harsh, ragged note in his voice. Kamil turned away from his last examination of the patient to study the anesthesiologist more carefully. Gowned and gloved, there was not much to see. Gillespie had already pulled his mask up, and the only skin exposed was a strip about four inches wide from his forehead down to the top of his nose. The dark, burning eyes stared at him intently. Gillespie's skin was waxy, faintly sheened with oil. Just at the hairline, a cluster of pimples stood out angry red against his pale skin.

"I doubt Carter was telling the truth," Kamil said neutrally. Now was not the time or place to get into a discussion of the peculiar incidence. Not with a patient already staring groggily at them through a haze of preop medication. Kamil gestured to the patient. "Ready?"

Gillespie nodded, appeared to be about to say something else, then thought better of it. He slipped the oxygen mask over the patient's face with a few perfunctory words, then quickly slid the needle into the IV tubing to inject the first anesthetic.

The patient started counting backward from one hundred. His voice trailed off at ninety-four as the fast-acting anesthetic induced unconsciousness. Gillespie followed that with a small titration of paralytic agent, then proceeded to induce deeper states of sleep. Finally, he looked up at Kamil and nodded. "Ready when you are."

Something about Gillespie's comment nagged in Kamil's mind, distracting him from the patient in front of him. He paused, scalpel poised over the exposed abdomen. What was it?

"Doctor?" The instrument nurse, the one he'd snarled at just a few days before.

It hit him with the force of a nuclear explosion. He paused, the scalpel suspended over the patient's neck. Then he laid the scalpel down carefully, took two steps back from the table, and stared at the assembled surgical team. "I'll be right back."

Thorne listened to the answering machine pick up the call. He was past tired and into a state of deep, bone-drenching weariness that precluded responding to even the most simple outside stimulus. He listened in a daze as Kamil's voice ground out in frustration at the recorder. "C'mon, Thorne, I know you're there. Pick up, pick up."

A few seconds' silence, and Thorne could hear Kamil breathing heavily. "Okay, maybe you've gone to bed. I hope to God I'm not too late. Thorne, something's going on with Gillespie. He's far too interested in Carter. And he knows about the rats. And there's more. Thorne, call me. Have them get me out of surgery if you have to. Jennings is assisting and he can handle it. But I've got to talk to you as soon as you get this message. Call me."

Thorne heard the receiver on the other end slam down. He spooned the rest of the microwaved meal into his mouth, his eyelids already dragging down and shrouding his eyes. Finally, he pushed the tray away and stumbled down the hallway to his bedroom. He fumbled with the covers, pulled them back, and fell into the bed. Seconds later, he was oblivious to the world around him.

The Korean air was redolent of mud, vehicle grease, and the wild, fresh green of the forest. The tarmac steamed from the recent deluge, thin tendrils drifting up to claw at the aircraft.

The Gulfstream jet sat near the air terminal, its self-contained stairway already extended for boarding.

Boothby's aide hefted up two bags, one an expansive suitcase and the other a suit bag, then preceded the general to the aircraft and made arrangements for the luggage to be stowed in the rear compartment. Boothby himself was greeted by the sergeant flight technician, and escorted to a spacious seat near the front of the aircraft.

"Is there anything I can get you, General?" the sergeant asked. He was clad in a neat class B uniform, a concession from the flight suit that he would normally have worn for lesser passengers.

Boothby shook his head. He patted the briefcase at his side. "Doing some work on the way over—don't wake me."

The sergeant nodded. "Yes, General. If there's anything I can do for you—"

Boothby dismissed him with an abrupt gesture. He heard the engines begin to spool as the air crew ran through their preflight and prelaunch checklists.

Ten minutes later, the aircraft taxied to the end of the runway. It poised there for a moment, brakes set and engines screaming, then with a slight jolt slid free and trundled down the runway. It departed the ground smoothly and gracefully and soared up toward cruising altitude.

In the back of the Gulfstream, Boothby was already deep in the paperwork contained in his briefcase, putting the final touches on his presentation to JCS.

Thorne was dreaming again, his mind twisting down strange pathways that would have been ludicrous during waking hours. As was often the case, the spectral figure of JFK intruded into many scenes—often not a key player, hardly partaking of the action at all, but a waiting, watching figure. At first, these dreaming intrusions had disturbed Thorne, particularly during the early stages in his interest in the JFK assassination. After years and years of study, however, he'd come to regard the ghostly figure as almost a guide. A guardian angel of sorts who watched over his dreams.

This time, JFK was far closer to him than he normally was. Instead of the normal, campaign-picture-perfect image he usually presented, this was the JFK immediately following the assassination. The face: the wounds that he'd memorized from so many studies of the photos, the haunted, haggard expression. Part of his skull was missing, and blood trickled down the side of his face, an ugly mar on the otherwise regular and handsome features.

It was the eyes that truly caught his attention—not as they'd been in death, but bright, alive with the powerful intellect that had been housed in that skull. JFK was staring at him, and Thorne had the sensation that the man was trying to communicate with him, trying to pass on some message. But what?

He saw JFK's chest expand as he tried to breathe, sucking in a deep, hard breath. Thorne felt his own chest move in response, unconsciously falling into the rhythm of JFK's breathing. A pained expression crossed JFK's features, the first hints of panic. Had it been like that for the dead president? A moment—perhaps only a microsecond—after the bullet had blown his skull to shreds, the last fantasies of a fading consciousness? How had he felt at that moment? Had it been an abrupt transition from complete consciousness— staring at the screaming and cheering crowds, feeling the massive convertible roll gently down the street—to the simple nothingness of death? Or had there been moments, some period of time however brief, when the president was aware that he'd been fatally wounded, felt his life blood pouring out from the back of his exposed brain? Had he seen Jackie, and her last frantic scrabble across the back of the convertible to retrieve the portions of his brain? Had he had a chance to wonder at the futility, perhaps even wallow in panic before oxygen starvation deprived him of even the most rudimentary intellectual functions?

JFK's chest heaved again. His mouth opened wide, impossibly

wide, and Thorne could see the expansive smooth, healthy tissue inside his mouth, count the regular, gleaming teeth. The mouth opened wider, even wider now, obscuring his nose and finally his eyes. All that remained of the president was the gaping mouth, topped by that short, slightly curly crop of hair.

Thorne felt his own body mimic the president's motions, his mouth stretching wider and wider until his jaw joint creaked. The pain roused him where terror could not, jerking him out of REM sleep and into the first light stages of doziness.

He couldn't breathe. A smothering, heavy material covered his face, eyes, and nose. It pressed down on him with sufficient force to be painful, stretching the delicate cartilage in his nose to the point of breaking.

Panic. Thorne was now completely awake, suffocating, struggling to breathe. He flailed violently, trying to reach past the pillow plastered to his face.

The pillow slipped down slightly as the result of his movements and one eye was exposed. In the dim light pouring through the outside window, he saw a figure, one hand held tightly against his body while the other bore down heavily on the pillow. The man's fingers were just inches away from his eyes, and Thorne's gaze traced up the fingers to the face, trying to discern the identity of his attacker.

He bucked, twisting violently, trying to throw off the man. But the man's knees were planted on either side of his body, his groin just inches above Thorne's gut, the weight of his body trapping Thorne in a vise.

The man used one arm. Why? Suddenly, as his hand groped toward his attacker, trying to pull the hand off the pillow, Thorne realized. It had to be Carter. The right shoulder injury, the sling still awkwardly tied around his body.

Reflex drove him to grapple with the immediate source of his discomfort, the hand holding down the pillow. With a massive effort, Thorne shifted the focus of his efforts. There was no way he could overpower the man, none at all. He was simply too large, too massively muscled and built to fight one on one. But he had his weak spot. The shoulder.

Thorne redirected his attack, striking with his rapidly fading strength at the highest point on the triangle. His fingers clamped down around the sling, scrabbling for a handhold. With all of his strength, he pulled Carter forward.

The unexpected move caught Carter off guard. He leaned forward, off balance. Thorne drew his arm back and slammed his open hand, leading with his heel, into the exact point where the incision was.

Carter howled. The force of the blow threw him back, and wrenched his hand off the pillow. Thorne gasped, almost choking on the sweet, fresh flood of air that streamed into his tortured lungs. His strength returned almost immediately. He rolled off the bed, got to his feet, the last vestiges of grogginess now fading.

Carter was crouched near the door, his good hand supporting his injured arm. The sling had torn free in the violent motion, and dangled uselessly from its strap.

"You think you're so smart." The words came in a ragged, harsh stream. "You don't know shit. I know that about you."

Thorne shook his head. "Why are you—"

Carter laughed, an amused sound that was at odds with the situation now slipping out of his control. "Could've taken you with one arm."

Thorne stood at the far end of his bedroom, his back to the window behind him. The deranged soldier crouched between him and the door, the only exit from the room. Off to Thorne's left was the bathroom. His mind skittered, trying to think of something that would be of use there.

"I'll be back." Evidently reaching some decision, Carter slipped out of the room soundlessly.

Thorne stood where he was, paralyzed by the rapid sequence of events. From dead exhaustion into terror, then suffocation. In his mind, he saw the battered, bleeding face of JFK smile at him slightly.

The police arrived five minutes after he called them. The patrolman politely accepted his invitation to come in, and followed him up the stairs to take a look at the bedroom.

"Looks like somebody's been here, or it was a hell of a nightmare." The cop poked one curious foot at the sheets and blanket crumpled on the floor. He glanced over at Thorne. "You're certain you didn't just dream this?"

"Of course I'm certain. Look, I even told you who the fellow was. I know him—he was a patient at our hospital."

"I know who you are, Dr. Thorne. And so does my shift sergeant." The patrolman eyed him with a steady, sardonic gaze.

"He was here, I tell you." Furious, and running on nervous energy, Thorne snatched the sheets up off the floor. He searched through them frantically, his hands running over the smooth, cool fabric. "There." He pointed to a splatter of bloodstains. "That's from where I ripped the bandage off and hit him. It's his blood, not mine. Don't you believe me?"

The patrolman took a step back from the sheet Thorne held out. "I don't touch nothing without gloves on," he said. "And the only thing that will prove it's his blood and not yours is a DNA test. Maybe a blood test, if you're different types."

"Then do it." Thorne thrust the bloody sheet at him.

"Put it in a plastic bag for me. I'll take it down to the station, see what the sergeant says."

Thorne led the patrolman back down into the kitchen and complied. The patrolman accepted the green plastic bag containing the sheet and seemed about to say something. Finally, he pulled out his notebook, "Let's go over the facts again, Dr. Thorne."

"Why weren't you writing them down the first time?"

"Listen, I don't tell you how to do surgery. Don't tell me how to do my job."

Thorne slumped into the kitchen chair he'd vacated just hours earlier. He gazed up at the young, heart-faced cop. "Okay, here goes." Briefly, he recounted the details.

A knock on the front door brought a look of relief to the patrolman's face. "Wait here." He left the kitchen and was back moments later. The massive, hulking figure of Tom Wallinger loomed behind him.

"Good evening, Doctor. Or, uh, should I say good morning?" Wallinger made a small gesture at the patrolman, who gratefully fled the room. Wallinger slumped into the chair next to Thorne. "What happened?"

"I'm not sure it's any of your business," Thorne snapped. "What are you doing here?" Wallinger shook his head slowly. "Merced isn't that big a town. Something comes up involving one of our docs, I get a courtesy call from the local forces. Just a matter of professional courtesy."

"Carter was here. Don't try to lie to me, I know he left the hospital."

Wallinger seemed unsurprised that Thorne was aware of that fact. "So you say he was here." He glanced back at the front door. "I take it the patrolman wasn't convinced."

"And you?"

"Where have you been since your lady friend got you out of jail?"

"What business is it of yours?"

Wallinger started toward him. The patrolman grabbed him by the elbow and held him back. Wallinger started to shake him off, then took a deep breath. "One of these days, Thorne, I'm going to— Listen, I've got a dead orthopedic surgeon in the parking lot, and a guard who was almost decapitated in the garden. A missing patient who says you tried to kill him in Korea, and a general confirming it. And now you're claiming that the same patient—one who's seriously handicapped by recent surgery, mind you, and has every reason in the world to want to stay *away* from you—quietly sneaked into your room and tried to suffocate you. Why the *hell* do you think I want to know where you were?"

Thorne shook his head, almost feeling his brain rattle within the hard skull that protected it. "Carter. It had to be him. He already sliced up an orderly, what makes you think he would balk at taking out a couple more? Look, all I can tell you is that he was here. What you believe is up to you."

"Mind telling me why Dr. Gillespie ordered you to stay away from the hospital?"

"Medical leave."

"Psychiatric in nature?"

"*No.* I don't have to—"

Wallinger stepped forward again, slowly this time. "I'm afraid you do." He held out a hand to Thorne. "Why don't you come on down to the hospital with me, Doctor? At the very least, we need to check you out after this attack. Make sure there's no permanent damage."

"And I suppose you'll be requesting a psych eval as well?" Thorne asked bitterly.

Wallinger shrugged. "Same question: What would you do in my spot?"

Thorne sighed and got to his feet. "What if I say no?"

"Then this patrol officer takes you into custody for an involuntary commitment." Wallinger appeared to consider something. "Actually," he admitted, "I can't be certain he won't take you straight to jail. I have to tell you, your credibility with the local cops isn't very high right now. But if you go with me, it will be a voluntary admission, with discharge subject to Dr. Gillespie's discretion."

Thorne's shoulders slumped. It seemed like he had no choices. At least the hospital was safe, familiar ground. With Carter on the loose, it might even be safer than his own house. Finally, he nodded. "Okay, I'll go with you. But I'm not promising anything."

Wallinger smiled. "A good choice, Doctor. Let's go."

The patrolman waited outside until he saw Wallinger's car leave the premises, complete with a second occupant. He shook his head, wondering just how crazy most of those doctors were. The doctor seemed like a nice fellow, for somebody who was psycho. It didn't make sense that he would have tried to shoot that guy—he didn't seem like the sort of fellow to do it. Still, one never knew. He thought back to his own days in the Army, how the condition of incredible deprivation, constant danger, and hours of preternatural alertness could transform reality into something completely dangerous and alien. Maybe that was what had happened over in Korea, although he wouldn't have supposed that the doctor would be the one to crack.

Too far above his pay grade, he thought, invoking the old Army rationale for evading responsibility.

TWENTY-ONE

Terrain matters.

General Boothby stood outside the door to the war room, waiting for his chance to brief the Joint Chiefs of Staff. Inside, the chiefs were thrashing out priorities for the programmed budget, wading through the intricacies of technology and service requirements to arrive at a unified front before Congress. He knew the drill, had been through it himself during a staff tour at JCS. While the American public thought of the military forces in terms of conflicts that they saw plastered over CNN every day, military professionals knew that the hardest battles were fought here, within the constraints of the budgeting and programming government system.

Terrain matters.

The thought surfaced again, niggling at him as it had for the past two weeks. He focused on the idea for a moment. It served to center him, to calm him as he realized the cause for the muscle jumping erratically at the corner of his jaw, the odd, creeping feeling at the back of his scalp. He consciously slowed his breathing, taking deep, oxygenated breaths into his lungs. That was the point his subconscious was trying to make— and the one he'd ignored. The physical sensations were reminding him that the briefing he was about to present was a battle just as surely as the last sniper attack in Korea. Body count was measured in careers rather than corpses, but the basic principles of conflict applied.

A battle, that's what it was. Not a subordinate commander's briefing to the JCS, but a winner-take-all, zero-sum game.

The door opened. "They're ready for you, General," the other brigadier said.

Boothby nodded and stepped into the room. His stride was confident now as he understood the true nature of this meeting. It was not just a briefing, it was war. He took one final deep breath, and began.

The past two days in the hospital—a thorough psychiatric evaluation and an extensive series of tests—had been Dr. Gillespie's condition for allowing him to retain his privileges at the hospital. He'd been too tired to argue the first day, too scared to do it the second. Now, at noon on the third day of his stay there, he'd decided enough was enough.

"I *am* leaving," Thorne insisted. His finger continued clicking on the channel changer, cycling the small color TV mounted high on the wall through its selections. At the foot of the bed, Debbie Patterson glared down at him, hands on her hips. Thorne recognized the signs of postcall exhaustion, the faint, purple circles under her eyes, the frown permanently embedded in her forehead. Debbie stood virtually motionless, not deigning to waste precious energy on nervous movement.

"One more day."

"Not a chance." Thorne switched his gaze back to the TV, his finger suddenly freezing above the clicker as a familiar figure strode into view. "Damn it," he said, wonderingly, almost to himself. "He's here."

Patterson walked to the left side of his bed and followed his gaze up to the TV. "Who's here?"

"General Boothby. I worked for him in Korea." Thorne hesitated, uncertain as to how much to say to her. "Korea?" Patterson took a step closer to the bed. "You haven't told me your side of it yet."

"Never mind. It's not important." Even as he dismissed her question, he thumbed the button that would increase the volume on the TV. The announcer's voice was now audible.

". . . arrived in DC early this morning to brief the Joint Chiefs of Staff on the recent events in Korea. According to unnamed administration sources, the general is bringing a cautionary message about this troubled country to his superiors." A file photo of General Boothby, looking younger than he had in Korea, flashed up on the screen. "Noted throughout the Army for his tactical brilliance, and a keen student of the strategic political intricacies of that country, Boothby is viewed by many as the foremost expert on this troubled region. Whether or not his recommendations will be taken for action by the Joint Chiefs of Staff remains to be seen." The camera pulled back to allow a full figure view of the reporter with his name overlaid on the picture.

Washington. Now why would Boothby be in the United States, given the escalating conflict in Korea? Thorne shook his head, trying to recall if this visit had been scheduled before he left Korea. Not to his knowledge, but then, he wouldn't have been told much, not as a reserve doctor on temporary duty in Korea.

"Thorne?" Patterson said, still staring at the screen.

Thorne shook his head. "Nothing happened. Carter is lying, of course."

But something did happen. Something I don't want her to know— something I don't even want to know about. And there are just two other people in the world who do know: Boothby and Carter. What are the odds of both of them being in the United States at the same time?

Thorne thumbed the volume up slightly higher as the anchor reappeared. "What's the next step, Carl?"

The figure on the screen, clad in the obligatory Burberry overcoat, nodded as though he'd been expecting the question. "The general's office tells us he's eager to return to Korea, but of course he's at the beck and call of the joint chiefs. Depending on what the decision is today, General Boothby may be staying over a couple of days in order to brief members of Congress and perhaps the president himself. Only time will tell, Jim. Back to you."

The anchor turned back to face the camera. "In other news—" Thorne clicked the sound off.

Brief the president? Why did that sound wrong? Wasn't that normally the job of the chairman of the Joint Chiefs of Staff, or the secretary of defense or someone? Aside from an odd interest in Thorne's own assassination theories, Boothby had shown no particular interest in politics. So what was it that bothered him?

Thorne closed his eyes and replayed the scene in his mind. Boothby, striding confidently past the camera, his gaze fixed on the future, a slight hitch in his walk as he favored the still-injured shoulder, but otherwise a confident, capable general. Brilliant, some said. His hair cut short in the normal military fashion, his uniform sharply pressed and fitted, his—wait. His hair.

The rats. Skin beneath the gashes mottled with petechia and blisters.

234

That was it. He opened his eyes and saw Patterson leaning forward over the bed, a look of concern on her face. "Where were you just then?" she asked softly. "Back in Korea?"

"He has a rash on his neck." Thorne pointed to the television. "General Boothby, I mean. A rash."

A guarded expression crossed Debbie's face. "And that's important?" she asked, her voice calmly interested. A professional tone, one Thorne had used himself many times when talking with patients.

He nodded. "It could be." Briefly, he debated telling her about his conversation with Kamil, the odd, speckled rash that had warped the dead rats' bodies. Again, for reasons he couldn't exactly decipher, he decided against it. "Or maybe not." He tried for a casual chuckle. "It might just be a rash."

Dubiously, Patterson regarded him. "I really think you should stay another day."

"No. Look, I'll make all the follow-up appointments, but I've got to get out of here now." He flung back the bedclothes. "I've got to make a telephone call—I'm getting dressed."

Thorne dressed quickly, repeated his assurances to Patterson, then eased out into the hallway. He walked confidently past the nurses' station and to the corridor that led over to the professional building.

His office space was untouched, everything just as he'd left it. He turned his computer on, drumming his fingers impatiently as it cycled through its start-up routine. As soon as the software logo appeared, he clicked and moused into his telecommunication program.

There it was, in the folder in which he thought he'd left it. The note on the effects of the folic acid deficiency on adults. He skimmed the article again, then raced down to the end of it to read the writer's biographical information. Johns Hopkins. "Yes," he crowed when he found the phone number attached to her bio data.

He placed the call, now feeling fully alive for the first time in three days. It was a long shot, but it was just possible. Finally, he got her on the phone.

After identifying himself, he said, "I'd like to talk to you about some of the more subtle effects of your study."

"Sure, what are you interested in?"

"Subclinical neurological damage. Something that might not be picked up with standard testing but could be potentiated by an adverse drug reaction. Is that possible?"

"Depends on the drug, of course. Anything particular in mind?"

"Anesthetic agents. I'm wondering whether traditional studies take into account a wide-enough range of metabolisms. It's possible that people with folic acid deficiencies during early development might respond differently to longer hydroxyl molecules."

"I see. Well, I certainly wouldn't rule it out. Statistically, we find that approximately one in every twenty people we test has some degree of folic acid deficiency. If the results on neurological development are as subtle as I think they are—and that is tending to show—then yes, that could account for a wide range of responses to any anesthetic, even the proven ones." Her voice then took on a cautious note. "But do you have something different in mind?"

"It's all hypothetical," he tried to reassure her, his words sounding hollow to his own ears. "I just read your paper and was curious."

After a brief discussion of possible side effects, Thorne thanked her for her time and hung up. He stared at the screen, his eyes searching the paper for any more clues.

Stupid, all too stupid. Just think about what you're postulating: a new anesthetic drug that seems to be the perfect agent for almost any patient. Sure, Boothby was treated here, but you've got no proof that Anaex was used on him. Or on Carter, for that matter. There's no record of a prior admission on him, and he's as crazy as Boothby is. So where does that leave you?

With a rash. A rash that could be anything on a man, and that could be nothing on a rat.

Wallinger switched off the tape recorder and steepled his fingers in front of him.

"And you're certain about this?" General Huels asked. "Certain enough that you think there's an imminent danger to national security?"

Boothby held completely still, aware of the energy coursing through his body. He laid it out carefully for them, feinting with his concerns over the sniper attacks, counterattacking budgetary questions with data on increased efficiency, and finally launching his frontal assault. "There's little doubt in my mind, none of any appreciable level," he answered, careful to acknowledge the possibility, however remote, that his data was incorrect. To do otherwise would have immediately aroused their suspicions, brought down on him a flurry of questions he was not prepared to answer. But in this town, striking the right balance between confidence and reality was the absolute perfect ploy.

"Until proven otherwise, I'm operating on the assumption that the North Koreans have mobilized their nuclear weapons to within easy striking range of my forces. While there are dangers on relying on indigenous intelligence, the degree of risk and the extent of damage possible certainly warrants the increased measures I propose."

"Escalation," the chief of naval operations said simply. He let the one word stand for the specter that all but drove them away from a mobilization to Korea, the possibility of embroiling the United States in another Vietnam-type conflict.

"Deterrence." The Air Force chief of staff rapped the word out as an equally abbreviated shorthand for his position. Forces in theater, the capability to mobilize immediately, had been known to deter more than one tin-pot dictator from invading an otherwise peaceful neighbor.

Not that Korea would be as easy as that. Never.

Boothby stepped back slightly from the podium and felt the tension drain from his body. He'd done his part, fought his war. The discussion was going to get kicked up to a higher level and all he could do was stand by and wait for the body count.

Finally, General Huels appeared to arrive at a decision. He turned away from his fellow chiefs and back to the junior general. "I will brief the president tomorrow," he said. He pointed one finger at Boothby. "And you will accompany me. Based on your data—and solely on your data—I have serious concerns about our readiness posture in Korea. But given the political implications for our forces there, it's the commander in chief's call."

Boothby nodded, and felt for the first time a faint sheen of sweat break out on his forehead. Wars were won campaign by campaign—in more ways than one.

TWENTY-TWO

"No. Another two days at least," Dr. Gillespie said.

"Give me a reason I need to stay, sir," Thorne responded immediately. Evidently the floor nurse had notified his superior of Thorne's unscheduled departure from the ward, and Gillespie had tracked him down to his office.

"Because you don't want me to discuss this little matter of your assault upon a patient with the state licensing board," Gillespie shot back. His face was wreathed in an expression of triumph.

"Maybe I'm not the only one they'd like to hear about," Thorne countered quietly. "There are matters more serious than the unsupported allegations of a paranoid violent patient."

"What's that supposed to mean?"

Thorne stood up from behind his desk and stepped into the middle of the room. Gillespie was slouched on the long couch against one wall. "I think you know what I mean. Anaex. You're way outside the protocol, Doctor."

"I don't know what you mean." Gillespie's expression darkened immediately to sullen, the speed of the change surprising Thorne.

"You told me Prime Minister Danoff was the first. That was a lie. Admit it."

"Are you implying that—"

"How many so far?" Thorne asked. "I can count a couple." He held up his hand and started counting names on his fingers. "Dr. Kamil's uncle. General Boothby. Hannah Greener's husband." He folded the three fingers one by one into his palm, leaving the small and ring finger of the hand extended into the air. "Care to name the others for me? Or shall I tell you myself after I've questioned all the recovery room nurses? As rapidly as your Anaex patients emerge from anesthesia, I don't doubt that they'll be able to remember them with a little prompting. If not, the nursing notes will."

"This is complete nonsense. I didn't use Anaex on Danoff, you did. The records will back me up on that."

So Kamil had been right. Gillespie had a backup plan, one that involved blaming on Thorne the unauthorized use of Anaex on Danoff, and blaming the earlier instances on his predecessor. Had the other doctor really sabotaged the Anaex trials, as Gillespie had claimed when he'd denied Thorne solo access to the lab? Or had that been part of the plan as well?

Patterson would remember it too, if anyone started asking questions. He'd pointed out the rapid emergence to her himself. That had led to coffee, and later to— He pushed the thoughts of Patterson and what she'd come to mean to him out of his mind.

"I wouldn't have agreed to use it if I'd know about the others," Thorne said finally. "Not without knowing how they did. You told me he was the first clinical trial. You *told* me that."

Gillespie chuckled, an evil-sounding snort. "Do you think the state licensing board will buy that? After what you've been up to lately?" He stood, slightly taller than Thorne and using every inch of his height to his own advantage. Despite himself, Thorne felt the pull of the man's presence, his commanding, professional charisma. "Do you really think it will matter, Dr. Thorne?" Gillespie waved one hand at the Thorne's office. "All this, gone. The moment I fire you. Is that what you want?"

"How many others?" Thorne said stubbornly. "Just those four, then?"

Gillespie studied him for a moment, an odd expression of glee creeping across his face. "What could it hurt? It's the word of a discredited junior doctor out to save his ass against mine. Yes, just those four."

Thorne stepped toward the door, intending to head immediately for Wallinger's office. Despite the disagreements he'd had with the security officer, there was no doubt in his mind that that was the only course of action.

"I may go down for administering Anaex to Danoff, but I'm taking you with me. How could you, Doctor? Try the stuff on patients without their informed consent, before you'd done a full-scale lab protocol? What gives you the right to play god with them? What gives you the right?" Suddenly enraged beyond all reason, Thorne stepped forward as though to seize the other man by his lab coat. Gillespie held up one hand in front of him, his self-confidence and power almost palpable. It stopped Thorne short. Reality sunk in.

What were the chances that Wallinger would believe him? Slim to none. Hell, he wasn't sure he even believed himself. The entire thing sounded ludicrous.

A deep-seated weariness flooded his body, almost as overwhelming as it had been the night he'd checked into the hospital. He saw Gillespie beam at him as the older doctor recognized his dilemma.

"Go home, Dr. Thorne. Get some rest. Eat," Gillespie urged softly. "Think about what you're saying. Then we'll talk." He reached out as though to touch Thorne on the shoulder, then evidently decided better and pulled his hand back and put it in his pocket. "We'll talk," he repeated. "Despite everything that's happened, there's a place for you on this project, Doctor, one that will make you the most famous person in your medical school class. You think about that, and think about what you'd like to do instead of practice medicine." It was Gillespie's turn to reach for the doorknob. He pulled it open and stepped out into the foyer. Just as he reached the door to the outer office, he turned back to Thorne. "Just think about it."

Gillespie strode down the corridor toward his office, confident that he'd made the right decisions. The young doctor simply had no options. He should realize that at any moment. That Thorne had even dared to threaten action against Gillespie was simply more than he could bear. The arrogance of the young doctor, the sheer fucking arrogance. The more he thought about it, the more certainly he was convinced that Thorne had no future in the Anaex project. Or at the Murphy.

Besides, there was one other fact that Gillespie had failed to admit to Thorne. One that worried him on a level that he couldn't even begin to describe. It was a deep, gut-sucking fear, so pervasive that the only way to deal with it was to shut it off in the farthest corners of his mind.

There's no way Thorne could find out. None at all.

Dr. Gillespie was not nearly as irresponsible as Thorne believed. Before using it on surgical patients, Dr. Gillespie had tried Anaex on himself.

Angie Duerkin was pissed. Seven hours and fifty-five minutes into her evening shift on the front desk of the ER, she was confronted with a thin, wan woman holding her stomach and complaining of pain. Of course with no insurance, and no sign of Duerkin's relief.

Duerkin sighed, glanced up at the clock again, and wondered if there was any way she could finish this triage admission before the long hand on the clock reached twelve. Not a chance, the way things were going.

"So where does your husband work?" she said, looking back down at the sheet in front of her. She heard the slow, hesitant voice start, barely audible above the normal commotion in the ER waiting room, and sighed. Most of these questions she didn't even need to ask—she could already tell what the answers would be. No insurance, husband unemployed, no prenatal care, and no obstetrician of record. Only completing the required paperwork had prevented her from hustling this lady through. She checked the first block again, more out of something to do while the woman struggled with the inevitable explanation of her husband's unemployment, than of any real curiosity. Hannah Greener. A plain name for a plain woman, and both would surely slip her memory as soon as Angie's shift was over.

"I was here earlier this week," the voice said, adding that statement onto the end of her litany of woes. "Here."

Maybe a shortcut. Angie typed the woman's Social Security number into the computer, cynically amazed that Greener could even manage to remember that, and felt a surly sense of gratification as the file from her last admission popped into view on the screen.

Admitted overnight for observation. Notify Dr. Gillespie if the patient returns to ER.

Had she been of a more questioning mind, Angie Duerkin might have bothered to wonder why a senior anesthesiologist on staff was interested in this particular woman. But with three minutes before her shift was over, Angie's only real interest centered in seeing the dark shape of Jaimie Callis, the night-shift woman who would relieve her, appear in the glass doors that led outside.

Angie quickly copied down the rest of the necessary information from the screen, saving her the bother of talking to Greener herself. "Sign here," she ordered in her best bureaucratic tones and shoved the papers over to Greener. The other woman took the proffered pen, gasped and grimaced, her hands going reflexively to her abdomen. Angie sighed, tapped impatiently on the counter with her fingers. "The sooner you sign, the sooner I can get you seen," she said.

Hannah Greener tensed for a moment longer, then sighed in relief as the spasm passed. She scribbled her name hastily on the bottom of the form and pushed it timidly back across the counter. Angie snapped it up, rose from her chair to start a treatment file on the woman, then turned back to Greener. "Just have a seat. Someone will be with you soon."

"But I'm—"

"Just have a seat," Angie said again, pointing at the row of plastic chairs fixed to a single steel bar. "Soon."

Hannah walked laboriously over to the waiting room chairs. She collapsed as she sat down on the plastic chair, wedged in between a truck driver holding a bloody towel to his wrist and an eight-year-old boy wailing that he was going to throw up again.

As the big hand of the clock reached twelve with an audible click, Angie swung the window shutters closed, latching them from her side. As the wooden slatted frames blocked out the view of the ER waiting room, all thoughts of Hannah Greener and Dr. Gillespie vanished from her mind.

Hannah Greener's world was a small bubble of pain centered on her abdomen. The screaming and cries around her bounced off it and were refracted back into the bedlam of the waiting room. The faint scent of gasoline and sweat from the truck driver, the thin, mewling whine of the child next to her barely even registered, and then only in the period between the contractions.

Another one was starting, she could feel it in the quivering of her muscles, building into agony that engulfed her, carrying her along with it to some unseen destination. She was barely aware of her own cries, much less the truck driver's disgusted snarl or the child's wailing. There was pain, only pain, hard, demanding, devouring her entire consciousness as the black-and-red laced void that loomed before her.

It was worse than before, forcing a groan that crescendoed up the scales to become a scream. She gripped her belly, trying to double over, screaming as she tottered on the edge of the chair. She felt herself start to go forward, still barely aware of it, and the hard linoleum floor rushed up to meet her. She hit on her side, the impact registering for only a moment before the pain redoubled its efforts.

She was howling now, her voice rich and strong, cutting through the rest of the noise, reaching back into the treatment cubicles that were rabbit warrens behind the admitting desk. A side door popped open, a nurse appeared, her face shocked out of its normal professional impassivity.

Hands reached for her, drawing her up straight, and she screamed again in protest. Finally, just as they were lifting her to a wheelchair, she passed out.

Thorne's beeper went off just as he reached the elevator. His hand moved by reflex to still the sound and he looked down at the number. The ER. He grimaced. Evidently at least one department hadn't heard that he was suspended. He closed his hand around the beeper. Should he go down and notify them himself or simply call in later from home?

Better do it now. Otherwise, there was every chance they'd keep beeping him all the way home until he answered.

He stepped into the elevator. Kamil might still even be down there—he'd find him, see what it was that had been so important earlier, and then get home. Mortifying, having to tell them that he was no longer allowed to respond and practice at Murphy, but best to go ahead and get it over with.

He leaned against the back wall of the elevator and tilted his head up, closing his eyes for a few minutes. Two days' rest had not yet washed away the traces of exhaustion that had been building from the first moment he'd stepped on the plane headed for Korea. What he needed was weeks, maybe even months, maybe more than that. All around him, everything that he'd thought was good and great and wonderful about Murphy was turning to ashes, bitter shards of his med school and residency dreams. How was it possible that things had gone so wrong, so quickly?

The resident ran his hands over Hannah Greener's belly, felt the muscles contract and pull under his fingers. At least the reason for her discomfort was obvious, if not the cause behind her miscarriage. What form of denial enabled women such as this to fail to seek out prenatal care? If it had been his wife, his sister—no, there was no way he'd ever understand it. He studied her for a moment, seeing the harsh lines that poverty had etched in her once-attractive face, the sheer anguish in her eyes. "I see you've been here recently," he said quietly. "Don't worry, your baby is fine. We're going to get you up to the OB ward and get you something to make you a little more comfortable. Are you allergic to any medications?"

Hannah Greener shook her head, her teeth too tightly gritted to answer.

The resident studied the computer screen again, paged down for the follow-up instructions, and noted the request that Dr. Gillespie be called were this patient seen again. He walked to the door of the treatment cubicle and stuck his head out to see if Dr. Gillespie were in sight. "Julie, do you know if Dr. Gillespie's been paged?" he asked the charge nurse.

Julie shook her head. "Maybe the admitting clerk did it, but don't count on it. Shift change."

The resident sighed and stepped back into the cubicle. "I'm going to call one of the doctors who wanted to see you if you came back," he said to Hannah as he crossed to the room phone. "Dr. Gillespie. Do you remember him?"

"No." The word slipped out between her clenched teeth. "Husband's doctor."

The resident paused for a moment, confused. "He was your husband's doctor?" he asked.

Hannah nodded, almost overcome again by the pain. "Husband's doctor. Dr. Thorne—he—"

So which one to call, Dr. Thorne or Dr. Gillespie? The resident wavered for a moment, then decided on Dr. Gillespie. After all, it was his note in the database, not Dr. Thorne's. Regardless of what Mrs. Greener thought, Dr. Gillespie may have been the last one to treat her. Certainly, as indicated by the notes in the file, she might not have been in a condition to notice when she was last in the ER.

Reaching a decision, he reached for the house phone and called the operator. "Page Dr. Gillespie to the ER."

It was her frailty that annoyed him the most. Gillespie stood at the door, assessing the woman from a distance of six feet away, felt the combination of rage and exultation building into an intense, pounding surge of euphoria. Here was one link that could be eliminated, even if her husband was temporarily beyond his reach. At any rate, she was the cause of the problems now, the one who'd accused her husband, the one who'd set Thorne onto his trail. Without her interfering, there would have been no danger. Greener and Thorne. He stepped into the room, the blood pounding in his head, quietly confident that he could eliminate at least one of the threats now.

"It was unlike anything I'd seen before," Kamil finished, recounting again what he saw of the rats in the lab. "Not only the patent wounds but the general physical condition as well. The skin, Thorne, that was some ugly shit." An expression of distaste appeared on Kamil's face.

"I saw it on the rats I dug out of the Dumpster," Thorne said. "No chance it's related to some sort of biopsy?"

Kamil shook his head slowly. "No. There you're cutting through cleanly. The wounds—at least after I get through with them—are supposed to be there. Clean edges, not that."

The two men were standing in the central passageway to the ER, oblivious to the flow of patients, physicians, and health-care workers around them.

Thorne sighed heavily. "But they've got the rats now."

Kamil nodded.

"I'm going to answer this page, then I'm going home." Thorne said. "Man, I'm beat. And there's nothing else I can do here. Especially not here."

"The committee will never let him get away with it," Kamil said, referring to the credentialing committee that controlled the ability of physicians to practice at Murphy. "Not on just that."

"I'm not so certain about it. Gillespie swings a lot of weight around here, and then there's Carter's statement."

"Now I know you need some sleep."

"Maybe you're right."

After assuring Kamil that he was going straight home to bed, Thorne headed for the ER exit. He cut across the central corridor to the far string of rooms, trying to avoid two trauma patients that were being wheeled into adjacent rooms. Out of sheer reflex, he glanced into the rooms as he past them. What he saw in treatment room three brought him to a dead stop.

It was Hannah Greener, he was certain of it. She was on the treatment bed, her face turned slightly toward the window. Standing behind her and facing Thorne was Dr. Gillespie. The sheet was pulled down, exposing the middle of her back. Gillespie's right hand was out of view and his left hand was gently palpating her spine.

Without thinking, Thorne slammed into the room and jerked Gillespie away from the table. He stumbled over the base of an instrument tray just as he reached Gillespie. Gillespie pivoted and shoved Thorne away. Thorne fell and sprawled over the next bed.

"Just what the hell is going on here?" the resident demanded. As the identity of the two struggling men sunk in, he belatedly added, "Doctors."

"Call security," Gillespie ordered, his voice cold and hard. "Dr.

Thorne's credentials are suspended. Make sure the rest of your shift knows that."

Thorne struggled to his feet. "Wait."

The resident barely hesitated.

"There's more to this than he's telling you," Thorne said, his words coming out fast and furious, tumbling over each other in a desperate effort to save Hannah Greener's life. "Don't let him treat her. Yes, get security down here. But not for me." He pointed at Gillespie. "Dr. Gillespie was attempting to administer an unauthorized drug to this woman," he said. "That file on the treatment table next to her—"

"You're completely insane," Gillespie said coldly. He turned back to the resident. "Now move. I want security here in five minutes or your ass is grass." The resident bolted out of the room and headed for the nurses' station.

Thorne couldn't blame him. Faced with a choice between believing the senior anesthesiologist present on staff and a junior research doctor, he knew what he would have done. But that didn't change the facts. With Gillespie on the loose, Hannah Greener was in deadly danger.

The concerned, aghast face of Kamil appeared in the treatment doorway. "What the hell? Thorne?" Kamil turned a puzzled, open face to his friend, searching for an explanation. "What's going on?"

"I don't have time to explain," Thorne said quickly, aware that he had only moments before security appeared and hustled him off the premises. "But watch Hannah. It's Gillespie," he said, struggling to slow down enough to make himself understood without repeating the entire extent of his suspicions here in public. "I treated her last time she was in the ER. She's my patient," his voice now strong and confident. "Kamil, take her up to the OB ward. Do it yourself. And don't let Dr. Gillespie anywhere near her."

"Now see here," Gillespie began.

Thorne cut him off with a quick gesture. "You do that and I'll leave immediately, Doctor. Immediately. And," he added, surprising even himself, "my resignation will be on your desk in the morning."

Gillespie looked surprised, then self-satisfied. "That would be very acceptable." He turned back to Kamil. "If it will resolve this situation more quickly, you have my permission to accede to Dr. Thorne's outrageous request. Anything to get him off the premises and away from our patients."

Kamil stood there, evidently completely bewildered.

"Get her up to OB," Thorne repeated. He picked up his wallet and the rest of the contents of his pocket from the floor, where they'd fallen during the brief struggle, and walked to the door. "Just get her up there, Kamil. I'm leaving."

The maintenance foyer was on the lowest level of the Murphy. Corridors radiated off from its central circular area, providing access to the major engineering spaces that supplied emergency power, temperature control, and disposal services for the rest of the hospital. It also served as a shortcut to a parking garage as well as an underground access to the professional building. Thorne usually parked in the lot out in front of the hospital, which allowed him easier access to his office. Today, however, he'd been lucky enough to find a vacant spot in the garage.

Like most doctors, Thorne used the maintenance foyer as a shortcut between all the areas, particularly when he wanted to avoid contact with other members of the hospital staff. It was an unspoken but well-recognized fact that a doctor transiting the maintenance corridors was granted a degree of privacy. Eye contact was discouraged and casual conversations rare.

Now, more than ever, Thorne appreciated the maintenance corridor protocols. The last thing he wished to do was stop and talk to another doctor. He couldn't decide which would be worse, having to reveal his utter disgrace to a colleague and watch the shock and horror dawn in the person's eyes, or endure the forcibly hearty condolences from one already in the know.

He saw the other man first as a distant figure at the far end of the corridor that led to the hospital proper. Saw him coming and dismissed him, relying on the maintenance corridor protocol. It was only after the footsteps picked up in pace and intensity that he glanced up, startled, and recognized who it was.

Gillespie. Anger raged through him, burning away the depression

seeping into his mind. It was Gillespie who had substituted his judgment for that of his patients, practiced medicine in a manner so foul
that it defied any rational explanation. In the face of confronting his
own moral weakness in Korea, Thorne had wavered—wavered, then
done the right thing. But the opposite was true of Dr. Gillespie, the
man he'd looked up to and dared to hope would be his mentor.

Anger, then a small, niggling fear. He'd never seen Dr. Gillespie
move as quickly, not even during a code in the ER. The other doctor
moved purposefully, heading straight for him.

As Gillespie grew closer, Thorne could see that his eyes were
darting back and forth, lingering more and more often on Thorne.
Cold fire burned behind the constricted pupils, radiating out a sense
of malevolent intent.

Gillespie barreled up to him, then transformed his forward motion into a stunning full body tackle. He caught Thorne around the
midsection, wrested him into flight, and then slammed him down to
the floor. His vagus nerve constricted and Thorne felt his diaphragm
seize up. He struggled against the choking sensation, one part of his
mind clinically noting that his breath had been knocked out of him
and would return shortly. Another part insisted he was suffocating.

Thorne fought off the other doctor and managed to land an upward jab of his knee in the other man's groin. Gillespie grunted and
curled up reflexively, but his hands continued to scrabble up Thorne's
coat toward his neck. Thorne backpedaled on the floor, shoving himself away from Gillespie with his heels and trying to get out from
under the larger man.

Thorne finally planted one sneaker on Gillespie's forehead and
shoved back hard. The motion peeled Gillespie off him, but the other
doctor quickly recovered. With another guttural monosyllable, one
that might have been a word or simply an expression of anger, Gillespie lunged at him again.

Finally, Thorne understood just how dangerous his situation was.
At this hour of the night, the maintenance corridors were deserted.
Gillespie was clearly insane and seemed to possess an almost inhuman
strength. While Thorne's reflexes were quicker, Gillespie was stronger.
In a one-on-one encounter between the two, the odds were far too

close for comfort. In the split second before Gillespie reached him, Thorne made his decision. He ran.

Even this far from the public eye, the floors were spotlessly clean and waxed. Thorne pounded down the hallway, aware that the tile beneath his feet could turn dangerously slick in a heartbeat, aware of how close behind him Gillespie was.

The Murphy complex covered almost three square acres of ground. The corridors below it wove back and forth in an intricate maze. Once he was away from the well-beaten track between the ER and the parking garage, Thorne's sense of direction quickly deserted him. He could hear Gillespie falling farther behind, but not far enough to give Thorne time to slow down. He needed to find safety, either in the company of other people or in the form of some barricade.

Reaching a fork in the corridor, the light now fading as light fixtures were further apart, Thorne made a decision. He veered off to the righthand corridor, only half-certain that it would lead him where he thought it would.

Sixty steps later, he saw it. Not another elevator, but a set of stairs that provided access to the upper floors. There, at least, he was likely to find other people.

Thorne darted up the stairs, jerked open the door to the upper level and stepped into it. His anticipation immediately faded to fear. He had thought he was coming up on the radiology department, a twenty-four-hour facility that would have provided some measure of security. Instead, he was faced with the cool, light-green double doors that led to the morgue.

By the time he reached the top of the stairs, Gillespie's heartbeat seemed to drown out his own footsteps. He stopped, forced himself to hold his breath for a moment, and listen for Thorne's footsteps.

Nothing. How could the man have gotten so far ahead of him in the brief moments that he'd been out of view? He couldn't have continued running, not and remain so silent. No, he must be somewhere nearby—nearby and hiding. Gillespie raised one hand unconsciously to scratch at the burning itch at the base of his neck.

He had to be in the morgue, had to be. A peculiarly appropriate choice for Thorne, but then again, the younger doctor had always had qualities that surprised Gillespie. If only Thorne hadn't poked that keen intellect into places where it certainly shouldn't have gone. He was too young, he could never understand the pressures and forces at work within the hierarchy at Murphy medical. Publish or perish, grantsmanship, the whole slew of administrative and political duties that went along with being a department head at the prestigious institute. So what if he'd taken a couple of shortcuts? It was nothing more than he was due, in fact the idea suddenly made complete sense as he considered it: He'd actually been encouraged to do just as he had, experiment with Anaex on existing patients. Of course he had. Hadn't the hospital administrator himself pointed out that daring and innovation were two of Gillespie's best qualities? Hadn't he been asked repeatedly, coerced even, into speeding up the Anaex trials? Now that he thought about it, he was almost certain that he'd even discussed human trials with the chief of staff. Hadn't he?

No matter. What he'd done had been guided by the same principles that had guided him through twenty-five years of medical practice—he'd been acting in the best interest of his patients, not only those on the table in front of him at that moment but the ones who would come later. Anaex was the answer to too many surgical and anesthetic problems, too perfectly elegant a solution. A single extra hydroxyl chain on the end of Ketamine and voila: the perfect drug.

His anger was back now in full force, seething and bubbling inside like a massive stew of old wrongs.

The morgue. An entirely suitable place to end this. Gillespie shoved open the door and stepped into the receiving area.

Now. As soon as the door had completed its backward arc, Thorne sprang. He caught Gillespie's throat in the crook of his arm, jerking back hard without concern to what damage it would do to the cervical vertebrae. He slammed the larger man into the tiled wall, putting his free hand on the opposite side of Gillespie's head. The thud that Gillespie's head made when it hit the wall sickened him, as did the odd undertone of joy that he felt at the sound.

The older doctor's bellow of rage at the surprise attack was quickly transmuted into a yelp, then a groan. He staggered for a minute, pulling Thorne off his feet. With one arm crooked around Gillespie's neck, Thorne's other hand darted into Gillespie's pocket and seized the syringe he'd seen Gillespie put there.

Gillespie was frantic now, slamming into a wall and trying to dislodge Thorne from his back. Thorne jerked back with his arm, trying to cut off the flow of blood to Gillespie's brain. He hit the wall again as Gillespie threw himself into it, and felt his own head strike the cool tile. The shock stunned him for a moment and he loosened his grip on Gillespie. In one mad dervish whirl, Gillespie threw him across the room.

Thorne hit the autopsy table. The granite slab caught him in midsection, doubling him down and slamming his chin into it. He rolled, throwing himself off the end of the table then rising on the opposite side, interposing it between himself and the other doctor.

With a howl of rage, Gillespie sprung across the autopsy table at him, grasping for him. Thorne stepped back and Gillespie's fingers barely grazed the front of his shirt. He waited until the man was fully extended, then stepped in to bring his elbow down in a hard, sharp blow to Gillespie's spine. That slowed him for a moment. When Gillespie stood again, his motions were noticeably slower, and Thorne evaded him easily.

Another few moments. Thorne danced out of reach, now careful to keep his own body between Gillespie and the exit door. Gillespie charged again, and Thorne stepped aside easily. It seemed like an arcane game of matador and bull, with the same deadly objective.

Gillespie twisted and bellowed. He lashed back with his elbow, burying it deep in Thorne's gut. He pivoted, throwing Thorne off. Thorne staggered across the room, desperately holding on to the syringe. With a quick jerk, he flipped the plastic cover off the needle.

Gillespie charged. Thorne waited for him, the syringe behind his back. Gillespie plowed into him and drove him the rest of the way across the room into the far wall. They hit with a sickening thud. The impact knocked the breath out of Thorne.

Thorne stabbed through the thin surgical scrubs to jab the needle into Gillespie's flesh. He slammed the plunger home, felt it give way easily beneath his fingers.

What was in it? No way of telling, but if Gillespie had been about to use it on his female patient . . .

Gillespie's fingers found Thorne's neck and curled around it. Thorne jerked his knee up, aiming for the groin, but Gillespie blocked the movement with his leg.

There was a dull, ringing noise in his ears, and Thorne's field of vision crept inward from the edges. He wrenched himself sideways, trying to escape the hands knotted around his neck, but Gillespie held him pinned against the wall.

The pressure loosened abruptly and air flooded his windpipe. Gillespie reeled away from him, hands now clutching at his own throat. His face was purple, suffused with blood and steadily deepening in color.

"Heart attack." Gillespie gasped the words out, as deprived of oxygen as Thorne had been moments before. "Get—" Gillespie collapsed on the floor.

Thorne darted to the telephone and dialed the operator. "This is Dr. Thorne. Code blue, in the morgue."

"In the—"

"Call it, *now.*"

Panting heavily, still dizzy from the repeated blows to his head, Thorne rolled Gillespie onto his back and began CPR. Three minutes later, the crash cart arrived along with the staff responding.

Thorne moved away and watched them work on Gillespie. He'd given the syringe to the doctor leading the charge, but without knowing what was in it, it was of little use. Gillespie's fate would be decided long before that.

He backed out of the room, watching the team still working on Gillespie, and found a telephone in an outer office. He dialed Debbie Patterson's home number. When her sleepy voice answered, he said, "I'm on my way over. Don't call anybody, don't do anything. Just trust me, this once. I'll explain when I get there.

TWENTY-THREE

Patterson opened the door and pulled him inside before he could even ring the doorbell. "My god." She stared at Thorne's battered, swollen face. A few streaked smears indicated where he'd tried to clean off the blood, but he'd missed several spots. His right eye was already swelling shut, and angry red blotches decorated his neck. "The kitchen—my bag is on the table."

Her protestations that he needed medical care had quickly faded to intermittent weak objections as the story unfolded. Finally, when he concluded with leaving Gillespie unconscious on the morgue floor, she shook her head.

How much of the tale was Thorne's own distorted version of reality and how much was truth? At this point, having observed him earlier as an inpatient in the hospital, she simply wasn't sure. Over the last week, she'd noticed the change in him, the increasing restlessness, the uncharacteristic irritability. Now was she hearing the root cause of all of it, with final manifestations of serious psychiatric elements?

"You don't believe me." Thorne's voice was flat and controlled. She saw the resignation in his eyes, the grim determination evident despite his battered features.

"It's not that I don't believe you," she said carefully. "It's just that you're asking a lot."

"I'm not asking, I'm giving you the opportunity to help me stop this before it goes any further." He stood up abruptly from the couch, wincing slightly as he paced. Energy seemed to pour out of him, vibrant and healthy despite his physical condition. She marveled at his resilience, his sheer dogged persistence.

Marveled, but wasn't convinced. "I might know someone who could help" she said slowly. She filled him in on her uncle's position on the Joint Chiefs of Staff. "What do you think the chances are that he'll believe this? It's different for me, at least I know you."

"I have proof."

"The rats?" Debbie's skepticism deepened. "I thought you said security had them."

Thorne nodded. "But they'll turn them over to the proper military authorities." His voice took on an ironic note. "Without the military, the Murphy isn't anything. I'd never realized how much that connection constrained us. All I saw was that there was funding, political support for what we were trying to do. Oh yeah, good old Thorne, true believer."

The bitterness in his voice cut painfully to her core. "We *are* doing good work. The best in the country in some areas," she answered. "This Anaex thing, just how certain are you that Gillespie's been using it on patients?"

"I'm certain. You have to believe me on this."

"Suppose I do. Big deal, a surgeon believes you. The person you have to convince is my uncle."

"I know. But I need you to put me in touch with him."

Again, the dilemma she'd been circling around for the past five years. Her connection with her uncle was that of favorite niece and adored uncle. The first time she'd realized just how powerful a man he was had been shortly after her interview at the Murphy. Uncle Jerry had followed her entire application process with avid interest, insisting that she debrief him daily on responses to her telephone calls and application. After she passed the initial screening interview at Murphy, his interest had grown even more keen. After the final interview, he called her before she could even reach him and said, "You're going to get it, Debbie. I know it."

"There are a lot of qualified applicants," she remembered protesting. At the time, she believed that his comment was simply the normal function of the cheerleader that he'd served in her life for so many years. Later, after she'd understood who he was—and what Murphy was—she began to suspect otherwise.

She'd pushed herself hard before the Murphy, and even harder afterward. The issue of just how much her uncle had influenced the selection had never been discussed. Finally she'd started to believe that she'd earned the position on her own merits. And lately she'd added the corollary that regardless of whether he'd rigged the selection process, Murphy had gotten the best candidate anyway.

And so what was Thorne asking her? To back-channel information to the one man who might most need it? Or to impose on a family connection in an overt way that she'd never attempted, to perhaps cross some line from family concern to nepotism? And once crossed, would she ever again be able to be certain that she made her way on her own? Or would there always be the question in her mind: Was it her or her uncle's influence?

She took a deep breath, held it for a few moments, then let it out slowly. "And you think General Boothby was one of them?" she asked again, hoping against hope that he would change his story.

"I saw him, Debbie. In Korea. I saw him and followed him, and damn near lost myself. He's in the States now, briefing the JCS on Korea. From there, he'll go to talk to the president, if the situation is as serious as I think it is."

"We're not going to stop that."

Thorne shook his head. "Everything the general *tells* them will be true."

"Then what's the problem?"

"Because he won't tell them *everything*. Because he won't admit that he's the one behind the escalating violence there, that he's the one provoking it. It's all part of his plan, Debbie. Don't make the mistake that I made: knowing the man is brilliant but thinking that I was in his class. That I could understand what he was doing, plan as far ahead as he does. No matter how smart we are, that's not our line of work. The general's got this whole thing planned out like a military campaign, and no matter how hard we try, we are not going to be able to break the code. It's as impossible as Boothby walking into OR three and performing a heart transplant. He might be smart, but I don't think he could do it."

"Don't think?" Debbie asked, trying desperately to use humor to break the dull foreboding that had settled over her.

Thorne half smiled, acknowledging her attempt. "If anyone could, it would be Boothby. But no, I don't think he could."

"I don't know if—"

"Yes, you do." Thorne's voice held a note of sadness. "I know you know how to get in touch with him. I heard you on the phone the other night."

"You were eavesdropping?" Debbie demanded.

"No." Briefly, he summarized how he accidentally overheard her as he got out of the shower chasing an errant towel. Debbie felt her own face flush, whether in reaction to being caught in an evasion or in reaction to the overwhelming animal vitality she felt radiating out from Thorne. Finally, she said, "Let me think about it." Raising a hand to forestall his protests, she continued, "Not for long. Just a little while. Go get some sleep. I want to think about it. You have to know what you're asking."

Thorne sighed and stood up. "I'm sorry it's come to this, Debbie. But if you can't help me, then I have to find someone who can." He picked up his coat and headed for the door.

"Wait. Where are you going?"

He answered, his back still to her, "To the police. And if they won't listen, to the FBI, or to any other organization that I think has the slightest chance of giving me a fair hearing. All I want is for them to check it out."

"They'll never believe you," Debbie said, arriving at a decision. "They'll call the hospital, check up on you. Hell, the local police will have Wallinger down there to collect you again before you can even finish telling the story. You know that."

He whirled on her. "Then what would you have me do?" he said, his voice harsh. "Stand by and do nothing? Protest that I'm a doctor, not responsible for anything outside of the Murphy complex? Just what would you ask of me, Debbie?"

She lifted her chin and stared him straight in the face. "I'd ask you to be who you are," she said softly. "The man I first met at Murphy, the one I slept with two weeks ago."

"You don't want to know that man, Debbie. He's not who you think he is." Thorne's voice carried a note of infinite disgust. "I found that out in Korea. Part of Carter's story is true. I killed a man there. Not Carter, but a Korean."

"Intentionally?"

He nodded. "I was on patrol. They left me alone out there, maybe

257

just to see what I'd do, maybe for some other reason. Like I said, I'm never going to be able to really understand Boothby, not when he's operating in his own element. But for whatever reason, I was there. This guy, he came out of the trees. His rifle—at the time, I knew if I didn't get him, he'd kill me. So I shot him. Hell, I barely remember pulling the trigger. It's like I was on automatic, like I *knew* what was happening and was watching it from outside myself."

"It's no sin to kill someone who's trying to kill you, Scoot. If you didn't have a choice."

"There's always a choice. I'm a doctor. I should have—"

"Have *what?* Let him kill you instead? Nothing in the Hippocratic oath requires that. Or just not have been there in the first place? Agreed, but it doesn't sound like you had a choice at that point."

"You don't know. You weren't there. Listen, I appreciate what you're trying to do, but it's something I have to live with. I'm the one who killed that man."

"Anyone in the same situation would have done the same thing. Get over it, Thorne. You're not some godlike creature, no matter what they taught you in medical school."

"I know I'm not. But Boothby thinks he is. Debbie, if I can do something about this, stop him before he kills thousands of people over there, at least I might be able to justify what happened. Don't you see that?" Thorne was pleading now, a man stripped down to the most fundamental of choices.

"Okay." The words were out before she'd considered them, the decision settled on her as completely right and true. "Okay, I'll call him."

"And what will you tell him? That an insane doctor is raving in your apartment and you're just calling to get him out? To satisfy some odd obsession of his?"

She shook her head, felt a returning flood of confidence. "No. I'll tell him I know you and your work, and that he needs to listen." She shrugged again, aware of the limitations of her relationship with her uncle. "Past that, you're on your own. He either believes you or he doesn't."

Thorne crossed the room and took a seat next to her on the couch again.

"Let's do it now, before I start doubting myself. Again." Puzzled, she looked up at his last word, and saw his eyes opaque and unreadable. She picked up the telephone and punched in the numbers for her uncle's pager. She answered with her own telephone number, followed by the pound sign, and then waited to hear the acknowledgment from the national paging service that her message had been transmitted. She replaced the receiver in its cradle and said, "Now, we wait."

Wallinger walked the halls of Murphy, his crepe-soled shoes silent on the glossy tile. He passed the nurses' station, nodded familiarly to the nurse leaning on the counter scribbling patient notes, and proceeded on down the passageway to the west exit. He passed the elevator foyer, quickly assessed the woman and man waiting there. No threat, relatives or friends of one of the patients from their expressions. And one that wasn't doing well.

At the end of the passageway, a concrete set of steps led down to the ground floor and then into the subterranean spaces of the hospital. He paused in front of it, his hand resting on the shiny enamel-painted door. The stairways, that was the main purpose behind this little tour.

Not that it was unusual for him to walk the corridors, taking the security temperature of his domain. But the recent unexplained departure of Sergeant Carter had revealed a major shortcoming in procedures. The Murphy was well protected from uninvited intruders, but had few precautions to insure that people inside the hospital couldn't leave. It would require a delicate balancing of safety and security requirements to find a solution. The Murphy had to be able to maintain control of patients who posed security risks in one form or another. Especially military patients. Especially the military.

His rationale would be that the new precautions were necessary to insure that intruders could not leave the building without being detected. The idea would provoke heated response from many corners, he knew. It was not only untenable to lock the doors, given most of them served as fire escapes, but he suspected most of the board would also argue that it was in the patients' best interest that such people left quickly anyway. Better to transfer the problem to the outside world, to put the local authorities on the spot, rather than risk escalating problems inside the hospital proper.

The military would have a different take on it. Of that he was certain.

And it was not only the patients. The problem with Dr. Thorne and Dr. Gillespie stuck in his craw, an ever-increasing annoyance. Wasn't it enough that he had to cope with the security requirements of, on this particular day, fifteen different nations without having to prevent physical confrontations between the physicians? He shook his head, getting madder and madder the more he thought about it. Two doctors, tussling like common street thugs. And whose fault had it been? Neither doctor had given him a particularly satisfactory explanation, and Dr. Thorne's credibility was questionable at best.

He thought about it for a moment, and found his thoughts veering off toward Dr. Thorne. There were plenty of objective reasons for his suspicion. The statements by Carter, the reports from Thorne's co-workers that he'd apparently undergone some traumatic event in Korea that had resulted in a change in his personality. And that surgeon—Patterson was her name. He smirked a bit as he thought about the sparks that flew when he saw the two of them together. Something going on there, a little nonviolent exploratory surgery, he suspected.

Yes, if pressed, he'd have to admit that Thorne was uppermost in his thoughts as a security risk.

He pushed open the door and started down the steps. There was something odd about Carter, as well. That alone bore more investigation before he placed too much weight on the man's claims that Thorne had shot him.

He paused on the middle landing, shut his eyes for a moment, and tried to recall the security admitting information on the renegade sergeant. It had been oddly worded, but the implications had been clear. Somebody high up—very high up—had wanted Carter at the Murphy. Perhaps it was time to find out exactly what that was about.

He made up his mind and continued his descent. He'd finish his rounds, have his staff start drafting a preliminary plan for increased surveillance and control of egress points, and then make a few phone calls. Perhaps his compadres over at CID would be more forthcoming than they usually were. He'd try them, and also try to get through to the highest ranking officer he could in Carter's chain of command.

Boothby parked his car down the street from the stately house that served as the family homestead during his tours of duty in Washington. The upstairs lights were on, and the lower floor was obscured by shrubs and low trees. Coupled with the dim moonlight and partially overcast sky, it gave the impression that the second floor was floating suspended in midair. He saw a figure move in front of the window, backlit by the room light. After so many years of being married to her, he could recognize her by the way she moved, her shape even in the dimmest light. Alicia, the traitor. The one who should have been with him in Korea at his side, standing by him until the last possible second before civilians were evacuated, the moment before the ultimate confrontation. Her absence served to create disorder among those families on post in Korea, made them uneasy in a way that they found difficult to define. In some ways, it was as though he himself had fled the theater of combat.

He sat for a moment longer in the dark, then got out of the car. It wouldn't hurt to talk to her, to try to explain. To make her see reason the way he'd always been able to before, to convince her that one more overseas tour was absolutely necessary to further his career— their career—in the Army. She'd been increasingly resistant over the last few years to overseas tours, whining and mewling about the effect on Brett. And Brett—another problem altogether.

Boothby stood outside the house now, shadowed by the two large juniper trees at the entrance to his walkway. Avenues of approach, his tactical plan for the discussion with Alicia rode through his mind like a ground combat maneuver scheme, the possibilities and permutations shifting as rapidly as he could assess them. Finally, he felt the mental click that always signified to him that the right course of action was in front of him. He moved out of the shadows and around to the back door of the house, taking advantage of the cover to mask his approach. Not that it really mattered. He had no doubt that both his wife and son had retired to the upper floor, but it was never smart to make too many assumptions about the preparedness of the enemy.

"No, of course I understand. Do you know where I can reach him there?" Wallinger asked. His fingers drummed out an impatient rhythm on the top of this desk. Military bureaucracy and security—while he appreciated the necessity for both, dealing with proper channels was always a pain in the ass. He waited, musing at the oddity of listening to Kenny Rogers while on hold with Korea, as the major to whom he'd been speaking bumped him up to the colonel. Finally, he spoke to the chief of staff.

"It's imperative I speak to him." Wallinger mustered a degree of officiousness that had followed him from his Army career into civilian life. No matter that the colonel would have once been so senior to him that all he would have rated was a quick salute. Now, things were different.

"Read the newspapers," the colonel replied. It was evident from his tone that he had far more important things on his mind than the queries of a rent-a-cop at a hospital in California. "We're a little bit busy over here."

An understatement, Wallinger could tell. He grimaced, thinking of the preparations that would even now be under way in that god-forsaken hellhole. "He's got to have a point of contact here," Wallinger tried. "I've got to get through to him. His personal safety may be at stake."

"What's that?" the colonel said, his voice now wary. "I thought you said this was about Sergeant Carter? His captain can answer any questions about him."

"It's about Carter, and more. Listen, I spent twenty years in the Army. I'm head of security at Murphy Medical Center in Merced, California, and I have reason to think your boss's life is in danger. So are we gonna dick around with your standing orders or are you going to tell me who I need to talk to back in the States?"

A long silence ensued, broken only by intermittent spikes of static from the overseas line. "Give me your number," the colonel said finally. "I'll pass it on to someone over there. He can call you if he's interested."

"You're making a mistake," Wallinger warned. "I'll find him somehow, and it's gonna be embarrassing as hell when I do find him and tell him about our conversation today."

"Try the Joint Chiefs of Staff. They'll know where he is." The line went dead.

"Big deal. That was my next call anyway." Wallinger picked up the phone and started dialing.

Debbie pulled Thorne's feet up onto the couch and straightened out his torso. She made sure that he had good circulation to his arms. As exhausted as he was, he could lie on one and cut off the circulation completely, just like a man in a dead drunk.

But drunk he wasn't. Perhaps there was some other mental problem, although she was beginning to believe that Thorne was far more sane than anyone at Murphy thought. Well, no matter. She'd done what she could, and now they would both have to settle in and wait for her uncle's return call.

She stood up and crossed the room to a cabinet located at the end of the short passageway. She pulled out a blanket, shook it out, then recrossed to the couch and tossed it over him. She stood there for a moment, gazing down at him.

Thorne had already shifted over to his side, curling his hands up under his face. In sleep, he was oddly vulnerable, yet relaxed in a way she hadn't seen in days. The tiny lines and muscles in his face were relaxed now, falling into a natural, composed look. She watched his eyes move under his eyelids, indicating he was in REM sleep. Suddenly, she was curious as to exactly what Thorne could be dreaming of. Of her? She was surprised at how quickly the possibility sprang to mind, tinted with an eagerness and longing she hadn't suspected existed. No, probably not. Something at the hospital, maybe something in Korea. She studied him again, and then decided that whatever he was thinking had nothing to do with Korea. His face was too smooth, his breathing too even. Whatever he was dreaming about, it was of a peaceful, untraumatic nature.

She curled herself up in one corner of the couch and pulled the far end of the blanket over her. Thorne moved slightly, snuggling his feet up to her thigh and hip. She smiled ruefully. That was probably the most physical contact she could expect for a while. She pulled the blanket further up and settled in to wait for the phone to ring.

Boothby slid the key out of his pocket and slipped it into the backdoor lock. He'd already removed it from his regular string of keys and coated it with WD-40 to insure there was no noise. The lock turned easily and he pushed the door open, freezing at a slight squeal from one hinge. He waited for several minutes, wondering if there would be a reaction. Finally, when he was convinced Alicia had not heard it, he shoved the door open the rest of the way and stepped into the mud room attached to the kitchen. Two plates and a cooking pot filled with water were in the sink. A paper napkin smeared with barbecue sauce lay on one end of the counter and the chairs were still pulled out from the table.

Disorder. Neglect. The dishes that should have been done before Alicia retired for the evening, Brett drying them and placing them back in the cabinet, the chairs neatly tucked under the table, the napkin . . . just how far had the household routine degenerated in his absence?

Even the family room, with souvenirs and mementos from all of his last tours arranged in the graceful pattern called Army eclectic, was cluttered. Bills lay piled carelessly on one shelf of the bookcase. And just how long had that TV tray been positioned next to his own recliner?

Getting on with her life, was she? Forgetting her responsibilities? Just as Brett had. Was he the only one in the entire family who understood what the word responsibility meant?

He moved slowly, passing through the kitchen and living room on silent feet. The stairs leading up to the second floor were carpeted, and he walked close to the joint with the wall in order to avoid a few chronic squeaky boards underneath. His boot scuffed against a child's shoe, sending it clattering down to the next step. He froze again, waiting for any reaction.

Outside the door to the master bedroom, he stopped again. He quickly undid his shirt, unzipped his trousers, and let them fall to the floor. No matter if she heard a noise now, he was too close for it to matter.

The bedroom door was partially open. He eased through the crack and padded quietly to her side of the bed, and felt a grim satisfaction that at least that much hadn't changed.

His precautions had been unnecessary. Alicia was firmly committed to slumber. He studied the familiar curves beneath the bedclothes, the oddly childlike way she curled up in sleep. It evoked a fleeting surge of tenderness, of some emotion that felt ancient and distant. He shoved that away, focusing on his purpose. Maybe there'd been time years ago, when he was still young and on his way up in the Army for that sort of nonsense, but not now.

He moved around to his side of the bed, pulled back the covers, and slid between the sheets.

Alicia awoke instantly, raised up in bed, and stared at him with shocked eyes. He saw her draw in a sharp breath, a preliminary to screaming, and her hand flailed blindly toward the bedside table where he knew she kept a gun.

"It's me," he said, moving quickly to catch her hand. The beginning of the scream started, quickly cut off as she realized who he was.

"My god, what are you doing here?" she said, her voice panicky. "You're supposed to be—"

"In Washington," he concluded calmly, finishing her sentence. "Briefing the Joint Chiefs of Staff."

"Thurmond, I—"

He shushed her quietly, then pulled her toward him. "Later." Her body went stiff, then she pulled back from him slightly. He tightened his grip on her, his fingers roaming over her body. How long had it been? Too long, he realized. Too long to carry out the plan of gentle seduction he'd planned, too long to endure the emotions flooding in now, replacing the rage with something dark and ugly.

He jerked her toward him. A harsh, whispered protest that he silenced with his mouth, and then he was on her, hard callused hands holding down soft flesh, his knee shoving apart her legs. He was hard, so hard, almost unable to contain himself as he poised his body over hers. He stopped for one second, long enough to savor the sheer terror and anguish in her eyes, then slammed into her, reclaiming his rights.

The Army CID duty officer suppressed an irritated sigh. Bad enough that his weekend was ruined with duty at the central office. Worse that the coming celebration of the Army's birthday began on Monday, necessitating extensive coordination with the other law enforcement agencies in town as well as personal security arrangements for a covey of senior officers. Now, the phone call that had finally been routed to him through his underlings, kicked up the chain of command as a problem too tainted with the possibility of a foul-up. It had been the right decision, but that made his decision no easier.

"The name of your hospital again?" the major asked, scribbling on the legal sheet in front of him. "And the phone number?"

He listened as the voice, a harsh Midwest drawl tinged with Chicago undertones, repeated the information. A touch of impatience, he thought, and was ashamed to find that the thought of ruining some else's day made his own trials a bit less lonely.

"Okay. I'll check into it and call you back." He could tell from Wallinger's response that the hospital security officer was not satisfied. Well, fuck him. There were written procedures for dealing with threats against senior officers, an entire checklist of messages to be sent, officers to be notified, and preparations to be made for including the information in the morning brief. If the civilian didn't like it, then he could go to hell.

"No, no promises," he said, forestalling a litany of requests that he could tell was just beginning. "Listen, let me do my job, okay?"

As he hung up the phone, he reached for the binder located in a small rack next to the duty desk. He thumbed through the pages, the tabs worn and grimy from constant fingering, and reached the relevant portion. He ran down through the list of names, found the correct point of contact, and picked up the phone again. His underlings had been right. The man might be a crank, but he sure as hell wasn't going to take the responsibility for it. Instead of passing it up through the chain of command, this one was going to be a lateral pass. He dialed the number for the Joint Chiefs of Staff security officer at home and sat back with a smile.

The first ring of the phone brought him instantly awake, but he was confused about where he was. The pillows and blanket covering him felt wrong. For a second, the appearance of the room befuddled him.

Debbie Patterson's voice reoriented him. He heard her answer the phone, begin a low, quiet exchange with the person on the other end. Family pleasantries, a few words of gossip about relatives, then he heard her cut to the chase. "I have a friend who's concerned about the mental stability of General Boothby. He's here at the house, could you talk to him?" The silence stretched on too long to be a simple yes or no, and he saw Debbie nod and make murmurs of assent twice. Finally, she turned to look at him. She held out the receiver. "It's my uncle."

Thorne took the telephone, forcing himself awake. His muscles felt heavy and leaden, lagging behind the adrenaline surge already hitting his brain. His one chance.

He took a deep breath.

"I realize what I'm about to tell you may sound incredible," he began. He stopped suddenly, damning himself for being a fool. Trite phrases and a thousand arguments to prove his authenticity flooded his mind. Desperate to establish his credibility with his only chance, he found himself unable to phrase a single sentence that didn't sound like it had been lifted from a bad movie.

He stuttered for a few moments, floundering, aware of Debbie's deepening expression of dismay. Finally, he said, "Let me tell you what happened in Korea."

He started with Korea and his mobilization then cut back to fill in his own background at Murphy. He ran through the data on the rats, including the bloody massacre and odd disposal of the remains. Finally, he ventured a few tentative opinions on the reason for the escalation in Korea. At that point, Debbie's uncle cut him off.

"Stick with what you know. I'll check it out."

Thorne felt his jaw drop. His presentation had been anything but compelling, and he felt the sense of despair deepening as he heard his own voice stumble over the story. Not a bit of it had been embellished, and he'd been careful to distinguish between fact, his professional opinion as a doctor, and his opinion as an untrained observer.

"I—I can't thank you—what can—" Thorne stuttered.

"Debbie vouches for you. That's enough for me. You stick to what you know, medicine. Don't talk to anyone else until I get back to you. You got that?"

"Yes. I'll do that. Not talk to anyone, I mean. Just look at his skin, sir, if you have the chance. Please, if there's any sign of a serious rash, eruptions, a bandage of any sort, find out if it's in his medical record. See what they're calling it. And, if it's there, be careful. Be damned careful." Thorne shuddered, his memories of Korea flooded his mind. He saw again the bloody corpse, smelled the acrid scent that eddied and drifted in the night air, saw the bright, almost gleeful expression on Carter's face.

"There are some other things I should tell you," he said, remembering just what this man would hear from other sources. About Carter. About Gillespie and his problems at the hospital. About the suspension of his medical privileges at Murphy.

"Go on."

Briefly, Thorne outlined the horror stories he was sure the man would hear.

"Goes one of two ways. Either it proves you are the ultimate in unreliable sources, or it shows that you're an honest man."

Thorne heard the sigh from the other end, and asked, "Is there anything you can tell me? Anything at all?"

A grunt this time, noncommittal and void of emotional content. "Put Debbie back on."

Thorne murmured his thanks again, then handed the telephone to Debbie. She took it and turned away from him, and he felt his heart sink as he stared at her back, the lean, smooth arc of muscle shaping the thin cotton robe, the barely visible swell of her ass under it. A line of white skin at the edge of her haircut, indicating a recent trim. The smooth, deceptive lines of the muscles in her arms, arms that he'd seen move with the most delicate deftness and authoritative strength of any surgeon he'd ever observed.

"Yes, I understand," Debbie said. She twisted to look back at him, her eyes unrevealing. "He will. And thanks."

She replaced the telephone and shook her head for a moment, then turned back to him. "He'll do what he said, you know." She said it in an offhand manner as though there were never any doubt of it. "Check it out, I mean."

His body seemed suddenly lighter, as though he'd lost twenty pounds in the last ten minutes. Wordlessly, he opened his arms to her. She slid into his embrace, as warm and fragrant as the night.

"Thank you," he whispered.

"Is this how you thank all of your surgeons?" She moved closer, pressing against him until the cotton robe between them was alive with her heat.

"No. And this is not about your uncle, either," he said, gesturing at the phone with his head. His arms wrapped firmly around her. "Thank you. For being here. For listening. For all of it."

"Prove it." She pulled away slightly from him and looked up with a challenging stare.

He watched her sleep, savoring the scent and the smell and the sound of her. And dismayed at what he was about to do. Had there been any other way, he would not have left her, not for a single day. He slipped quietly out of bed, watching her the entire time. Debbie stirred briefly, half opened her eyes to look up at him, and smiled. "Go back to sleep," he said softly.

She murmured something unintelligible, and her eyes shut.

Thorne waited for five minutes, then carried his clothes out to the living room to dress. He left the apartment, returned to his car downstairs, and pulled out on the highway.

Despite the assurances of the phone call, he could not take any chances. Sometime during his brief postcoital slumber, the final piece of the puzzle had clicked into place. Korea, Boothby's fascination with his JFK assassination theories, and the general's recent return to DC.

Eerie signposts on the landscape of a delusional mind. The signs were all there, if you knew how to read them.

Thorne hoped he did. The red-eye flight to DC left in three hours.

TWENTY-FOUR

The next morning, General Boothby arrived at the Pentagon early for his meeting with the chief of staff. Everything was well at home now. He'd seen it in the way Alicia had behaved as she fixed his normal breakfast of orange juice, a bagel with cream cheese, and French roast coffee. That she had refused to meet his eyes, that her hands had trembled slightly as she served the meal, he attributed to the aftermath of passion, and perhaps a bit of embarrassment at her own conduct. No matter. She'd had bagels in the freezer, just as she always did when he was on a tour in DC, and that proved that she knew that their current state of affairs was simply a mistake. And totally, and completely, hers. At some fundamental level, she'd known he'd be back, and had done her duty as a wife to prepare for his return. A good Army wife was always ready.

The corridors were already teeming with junior officers, each bent on arriving before his or her boss, insuring that the coffee and morning donut messes were well stocked, and generally doing anything they could to break out of the pack. He nodded greetings, returned salutes as required, savoring the respect and awe that the one star on his shoulders rated. His last tour at the Pentagon had been as a junior colonel. He'd been senior enough not to actually make the coffee, but junior enough to assure that it was done. Such was the life of a four-striper in the world's largest office building in the center of American military power.

Ah, but Korea. Command of the forces there was even headier, and he took grim pleasure in the fact that most of the people who recognized him knew exactly who he was. Not a junior flag officer stashed in the Pentagon for seasoning and staff work, no. An officer in general command, one with an entire division under command. An officer at the pointy end of the spear, one whose daily decisions spelled the difference between peace and war.

At least he hoped so.

"Good morning, General." The master sergeant at the front desk was on his feet, immediately responsive to his presence. "May I get you some coffee, sir?"

Boothby nodded. He knew that the sergeant would know how he took it without being told. Master sergeants were good at that sort of detail. Not that the master sergeant would do it himself—even within the enlisted troops in the Pentagon, there was a clearly established pecking order.

Moments later, a fresh mug of coffee was politely tendered by a staff sergeant. Boothby took it appreciatively, marveling at the way the Army maintained a consistent, peculiar bite to the brew in every unit in the country.

"You're scheduled for 0900," the master sergeant said. He had one stubby finger planted on the day book before him. "You know where the chief of staff's office is, of course."

"I certainly do, Master Sergeant," Boothby answered. He drained the coffee in one, long appreciative swig. He handed the empty mug back to the staff sergeant. "In fact, I'll head down there now."

At the chief of staff's office, the normally respectful greeting was tinged with awe. He held back the smile, suppressed the glee bubbling up inside. There could be only one reason for the flurry of activity around him, the grave courtesy and straightforward demeanor of junior officers intended to pander to an overblown flag officer's ego, and the delicate traceries of power he now felt flowing out from himself to the rest of the room. He'd succeeded. The reaction of the staff was a sure indication that he was on the White House's calendar.

He greeted a few old friends, then was shown to the visiting flag officer's spaces to wait for the chief of staff. Ten minutes—a short wait in the Pentagon by any standard—and he was ushered in to see the man himself.

"You're on. Two o'clock this afternoon." The chief of staff's congratulatory expression held a note of doubt. "Thurmond, you're absolutely sure about this?" It was a request not as much for Boothby's tactical analysis of the Korean scenario as for reassurance that the junior general was not going to be an embarrassment at the briefing. On such intricate political maneuverings were built entire careers. Boothby personally knew of two generals who'd been urged into early retirement for mild disagreement with the president over some minor matter of national strategy.

"Ready and willing, sir," Boothby replied. "You won't be disappointed." And that, he knew, was the real reassurance the chief of staff was asking him to offer.

"You'll brief the chief first, of course," the chief of staff continued, referring to the chairman of the Joint Chiefs of Staff, Jerry Huels. "He'll want to know. And any problems we discuss in house first, before it leaks out to the rest of the flunkies."

Or before I step on my dick in front of the president. Boothby nodded humbly. Such a session, commonly referred to as a murder board, was intended to insure that the briefing officer was drilled on current policy and able to respond to off-the-wall questions or requests for greater detail.

"One o'clock. The murder board."

Thorne woke as the flight attendant made her customary final approach requests for seat belts fastened and trays in an upright position. Oddly enough, he'd slept well, deeply enough to clear the remaining fog from his brain.

In the harsh morning light that spilled over the runway, this frantic dash to Washington seemed like the futile pipe dream of a doctor way out of his league. What could he hope to accomplish with this? Did he really think that a personal argument would be any more persuasive than he'd been on the phone? No, he had to face facts. He'd blown his one chance. Blown it, and in front of Debbie. Whatever impulse had sustained him through the two-hour drive to San Francisco, the hour wait for the aircraft, and the final boarding with no luggage, it had vanished now.

"Sir?" The flight attendant stood next to his seat, a professionally cheerful expression on her face. "Is your name Thorne?"

Thorne nodded, an uneasy wariness quickly building to fear.

"Good, I'm glad." Confusion replaced his fear as he studied her face. She smiled even more brightly and said, "You were asleep when we did our final head count while airborne. I didn't want to wake you to verify our manifest."

Thorne could only nod.

Hard rubber on runway, the cattle call of disembarking—people jamming the aircraft's narrow aisle as they reached for their carry-on luggage—Thorne chafed at each delay, now committed to this course of action, unable to persuade himself that it would do any good. Still, he had to try, had to be able to know that he had done everything possible.

"Where to, buddy?" The cab driver glanced at him curiously. "Got any luggage?"

"The Pentagon," Thorne said, ignoring the question. "If there's a special entrance for the Army, that will do."

"You started this whole mess by fortifying." Jerry Huels hammered the statement out in a hard, angry voice. "I want an explanation, Boothby, now."

"Mr. President, if I may?" Boothby extracted a chart from a brown manila folder. "I've outlined the time sequence of events here." He handed the graph to the chairman of the Joint Chiefs of Staff. "As you can see, there were three sniper attacks on my men before I ordered the additional sandbagging. Patrols were increased immediately after the first, but only after the first."

"And that provoked them into further retaliation, didn't it?" Jerry Huels showed no signs of relenting.

"As our security measures in the Middle East resulted in the Khobar Towers bombing? Thirty-two American airmen dead, Mr. President." He shook his head. "I wasn't willing to take that kind of chance with my people. Not over there."

The tension in the air was palpable. Boothby met Huels's glare with a calm, confident expression. Neither flinched.

Finally, Huels nodded. "It'll do, Thurmond. But tone it down a little bit, okay? Lead off with an apology for the press misreporting the actual sequence of events or something. The president will take going toe-to-toe pretty well, but there's no point in getting to that point when there's a way around it. That he's got that information from the press works really well, particularly after they misreported his visit last week to Japan."

Boothby nodded, trying not to let his relief show. This was the essence of a murder board, a pressure cooker to see how he handled himself under attack, off the cuff. From the expression on Jerry Huels's face, he knew he'd passed.

"Time for lunch before we go?" Huels asked of no one in particular.

"Of course, General," Boothby said, surprising even himself. "I'll have the steak tartar."

An unexpected grin flashed across Huels's face. "You pull this one off, and I'll see that that makes it as a regular entrée on the flag officer's mess."

The Army CID officer was bone tired. Two terrorist threats overseas, the normal personnel emergencies within their own small staff, and the spate of messages overclassified by some absurd lieutenant in Germany had kept him up most of the night. Now, the last thing he wanted to deal with was the officer—the reserve officer—standing across the desk in front of him.

"A rash, you say?" He leaned back at his desk and laced his fingers behind his head. "On the general's head."

Thorne nodded. "It's the first sign. I've proven it in clinical tests."

"Tests." The major filled the word with doubt, conveying the totality of his opinion to the doctor in one single word.

"Get the highest-ranking doctor around here," Thorne continued, even now aware of the futility of continuing. The major had neither the background nor the interest to understand the danger. At best, Thorne would be glad-handed out of the office with reassurances that they'd look into the matter. At worst—he glanced back at the outer door. There'd been two security men there as he'd come in.

"You're obviously not aware that what you ask is completely impossible, not today." The major appeared to take some satisfaction in ignoring Thorne's request and dismissing the issue out of hand. "Not at all today."

"Why not?"

The major pointed at the newspaper folded on one corner of his desk. The front page above the fold shouted warnings of imminent war in Korea. "General Boothby's a bit busy today. He'll be briefing the president on Korea, then probably drawing up war mobilization plans."

"He can't."

The major smirked. "Oh, I think he can. The commanding general of Korea hardly requires permission from his dermatologist to do that."

"But you don't understand. Nothing's happening over there— nothing is. The general's starting it, he's behind everything." Thorne caught himself, took a deep breath, forcing his voice back down into a normal register. "Just get me a doctor, please?"

It was the major's turn to look concerned. He stood, came around from behind his desk, and laid one hand on Thorne's shoulder. "Maybe you're right. After all, he is the general, isn't he? We have to make sure everything is all right with him. Especially with the way things are going in Korea. I'll get the doctor over here right away. You just wait in the waiting room." He put gentle pressure on Thorne's shoulder, urging him off toward the office door. "Just wait here," he continued, pointing at a comfortable chair in one corner of the room. "I'll call the doctor, he'll come up and we'll talk about this again."

Thorne allowed himself to be led to the chair and settled uneasily into it. The major cast him one last reassuring look and then headed back into his office, shutting the door behind him.

Thorne looked across the room at the secretary sitting there. She was a civilian, one of the many that populated the Pentagon. There was an uneasy expression on her face as she looked at him, then quickly cut her eyes away. She picked up her purse, edged around her desk, and headed for the door. "Bathroom," she said by way of explanation, and then fled the room.

It took him a moment, but the insight finally came. The major was calling a doctor, but not to discuss the possibility that the commanding general in Korea was insane. No, the major had someone else in mind—someone considerably more junior.

Thorne bolted to his feet. If they were coming to get him, it would take hours to unravel the web of restraints they'd weave around him.

The two security men looked up at him with bored expressions, then returned to their reading material. They hadn't been told, then. Thorne glanced back at the door. It was only a matter of time until the major summoned them to his office, told them to keep an eye on the doctor while the psychiatrist arrived.

As casually as he could, Thorne picked up his briefcase and walked over to the door. "Sir?" one of the guards asked.

Thorne stopped, certain that he was about to be forcibly subdued. He eyed the door, glanced back at the security guard, and assessed his chances. Minimal, at best.

"If the major asks," the security guard continued, "should we tell him you'll be right back?"

"Yes. Right back." Thorne was surprised he could get the words out. "I'll be right back."

They traveled to the White House in two official staff cars. The guard at the gate, after checking identification and verifying their appointment against a master roster, waved them on through. Huels's driver pulled up in front of the White House's east wing, left the engine running as he jumped out of the driver's seat, and headed around the car to open the door for his VIP passengers. Boothby beat him to it, and was already leaving the vehicle as he arrived at the side door.

"Wait for us," Huels ordered as he exited. "The usual place."

The search by the Secret Service agents in the anteroom to the business section of the White House was brief but thorough. They passed through a metal detector, and the contents of their briefcases and folders were thoroughly examined. Finally, they were admitted to a shabby exterior waiting room, one hour prior to their appointment.

Weapons. The search would do them no good, Boothby thought. There was no metal detector in the world that would sound the alert on the techniques that Sergeant Carter had taught him.

The waiting wore on him as combat never had. Thurmond Boothby called on the hardest lessons he'd ever learned, waiting immobile and in the shadows for hours on end while in the field. Every muscle in his body ached, urging him to move, to somehow release the enormous pressure building inside him. Yet to do so in front of these four other officers would be to reveal his nervousness, provide grist for the inevitable rumor control debriefing that would follow his visit to the White House. He schooled himself to silence and immobility. Not even glancing at the charts in his folder.

Not that it made any difference. He'd made up most of the data in them anyway. They were simply props, tools to gain him access to this one particular briefing room.

The president's appointment secretary strode into the room and walked directly to the chairman. "We're running a little ahead of schedule," she said. "Are you ready now?"

General Huels stood. "Of course." Leading the way as the senior officer present, he followed the appointment secretary down the carpeted corridor to the briefing room.

Boothby brought up the rear.

"There you are," the cabby said as he deposited Thorne at the front gate to the White House. "Enjoy the tour and make sure you get a good look at the silver collection. Hell, you and I are paying for it, aren't we?"

The cab pulled away, and the booming echo of the cabby's laughter echoed in his ears. The guard directed him toward the public entrance to the White House. Thorne threaded his way between the white columns that he'd seen so often on news reports and postcards.

At the front reception area, it was a different story. The well-dressed woman who took his pass and examined it carefully was frowning. "You're too late for the tour that just left. The next one starts in forty-five minutes." She looked at him over half-rimmed glasses disapprovingly, as though every citizen in the U.S. should know what time tours through the White House began.

"I need to see a Secret Service agent," Thorne blurted out. "Immediately."

She took one step back and her frown deepened. Thorne noticed that she edged behind her desk, placing the massive wooden furniture between them.

"Hold on, let me get one for you." She started to reach for the telephone, then evidently changed her mind and turned back to her desk. Thorne saw her hand slide under the highly polished surface.

Seconds later, two men moved quickly into the room and took station on either side of him. Their hands were near his arms, and Thorne made certain his hands were in plain view. "We have a problem?" The older of the two men directed the question to the secretary rather than Thorne.

The receptionist nodded. She pointed at Thorne. "He asked for the Secret Service."

The man turned back to Thorne. "You've got it, sir. Now what is this about?"

"I'm worried about the president," Thorne began. He saw the older man's expression change slightly, and could hear it as clearly as though he could read the man's thoughts. Another nut, maybe a harmless one. Maybe not. Hands encircled his upper arms, edging him gently away from the secretary's desk.

"Why don't we go down to my office and discuss it?" the Secret Service man said calmly. "I'm Special Agent Georges. And you are?"

"Dr. Christopher Thorne of the Murphy Medical Center," Thorne said, and made a small motion as though to reach for his wallet in his back pocket. The grip on his arms immediately tightened.

"Let's go down to my office, Doctor," the man said. "And if you don't mind." Thorne felt hands slide over his body, conducting a cursory search of his pockets and pants legs. The junior agent fished his wallet out of his back pocket, flipped it open, and examined the identification there. "That's who it says he is."

"Well, let's go have that little talk."

"The president has decided to see you in the Oval Office rather than the briefing room," the appointment secretary said. She smiled, inviting them to acknowledge an honor. "Girl Scouts due in thirty minutes. We will stay on schedule, won't we?" The smile hardened into the expression of a seasoned bureaucrat determined to maintain order. "Even now, it's important that we don't disrupt the president's schedule." Clearly, the escalating conflict in Korea would not justify that in her mind.

General Huels nodded politely. "Of course we will."

The office was smaller than Boothby had expected. Much smaller. It was, as advertised, quite oval. The president was seated behind his desk, skimming through the folders and rapidly scrawling his well-known signature over documents laid out in a neat pile for him, only the signature line exposed.

The president stood as they entered the office.

"General, good to see you." He looked past Jerry Huels to Boothby. "And General Boothby, of course. I'm glad you're here, General. It's always of incredible value to me to hear firsthand the opinions of the man actually on the spot. Do sit down." The president motioned to the ring of chairs aligned in front of his desk.

Hardly daring to breathe, Boothby slid into a position in the center of the semicircle. Jerry Huels flanked him on one side and the Army chief of staff on the other.

"Tell me about Korea. How bad is it?" The president shook his head, giving a clear indication of his opinion of what the answer should be.

"It depends, Mr. President," Boothby began. He'd made note of the two Secret Service men standing along the wall as he entered, had seen the almost imperceptible relaxation in their posture as the four men in military uniforms had entered the office. Of all the threat priorities they constantly reviewed and ranked, senior generals would be the least dangerous.

At least that's what Boothby hoped they thought.

Quickly, Boothby summarized his position on the escalating events in Korea. He saw the president's frown deepen, became aware that his eyes were drifting away to examine the walls of the Oval Office as though he had not seen them all a thousand times before. Finally, the president held up one hand. "Are you sure we didn't start this?" he asked.

Boothby heard Jerry Huels make a small satisfied sound beside him. The same question, but in a far less virulent form, that Huels had posed during that morning's practice session.

"No, Mr. President. If I may show you—" Boothby withdrew the briefing chart Huels's staff had drafted for him. "You can see by the bar here that Korean aggression preceded any action by my forces. The yellow line indicates the increased fortification measures I took. The blue line is sniper attacks, the purple is—"

The president held up one hand. "Hold on, I surrender." All four officers smiled politely at the small joke. "These charts, they're more like an eye exam, aren't they." The president laid the chart flat on the desk and pushed it back toward Boothby. "Show me in simple language what you're trying to say."

Boothby stood and leaned forward over the desk. He was aware of a small motion behind him, something he'd just caught out of the corner of his eye, and he moved slowly so as not to arouse any suspicion. "I'll point out the critical points for you, Mr. President," he began, slowly easing around the desk so that his body was at a right angle to the president's. "Here, two months ago, was the first sniper attack." Boothby droned through the rest of the explanation of the intricate graph, slowly edging around the desk until he was almost on the president's side. He stood there, continuing his explanation, pointing out time periods and actions on the chart as he waited for the other men to relax.

"So you think General Boothby poses a danger to the president." Thorne couldn't tell from the Secret Service man's voice whether or not he believed him. In a desperate effort not to waste this one final chance, he'd started with the strongest lead-in, one that he knew was sure to attract their attention—that the president was in danger.

It had exactly the reaction he'd expected.

The man picked up a small walkie-talkie and spoke into it quietly, turning away from Thorne to muffle his words. The smaller, younger Secret Service man at Thorne's side was a coiled spring. Thorne overheard the brief murmurs, tried to decipher the words, but the message was delivered in intricate slang and code words. Still, they'd done something, that was all he could ask for.

"Just let me examine him," Thorne pleaded. "Please, it's absolutely critical."

The Secret Service man moved back slightly and regarded him gravely. "Taking care of the president is what we're all about, Doctor. And we don't take chances."

"Is General Boothby with him now?"

The two Secret Service men exchanged glances, then the older one nodded. "But I just spoke with the agents monitoring the Oval Office. Everything is entirely under control up there, Doctor."

Thorne stormed to his feet. "You don't understand, I have to see him. Have to. I'm the only one who knows what the symptoms look like, the only one who can see the signs. If I don't see General Boothby and something happens to the president, I'll make sure the story gets told."

There was an odd, electric silence in the room. Thorne waited, desperately aware that he stood no chance of darting out of the room and up to wherever the president was. Hell, he wouldn't even know where to start. Since he hadn't done the public tour, he had no conception of which areas of the White House were office space and which were administrative.

Finally, the senior Secret Service man nodded. "Okay, you can see him—as he comes out of the office. I'm sure the general will make time for it if we insist."

"That might be too late," Thorne said, struggling to sound professionally calm.

The two Secret Service men stood as one, arraying themselves on either side of Thorne. They guided him out of the office, and another three agents fell into step with them. "This way, Doctor. We'll be waiting out in the reception area."

Two feet separated the general from the most powerful man in the world. He was so close he could see each individual presidential hair glued neatly in place. The president wore an aftershave, he noted, a faint undertone of musk that was barely discernible from the smell of soap and clean skin.

Even with the moment upon him, Boothby hesitated. It had been so long in coming, such a very improbable long shot that he'd hardly dared to hope this moment would arrive. It was proof, the final proof, as if he ever needed it. His entire life spread out before him, the earlier triumphs, his recent reconciliation with Alicia, and the glowing approbation that history would award him. How many honors could they give the man who'd taken out this most treasonous of presidents? Everyone knew it needed to be done, but no one had the guts. Nor the ability. No, it was up to the military, as it had always been.

Boothby listed off the president's crimes in his mind as he studied the face turned up to him. The president wore a thin veil of makeup, something that surprised him even more. Even among what should have been his most trusted advisors, a false face to cover the treachery in his own soul. The thin coating of flesh-colored makeup decided him as much as anything else had.

Boothby made a motion as though to point out something else on the chart, then reached out and clamped his steel fingers in the mass of carefully coifed hair. He yanked the president up, twisting him around so that he shielded himself from the Secret Service men who were already moving, already charging toward him. He clamped his other arm around the president's waist, put his shoulder to the president's back, and pulled back on the head, exposing the president's lightly tanned and slightly crepey neck.

"Thurmond." He heard the word torn deep from General Huels's gut, and glanced over to see the anguished expression on his superior's face. "Stop this immediately." The words were frail and meaningless, a mere pro forma protest from an officer who knew what had to be done. Boothby felt a moment of disgust at the chairman's cowardice.

He jerked back even harder on the head and could feel through his fingertips the small, creaking noises that cartilage and bone made as they gave way under pressure. He gloried in the feeling, let it surge over him like a tidal wave, carrying him along to the peaks that awaited him. The Secret Service men were almost frozen, guns out and drawn, but Boothby kept the president in their line of fire.

He'd waited so long for this moment. He cleared his throat, started to speak, and was aware his voice sounded gravelly. For the briefest second, he wished for a glass of water to clear his throat, that his exact words might echo down through the generations.

"The punishment for treason is death." He took a deep breath, almost wishing he could prolong this moment for hours, even days, basking in the surge of power and energy that radiated through his every inch. He must be glowing, shedding a strange light in the room that the others could see. There was no way mere human flesh could control this heavenly mark of divine favor otherwise.

The door to the Oval Office slammed open, startling Boothby just enough for the president to twist out of his grasp, wrenching Boothby's still-wounded shoulder painfully. The room filled with thunder as the first Secret Service man shot.

Boothby howled, as much in anger as anything else as his grip weakened and he felt a warm surge of blood gush from the almost-healed incision. His strength in that arm decreased visibly, and he quickly calculated the odds. Enough, just maybe.

Not good enough. In an instant, Boothby changed the plan. He hurled the president to the ground behind the Oval Office desk, and landed squarely on top of him. He planted one knee in the president's back, and grasped his hair again with his good hand, pulling it backwards.

The president rolled, catlike, and Boothby remembered with some degree of wonder the reports of the president's early days on the college wrestling team. The president landed a solid punch in his gut. It wasn't enough to break Boothby's hold on the president, but the movement placed the president in the line of fire. Something hit Boothby from behind, a hard hammer to the back of his head. The general gasped and sprawled forward over the president, feeling his chance of history slip irretrievably from between his hands.

The president scrabbled across the floor to safety, and two Secret Service men virtually carried him from the room immediately. The other five fanned out, forming a grim circle around Boothby. Guns drawn, staring down at him, rage circling the room like a twisted tiger.

Boothby howled, shoved himself up to his knees with his good hand, and started to rise.

Pain, this one sharp and hard, slammed into his buttocks. He turned to face the new aggressor, and saw Dr. Thorne.

"You would have understood," Boothby said, grabbing at his butt to pull the hypodermic needle from it. "Of all of them, you would have. If you'd stayed." He looked up at Thorne as the drug took effect, stealing his consciousness from him. "You can't run, Doctor. I know who you are—and so do you."

"So do we." The senior Secret Service man spoke up. "He's the guy who warned us about you."

TWENTY-FIVE

Two doctors and a nurse swarmed around him, repeatedly demanding that he submit to a full physical examination, to lab tests, X rays, and every other diagnostic tool that they could imagine. Thorne waved them off, already aware that he was not seriously injured. At most, what he needed was sleep—and lots of it.

Unbidden, thoughts of Debbie Patterson rose to his mind. Maybe something besides sleep, he amended. For the moment, all he wanted was his life back, his future at Murphy, and the quiet stream of surgical patients who would not demonstrate any rapid emergence from his anesthetic art.

A side door to the Oval Office opened, one that was indistinguishable from the pattern of moldings ringing the room. Two Secret Service men stepped in, hands already on their guns, and surveyed the room as though there was some other danger lurking there. Finally, one of them motioned behind him.

President Williams strode in, the pale, shaken look that Thorne had last seen on his face already fading away to be replaced by a wide, congenial smile. The president gestured toward the Secret Service men. "They're furious with me, not that they'd ever admit it. I insisted on coming back in here, though. When a man saves your life, that's the least that you can do."

Thorne stood, pulled to his feet by the inherent dignity of the office of the president. His hands were still jittery from the close encounter with Boothby, but he reached out to take the president's offered handshake with what he hoped was a decent grip. "It was your men, Mr. President," he said, fumbling over the words as long-forgotten courtesies drilled into him in elementary school on addressing the president of the United States came back. "They acted quickly."

"According to Max there, not quickly enough. They'll be beating themselves up for six months over not listening to you right away. It could have saved a lot of trouble."

"I wasn't even certain myself," Thorne answered. "Not about Boothby."

The president sat down at the coffee table, wincing slightly as he did so. "I don't mind telling you, it shook me up a bit." His grimace deepened as something painful spasmed.

"Mr. President, it was very kind of you to come back to thank me. It certainly wasn't necessary, and I'm sure your own doctors want to have a look at you."

The president waved them off. "Sure, sure, soon enough. So what are your plans, Doctor? I understand you're in a bit of trouble at Murphy." He glanced over at the chairman of the Joint Chiefs of Staff, who was standing at the far side of the room. "I imagine that can be cleared up, can't it, General?"

"Of course, Mr. President," General Huels answered. "It'll be done immediately."

"You want to go back there, don't you?" the president asked. He hesitated for a moment, and then said, "I could understand if you didn't want to. After everything that's happened." It was General Huels's turn to come under fire. "I imagine there'll be plenty of funding for whatever you want to do. Right, General?"

"Of course," the general answered immediately.

Thorne nodded. "I'll need some time to think about it, Mr. President."

"Well." The president stood, now clearly in considerable discomfort. The two doctors were at his side immediately, reaching for him to assist him out of the room. "If you don't want to go back to Murphy, you call my office. Talk to Jerry over there," he said, nodding at the JCS chairman. "I could use a good anesthesiologist on the staff here at the White House."

Thorne's jaw dropped. "You're offering me a job? I didn't even vote for you, sir."

The president laughed, a sound clearly forced through pain. "Neither did almost half of the country, but I'm here anyway. And you can be too, if you want it."

With one last handshake, he let the doctors lead him away to another room. He paused at the concealed exit and said, "I mean it, Dr. Thorne. There's a spot here for you, and your surgeon friend, too, if you want." The president gave Thorne a knowing look. "But I'd be careful around her. She's got a powerful uncle."

So he knew about Debbie. And about everything else that had happened at Murphy. With an intelligence service that worked that well, how had they not known that events in Korea were being driven by the man who just tried to kill the president?

"You let me know," another voice said, and he turned to find General Huels standing next to him. The Secret Service had followed the president out, and the two were alone. "The president means what he says."

"Maybe later," Thorne said, uncertain as to whether or not this was an offer that could be truly turned down. "Why didn't you do something? I told you he was dangerous."

Huels sighed. "Tom Wallinger—you know him? CID called me this morning, and I talked to him. He said you'd attacked a senior physician, that you'd been hospitalized for a mental breakdown not long ago. Frankly, after hearing what he had to say, I had doubts about your reliability. If I'd thought you would show up here, I would have alerted the Secret Service, and you'd have been taken into custody."

"How is he? Dr. Gillespie, the man I'm supposed to have attacked?"

"He's okay. Unconscious, but they think it will wear off. Will it?"

Thorne nodded. "For the short term. There are long range consequences, though."

"Like with Thurmond." Huels sighed. "He was a fine officer. One of the most brilliant leaders I've ever known. Eventually he would have had my job."

"I believe that. So you probably wouldn't have taken me seriously anyway."

Huels shook his head. "Even if there were a problem, I thought I could handle him. I've know Thurmond a long time." Seeing Thorne's accusing gaze, he added, "I even had the Secret Service in the room for backup. They're usually stationed outside the doors and monitor the President on closed-circuit TV, not in the Oval Office itself. I thought it was enough."

"It wasn't."

Huels studied him for a moment. "I see that now, thank you. So what about the President's offer?"

"I have another project right now: tracing out the causes of the rage reaction that Anaex evidently induces in patients. Finding out why, and finding a way to stop it."

"And as the president said, there'll be money for anything you need funded. Our mess, we help clean it up." General Huels paused for a moment. "I'm going to take a chance here," he said finally. "As of this moment, consider your security clearance approved. Understand, if you breathe a word of what I'm about to tell you—and to propose—your ass is grass. Got it?"

Thorne shook his head. "I'm not interested in anything classified. Not anymore."

"You will be." General Huels laid his hand gently on Thorne's forearm. "Just for a few minutes. Trust me, okay? We've got some mutual interests."

"As long as I can call it quits and walk away if I don't like it."

General Huels smiled. "I'm going to remind you that you said that. Now, you agree to the security restrictions?"

Thorne nodded, tired of debating the point.

"What do you think about assassins, then?" Huels asked. "Is there any common factor in their personalities? In their physical makeup, perhaps?"

"Maybe," Thorne answered slowly. "It could be a lot of things."

"What if I gave you the chance to find out?"

Stunned, Thorne could only stare at him. The implications of General Huels's question were enormous.

"You've got them?" Thorne asked, hardly able to speak. "Assassins?"

Huels nodded. "Most of them are dead, of course. The older ones. But we've got the most complete set of autopsy slides and actual tissue samples available anywhere in the world. It's been a black project for years, funded under a joint military and Secret Service code name. What we need is a fresh look at the data, though. Maybe, with the Anaex Protocol stymied, you might be interested in heading the project up? All this is conditioned, of course, on your taking perfect care of my niece."

"My god, I—of course!" Thorne was at a loss for words.

Huels tightened his grip slightly, then removed his hand from Thorne's arm. "Good. It's settled, then. My people will talk to you, and probably the Secret Service as well, about the details. I'm going to be a little tied up for the next several months myself."

"What about Korea?" Thorne asked. "You're going to clean that one up, too?"

The general sighed. "That will take a little longer, I'm afraid. Some diplomatic concessions, some quiet work to eliminate the Sergeant Carters still over there. There'll be more than one, I'm willing to bet. Thurmond Boothby never did anything by halves."

"One last question."

"Shoot."

"Can you get me a ride home?"

General Huels looked startled for a moment, then amused. "At last, you ask something easy."

"You all right back there, sir?" The pilot's voice sounded tinny over the internal communications circuit. "Not feeling sick or anything?"

"I'm fine. Where are we now?"

"Still over Texas. It's one hell of a long state, Major."

I'm not a major anymore. Never should have been. It was—it was too easy.

On behalf of the United States Army, General Huels had gracefully accepted the resignation of one Major Christopher Thorne. Effective immediately.

And what now? Back to Murphy, he supposed, although in exactly what capacity was unclear. The assassin project—he was already starting to think of it as his.

And there'd be the research into exactly how Anaex interacted with the sleep process to produce the rage state, and General Huels had hinted that the Army was particularly interested in that process. Thorne had no doubts that the good general saw enormous military potential in being able to generate temporarily a killing rage state in soldiers. The problem, of course, was stopping it once it got started.

Maybe the B-6 deficiency was the key. The article he'd read on neurological deficiencies resulting from it weren't definitive, but it was someplace to start. Maybe massive doses could clear up General Boothby's mental state. Or it might just be a question of thoroughly flushing out the tissues of whatever remaining residue might lurk in them, probably in the fatty tissues. Hyperbaric chambers and O_2, maybe?

Another thousand miles slipped by while Thorne contemplated the avenues of research and planned out his approach. Finally, as the military jet slipped over the border of California, he faced the question that had been plaguing him.

Was this the first time?

It was a given that anesthetic agents did not produce this kind of longterm subtle effects. What you saw in recovery was what you got. The body flushed the rest of the drug out through normal metabolic processes.

Or did it?

Did other drugs, respected drugs in wide use for years, have undetected long-term side effects similar to the rage state? Could that be responsible for some of the atrocities men inflicted on each other? The Kennedy assassinations, the massacre at the San Ysidro McDonald's, and certainly Kamil's uncle's attack in Algeria, given that Gillespie admitted using Anaex on the secretary of state. Was there a possibility that anesthetic drugs had been at least partially responsible for other assassination attempts since the time that they'd first been used?

Maybe, maybe not. There would always be people like Sergeant Carter who simply seemed to live for violence, twisted and angry people without any degree of remorse or control over their own behavior.

Whatever the answer, it was going to be exciting to track it down. He'd need facilities—probably the old Anaex spaces—and a staff.

And a surgeon. For more reasons than one.

"You seem to be spending a lot of time picking me up at interesting places," Thorne said as he swept Patterson into a hard, tight hug.

"You *would* say that," she murmured. "And I thought I was so subtle."

"I meant the *jail* last time."

"Ah. That kind of picking up. Yes, that too."

He pulled back from her for a moment and ran his hand down the side of her face. She nuzzled against it.

"I'm glad to see you," he said finally.

"Same here. How's my uncle?"

"Fine. How's Kamil?"

"Fine." A devilish look came over Patterson's wholesome face. "Preliminaries out of the way now? Can we go to bed?"

He looked around the crowded military air terminal. "Not here, I think. Come on, I know a place nearby."

On the drive home, he finally talked about Korea. About the blood lust, the sheer surge of exhilaration that had swept over him as he'd fought his way back to the boat. How afraid he'd been, how determined he was to never ever let that part of himself out of the box again.

Patterson listened. His words finally stopped tumbling out of his mouth, jostling one another as he raced to get them out. Silence descended.

Finally, she said, "I appreciate what it took for you to tell me that. If you're worried about my reaction, don't be. We're all capable of surprising even ourselves, and life and death decisions aren't limited to the OR."

TWENTY-SIX

Nigel Carter waited in the closet. It was no different than spending hours in total darkness in the tunnels of Korea, and at least the air was fresher. The dark was comforting, the clothes that hung in the closet as concealing as the underbrush near the caves' entrances.

And the waiting was no different. It was one of the first things you learned to do as a soldier, wasn't it? Hurry up and wait. In line for chow, on watch or guard duty, or on patrol.

Or here. Deep in the back recesses of the good ole doctor's closet, hunkered down over shoes and boxes.

He could do time standing on his head by now, leaving part of his senses on guard while the rest of his mind roamed around in black corners, imagining the action that would come. Sometimes the real thing was better, oftentimes not.

This time it would be better, for sure. There wasn't the time pressure, the urgent need to act—to kill—before the enemy shot at you. The good ole doc, for that was how he thought of Thorne now, incessantly, just wouldn't be carrying any firepower.

Not that that meant he could be careless, oh no. He'd made that mistake last time. He'd known the bum arm would slow him down some, and he'd compensated for that, but he hadn't figured on what a dandy handhold the sling could give the doc.

And how much it would hurt. *Jesus,* how it hurt! The pain pills they'd given him at the hospital had worn off, fading out of his system like "Taps" wafting off in the air. It left a vacuum, one that the pain rushed back into fill.

He shifted slightly, easing the pressure on his tailbone. The area immediately around him was clear, he'd seen to that first off. No danger of a branch—*a shoe, dammit*—rattling around and giving his location away. No screwups this time. Just smooth, quiet killing, the way he liked it.

The way General Boothby liked it.

And just where had the general gotten himself off to? Carter had done his part, fingered the good ole doc. Disinformation, the general called it.

Whatever it had been, it had worked. For a while. Like the pain pills.

But not long enough.

Finish what you start. That's the first rule.

The hours passed, waiting hours. Longer that regular hours.

A click.

Carter came instantly alert.

A creak.

The front door.

He placed the sounds now, visualizing the house in his mind. The good ole doc would be in the foyer, shutting the door. Yes, there it was, the slamming sound. Now he'd—

What? That wasn't Thorne's voice. Higher, saying something teasing.

Well, well, well. A twofer, it would be. It didn't much matter to him, anything to get the damned waiting over with and get on with it.

Carter stretched slowly, careful to keep his joints from creaking. He stood crouched in the closet, waiting just a little while longer.

Footsteps. They were headed upstairs. Horny bastard, can't wait to get in her pants. Carter's hand strayed to his own crotch, rubbing gently. Maybe if there were time. Get the good ole doc first, then maybe just a little fun. He deserved it, waiting so long like this. It was almost like good ole doc had brought him a present. Maybe he wasn't such a bad guy after all.

He felt as much as heard them enter the bedroom, his senses so keenly attuned to the house that he could track them just by thinking about them.

The overhead light flicked on, outlining the door in thin glowing lines.

"Finally." It was the woman's voice, soft and breathy like he liked it. Carter scrunched over and peered out the crack between the door and the jamb, then drew in a sharp breath.

Man, oh man. Talk about a present!

She was short, blond, better looking than he remembered from the hospital. And maybe, if he could just get a better look—*yes*. Blue eyes. Yesyesyesyesyes!

"It's taken long enough, hasn't it?" Thorne now, the horny bastard. Touching her, kissing her.

Carter watched Thorne's hands move over her, his mouth locked on hers. They were pressed together tightly now, her hands scratching down his back, then busy with his shirt buttons, Thorne's hands under her shirt and reaching up. He heard Thorne moan, a deep, sexual sound. Carter damned near came right then.

"Get this off," the woman said. She shoved Thorne's now unbuttoned shirt back over his shoulders. "Now."

Clothes fell to the floor, equally quickly from both of them. Carter struggled to control his breathing, to maintain control. A few more minutes. The idea was growing on him, appealing to him with such a compelling intensity that he felt powerless to resist it. It was just right, *so right*.

They were on the bed now, hands moving faster, seeking out hidden places and the hard-soft combinations. Thorne's mouth was at her breast, and it was her turn to moan and gasp.

Carter waited. The moment, it had to be that one moment.

Finally, Thorne pulled back, supporting his weight on his hands as he moved back up her body. He was poised over her, just about to—

Now.

Carter slammed open the closet door and darted across the room. He vaulted onto the bed and slammed Thorne in the side with his body, knocking Thorne off the bed. Carter followed, rolling and guarding his injured shoulder.

The pain was screaming bright now, blocking out all other sounds. Carter ignored it, slashed out with the knife at Thorne's belly.

The blade bit into Thorne's skin, the motion converted from a stab into slash as Thorne continued his roll out of Carter's grasp. Carter swore and scrabbled after him, striking again at Thorne's exposed back. A thin, welling slice wound opened up.

Good, but not good enough.

Thorne was on his feet now. Carter moved forward again, aware that the advantage he'd had was slipping away, his shoulder slowing him up.

Thorne picked up the chair sitting in one corner of the room and swung it at him. Carter danced out of the way, keeping a tight grip on the blade.

Not going to work, not like this.

Carter shifted tactics. He let his motion carry him back to the bed and he reached for the woman. He landed on top of her, trying to get the knife at her neck. That would slow Thorne down if nothing else would.

The pain exploded. For a moment he was confused. He'd been guarding the shoulder, could take both of them with just one hand so how could—

More pain, overwhelming and dark, threatening to tear his consciousness away from his body. Not his shoulder, his groin. A small, strong hand was planted there, fingers anchored under his scrotum and palm hammering up against his balls.

She was trying to tear it off. Twisting, jerking. God, she was going to pay for this! Pay and pay and pay.

He felt the skin ripping, then suddenly the shattering pain moved to his shoulder. He was on his belly now, facedown on the bed, bigger hands around his neck. Woozy, he tried to figure out how that had happened.

"You told me, don't ever do what they expect you to do." Thorne tightened his grip on Carter's neck, depressing the massive carotid arteries that pulsed under his fingertips. He could feel the life beating there, the pressure building up against his fingers as the blood backed up, trying to fight its way up to Carter's brain.

Carter gurgled, trying to force words out.

"Here. Let me." Debbie leaned forward and cupped Carter's chin in her hand.

"No!"

She ignored him. "Now *this* is how you do it." She planted her free hand at the base of Carter's neck and jerked his chin up and back. There was a sickly, solid *crunch*.

Debbie held the broken neck in position for a moment, then released her grip on his chin. Carter's head fell forward and thudded against the hardwood floor. She ran her hand lightly down the back of Carter's neck, probing gently at the base of his skull. Finally, she straightened up and looked at Thorne, meeting his stunned gaze with equanimity.

"It snapped around the second cervical vertebrae, I believe," she said calmly. "High enough up, anyway, that he can't breathe on his own."

"How could—*Jesus*, Debbie!" Thorne dropped his hands from Carter's neck. "Help me stabilize his neck, roll him over. *Jesus!* We'll do CPR until the EMTs get here and maybe—"

"Stop it, Thorne," she said kindly. "I told you. You're really not so different from the rest of us after all."

Finally, Thorne remembered why Patterson's words had sounded so familiar the first time she'd made that point. He stared down at the dying Carter. "He said that, too."

TWENTY-SEVEN

The ambulance left first, light bar rotating and siren blasting. The police cars stayed longer, although one officer went outside after the first hour and turned off the light bars flashing atop three patrol cars. Thorne and Patterson were questioned separately, first by the patrol officer who'd responded with the ambulance, then by her supervising sergeant, and by a homicide detective. It had taken a confirming call from the Secret Service, invoking national security, before the detective relented.

Thorne slumped down the couch. His arms and legs were numb and his skin felt as though it had been sandpapered.

"Want some coffee?" Patterson asked. She was sitting across from him in an armchair, the same one she'd sat in for the last three hours answering questions while Thorne had been questioned in the kitchen. She stood and stretched. "Not much point in going back to sleep now. I'm due in surgery in two hours."

"You can't be serious. After all this?"

She nodded. "I'm all right to operate. Just a little tired, that's all. It'll be worse if I try to get a couple hours and have to get up again."

"Speak for yourself. No way I could trust myself on a case right now, and I'm surprised you feel like you could."

"Just something you get used to, eventually. I've taken myself off the schedule before, but only two or three times in the last five years."

Thorne yawned. "So we're not going to talk about this? About what happened?"

Patterson shrugged. "I will if you want to. But coffee first."

He heard her moving in the kitchen, grinding the beans, decanting bottled water. Was she really as unaffected by it as she claimed? He shook his head, unable to conceive of what inner strength—or callousness—could make her immune to it all.

Carter had that same capacity to commit acts that exceeded a normal human capacity for brutality, the keenly focused drive that blocked out all other considerations other than the mission at hand. The thought chilled him. Who was she, that she could walk away from this night as though nothing had happened? How could he even begin to think that he knew her in any way except the most physical?

The kitchen noises stopped except for the burbling sound of the coffeemaker. Silence—and then a choking sound pulled him to his feet and sent him running to the kitchen.

Debbie was standing in front of the sink holding two coffee cups, one in each hand. Her head was bowed and her shoulders quivered.

Thorne stopped, then walked across the Spanish tile to stand behind her. He put his arms around her and pulled her close to him, leaning forward to brush his lips across her cheek. He felt the moisture, saw the tears crowding her eyes. "It's all right now. Everything's all right," he said, his voice soothing and calm. "We're safe and he's gone."

Patterson continued to cry. He held her and waited.

"I would have let him die," she said finally, her voice hitching and choking on the tears. "Would have—if you hadn't been there."

"If I hadn't been here, he wouldn't have come." Not an answer, but the best he could do. "He's not dead yet."

"He will be. Or on a respirator the rest of his life. It might have been better not to keep him alive for the paramedics."

"We all make choices." He took the coffee cups from her hand, set them on the counter, then slowly turned her around to face him. "There's always a choice. It's just a question of what you want to live with. I've already killed one man. Maybe not much by Carter's or Boothby's standards, but more than I wanted. I didn't want you to have to live with that, too. Not ever."

Now the sobs broke hard against his chest, coming from deep within her. He let her cry, felt the tears start in his own eyes.

No, not like Carter. She never was and never would be. He'd saved her from that by starting CPR, then forcing her to help. He had hated it with every breath he'd forced into Carter, imagined a knife in his hand with every compression—but he'd done it. He'd known, as she had not, what it would be to live with it if he hadn't.

As she did now.

"Thank you," Patterson said when she could catch her breath. "Thank you."

He breathed a sigh of relief and held her close.